WE DARE:
WANTED, DEAD OR ALIVE
AN ANTHOLOGY OF BOUNTIES AND HUNTERS

Edited by Jamie Ibson

Theogony Books
Coinjock, NC

Chris Kennedy/Theogony Books
1097 Waterlily Rd.
Coinjock, NC 27923
https://chriskennedypublishing.com/

Publisher's Note: This is a work of fiction. Names, characters, places, and incidents are a product of the author's imagination. Locales and public names are sometimes used for atmospheric purposes. Any resemblance to actual people, living or dead, or to businesses, companies, events, institutions, or locales is completely coincidental.

Cover Design by J Caleb Design.

The stories and articles contained herein have never been previously published. They are copyrighted as follows:

We Dare: Wanted, Dead or Alive/Jamie Ibson -- 1st ed.
ISBN 978-1648553813

To you guys, the fans. It is your kind words, support, and reviews that have turned the We Dare anthologies from a slightly terrifying, "Hey wouldn't this be cool" idea into a labor of love. Thank you so much!

And as always, to my better half Michelle, for believing in me all the times that I don't.

* * * * *

Preface by Jamie Ibson

When you think about it, modern day bounty hunting is a pretty strange thing. To be granted bail, a certain amount of money gets put up as a security to ensure an accused suspect will turn up for court. Most folks don't have the kind of money required, so a Bail Bondsman loans them what they need and takes a percentage up front as their fee. The Bondsmen who know what they're doing have questionnaires and forms the suspect completes, which will then help the bounty hunter track down the suspect if he misses his court date (whether that's on purpose or by mistake.) When the suspect is handed off to law enforcement, the Hunter (and/or Bondsman) get the bail money back they put up.

At least, that's how it works for most folks. When someone who has the funds is able to put up their own bail and they abscond, it gets *very* lucrative, *very* quickly. Whoever presents the accused to the law gets the bail money, and that's where the big scores happen. Of course, if the suspect has the funds for hundreds of thousands, or even a million dollars in bail, they've got the funds and resources to make collecting that bail a very dangerous prospect.

In science fiction we gloss over a lot of that, of course. If an unwelcome space alien monster is preying on innocents in your station, offer a bounty. MegaCorps will pay cash for wageslaves who've fled the oppressive office for the freedom of the gutter. Got a rogue AI on the lam? Best hire a professional; they don't fight fair. Bounty hunters and fugitives have captured our imagination in science fiction for years, whether it's Din Djarin, Riddick, the crew of the *Bebop*, or River Tam aboard the *Serenity*.

Contained herein are fifteen science fiction stories about bounties and hunters, desperate men and women on the run, and the lone wolf operators whose job is to bring them in, dead or alive.

See you in the final pages,

J

Contents

* * * * *

Man's Best Friend by
Rick Partlow

The muzzle of the blaster yawned, inviting, tempting me with its silent offer to end my misery. Sighing, I shoved the weapon into its holster and dumped it into the locker, slamming the door shut. No matter how bad things got, I wasn't going to do that. I hadn't seen my son since my wife had left with him months ago, but I wasn't going to take the chance of him hearing what had happened to me. It was bad enough that Luke knew I'd been forced to resign from the Marshal's Service and knew why. I was sure Janie had told him. She'd hated me at the end.

The locker door clanking shut echoed through the ship's utility bay, a hollow emptiness that could have been the soundtrack for my life. And then it bounced back open, which wasn't some sort of cosmic portent saying I was going to bounce back, just a demonstration of what a beat-up piece of shit this boat was. Inside the locker hung a beat-up cowboy hat, and I hesitated, wondering if I should wear it. It was the last thing that Janie had given me before the arrest, before she'd left with Luke.

Naw. I look like a huge douchebag in that thing.

The ramp control had a short circuit, and it took three or four smacks on the button before the overworked, undermaintained motors chugged to life. It stopped a foot off the floor of the hangar bay, and I jumped onto it, forcing it down all the way while the maintenance crew stared, possibly horrified that anyone would attempt space travel in this thing. They didn't say anything when I walked past, though I wasn't sure if it was from professional or personal distaste. My money was on personal.

The dirty looks only got worse as I climbed the levels of the Epsilon Eridani Union Law Enforcement Headquarters. I'd taken the stairs to avoid being stuck in an elevator with anyone, but even the stairwell felt crowded. Every face grew more familiar the higher I climbed.

"This place is a fucking space station," someone behind me was complaining in a nasal whine. "It's got artificial gravity. Why don't they just make the stairwell zero gravity so we can just like, float up and down?"

"Because that's not how gravity generators *work*, Phil," the woman walking beside him explained with strained patience. "They have to make the field the same consistency the whole way through."

I recognized the woman, and, against my better judgement, I paused and turned back to her.

"Hi, Gracie."

Shock erased the older woman's semi-permanent smile for just a moment, but it reformed like a cloud after a strong wind.

"Grant Masterson! It's been months! How are you, honey?" Her smile didn't fade this time, but there was concern in the set of her eyes. "After what happened, I was so worried."

"Things have been rough," I admitted, "but I think I've got my ducks in a row now." I grinned and the lie hurt my face. "I'm a fully licensed bounty hunter, with my own ship."

It was even true. However, it was a grandiose way of saying I was in hock up to my eyebrows for a barely-spaceworthy piece of junk, committed to one of the most loathsome jobs I could think of. Bounty hunters tracked down fugitives the Union Marshals' Service couldn't locate or didn't have the personnel and resources to apprehend safely. Back in another life, six whole months ago, me and my fellow Marshals had called them the bottom feeders.

"Well, that's wonderful, Grant," Gracie enthused. "Is that why you're here?"

"Yeah, I'm looking for my first real bounty." I sighed. "I'd rather just download the data and be done with it, but the regs say that all bounties have to be registered in person." A shrug. "It's so they don't get yahoos dumping corpses at their doorstep and trying to claim the reward."

Gracie winced. "That's got to be… uncomfortable."

"I'll let you know when I get there."

If the awkward stares on the way up to the Law Enforcement Administrative Center had been bad, the hostile glares when I arrived there were targeting lasers boring into my back. Office workers whose names I barely remembered regarded me like I was a serial killer. I gave thanks to a God I wasn't really on speaking terms with that they were too busy to talk to me.

The biometric registration terminal was off in a corner, blissfully out of the way of the hustle and bustle of the squad room. A parade of weary and overworked Deputy Marshals hauled the scum of the galaxy through the booking center on their way to a holding cell. Then, maybe, a long trip to a federal prison if they were unlucky. Each was unique in their own way, but the faces all blended into one after a few years.

Except the cyborg being processed. He was pretty damn unique. Evolutionists, they liked to be called, since they insisted they were the next step in human evolution. The sick bastards cut off their biological parts and replaced them with cybernetics, which wasn't *technically* illegal except that they usually bought black-market boosted parts that made them living weapons. And *that* would have been illegal even if they hadn't financed the transition by trafficking in bootlegged organs and black-market drugs.

This one was nearly two meters tall, and nearly half as wide as he was high, and I doubt any regulation set of cuffs would have restrained him. He was wrapped up in an electromagnetic harness, expensive and bulky but absolutely necessary since he could have killed three or four people before anyone could have brought him down with their sidearms.

"Fucking Normie pigs!" the Evolutionist bellowed, his voice, like everything else about him, cybernetically enhanced until it had the volume of a megaphone. "You can't stop us! We'll outlast you! Eventually, you'll look around and find out we've replaced you!"

"Yeah, yeah, big guy," a familiar voice replied, the tall deputy pushing the Evolutionist toward the holding pen. "But you won't be there to see it because you'll still be sitting in prison."

I looked away, hoping he wouldn't notice me, but my luck was never that good.

"What are you doing here, Grant?" Larry Daniels was just as tall and improbably handsome as he'd been the last five years, which led to him getting a ration of crap from crooks we'd busted together... and getting the numbers of every single woman we'd ever taken a statement from.

"Hey, Larry," I said, nodding, trying to be casual. I patted the biometric registration console. "Just trying to find a stable source of income."

The tall man shook his head.

"Damn it, Grant, you're better than this."

"The review board disagreed," I reminded him. I offered him half my attention, turning the rest to the list of fugitives on the screen of the console.

Bradley Wegener, Wanted for Trafficking in Illegal Weapons. Reward: 5,000 Credits.

I grunted. 5,000 credits sounded like a good reward, but I'd heard that expenses could eat up more than half that... at least if the internet how-to videos had been accurate.

"Being a Marshal isn't the only thing you could do with your life," Larry insisted, and I made sure I didn't let him see me rolling my eyes. It was the fourth time he'd said it since the Board of Review had confirmed the decision of the Senior Marshal. "Local colony police forces are always hiring. You could get out of this system, make a fresh start!"

"Wherever you go, Larry, there you are. I can't start over until I get my head right, and running away won't do that."

And this was the fourth time I'd given him the same answer.

Katrina Flannery, Wanted for Sabotage of a Corporate Freighter. Reward: 8,000 credits.

Hmm... not bad. I checked her last known location and possible associates and discovered no, it *was* bad. She was last seen heading for Barataria Bay, the pirate holdout. Going there and trying to get out again alive wouldn't be a great choice for my first bounty.

Larry didn't say anything, and I thought maybe he'd walked away and left me to my task, but no, I wasn't that fortunate.

"You never did tell me why you did it."

"Did what?" I asked, scrolling down to the next name on the list.

"Punched out Representative Thomas Caty?"

"No, bugging his office without a warrant. I mean, you pled guilty. What the hell?"

"You know the system, Marshal; you figure it out. Or do you honestly think every single guilty plea you've ever got was because you pinched the right guy?"

Oscar Fuentes, Wanted for...

Hmmm. Wanted for illegal production of Artificial Intelligence. That *was* interesting. So was the reward, which was a whopping 20,000 credits. His face stared out at me from the end of the display, bland and mild and not at all a hardened criminal's desperate visage. Last known location was right here in the Epsilon Eridani system, on the Panicle, just a few light-seconds away. So, why weren't the Marshals just going through the floating city looking for him? Why was his name on the list?

Ah, there it is. He was suspected of working with the Evolutionists. Even the Marshals never ventured into the Evolutionist's section of the station without a fully-equipped strike team. Which was a good reason *not* to make this my first job, but that 20,000 credits would go a long way to paying down the fiendishly-high-interest-rate loan on my ship. Or maybe just turning it into something livable.

"Are you even listening to me, Masterson?" Larry asked, throwing up his hands. "I asked, how do you plan on doing this on your own? You're a cop! You'll be walking into all this without any back-up at all!"

I shrugged.

"I figure I better get used to it."

* * *

The Panicle was a cancerous growth grown around the original core built by the first union colony ships over a hundred years ago. In an ideal society, it would have been preplanned, neatly-organized, with all the services spread out evenly in every sector. The Union was far from ideal, and if anything personified the messy, slipshod, corrupt nature of the whole thing, it was the Panicle.

If there'd been any habitable planets in the system, the Panicle probably never would have been built, but the inner asteroid belt was a treasure trove of Bartoli crystals. Without them, we wouldn't have blasters, hyperdrives, gravity field generators or a dozen other things that make interstellar civilization possible. People had to run and maintain the mines, and all those people needed a place to live.

The Panicle wasn't just one city, it was an entire floating continent, a few dozen kilometers on a side… if it could really be said to have sides, since the term gave the hint of a regular shape. Which meant that there wasn't just one docking station and the wrong choice would mean an hour on a tram. I knew where the Evolutionist Enclave was—every Marshal did. But the fact that this Oscar fella was working for the Evolutionists didn't mean he was living with them. And even if he was, there was no way I was going to be able to get into the Enclave without an armed platoon or lots of money for a bribe, neither of which I had.

What I *did* still have, despite my recent troubles, were connections. I docked as near as I could to the connections, at the section of the station called *El Mercado*. If the Panicle was the heart of the Epsilon Indi system, then *El Mercado* was the rot at its core. Men and women came to the Panicle to seek their fortunes in the asteroid mines or in selling their wares and services to those who did, and the refuse, the failures, the misfits all seemed to wash out into *El Mercado*. The only good thing I could say about the place was it had artificial gravity.

"Independent Transport CSB-2901A, you are cleared for docking," a computer-generated voice informed me, not making any snarky comments about the ship's lack of a name. "Slave your controls to the beam, and we'll bring you in."

"Copy that, traffic control," I said, setting the autopilot and settling back into my chair with a sigh of relief. I *knew* how to fly a ship. They didn't let you graduate from Marshal training without learning. But I wasn't very good at it, and I definitely didn't like it.

I could have just let the ship's navigational computer do all the work, but I didn't like *that*, either. I didn't care for computers making decisions that could get me killed. I knew they did it constantly, every time I was on a space station, but there was a qualitative difference between lines of code carrying out "if-then" statements and an actual deliberation going on in a non-human mind deciding whether it was more ethical to plow my ship into an inhabited station or collide with a passenger transport in the event of a drive failure. There was a reason that any Artificial Intelligence was highly regulated, and I liked to think part of it was keeping decisions like that in the hands of humans.

The ship might have been old and nameless, but it followed the beam well enough, and if the touchdown was rougher than I would have liked, it was nothing that replacing the hydraulics in the landing gear wouldn't cure. That would only take 3,000 credits. A thousand credits for docking fees and berth rental, assuming this thing didn't take more than the seventy-two-hour minimum. Another thousand to register the ship with her official name, which I had another thirty days to do before I was in violation and would get fined. Five hundred for a safety inspection, and I had *ten* days to get that one. And of course, food. Eating would be nice.

El Mercado hit me like a wave the second I stepped out of the docking corridor. People rushed by, mostly because staying in one place too long meant having to fend off the obnoxiously aggressive street vendors, and the beggars and the pickpockets who worked in conjunction with them. I rested my right palm on the blaster holstered under my jacket and stepped out into the madness.

The wave of sound and smell and color crashed over me, overwhelming. Rainbow hair, skin merely a tapestry for holographic tattoos, clothes as colorful and ostentatious as possible to hide the fact they were cheaply fabricated flash. It was all a cynical attempt at camouflage, trying to hide their poverty and desperation from anyone stupid enough to dock at *El Mercado* without knowing what it was and who lived here.

I bypassed the train station. Most newcomers used it because the map menus were simple, and they definitely didn't want to get lost in the wrong section of *El Mercado*.

As if there's a right section.

I knew where I was going, and I wanted to attract less attention on the way there. I walked. There was no customs inspection, no passport control. Anyone could bring pretty much anything into *El Mercado* except nuclear, biological, or chemical weapons. At least, that's what the official rules said, and I assumed they had remote detectors for that sort of thing. They certainly had no problems with guns, because just about every third or fourth person I saw was carrying one openly, and I had to assume the others had them concealed.

Drugs were ubiquitous, the labs where they were made squatting in solitary ugliness, wrapped in protective fencing and insulation, guarded by men and women with guns. They watched me pass, not caring who I was or what my business was as long as I wasn't a threat. They sold in the streets, in stalls crammed into niches and corners, in fancy storefronts catering to the wealthier visitors. Guns were sold as openly, though their quality varied. Old-fashioned slug-shooters fabricated off patterns centuries old were spread across blankets on the ground on street corners, while blasters like the one I carried were restricted to storefronts, protected behind thick polyglass shields and watched over by an armed sales staff.

The rest was harder to spot. Dealers dealt in illegal, black-market virtual reality software. IP pirates sold stolen fabricator patterns. You could even find Bartoli crystals, although those were the most jealously guarded of all, kept in safes and carried out to ships or businesses by escorts. Nothing was marked, nothing was advertised. If you were there, you knew what you meant to shop for and where to find it.

I was looking for sex. Sex was everywhere, and like everything else here, for sale. Live companionship was available, but expensive. Once, there'd been actual human trafficking in places like this, but the Marshals hadn't tolerated it for long. Prostitution was legal; pimping was not. Any attempt by a house to take more than a fifty percent cut of companion's income was met by law enforcement raids, and no one here wanted that, particularly when the clientele for real, human companions tended to be wealthy.

Most lonely people tended not to be wealthy, which was why pleasure doll rental was a thing, though here they tried to get fancy and call themselves Lifestyle Companionship Providers. You could call it whatever you wanted, but the bottom line was, you were having sex with a robot, and a not too bright one at that.

Security was pretty stiff, no pun intended, at the live, human brothels. Not so much at the robot version. Their main concern was that none of the drunken spacers who stopped by tried to steal one of the dolls and take it with them on their ship for entertainment. At least not without paying for it.

The place I was looking for had a sign in bright, neon orange that advertised "Live Robot Sex," as if they didn't see the oxymoron inherent in the term, right beneath the imaginative name of the place: "Gears of Whore." Most of their clientele was probably too drunk to care. The woman behind the front counter sure was. Well, I was assuming drunk. High was also a possibility.

"Hey," I told her, nodding.

"Catalog is on the wall," she said, slurring the words, motioning to the holographic display dancing across the opposite wall, showing a variety of male and female images, human as well as animal. None of them were live humans of course... or live animals. I understood that the robots were quite lifelike nowadays, though I'd never tried one myself.

"I'm looking for Xander Free," I explained. She scowled deeply, her eyes focusing more sharply.

"You a cop?"

"No," I said honestly, fighting back a grin. "Just got some work for him. Extra money doing some tech stuff."

She shrugged, losing interest.

"He's in the maintenance room, third door on your right. You tell that worthless asshole that he better not be doing side jobs while he's on the clock."

I nodded and walked down the corridor, trying not to pay attention to the customers heading back for their cybernetic assignations. I was in no position to judge anyone else, but lonely people made me feel lonely. The maintenance room was well-lit, by contrast with the concealing shadows of the service chambers, and ducking through it was like walking into a surrealist painting.

Rack after rack of spare parts were mounted to the walls: heads, hands, feet, knees, all stripped bare of artificial flesh, the white plastic gleaming bonelike in the muted light.

Work tables were lined up in the center of the room, each occupied by a pleasure doll under repair, some with their flesh in place, others inhuman skeletons laid open, actuator motors and fluid-filled artificial muscles in full view. Maybe there was some deep, philosophical analogy to be made there to our society, beautiful and perfect on the outside but with a profane ugliness just under the surface. I don't know; I'm not that smart.

Neither was the guy leaning over one of the metal worktables, stretching synthetic skin on over the frame of a very well-endowed male robot. Nothing about the man's slack, sallow face screamed "genius" to me, though he had, at least, been dependable over the years as a Confidential Informant.

"Hey, Xander," I said, waving.

"Oh, shit," the little man moaned, letting his head sink down against the belly of the robot in a somewhat disturbing image. "I thought I'd seen the last of you. It's been almost a year, man."

"Things have been busy."

"When did you grow the beard?" he asked, squinting at me. "Are you like, undercover?"

"I'm so undercover, you should probably not talk about me being undercover," I suggested. I pushed the door shut behind me and leaned against the table he was working at, frowning as I realized the sex robot was staring at me. I stood straight, wiping my hand off on my pant leg. "I need some help. I'm looking for a guy who's doing some tech work for the Evolutionists."

Xander's eyes went wide, and he pushed away from the table, looking around the room as if he expected to find someone watching him.

"Dude, I don't fuck with the Evolutionists, and you shouldn't either! They won't just kill you, they'll cut off what they can sell and keep you living until they want to cut off the next part because it's cheaper that way! You can't ask me to spy on those guys!"

"I'm not," I assured him, raising a hand to forestall his burgeoning panic. "I just want to know if you've heard anything. The guy's name is Oscar Fuentes. He's an AI researcher, and we think he's trying to build off-the-books AI for the Evolutionists." I shrugged. "We don't know why, but we'd rather get him in custody before he gets the chance, you know?"

Xander didn't seem mollified, but he stopped retreating at least for the moment.

"Okay, yeah, I've heard of Oscar." He stripped off his work gloves and sat back on a wobbly stool set back against the wall. "He's a genius, man. Everyone who's in the business has heard of him. He's worked for anyone who needs any work done on advanced robotics and AI." Xander leaned forward conspiratorially. "I don't know that it's true, but I heard he used to work for the Union military, like in intelligence."

Oh, good. A former spook. No wonder the reward is so high.

"Have you heard where he is right now? Where the Evolutionists have him working?" I crossed my fingers and prayed it wasn't in their enclave.

Xander appeared hesitant, eyes on the floor for a moment before he gathered his courage.

"I'm getting paid for this, right?"

I sighed and reached into my jacket pocket, pulling out the five hundred credits I'd set aside for this eventuality, leaving me just enough to buy one more meal if I found a cheap street vendor. Xander counted it before hiding it away somewhere under his shirt.

"Okay, I don't know this is one hundred percent true, but I heard he was working out of an old, shut-down warehouse in the industrial district. I can show you where it is on a map, if you want."

"Thanks, Xander. You're the best."

And if he was lying, I was going to come back here and surgically remove that five hundred credits from his ass.

* * *

I should have taken longer to prep, but I only had seventy-two hours, so I just went straight to the warehouse. Not my brightest move, in retrospect.

The industrial district wasn't a dangerous place, not compared to the rest of *El Mercado*. Even black-market criminals have to work.

Fabricator shops, warehouses, and shipping centers were squeezed together into the real estate no one else wanted, not on the main thoroughfare, stuck into an isolated corner of this section of the station. Robots rolled and shuffled and hovered here and there, the only place you could find them in *El Mercado* outside the sex district. Personal robots were the toys of the rich, and the rich in this sector had different tastes, preferring human toys to cybernetic ones.

No one gave me a second look—the human workers not paid enough to double as security guards, and the goods manufactured here not worth enough to make it cost-effective to hire real security to guard them. *Except* for the one building. It was abandoned, the company that had owned it had gone out of business after a contract dispute, and, yet, it was the only place there that had humans watching it. They weren't being obvious, trying their best to look like normal workers, but there was a desperate edge to them, something only a cop or another criminal would notice.

I guess I'm a little of both.

The warehouse was in the center of the cluster of buildings, masked on all sides by the sheet metal walls of the other structures, which gave me a good approach without being seen. I hugged the walls of the fabricator shop catty-corner to the warehouse, concealed by shadows, watching the security guard on that side as he paced his area of responsibility. It was a sloppy job, I decided. Professionals would have overlapping patrol lanes, but these guys had just divided a side each. All I had to do was wait until this joker turned around.

And cardio. I needed to do more cardio. I barely made it to the shadows of the side entrance before he turned my way again. I was breathing hard and tried to hold it to avoid being heard, tried not to look at him for fear of the whites of my eyes giving me away. A shout would have meant the end of this operation and probably the end of my nascent career, but none came. The guard's shuffling, scraping footsteps turned away, and I let myself breathe again.

The door opened outward, and I slipped through, pulling it shut gently behind me. Inside was darkness. Night-vision glasses would have been nice to have, but they cost money. Staying tight to the wall, I closed my eyes and tried to let them adjust before I moved. This didn't make any sense. They were guarding the place, so there was definitely something important here. Why were the lights off? And why was it so damned cold in here?

I pulled my blaster from its shoulder holster, then zipped my jacket all the way up to my neck. I was pretty sure I could have seen my breath... if there'd been enough light for it. Shadows near the walls solidified and cohered into refrigeration coils as my eyes finally adjusted to what little ambient light there was. Refrigeration coils. That meant some serious quantum computer cores, which made sense for illegal AI research. Oscar was here and Xander had earned his five hundred.

Thank God. I didn't have the money to pay another informant.

Skirting the refrigeration units, I stayed close to the outside walls, trying to get an idea of the entire layout of the place before I did anything. No guards that I could see, just stack after stack of servers, wired together with superconductive cable, six rows across, taking up the entire center of the warehouse. The ambient light came from the power buttons glowing a steady green and the processor activity indicators, flickering red in a fitful, erratic pattern.

A brighter glow came from the other end of the warehouse, a shifting white and green that I recognized as the output from a computer display. A holographic one as it turned out, which was fancy for this area but what I expected if this was actually an Evolutionist operation. And one look at Oscar Fuentes told me it was.

That picture of him in his file must have been an old one. He wasn't a bland, boring man with a weak chin anymore. Now, his chin was metal. *Most* of him was metal. Prosthetics were a thing, of course. Most people can get flesh or bone or even whole limbs grown from DNA samples and assembled in a medical lab, but some don't have the nerve endings or the intact bone structure for the transplant, and, in those cases, the docs use prosthetics. But those prosthetics are designed to function and look just like the flesh and blood versions they're replacing.

What Oscar had done was well beyond that. He was a collection of shining, burnished metal, the limbs barely reminiscent of human arms and legs. Even his face was half metal, both eyes replaced by glowing red oculars, his lower jaw a steam shovel with metal teeth. He didn't have to sit at the station where he was hooked in, since his hips and legs were mechanical—he just stood, a statue staring at the holographic display with unblinking eyes.

Shit. I didn't have an EM dampening net or anything else that would hold this guy. I wasn't even sure if my blaster would take him out unless I aimed for the head.

Why the hell wouldn't they put in his file that he was an Evolutionist cyborg?

"I know you're there."

His voice was pleasant, not sounding artificial or automated the way some of the Evolutionists preferred, yet it sent ice-cold tendrils wrapping around my guts, squeezing. I was five or six meters away from him, half-concealed by the server stacks. I might be able to make it to the door before he moved.

"Don't bother running," Oscar warned me, as though he was reading my thoughts. "*They* know you're here, too. You run out that door, they'll shoot you down. Which would be a shame. You were a damned good cop, Grant."

I didn't raise my blaster, but I didn't set it down, either, as I moved closer to him, in front of him as though that mattered.

"Sorry, do we know each other?"

"Not as such. But you tried to save my life once. Before *this*." He waved at his body, as if to demonstrate what *this* was. "You weren't in time, but you did try. I suppose I owe you something for that."

"I did?" I blinked.

"And now, I'm saving yours."

A banshee screeched inside my head and everything went black.

* * *

*S*onic stunner.

I hadn't even pried my eyes open, but I knew what had happened. My head felt like someone had used it for batting practice, and the pins-and-needles sensation was still working its way down from my core to my extremities. I'd felt it before—every Marshal had to take a test-blast from the sonic stunner before they were allowed to use one.

Against my better judgement and the weight of the worst headache I'd ever had, I opened my eyes. I was in a small room, no more than three meters on a side, unadorned with so much as a chair. The floor was bare metal, the walls stark white, and the door was depressingly thick. I neglected to mention that the floor also made a horrible bed. Sitting up was a symphony of pain, but I decided that I'd rather face death on my feet than lying flat on my back.

What came through the door wasn't death, but it was close enough. It wasn't Oscar, or else I didn't *think* it was. I'm not an expert on Evolutionist fashion but this—*guy?*—didn't have metal teeth. Or hair, or a nose.

"Come with me." For an Evolutionist, that was practically a soliloquy, so I didn't argue.

The hallway outside was no less bland and sterile than the room where I'd been imprisoned, but at least it was more densely occupied. Through open doors, I caught glimpses of other cyborgs... standing. Doing nothing that I could discern, just standing there. Were they sleeping? They *could* sleep standing up, I was sure, thanks to the fact that most of them had at least part of their skeletal framework replaced by metal, and the noise and light wouldn't bother the ones who had cybernetic eyes and ears, since those could be turned off at will.

But I found it hard to believe that they'd leave the door open. The level of paranoia among these people was pretty damned high.

"You wonder what we do."

I glanced up at my cyborg tour guide in surprise.

"I do," I admitted, not elaborating since his people appreciated brevity.

"Interface."

He didn't offer anything further, but I understood. Their artificial eyes and ears were tied into the net—their own private nets and the general net of the station. They could experience a level of virtual reality no un-augmented human could reach, and I expected they'd take advantage of that.

"Do you miss human contact? Do you miss feeling other people?"

I don't know why I asked, but I did… maybe out of curiosity, maybe because I was hoping they knew a secret I didn't. I couldn't read his face any more than I could have read the face of a serving robot at a restaurant.

"You feel with your brain."

He was right, technically, but I didn't agree. There was something beyond the brain, beyond the flesh even. But you gotta choose your audience.

"You're a bounty hunter," he said.

"You know I am. Why didn't you just kill me?" Not that I was complaining, but there was no reason for them not to kick me while I was down.

"He asked us not to."

I didn't have to ask who *he* was, because we'd arrived at our destination. It reminded me of the warehouse. Same equipment, same refrigeration, and, thank God, I was still wearing my jacket. And the same person in the center of it all.

"Hello, Grant," Oscar said. It was so damned hard to identify with someone who didn't have real eyes to look into, but the voice helped. "Sorry I had to stun you, but if they'd found you holding a gun, you'd be dead."

"Why do you care?" I asked, looking back over my shoulder as the door closed behind us. The Evolutionist had left me here alone with Oscar. "Who the hell *are* you?"

"I did change my name since our last encounter. You knew me as Oscar, yes… Oscar Lemond."

I don't quite have an eidetic memory, but there are certain things that stick with me. Like a Union Marshal netdiver who'd been running cracking dives into the computer networks of organized criminal networks. He was damned good at it. So good, some of those criminals paid a lot of money to make him go away. They planted a bomb in his apartment on the Panicle. I heard about it from an informant, and I tried to warn him, tried to get over there, but it was too late. I'd done my best to shut out the memories of that day, of what I'd found in the wreckage, but it flooded back, and I nearly retched.

"I thought you were dead," was all I could choke out.

"After the bomb, there wasn't much left of me," Oscar admitted. "That I survived at all is a miracle, and when the doctors broke it to me that I would wind up with more of me artificial than natural, I was fairly close to taking up their offer of assisted suicide. But then, I had a thought. Perhaps this could be an opportunity. After all, the doctors and technicians were going to have to be connecting the new prosthetics directly into my brain, so why not give me the chance to get even with the criminals who'd tried to kill me? I suggested they go ahead and give me a direct brain-to-computer link, wireless capability, enhanced cybernetics, the works. All it would take was approval from the Union Navy, but I figured since I worked for the Marshals and was volunteering to use it in the service of the government, it should be automatic."

The biological half of his face twisted in a sneer.

"It wasn't, of course. The Navy turned down the request, and the Marshals opted to retire me. With a generous medical pension, of course. But I had other ideas, and, rather than sit around and wait for them to turn me into a full-body cosmetic prosthesis, I took the money and made other arrangements."

"I killed them, you know," I said softly. "The ones who planted the bomb. Tracked them down and raided their place. They wouldn't surrender."

"I know. I watched the security camera feeds and enjoyed every second of it." His smile reminded me of a great white shark about to take a bite from a seal.

"You were a cop. Now you're an Evolutionist?" Maybe I shouldn't have sounded so angry since Oscar was the one thing keeping me alive, but the part of me that was still a Marshal was outraged.

Oscar's laugh was a rumble deep inside his metal chest.

"Just because I chose this appearance does not mean I am an Evolutionist. Though they assumed the same thing when they first approached me and were quite disturbed when I refused to help them."

"This is what 'refused' looks like?" I waved at the machinery. "Because it sure looks like you're engineering AI for them."

"Even one such as I has weaknesses, Grant." Oscar sighed, a curious sound coming from someone like him. "And weaknesses can be exploited."

The door burst open and the same Evolutionist cyborg who'd escorted me to the room strode inside, making a beeline for me. I tried to step out of his way but ran up against a bank of servers and couldn't avoid the snakelike strike of his hand wrapping around my neck. Alloy fingers squeezed *just* hard enough to cut off my air without breaking my neck, which must have required great restraint from Mr. Roboto, but I was in no position to appreciate it. I slammed a fist against the side of his arm with all the strength I had, but it was like punching a brick wall.

"Weaknesses like this human." He must have been listening into our conversation, but he wasn't looking at me, staring instead at Oscar. "I have been patient, merciful. It's been weeks. Show me results or this human dies."

I could hold my breath for over a minute. I'd done it many times in a swimming pool, once in the ocean, even, but there was a qualitative difference between doing that and having a hulking cyborg choking me slowly to death. Unconsciousness crept up on me, a black presence squeezing out vision, a roaring in my ears that nearly drowned out Oscar's reply.

"Quinn, the system is ready, I am just preparing for the upload."

"Don't call me Quinn," the cyborg snapped. "Names are for mortals."

A flick of his wrist, and I was flying, hitting the floor shoulder-first and tumbling across the room until I rolled up against a server stand. The only good thing was, I didn't have any air left to get knocked out of me. Wheezing, I shook my head to clear it and didn't immediately try to get up; I just watched Oscar lead the cyborg formerly known as Quinn into the center of the chamber.

I hadn't noticed the gurney there because it was shrouded in darkness, but now that I saw it, the lines of it came into focus. It was a human shape and the hairs at the back of my neck stood up at the stillness of the chest. Had they brought a corpse in here?

Then I noticed the face. There wasn't one. It was the ceramic and plastic skull of a humanoid robot… and as my eyes adjusted to the darkness, it became obvious that it was a female sexbot, much like the ones in the brothel where Xander had led me into a trap. Oscar pulled a superconductive cable bundle from a spool in the center console and stretched it back to the bare skull of the robot, attaching the socket to jack in the back of the head.

"The quantum core is undetectable," Oscar warned, "but the Bartoli crystals are going to have a different thermal signature than a typical sexbot. Any in-depth scan will spot it."

"We don't need an in-depth scan," Quinn assured him, running his fingers just a centimeter over the false flesh of the robot, putting the lie to his assertion he didn't miss touching another being. "Just something smart enough to work for us and lacking the restraints of a robot."

I should have kept my mouth shut, but that's never been my strongsuit.

"You're going to turn sexbots into assassins."

Quinn didn't bother to look at me, though he did reply, which surprised me.

"Assassins, spies, saboteurs. They can go where we can't, not without attracting attention."

"And this is just the first, isn't it?" I pressed, scooting up into a sitting position, back against one of the server racks. "If it works, you can put AI in maintenance bots, food servers... whatever you want."

I didn't think an Evolutionist could smile, but I was wrong.

"You're a bright one, for a Norm."

"What do you have on him?" I was pushing my luck, now, but in for a penny... "I read Oscar Lemond's file after I thought he died. He had no family, no girlfriend, no close friends. He was a loner who buried himself in his work. And I can't think that's changed since he retreated into a metal shell."

"Oscar looks like us," Quinn said, scorn dripping off his words, "but he has the soul of a Norm. Genius, smarter than any of us, and what does he do?" Quinn's head cocked to the side, a very human gesture, one that I recognized as him using an internal datalink to send a message.

I wondered if the cyborg understood the concept of leaving someone hanging, but it was only a few seconds before another of the Evolutionists walked in, trailing behind it a... a *dog*. On a leash.

I'm not much on dogs, wouldn't be able to tell you any except the most popular breeds, but this one looked a lot like an English mastiff my grandparents had, if it had knocked up a golden retriever. Big, but fluffy and cute enough that the big wasn't intimidating. There was something strange about the collar attached to the leash. It was bulky and thick, with circuits embedded into its surface, ringed with what looked like electromagnets, and I had no clue why anyone would have something that complex wrapped around the neck of a dog.

Unless...

"A robot dog?" I guessed, coming slowly to my feet.

The dog looked at me, arching an eyebrow.

"Oh, look, the meatsack thinks he's a smart one. What else you got, buddy? Wanna tell us what the speed of light in a vacuum is?"

I was at a loss for words.

"An AI quantum core brain," Quinn lamented, staring at the dog, "as sophisticated as any I've seen, and the Norm puts it into a pet."

"A friend," Oscar said, and his tone held nothing of the light banter I'd heard earlier. "Dog is a friend."

Not an original name, but who was I to judge?

"Your friend," Quinn told him, "will have his memory core erased by an electromagnetic pulse if you don't do as you're told."

So, that was what the collar was for. And I bet the leash the cyborg held was the control for it.

"You know," Dog went on, seemingly unfazed by the threat, his brown-eyed gaze turning on Quinn, "for an Evolutionist, you sure are a big-mouthed shitbag. I thought you idiots were supposed to be the strong, silent types? I mean, I *expect* humans to be idiots, but aren't you supposed to be the next step in evolution or some such bullshit? Because to me, you look like a bunch of sullen, Goth teenagers."

"Dog," Oscar admonished tightly, "all it'll take is for that Evolutionist idiot to push the button on the end of that control and you're, effectively, dead. You know that, right? And since I neglected to give you opposable thumbs, you can't just reach up and take that collar off. So perhaps you should consider that discretion is the better part of valor."

There was something off about the tone of Oscar's voice, just a bit of a didactic edge. I'm not sure anyone else would have noticed it, but part of being a Marshal or any cop is not just hearing what people are saying but how they're saying it. The Evolutionists already knew about Dog's collar, and Dog already knew, so who was he telling?

Oh, darn, he's telling me.

"The robot is ready," Oscar said, shifting gears so suddenly, I blinked at the subject change.

The ex-cop yanked the cables out of the machine's head, then pulled the fake-skin mask back over its skull and stepped back. The robot was very female, dressed about as scantily as most sexbots, in a filmy negligee that did absolutely nothing for me since I required at least a pulse in my potential lovers. She moved with the seductive sway of a seasoned professional, the corner of her mouth turning upward as she saw me.

"Well, now," she drawled in an accent I couldn't place except that it was from Earth. "Who might you be, handsome?"

She sauntered up to me, one hand on a hip, the other tracing a line down my cheek. It was the typical sexbot talk, but something about it made my skin crawl, and I flinched away.

"Show me," Quinn ordered, looking at Oscar. "You could have just rebooted a sexbot for all I'm seeing."

"She's yours to command," Oscar said, motioning at the bot... and at me. "That's why I wanted him kept alive."

"Oh, let's not be hasty here," I said, checking the corners of my peripheral vision for any way out, or, alternatively, anything that could be used as a weapon. And finding neither.

"Her name is Candy. Go ahead, tell her to kill the cop."

I was going to just go ahead and run, try to get past them. It wouldn't do any good, but fighting 150 kilos of metal wasn't going to accomplish anything.

"Candy," Quinn barked, "break his neck."

Candy hesitated, glancing back at Oscar.

"You know what to do, Candy," he told her. "Follow orders."

The sexbot moved faster than even the Evolutionist cyborgs, grabbing me by the arm and tossing me as if I weighed nothing... right at Dog. I hit shoulder-first and expected fluffy dog-body but instead, got something rock hard that nearly threw my arm out of joint. But he did move. Physics couldn't be ignored and the robot dog went tumbling across the floor, with me wrapped around him. And the leash wrapped around me.

I was seeing stars—again. This was getting old and I longed for the days when I used to arrest people who weren't cybernetically jacked and capable of killing me with their bare hands. But through the stars came a blur of motion, through the roar in my ears the thud and clang of metal hitting metal and I gradually realized that Oscar and Candy were fighting the two Evolutionists. Oscar was engaged with the one who'd brought in Dog and was holding his own, exchanging punches that landed like hammer blows, but Candy wasn't doing so well. I knew why. She might be an artificial intelligence capable of violence, but she was stuck inside a fairly fragile sexbot.

She was fast and doing a good job of dodging some of Quinn's blows, but not all. Her lower jaw hung off her face by a strip of faux flesh and her left arm was disabled below the elbow. And once he was done with her, Oscar and I would be dead as well.

"Take the fucking collar off, meatsack!" Dog snapped at me.

Oh, yeah.

I fumbled at the thing for three seconds before it fell away, and that was long enough for Quinn to finish off Candy. He ripped her head from her body in a shower of sparks and tossed it negligently away, turning to Oscar. Dog hit him square in the chest, knocking him to the floor with a tremendous crash. I caught one glimpse of a mouth open too wide and teeth of shining metal flashing before the screams started and pieces of metal and flesh began flying everywhere.

Oscar and the other cyborg were in a tight clinch, and I dodged out of the way as the two of them tumbled to the floor where I'd been a moment before, rolling around, neither able to get the advantage. I looked around again for a weapon, and this time, I found one. Candy's right arm had been snapped off below the elbow, leaving a jagged shard of metal and I grabbed it by the wrist, ignoring the bile rising in my throat at the imagery of the severed hand.

The Evolutionist was on top of Oscar now, pummeling him from above, and there was only one vulnerable spot I could see. The back of the cyborg's skull had a bare spot, usually protected by a metal flange, but his head was down, chin on his chest and it was sitting there all nice and white and obvious. I used both hands to stab the jagged edge of Candy's arm right through the patch of actual bone and into the cyborg's very human brain.

Candy's hand waved goodbye for him as he stiffened and shuddered, then collapsed on top of Oscar. The ex-cop pushed him aside and jumped to his feet, grinning with bare, steel teeth.

"Thanks for the hand," he told me, and I stared at him in disbelief, but he'd already turned to Dog. "You finished playing with your food?"

Brown fur was matted red now around the robot's muzzle, blood dripping off his teeth to meet the rest of Quinn's arterial spray on the floor. Dog grinned, bits of metal and flesh stuck between the razor-honed fangs.

"I suppose it would be a good idea to get the fuck out of here."

"Grant," Oscar said, offering me a hand and pulling me to my feet. "Do me a solid and grab that collar and leash. When the two of us are through the door, hit the button on the handle and toss it into the room behind you." He waved around at the server stacks. "Don't want to leave all this behind for them."

I felt like I was walking in a dream, which might have been a sign of a mild concussion, but I found the collar and tried not to step into the spreading pools of blood when I grabbed it. I wasn't sure what bothered me more, the blood or the shredded, broken metal and plastic left over from the dead, but I averted my eyes from both and concentrated on finding that button. I hesitated, wondering if the effects of the EMP device on the human body would be any less unpleasant than what it would do to my cybernetic allies, but then shrugged. Oscar was right. I couldn't leave the means to build illegal AI in the hands of the Evolutionists.

I pressed the button and threw the collar into the center of the room, then ducked out and slammed the door shut. The click of the lock barely beat the snap-hum, still loud even through the thick, metal door, and I sighed in relief, though there was nothing to be relieved about just yet.

"Where are we?" I hissed at Oscar, following him and Dog down the empty hallway, hoping he wouldn't tell me we were in the middle of the Evolutionist enclave.

"In the middle of the Evolutionist enclave," he said cheerfully. "Don't worry, though, we know a way out."

They didn't seem at all concerned with the cyborgs standing motionless inside the side rooms, passing by as if the Evolutionists were statues rather than potential obstacles. I wanted to ask why, but I didn't want to talk. Despite Dog's insults, incessant chatter wasn't an Evolutionist thing and was much more likely to attract attention from those ViR-immersed cyborgs. I felt like I was tip-toeing through a cave full of hibernating grizzlies, though I honestly wasn't sure if grizzlies hibernated in caves. I'd never seen one except on video.

We passed at least two dozen of the rooms and I wondered if this was their version of a barracks, where they slept and did ViR immersion and ate whatever it was they ate. I had no idea because the Marshals Service had no idea... we'd never been able to get any intelligence sources inside the Enclave.

When we left the Hall of Standing Cyborgs behind, I wanted to feel relief, but I wasn't sure if it was justified. The bare hallways were gone, but now the three of us were in a huge, metal-walled chamber, lit up with harsh, overhead lights, filled with row upon row, stack upon stack of transparent, fluid-filled cylinders. I didn't want to think about what was in them, but I couldn't turn away. Organs. Human organs, preserved for sale. I bit down on the bile trying to come up my throat, and suddenly lost any vestigial guilt I might have felt for killing the Evolutionist back in the AI lab.

"This shit bother you, meatsack?" Dog asked, the slap of his paws on the metal obscenely loud in the empty chamber. "Spare parts? Make you feel like you're one of us?"

"It makes me feel like someone was murdered for every single one of those organs," I shot back. "Where are we going?"

"This is the hideout for some of the most wanted criminals in the Union," Oscar told me. "You think they don't have an exit plan?"

"I'd think they have electronic security," I told him, eyes darting around from one side of the chamber to the other as we crossed it. "How come we haven't been spotted?"

"Because those idiots gave me access to their systems to finish the work you interrupted when you busted into the warehouse in *El Mercado*. Thanks for that, by the way. And I guess I'll have to thank my old friend Xander, too."

Great. The whole damned thing was a setup from the word go.

"This was my first bounty," I lamented, but Oscar shushed me and yanked open the door to the next chamber.

It was a hangar. In the center of it was a starship, a transport about the same size as mine, but newer and less of a piece of junk. I goggled at it, trying to figure out how the hell it was supposed to launch... and then I noticed the elongated tunnel heading up from it at an angle... presumably all the way to the surface of the Panicle.

"We're stealing this," I assumed, following them to the open belly ramp.

There was no one around and why would there be? They wouldn't want people screwing around with their emergency escape plan, drawing attention to it. We just walked right inside.

"Technically," Oscar corrected me, "Dog is stealing it because I designed him to be very good at that sort of thing."

As if on cue, the canine-shaped robot trotted up the passage to the cockpit and hopped into the pilot's seat. His right eye opened up and a probe extended out of it, finding a socket in the control panel.

"And then I'm going to take it somewhere far away from here," Oscar went on, clambering into the copilot's seat, "and try to forget I ever saw this place."

"I'd ask if you'd drop me off at my ship first," I said morosely, falling into a chair between them, "but there's not really any point. Without the bounty from this job, she'll get repossessed in a month."

The belly ramp closed with a pneumatic sigh and deep in the guts of the ship, the main drives began to roar.

"I told you I owe you, Grant," Oscar assured me, smiling that shark smile. "I've made some money these past few years, leasing my talents to the highest bidder. How much was the price on my head?"

"Twenty grand," I told him.

His head tilted to the side as he used his implanted datalink, but before I could ask him what he was doing, I grabbed at the seat re-

WANTED, DEAD OR ALIVE | 39

straints, trying to steady myself. The ship was moving, rising slowly off its moorings and angling up through the tunnel.

"There. You have your twenty thousand," Oscar said, focused on me again. "That should give you a start in your newfound profession."

"You're awful generous, aren't you?" I asked, skeptical. In my experience, people didn't throw that kind of money around for no reason.

"That representative was dirty as could be, and then he sicced the system on you. That system chewed us both up and spit us out, broken physically and otherwise, because the system doesn't care. Pleading guilty to the misdemeanor charge meant you could, say, get bonded as a bounty hunter. Fighting it, and losing—and the rep would have made sure you lost—would mean a felony conviction. Believe me, I've seen it, I get it. You were a good cop, and if you live long enough, you'll make a good bounty hunter too."

The black at the end of the tunnel turned to light, a double lock folding silently out of the way, letting Epsilon Eridani shine through. The ship rocketed outward and suddenly we were shooting away from a side of the Panicle I'd never even seen before, heading on a curving course around the bulk of the station.

"Hah, yeah, *if* he lives long enough," Dog scoffed, not turning away from the screen—I was grateful for that, since the whole probe-out-of-the-eye thing made me a bit queasy. "Bounty hunting isn't like being a cop. You won't have any backup out here, no SWAT teams to call in. Some asshole's going to put a round through the back of your head inside a month."

"Not if you're watching his back, Dog," Oscar said.

"What?" Dog yelped, twisting around in the seat. The probe had retracted, and I might have mistaken him for a real dog if he hadn't kept talking. "What the fuck are you talking about, Oscar? I'm going with you!"

"I'm going to find a hole and pull it in after me," Oscar said, shaking his head. "My kind of business draws too much attention here around this many greedy people. I'll do better with a more remote location. But your talents would be wasted in a place like that, Dog. I gave you the gift of blending in. You're going to use it, but first, you have to learn how. Grant here is going to teach you that."

"Whoa, wait a second," I interrupted, hands raised palms out. "You expect me to take a highly-illegal and very dangerous unregistered AI with me while I try to be a bounty hunter? Are you nuts?"

"It's only illegal if they find out about it," Oscar said. "And yes, he's damned dangerous. Think how handy that could be in a place like *El Mercado*."

I did. I'm ashamed to say it sounded like a really good idea.

"Why the hell would I want to play second fiddle to some washout ex-cop?" Dog demanded, puffing his chest out like a real dog about to assert his territory.

"Because I'm asking you to," Oscar told him, resting a hand on the head of the scruffy mastiff-retriever mix. "And I'm your friend."

Dog sighed.

"All right, Goddammit." Dog rounded at me, his glare hard enough to melt steel. "But I'm telling you right now, meatsack, if you get an attack of conscience and try to turn me in as an illegal AI, I'll rip your fucking throat out before they can shoot an EMP at me. You got that?"

"Trust me," I said, unable to stop myself from laughing, "I am way past attacks of conscience. And if I tried to turn you in, I'd wind up in a cell for the rest of my life, even if I survived."

"Excellent!" Oscar enthused, clapping his hands. "To quote one of my favorite movies, 'This could be the beginning of a beautiful friendship.'"

Dog didn't seem convinced, and neither was I. But for the first time in six months, I wasn't alone.

* * * * *

Rick Partlow Bio

Rick Partlow is that rarest of species, a native Floridian. Born in Tampa, he attended Florida Southern College and graduated with a degree in History and a commission in the US Army as an Infantry officer.

His lifelong love of science fiction began with Have Space Suit—Will Travel and the other Heinlein juveniles and traveled through Clifford Simak, Asimov, Clarke, and on to William Gibson, Walter Jon Williams, and Peter F Hamilton. And somewhere, submerged in the worlds of others, Rick began to create his own worlds. He has written over 40 books in a dozen different series, and his short stories have been included in twelve different anthologies. He is currently writing the best-selling Drop Trooper series for Aethon Books and a mil-SF alien invasion series, as well as the Earth at War series for Pramantha Publishing.

He lives in northern Wyoming with his wife and two lovable mutts. Besides writing and reading science fiction and fantasy, he enjoys outdoor photography, hiking, and camping.

To subscribe to Rick's newsletter, go to this link: https://www.subscribepage.com/o1m0u1

# # # # #

The Oni and the Shadow by Quincy J. Allen

A Contractor Wars Story

The Oni

I held up a closed fist. Their eyes followed it as if it held the promise of riches and freedom. I shook it. The dice rattled like dry bones. I already knew what the number would be. I was *yamabushi*… *hijiri*—one with the dice like a monk atop the mountain. Tonight, I couldn't lose.

And for a change, I wasn't cheating.

A harsh glow of yellow, pink, and green filtered down into the alley, sifting over us from Takagi's Orgasm Emporium where anyone—human or alien—could get its rocks off for the right price. Men shouted beside me, looking like washed-out photos of broken souls. They were old *kobun* mostly—drivers, second-rate bodyguards, and street thugs sporting more salt than pepper hair. We were all miles beneath the Yakuza big shots they worked for.

The *kobun* and I were stuck in a no-man's-land between money, sex, and death. Back alleys and low-rent noodle-carts were where men like us were at home. The only real difference between me and them was that I'd chosen the bottom—floated down to it like a fish carcass bitten in half by a shark. They, on the other hand, had been born here—and knew they'd never rise. We were brothers at the bottom of a barrel named Shinjuku.

45

I'd chosen Shinjuku because a person can get lost in the smooth canyons of rain-drenched plascrete and searing neon—where there's enough anonymity and opportunity to satisfy any appetite. That's what I did—got lost here to satisfy an appetite—although not any appetite you'd expect from an ex-hunter of men. That was all behind me, and what I'd become was enough—barely. I could finally stand in the light after so many years in shadow.

It had taken me six weeks to get into Gorira's floating crap game behind the *Koroshiamu*. At first he'd said he didn't trust me. I couldn't blame him. New faces in Shinjuku made people nervous, and Gorira—a very minor *shatei* for the Yamaguchi-gumi—had to worry about his boss Takagi, a particularly nasty *kyodai* who didn't fuck around with mistakes and was gunning for a shot at being made some day. Takagi had a habit of having people beaten to death and the pieces fed to the kelp farms.

Gorira had good instincts. He'd sniffed what I *used* to be—at least suspected—but when I told him where to find the *bōsōzoku* thugs who raped his niece, I had an open invitation to his game. Shinjuku is like that. You pay to play, one way or another, and damn near everything is currency. Flesh and blood especially.

I stared down at a pile of about thirty-thousand yen scattered across the blanket as the dice rattled in my hand. I could feel it—the tension growing as everyone waited for the dice to hit the grimy, black blanket Gorira laid out whenever *Konnichiwa Koneko* broadcast their syndicate death matches to holo-arenas like the one inside the *Koroshiamu*. In Shinjuku, most people's lives revolved around whenever the syndicate's ultra-lethal combat tournaments were being broadcast. When it came right down to it, the primary industries of Shinjuku were killing and fucking.

The number to make was five.

I rolled the bones. I could feel it there, the five, slipping off the tips of my fingers like a silk glove. I knew it before the dice bounced, before they stopped tumbling.

I smiled.

"Five!" Gorira shouted. "Moto-san wins!"

The *kobun* who had bet on me cheered. The others glared as I reached out to pull in my money.

Glass shattered from somewhere high above. We all looked up. A woman—someone's escort, no doubt—screamed as a shadowy figure sailed through a sixth-story window of the *Koroshiamu*, bounced off the wall of the Emporium, and dropped onto the center of the blanket with a grunt that sounded more like a beast than a man. Dressed in black, he'd landed in a crouch, face down toward the blanket.

The men around me rolled back, panicking like rabbits when a fox slips into the den. Someone shoved past Gorira, sent him tumbling into a row of trashcans where he shouted a litany of curses at the man's parentage. Everyone else raced down the alley or through the open door leading into the *Koroshiamu* kitchen.

The man in black slowly raised his head and stared at me.

An oni mask.

Red irises set in yellow eyes bored into me. The mask was bone white, like a gleaming skull, but with the face of a demon. The face had stubby horns and long tusk-like fangs of obsidian. There was something peculiar about how it covered his skull, almost as if it was part of him.

"You're on my money," I said as calmly as I could. Part of me—the part with brains—wanted to walk away. The guy was trouble, a mountain of it, and he *had* just dropped six stories without a hitch. Only top-of-the-line chassis—Masamune WarBorgs and their like or serious custom augments—could crank out that kind of performance. The thought gave me pause. If he was that hard-wired, combat unit or not, he'd tear me apart. I wasn't what I used to be, but I wasn't ready to turn my back on all those yen.

Hell, I'd earned it for a change.

He snorted, a derisive sound that made it clear he didn't think much of me... or my money.

This is going to get ugly, I thought as I stood slowly. He came up with me, and his eyes never left mine. He towered above me, well over six feet. The black cloth of his shirt, stretched taut over his body, flowed like dark water over the cut of thick muscles. I could just make out an irezumi-style tattoo—an oni head—running down from the open neck of his shirt.

I shifted my feet and squared my weight. So did he. There was something odd about his posture. It was casual, careless, as if he feared me no more than he would a child. I'd seen it plenty of times during my years hunting criminals for the *Kage No Gundan*. Usually men who stood like that were simply overconfident—far too accustomed to beating down the meek without really knowing how to hurt another human quickly and efficiently.

I *know* how to hurt, even kill that way, and the guy in the mask was the other kind—the sort who *knew* he couldn't be beat... just like I had known about the dice.

"I just want my money," I said, holding up my hands. "I can't leave without it."

He shook his head slowly.

Sirens cried in the distance, echoing down the streets and alleys, headed this way. Yamaguchi-gumi cops, no doubt. Cops not on their payroll knew better than to come down here.

"I think those are for you," I added, hoping he'd rather avoid the cops than stick around to trounce me.

We both heard pounding feet just before Gorira sailed in from the side. The man in the mask blurred. He turned, caught Gorira under the arm, and sent the hapless *shatei* sailing into a wall where he dropped, unconscious or dead. I couldn't tell which.

My instincts screamed to take the opening. As he turned, I sent a kick toward his mid-section. He didn't block it—he punched it. I barely saw him move, and as pain shot through my leg, I found myself really wishing I hadn't disabled all my mods. I followed with a fast strike to his throat. I'd killed men with that punch, collapsing the windpipe and sending my victim to the ground to writhe and gasp until he died. Unfortunately, my punch didn't find his throat, it found his hand.

Did I mention I'm not what I used to be?

He just stood there for a few seconds, looking at me. Jerking my fist back, I sent a flurry of punches at the mask, stepping in each time, but nothing hit home. He shifted left and right, stepping back with me like we were dancing. It was like he knew what I was going to do before I did it. He caught my fist again, with a smack of flesh on flesh, and twisted my arm outwards. My elbow screamed with pain. He raised his other hand high, and I could see what looked like claws extending from his fingers. They were the same bone-white color as the mask that encased his head.

He smiled. I don't mean that he smiled behind the mask.

The mask smiled.

His hand came down like a scythe. The claws raked across my chest, burning like fire, as if red-hot blades had scored home. I knew he'd slashed down to my ribs, and I figured I was dead.

An agonized scream tore from my throat, and I never saw the right cross that put out the lights.

* * *

The Wakagashira

I opened my eyes to a beautiful, athletic woman in a gray pantsuit, accentuated by a silver belt. Her eyes were the same color, and as hard as Masamune steel. She wore no makeup, save for lipstick as black as obsidian, and her short-cropped hair rose like a black, spiky crown.

"You're awake," she said in a soft, almost regal tone. It had an edge to it, one even most royals can't muster—except, perhaps, the Emperor. *She doesn't like me.* I could see it in those eyes.

I lay upon a futon, the sheet pulled up to my chin. I could feel the rigid warmth of PK—*purasuchikkusukin*—that covered my chest from my collar bones to my navel. It was a sort of artificial flesh loaded with nanites that held people's insides together, stopped bleeding, and dramatically accelerated healing.

"Clearly," I replied. I shifted my jaw back and forth, wincing with pain but grateful the oni hadn't broken it. *She's Yakuza.* I thought. *And made.* I could tell right away. It's like walking down a street full of stray dogs. Most are just lost, looking for a home or a scrap to eat. They're domesticated. Meek. Then there are the dogs who own the street. They stand their ground. Look you in the eyes with their ears laid back. You can tell they're dangerous—they take what they want. Yakuza are the same way. They're not domesticated. Not meek. They're predators.

I had to be in a Yakuza stronghold. Next to the Emperor's palace, this was the very last place I would have wanted to wake up.

"Got a name?" I asked.

"You may call me Buki," she said, and there was a hint of menace in the word. It meant weapon, after all.

I smiled. "Got a cigarette?"

"There's no smoking in here." She stood motionless, like a statue, and her eyes held neither pity nor compassion.

"I know." I didn't actually. "Got a cigarette?" I needed to figure out who she was and what she wanted. I was alive because she—or someone she worked for—wanted me that way.

"I don't smoke." Her eyes held curiosity, but there was also a layer of distaste, almost contempt, that I couldn't figure out. I'd never met her before, and I'd been careful to avoid crossing paths with any of the Yakuza since coming to Shinjuku with my new face.

"I didn't ask you that," I said. "Do you have a cigarette?" I repeated slowly.

She raised an eyebrow as she opened a small purse, pulled out a pack of slim cigarettes, and flicked her wrist. *Point to me.* She worked for someone who *did* smoke. The pack shot across the room and hit me directly in the crotch. I could tell it landed *exactly* where she intended. I had no doubt she could do the same thing with a weapon if she wanted. You learn to spot things like that early, or you end up with a throwing dagger stuck in your chest. I'd seen it plenty of times... just not my chest.

"Thanks." I pulled one out, sniffed it—frowning at the burn of menthol—and then propped it into the corner of my mouth to dangle like an unfinished thought. I don't talk to Yakuza without a cigarette in my mouth. I'm funny that way.

"There's no smoking in here," she repeated.

I stared out the window at an almost ethereal blue fog whose light source had to be Neo-Kyoto. It had been a long time since I'd been this close to the sky. I could always tell the difference. Three-hundred levels beneath Neo-Kyoto, Shinjuku glows yellow and pink through a fog that seeps down from a plascrete ceiling that forms the floor of the mega city. Shinjuku's glow makes it look like a happy, carefree place—which, of course it isn't. Neo-Kyoto, on the other hand, is blue-gray and reserved, almost sullen, despite being open to the sky and stars.

"I heard you the first time," I said.

I wasn't in a hospital. It had to be someone's bedroom.

Or guestroom, I guessed. A sumi painting of a samurai adorned the far wall, and a jade dragon perched menacingly upon a black lacquer dresser beneath a wide window. The futon beneath me was firm and fresh. It felt new, like what you feel in places that sell them. The room was clean, tidy, and *unused*.

"Thanks for the patch-up," I said without taking my eyes off the window.

"You're welcome." There was no graciousness in her answer, only courtesy.

"So…" I let my eyes slide across the room to lock squarely with the steely eyes of a woman who clearly didn't take shit from anyone. I could tell by the way she stood—light-footed and ready for a fight. The way her blouse draped down her muscular neck and her suit rose and fell over corded muscles, it was clear she'd had years of training behind her. "You want to tell me what that was back there?"

She smiled. *Another point to me.* "How do you know I know anything?" she asked.

I cocked an eyebrow. *It's going to be like that, is it?* I thought. I gave her a wry grin. "It's a funny thing. When I wake up in a strange bed faced with a beautiful Yakuza staring down on me after a crazed, oni-mask-wearing thug with superhuman strength falls six stories and takes a big chunk out of yours truly… well, the odds are she knows at least some of what's going on. So, what the fuck was that?"

"A thief." That's all she said, and the silence hung between us like dirty laundry.

"A *thief*," I finally repeated with a heavy dose of cynicism. "That mask. It *moved*. Like it was flesh. That wasn't just some oni mask hanging on a man's face, was it?"

"No."

I waited for her to elaborate, but all I got was more dirty laundry. "Is that all you plan on telling me?"

"For now."

"I don't suppose you picked up my money, did you?" I asked.

"Money?"

At least I got some confusion out of her, I thought. "From the crap game," I clarified. "There was thirty-thousand yen on the ground. Your oni interrupted a game that I had just won, actually."

"No."

"Well, shit." I'd started the night with two-thousand, thought I was going to walk home with thirty thousand, and now I had exactly dick. "So what do you want with me?"

"I want you to track down the thief... and collect the bounty we've put on his head."

I guffawed and let a trail of laughter follow behind it. "The impossibly strong, unbelievably fast thief that cut me up like sushi?" I snorted. *"That* thief?"

She nodded.

"I'll pass. Thanks."

She turned toward the door. "Masaru!" The door opened immediately, and in walked a small man with beady eyes and a black suit. He had *shingiin* written all over him. The yakuza lawyer held out a file to the lady, and she flicked her eyes in my direction.

Masaru bowed crisply, set the file down on my chest, and walked out without looking at me.

"You hate the Yakuza," she said. It wasn't an accusation.

I snorted. "Hate is a strong word. Hating the Yakuza is like hating bad weather. It shows up whether you hate it or not. I choose to stay out of the rain when I can, or use an umbrella when I can't. In this case, I think I'd like to stay out of the rain."

"You may want to look at that," she said, nodding toward the folder.

I looked down and realized it had a picture of me clipped to the front. By that, I mean it had a picture of me *before* I changed my face and disappeared into Shinjuku. It scared the hell out of me. *Point to her.* She knew who I really was... or at least had been. That explained her contempt for me. Knowing what was in that file meant she knew I used to kill Yakuza for money and status. It meant she also knew there was a healthy price on my head, put there by the emperor himself. *Kage No Gundan*—Shadow Warriors—didn't leave the Emperor's Shadow Corps. We called it that because all of us worked in shadow and ended up disappearing into it... feet first.

I'd cheated that fate.

I opened the folder and realized it was my complete file from the Shadow Corps. I'm sure I paled as a wave of nausea washed over me. Whichever clan she worked for, they were *very* well connected. "You're not supposed to have this," I said quietly.

"No, I'm not," she said. "But based on who you were, you're exactly what I need to clean up a mess not of my making but which I find squarely in my lap."

"Mess or not, I walked away from that life... slipping through shadows and hunting... *people*. I left it all behind me. I'm not even connected to the Net. I had my mods and CPU disabled. I went dark so I could never be tracked. I'm a *detective* now... I snap pictures of cheating husbands and unfaithful wives. I find lost puppies. I trade information for bowls of soup and seats in floating crap games. And I'm *happy!*" There was more bitterness in my voice than I expected.

"No, you're not." She said it as fact, like saying the ocean is deep or mountains are stone. And deep down, I knew she was right. I might have found a degree of contentment in this new life, but it was just a waiting-to-die existence. I had been a slave to the Shadow

Corps, and the allure Shinjuku offered had been freedom and ano-nymity… even if it was a dead-end life at the bottom of the barrel.

"Well, I'm not unhappy," I replied. "More importantly, I'm free and *breathing*." I ran a hand over my chest and felt the rubbery layer of PK holding the four deep gashes together. They'd be healed by the end of the day.

Her expression didn't change.

"You're not giving me a choice, are you?" I asked, feeling trapped all over again.

"Turn to the last page," she offered, and it was the first time there was any warmth in her voice.

I did.

The last page was blank.

When I joined the Shadow Corps, they put in a warehouse of brain and body implants. They turned me into a weapon that could beat any street-legal Masamune chassis. To make room, I let them take out who I'd been. When I left, I'd paid a tech to wipe out all the software in my head. The hardware was still in place, but with noth-ing to run it, I was just another meat sack—disconnected from the digital world with no more strength or speed than your average hu-man. It cost a fortune, but it also meant the Shadow Corps couldn't pick me up on the net. But I was still on the run… hiding from pry-ing eyes.

"Do you want a clean slate?" she asked. "Freedom to go any-where. Be anything you want."

"Of course." I looked at her thoughtfully. "And to get there, I just have to hunt down and kill this thief of yours? I'll also assume I don't have much choice?"

She smiled. The answer was yes to both, but she was polite enough not to slap me in the face with it. "There is one other thing," she said.

The hairs on the back of my neck stood up. The way she said it, the look on her face—she knew I wouldn't like it.

"What's that?"

"To beat the oni—you'll have to turn everything back on. You'll have to become Kage No Gundan again."

My blood went cold. "There's no way. The second I'm back online, the Shadow Corps will drop an anvil on me. The ID is hardwired into the CPU, and it'll link up and hit their mainframes in a couple nanoseconds."

"There is a way. The signal is hardwired. The ID is not."

"What?" How could she possibly know that? I'd always been told it was *im*possible.

"I can't tell you how, or why you don't have to worry about it. You'll just have to trust me."

I felt like a rat in a trap. I knew the instant my ID hit their system, a thousand alarms would go off and a dozen hunters would come after me until my corpse was shredded in an industrial scrap grinder. I didn't really have to think about it, though. If I did nothing, I was dead. I had no doubt she'd turn me in if I refused. If I did what she asked, however, I only *might* be dead. I'd have to figure out the rest as I went along. Maybe I could turn the system off and disappear again.

"If it makes a difference," she added, "I'll be going with you on the hunt. *Both* our necks will be on the chopping block if they come after you. And I'll pay you fifty thousand when the job is done."

I kept the surprise off my face.

"You?"

"Let me explain something. My oyabun named me Buki for a reason. I was his greatest weapon. You watch my back, and I'll watch yours. I can't take the oni alone, but with a Kage No Gundan beside me, we have a chance. I won't let them destroy everything Satō-san built."

That caught me off-guard. "Satō-san? As in Satō Akira? Of the Seiko-kai?"

She nodded.

I knew them. They were the one clan the Shadow Corps had never messed with. It wasn't that we were prohibited from hitting them, it was that none of their members ever came up on the Emperor's hit list. I'd always wondered about that. And then a few things clicked into place. The file. Spoofing my ID. And why the Shadow Corps had left the Seiko-kai alone. They were working either with or for the Emperor.

What the hell am I into? And why am I still alive? I knew Buki wouldn't tell me. Probably couldn't. I smelled a shadow-op… like the ones I used to lay down to get bad people to do what I wanted. Leverage is *everything*. The old part of me desperately wanted to dig deep, find out what was all really going on here. Good sense, however, won out. I'd play along. Play dumb. The best move for me was to do this job and hopefully find a way to get as far away from Buki, the Seiko-kai, and the Shadow Corps as I possibly could. Off-world, no doubt. But like Perdition, I'd have to go through Hell before I could get out of it.

I let out a long, resigned breath and then met her gaze. "What did he steal?" I finally asked.

"A statue… and my oyabun."

I raised an eyebrow, a bored expression on my face. The way she said it—Satō-san wasn't a hostage, he was a corpse, and the oni had made him that way.

"Look. If I'm going to do this, you need to do more than give me that cryptic bullshit. If I ask you a question about this job, you give me all the information you can. Either that, or we quit now and you turn me in for the bounty."

An irritated sigh slipped past her lips. I knew she was weighing how much she could tell me against how much she figured I needed to know to get the job done. I had no doubt she wouldn't tell me everything, but I sure as hell needed more than she was giving.

"The statue is called *Kitsuneribenji*. It depicts a nine-tailed *kitsune*. It's thirty centimeters tall, made of jade, and is the storage unit for a very dangerous prototype. Satō-san facilitated its creation, and if word of that got out... the consequences would be dire for more than just the Seiko-kai. The thief showed up at a meeting he shouldn't have known about, killed four people, including my employer, and took it."

"Why?" I asked.

"I don't know." She'd answered too quickly. She knew *something*.

I looked bored again.

"My best guess is that he wants to sell it to one of the other clans."

My expression didn't change.

"Really," she insisted. "I'll admit, there's more to it than that, but I have no intention of telling you what. You don't need to know, and such knowledge would have consequences. If that's a deal-breaker, then I'll kill you right now and bring your head in for the bounty. I can assure you that the rest has no bearing on getting the job done. Take it or leave it." *Point to her.* She'd given me all she was going to on the motives. And she was right. With something like this, the motives didn't matter as much as the who and the what. Besides, I already knew I was way in over my head.

"Why are you really doing this?" I asked. "And if, by some miracle, the two of us manage to take it back, what happens then? You just cut me loose? What's to stop you from handing over my head once I've helped you?"

She looked disgusted, as if I'd stuck my chopsticks point-down in a bowl of rice. I'd touched a nerve, and I almost felt bad about it. She closed her eyes and took a deep breath. When she opened them, her face went hard, and I saw the killer peek out from behind the beauty. "I want *revenge* for what he did."

I could tell she was weighing her words carefully. I knew that look. I'd seen it. Hell, I'd even worn it once or twice. Her employer had been more than just an oyabun who paid her well. She'd cared about him. A great deal. I realized she was more than just a member of the Seiko-kai. She was one of the senior members, perhaps even a *saiko-kommon*—Satō's senior advisor—or maybe even his *wakagashira*, his right-hand. The look on her face got me to shut up and had me thinking she was probably the latter, *wakagashira* for the Seiko-kai.

"And if we find it," she continued, "I'll take possession of the prototype for reasons that are entirely my own." She narrowed her eyes. "As for you, the Seiko-kai has never broken an agreement, and we never will if I have anything to say about it. You'll be paid, have a new ID, and you can go back to low-rent crap games in back alleys, if that's what suits you."

She was right about the Seiko-kai not breaking deals. It was a hallmark for them. Everybody knew it.

"Before I commit, I want to know who—and what—I'm dealing with," I replied. "You were his *wakagashira*, weren't you?"

Her lips pressed into a thin line. "Yes. I served as his right-hand for twelve years." She didn't look that old to me, but skin jobs were an easy thing when you have the resources of the Yakuza.

"Are you in line to take over the organization?"

"I should be," she replied slowly, and there was something strange about the way she said it. "But the reality is… problematic."

"So, who is likely to take over the organization? The *saiko-kommon?*"

"Yes," she said, and there was no missing the venom in her voice. "Okamoto Touma. He was Satō's senior advisor. He's clever and dangerous and made all the right moves to fill the vacuum."

"Does he know what you're doing with me?"

"No."

"Why not?"

"Because I don't trust him—and he doesn't like me."

It was a bit unusual that the *wakagashira* wasn't the next in line, but the answer didn't really matter—not to me, anyway. If she didn't trust him, that was something for her and the Seiko-kai to sort out. It had nothing to do with me. As the *wakagashira*, she could make good on her offer, but I needed to up the price of tea a bit.

"I'll do it, but fifty-thousand isn't enough. Make it a hundred grand, and I'll have enough to get off Neo-Kyoto… even out of the Hegemony. If that's acceptable, then I'm all yours."

"Done," she said without hesitation. "Now, you might want to lay down."

"Lay down? Why?" For a split-second, I thought she was going to off me.

"Because I have no idea what this is going to do to you."

"What?"

She pulled a slim device from her purse, stepped back, and stared at it for several seconds.

A holocaust exploded in my brain. My body went rigid. Whirlwinds of light—every color, every hue—swirled past my eyes. The sum of all knowledge poured into my soul and filled it to bursting.

I'm sure I screamed, but there was as much sound pouring into my mind as there was data. I'd forgotten what being connected felt like. With my hands pressed over my ears, I focused on the firmware that was still booting up inside my skull. Filters... where were the god damn filters? Threads floated up out the rapidly activating system that had lain dormant for years. One by one, I yanked on the filters I wanted. I don't know how long it took. It felt like hours, but eventually I'd laid down a rough and dirty array of filters to keep everything out.

Kuso! I'm out of practice.

When the thunder faded and the lights dimmed, I initiated a scan of all connections my systems had made or were trying to make. I immediately found the root signal that covered every planet in the Kagoshima Hegemony. Everything digital connected to it by default, which is why my brain had gotten singed by the avalanche of data. There was also a connection to the device she'd used to re-initialize my system, and I could feel it, in turn, connected to her. For the briefest of moments, I connected to her system. It was only a flash, mere nanoseconds, but in that barest fragment of time, I knew that there was something different about her. I couldn't put my finger on it, but it was there. Her own software slammed down a firewall, and the contact was thrown back in my face like a bag of old fish heads. *We all have our secrets,* I thought. I kept scanning connect-points.

The building around me was heavily latticed with encrypted connect-points. My system banged up against them like a moth against a street lamp. I instinctively pulled up an arsenal of decryption protocols to tackle them but then stopped. Now wasn't the time. I let out a long, slow breath and met her gaze once again.

"So, do you have any idea where we can start?" She was assuming I was one hell of a detective.

I smiled... mostly because I am. "Souma," I replied.

"What?"

"Take me back to Shinjuku."

* * *

The Horishi

Buki's grav-limo rose away from the curb as we stepped into the tattoo parlor, grateful to be out of the downpour. The place smelled of real ink and sweat. Souma started to rise from the big, red leather chair at the back of the parlor but leaned back when she recognized me. She knew I didn't want ink. She was an irezumi tattoo artist, the best in Shinjuku, and a prized asset of the Yamaguchi-gumi. She inked anyone though—anyone who could pay—not just the Yamaguchi. She was also a better source of information than any of my other informants. It's remarkable what people will talk about when they're under the needle.

Souma was a kid to my eyes—thin, devoid of curves. I figured that was the reason she worked the parlor rather than touting Yamaguchi-funded breast and butt implants at one of their nightclubs. She was as street-smart as they come. It's one of the reasons I liked her. She knew the score... knew how to the play the game. I could only hope the Yamaguchi didn't chew her up and spit her out like they did so many others. She was also one of the few people I knew who had no implants whatsoever—full organic. In fact, her entire studio was devoid of connect-points. The only signal I could pick up was the root broadcast to the planet, but nothing in her shop was connected to it.

I glanced around, thankful to discover the place empty for a change.

"Souma," I said, nodding. I pulled over a chair and set it in front of her. "How's business?"

She looked around the empty studio, a wry grin on her face. "Booming, clearly." She sat up, straightening her green and gray *yukata* and exposing heavily tattooed skin that I had no doubt covered her entire body except her hands, feet, and head. She pulled an errant strand of purple hair from her thin face, tucking it behind her ear as she leaned forward. She looked Buki up and down, probably coming to the same conclusion I did when I saw the *wakagashira* for the first time.

"Who's your friend, Moto-san?" she asked.

I smiled. "A client."

She shrugged. "Fair enough." Looking back at me, she asked, "What do you want? And what's in it for me?"

"A name. Five-thousand yen," I replied. It wasn't that unusual a request. Souma had helped me track down Gorira's rapists. She'd done that one for free, though. Getting guys like that off the street was in her best interests. The only thing worrying me was if Buki's thief was already working with the Yamaguchi-gumi. If Souma refused to help, at least I'd know what clan the oni worked for.

"You know the rules," she said, "who I work for and who I can't roll over."

I nodded. "I need black and red pens… and some paper."

"In that drawer." She pointed to her station beyond the chair where she inked her clients. Buki retrieved what I needed and handed it to me.

I set the pad on my knee and pulled out the black pen. Closing my eyes, I visualized the red oni head I'd seen on the thief's chest. With quick, mechanical motions, I drew the outline of the artwork. The image was precise—exactly as I'd seen it. My newly activated implants let me put on paper anything I'd ever seen. Souma got an impressed look on her face. "That's a neat trick," she said. "If you ever decide to change careers, I could probably put you to work here."

"Pass," I said as my hand skittered across the paper.

I'd filled in about fifty percent when she held up her hand. "Stop. Let me see that."

I handed it over. "Recognize it?"

She nodded. "It's my work."

"Do you remember the guy you gave it to?" Buki asked.

She hesitated for a few heartbeats, and I worried the thief *was* Yamaguchi. Then she nodded again. "Yeah. About a year ago. He was a mean bastard. Cold. One of the *Inagawa-kai* enforcers. They call him Shard."

"A year ago?" Buki asked, not hiding her skepticism.

"I remember them *all*, lady," Souma said, narrowing her eyes at Buki. "*Every. Single. One.*"

Buki got a respectful look on her face and nodded once. It wasn't an apology, but she made it clear she knew she'd at least brushed up against the line.

"I don't suppose you know where we can find Shard," I injected, bringing her attention back to me.

"No idea, Moto-san," Souma replied. "Sorry."

"I think I can help there," Buki spoke up, placing her hand on my shoulder. "We should go."

"Pay her," I said as I stood. Buki opened her purse, pulled out a money clip, and peeled out seven crisp bills. She handed them over, and Souma quickly slipped them inside her yukata. She'd paid her seven grand, not five. *So Buki knows how to apologize after all*, I thought.

We stepped out of the parlor and stood under the awning, a throng of people grazing by us as the rain fell. With my system back online and even with the filters on, the street was awash with adverts, connect-points, and IDs floating over the heads of the passers-by. Many of them had one or more live connections darting out from the connect-points that were literally everywhere. It was strange to once again see the digital overlay of a world that I'd put behind me. I adjusted my filters to lose more of the distractions but kept the IDs active in the display overlay. I was tapped into the Shadow Corps system and had been since I first fired up. Nobody had come for me yet, so I'd stopped worrying about it. I saw a few warrants attached to a few names, several low-end bounties that regular hunters would track down soon enough, and even a few masked IDs that my decryption system automatically translated into IDs of known yakuza hitters. None of them seemed interested in us, though. I turned to Buki.

"So what's your plan?" I asked, leaning in so she could hear me over the rain.

She held up a finger. "A name often leads to an address." I saw a connection dart out from her and bore into an encrypted connect-point nearby, showing up in my sight like a lance of red light piercing the building across the street. I instinctively called up a ghosting protocol and piggy-backed her connection. It would be undetectable to her and who or whatever she connected to. I felt along the connection like a wisp of wind, feeling my way to the other end—and crashed into the digital equivalent of a concrete wall.

That had never happened to me before. I kept any expression off my face, but it worried me. Whatever was on the other end was as high-end a firewall as I'd ever encountered.

A moment later, she severed the connection.

"I take it you just requested a trace on Shard?"
She nodded.
"Want to go get some lunch while we wait?" I asked.

She met my gaze. "We may not have ti—" A lance of light flared out from the same connect-point and bored into her. Before I could call up another ghost protocol, she met my gaze. "Koda Hiroshi. Apartment #3305, 7-20-1, Nishi-Shinjuku, Shinjuku-ku, Neo-Kyoto." She smiled. "And—apparently—he's home. Trace-connect shows him tapped into the building."

Nobody's that fast, I thought. An enforcer like Shard would have had three or more layers between his alias and his real identity, assuming there was a connection at all. Whomever had gotten my file for Buki had to be the same one who got Shard's ID and address, and he—or she—was *really* good… better than anyone I'd ever even heard of, even at the Shadow Corps. And then I started to suspect who she was working with—and it scared the hell out of me.

"Have your driver circle the Nishi-Shinjuku building in standard sled lanes and wait for your call."

"We're not taking my car?"

"No. We'll take the Metro. It has a station practically in the basement of the Nishi-Shinjuku, and he may have surveillance or alerts for non-standard vehicles in the area. Your grav-limo sticks out like a sore thumb around here." The entrance to the subway tubes was just around the corner. I knew because I'd staked out that apartment building a few months earlier. I was getting photos of a Sony exec and his mistress.

I also had an ulterior motive.

"But—" Buki started.

"It's your turn to trust me," I said and strode away before she could answer.

* * *

The Uragirimono

The rain slid off my ionized coat like it was made of glass, and the rain felt good on my face. I moved between the other pedestrians easily, barely brushing them as I passed by. A quick glance over my shoulder showed Buki right behind me.

We dashed down the steps, passed through the gates, and boarded a magtrain packed tightly with passengers who smelled just like a dirty under-city. With a lurch, we were off, Buki glaring at me from beneath a crown of soaked hair. Her suit was dry though, ionized just like mine.

As the doors opened, we slid out. "I need to use the restroom," I said.

I got another glare.

I shrugged an apology. "I gotta go." I angled toward the restroom I wanted. I knew she'd stay close by. She wasn't about to give me an opportunity to cut out on her. Not that I planned on ditching her. When I take a job, I see it through.

I went in, did my business, and then stepped up to a wall of Metro lockers. I ran my thumb over the reader of locker J374 and heard it unlock. Making sure no one was watching, I slipped my hand into a black nylon gym bag and pulled out a Miroku TK60 needler. Small enough to fit into the palm of my hand, it disappeared into my coat pocket. The TK60 is nearly silent, undetectable to your average metal detector, and can fire 60 rounds per second on full auto. With an adjustable burst-fire selector I keep on five needles per trigger, it's a mag-accelerator pistol of exceedingly lethal design. Most of the Miroku line is illegal as hell, with the TK60 a standard issue sidearm with the Shadow Corps. If I got caught with it, cops would shoot me on sight, but I had no intention of facing the oni mask without it.

Reaching into the bag again, I felt around and found a few more devices I figured I might need—including a scatter-bomb—and slipped them into other pockets. Double-checking the gear, I closed the locker and walked out of the men's room. I spotted Buki standing just outside, oblivious to the stares from a river of commuters flowing by.

Her eyes slid down my body as I stepped out, pausing for an instant on my coat pockets. She looked at me with a raised eyebrow. "It seems you came out with more than when you went in, Moto-san."

"I don't plan to just knock on the guy's door," I replied.

"I figured you'd have a stash of tech." She turned and headed for the stairs heading out of the station. "Guys like you always do."

"Stashes," I corrected. "And you'll thank me once we're up there."

At the top of the stairs, we circled around the station entrance and walked through the front doors of the Nishi-shinjuku. The lobby was empty, although we did see several young ladies behind the glass walls of the management office. I waved and smiled, as if we were supposed to be there, and we walked up to the bank of elevators.

"Thirty-two," I said as we stepped into an elevator. I placed my back to the control panel, pulled a slim hacker from my pocket, and set it on the panel without looking. The device activated automatically as the doors closed and linked my internal system with the building's security protocols. The elevator lurched upwards as data scrolled before my eyes. It took only seconds for me to crack through their firewalls and disable a dozen system alerts that terminated in apartment 3305. I accessed the feeds for the 33rd-floor cameras and, making sure the hallways were empty, set them into a three-second loop. Someone would find the override eventually, but not until well after we were gone—I hoped. I then changed the destination from the thirty-second to the thirty-third floor.

I tried to access the cameras for the apartments and found all of them locked out with some pretty serious encryption. Given time, I could crack them, but we were almost to the top. I wanted to get in and out as fast as possible, and I had a plan for seeing who and what was in Koda's apartment.

The elevator doors opened, and Buki hesitated, looking at me expectantly.

"We're clear in the hallway," I said as I pulled the hacker off the panel and slipped it into my pocket.

She nodded and stepped out, heading straight for 3305. She reached the door and stood next to it, waiting for me. "If he's in there, we need to keep it quiet. If the authorities come, we'll have a problem."

"It'll be fine," I said easily.

She rolled her eyes. "So, what's next?"

With a smile, I pulled another device out of my pocket and held it up for her. It was a bug in both name and function. An inch long, it resembled a cockroach made of smooth, black metal. I activated it and felt it link up to my internal system with a ghost-protocol that would piggy-back whatever CPs were in the apartment. Its color shifted, changing quickly to reflect my skin tone and the color of my jacket. The thing had a camouflage coating that would change to whatever surface it walked upon. As it came online, a small image appeared in the upper-right-hand corner of my vision, showing me whatever the bug saw. I dropped it to the floor, tapped into the control matrix, and sent it skittering under the door.

"Do you have a link?" I asked.

"Of course," she replied. "Open a gateway."

I felt her system prompt for a connection and synced up the A/V feed from the bug to her gateway. She connected, and there it was again—something different about her. I couldn't put my finger on it, but it was there.

"Got it?"

"Yes."

Two men stood just inside the door, one on each side, and they held slim, gray, auto-needlers cradled in their arms. A short hallway stretched away from the door, and there was a kitchen off to the right. I sent the bug scurrying up the wall behind one of them, onto the ceiling, and down the short hallway. We heard voices coming from the next room.

"*—worry, it's all there,*" said a man with a deep, artificially altered voice.

"*I was tempted to keep the mask,*" said another, followed by a chuckle. "*That thing is unbelievable.*"

"*I would have killed you if you had,*" the deeper voice warned.

"*Which is why I'm handing it over. Where the fuck did it come from?*"

"*The Gishi.*"

"*The Engineer? I've heard of him. Supposed to be one of the best, but a real whack-job.*"

"*He was. That fool Satō was just going to hand it over to Fukuda, like a sniveling lap dog.*"

"*Who's Fukuda?*"

"*Don't worry about it. You've got your payment. What's your plan now?*"

"*I'm done with those bastards in the Inagawa-kai. I'm hoping this job earns me a spot as a* Fuku-Honbucho *with the Seiko-kai. I'd like my own region.*"

"*When the dust settles, and my new status is formalized, I think we can work something out.*"

"*What about Buki?*"

"*She'll be retired just like the Gishi was, so don't worry about it,*" the deep voice replied.

We heard the clicks of briefcase latches closing, and then the bug came around the corner of the hallway, revealing a lavish living room with floor-to-ceiling windows along two sides. They'd been set to opaque to prevent anyone from seeing inside the apartment. I recognized Koda Hiroshi immediately. He wore a gray suit with a wide-collared burgundy shirt open, exposing the red oni tattoo that had led us to him. The other man's back was to us. Tall, wearing a black suit with a long, salt-and-pepper ponytail draped down the middle of his back, he held the oni mask in his hands. Hiroshi settled onto the sofa and picked through an open, silver briefcase. I could just make out the flash of currency bundles. A jade statue of a nine-tailed *kitsune* sat upon the coffee table next to the briefcase.

"Is that it?" I asked Buki as the man with the ponytail looked back toward the hallway. "Next to the briefcase?" I felt Buki stiffen beside me.

"Okamoto Touma…" she hissed. "*Uragirimono!*" Okamoto was the *saiko-kommon* of the Seiko-kai, and had been behind Satō-san's murder.

I heard the telltale *buzz-snap* of a flex-blade—an assassin's favorite. It's an easily concealable hilt and blade of soft metallic-fabric that goes rigid and is as strong as titanium when a current passes through the fibers. Before I could do anything, she shoved me aside, kicked the door apart like it was paper, and leapt through with a flex-blade katana in her hand. She was moving so fast, I almost couldn't keep up with her.

"*What the—!*" Koda shouted from inside as I heard two quick *THUNKS* from just inside the door.

"Shit," I muttered, and yanked the Miroku out of my pocket. I stepped in and saw the two decapitated guards just inside the doorway, blood still pumping from their exposed necks out onto the floor.

In the feed from my bug, I watched Okamoto slam the mask onto his face just as Buki rushed into view with the flex-blade held low, point forward, ready to attack or block. The white mask flowed around his head, becoming a complete helmet of sorts, and looked like a gleaming, white skull. A deep, bone-shaking growl filled the room, like when Koda had worn the mask, but deeper, more throaty. The stranger turned. The mask bared a mouth full of fangs. Buki pulled something from within her sleeve and snapped her wrist. A throwing dagger appeared in the center of Koda's chest, and he grunted. Buki leapt past Okamoto with a flying side-kick that caught

Koda in the chest, sending him back over the couch with a rib-cracking impact and putting him out of the fight for good.

I cleared the hallway just as Koda crashed into the window with a staggering impact that fractured the pane, but it didn't break. Buki landed in a crouch, blade held high just as Okamoto roared his fury and blurred into motion. The coffee table shattered as a massive claw came down. I'd feared for Buki but realized she'd already stepped back, moving almost as fast as the mask. *She must have some cutting-edge implants for that kind of speed,* I thought.

I snapped the Miroku up and fired a near-silent burst into Okamoto's leg. I didn't want to kill him if I could avoid it, but he was faster than Buki. I just wanted to give her the chance to do her job… and take the murder rap if we got caught.

I felt the Miroku vibrate in my hand. I *know* I hit my target. The mask didn't even flinch. He went straight for Buki, his claws a blur as they slashed against her flex-blade. She was still in one piece, but he drove her back with each slash, his smile predatory—triumphant.

The blade danced in her hands as he came at her. She blocked three attacks and came back with a quick strike. She connected with his arm, but drew no blood. The suit he wore was armor—made of the same stuff as the flex-blade. The flex-blade, like the Miroku, was useless against it, so I dropped the weapon and hoped Buki and I could take this bastard.

"Moto-san!" Buki shouted as she sent three quick slashes against Okamoto's guard. He blocked every swing and then sent a lightning-fast snap-kick into her midsection. She sailed back into one of the windows. It starred out but didn't break.

If Buki hadn't activated my mods, I'd barely be able to see them move. But I was Kage No Gundan again—a Shadow Warrior. I felt my mods singing beneath my skin.

I leapt across the room, clearing the eight feet between us just as Okamoto turned. I'd never seen anyone move that fast, but I didn't care as he swung back at me. I dropped beneath it into a crouch, sending a flurry of rabbit strikes straight into his midsection, driving him back as he grunted with the impact. Sliding forward, I came up with a fast, hard uppercut, looking for a chink in his armor—there, just beneath his chin. He stepped back and brought up a hard knee. I partially blocked it with my forearms but still took the brunt of a blow that sent me sailing across the living room to smash into a far wall. I hit the floor, rolled forward, and came up just in time to see Buki come at Okamoto again.

She slashed at him again and again, the katana a blur. Okamoto slapped the blade away several times, caught the edge on the sleeve of his suit, and then wrapped a claw around the blade, holding it firm. Buki instinctively tugged to free the blade, and it was all the opening Okamoto needed. His other hand swung around and then up, raking along her body from waist to chin with such force that she slammed into the ceiling and dropped to the floor, motionless. I'd expected blood to spray with the blow, but there was none.

It didn't matter. I had to end this—and *now*. My only option was to grab the tiger by the tail and hope a Kage No Gundan could beat the oni. I charged in, my focus on those claws. My timing would have to be perfect.

Okamoto turned in a blur, set, and raised a claw. It came down like a lightning strike. My mods screamed in response. I caught his wrist and tightened my grip for all I was worth. The other claw came at me, low and fast, and as it did, I felt a connection I didn't expect. I caught his other wrist and went rigid, holding his arms out.

The mask smiled. He started to squeeze. I don't know if it was his mods, or the mask, or both, but those claws stiffened into daggers and he began pressing them in toward my skull. I strained against his grip, but even with a Kage No Gundan warframe, I couldn't hold him off.

"You're about to die," Okamoto pronounced.

The connection I'd felt, a tickle at first, solidified. My CPU sent out a command that I didn't even know existed and burrowed into the firmware of the mask. The thing was nanotech. A flash of data poured into my brain—straight out of the oni mask and into my brain. In a flash, I knew what it really was—why it existed—and it put the fear of god in me. It had been designed to enhance Shadow Warriors... so they could *kill* Shadow Warriors.

If Okamoto's mods had come from the Shadow Corps, what my CPU was doing would never have worked, but for me it was almost automatic. I willed the mask to tighten, collapse in around the skull that supported it.

Okamoto went rigid. He screamed. His cry of agony was cut off as the mask tightened in around his neck and the claws retracted. He started jerking and flailing in my grasp as blood poured out from the edge of the mask and it slowly crushed his skull.

With a sickening *CRACK,* the mask closed in on itself. Okamoto jerked once and sagged in my grip. The oni mask seemed to melt away from his features and flow down his arm. Before I knew it, the material—looking like melted wax—slithered up my arm and around my head. For a moment, panic took me. My CPU linked fully with the mask. A surge of energy flowed through my body, as if my adrenals had suddenly dumped everything they had into my nervous system. The world slowed around me, and every detail stood out in sharp contrast. I looked around the room, saw the array of encrypted connect-points that filled the area, and tapped into one. The encryption gave way before my touch like hot iron cutting through silk.

A dozen alarms along this floor blared in my vision from other tenants reporting a disturbance. With a thought, the protocols built into the mask let me disable those alarms, send a dozen authenticated all-clears to the cops, and light off an armed robbery alert in a bank around the corner. I just needed to buy enough time for Buki and I to clear out of the apartment and disappear.

I glanced at where she had fallen. She was unconscious, but her system was still active. The mask cut through her encryption too, and I instantly realized what I'd felt before—what made her different.

The mask let me move through her memories like a bird through the air. I froze—pulled back the connection I'd made with her. It was a violation, one I had no intention of committing, despite what I now knew she was.

I took a deep breath and let it out slowly.

This mask was the most dangerous weapon I'd ever even heard of—and it needed to disappear. This thing was too much for any one person to wield. It would make a Kage No Gundan nearly unstoppable. I knew it had been created specifically for a Shadow Warrior. The fact that I'd been able to take control of it while Okamoto had been wearing it was proof. I called up a function within the mask's OS and deactivated it. As it flowed off my skull, I felt that surge of energy fade. The world went back to normal, and I looked at things the way a human was supposed to.

I held the mask in my hands, staring down at it. Who was Fukuda? Why had Satō-san, the oyabun of the Seiko-kai made it for him?

What the fuck am I into?

Buki stirred on the floor and let out a groan. Maybe she had those answers. I knelt down beside her. Four gashes had separated her "skin," exposing a metal and polymer chassis beneath. Her eyes fluttered open as her system finally rebooted from the blow she'd taken. Her gaze met mine, and then her eyes drifted down to the mask in my hand. She let out a slow sigh of relief.

"You got it—and him."

"I did," I said, "but it was close." I stared into her eyes for several seconds, looking for—I don't know what. "If I wasn't who I used to be, we'd both be dead, and your saiko-kommon would have taken over the Seiko-kai like he planned."

She nodded.

"You're an android," I said quietly. "Which means you can't own anything."

Her head snapped toward me. "What of it?" There was anger and fear in her face.

"It doesn't matter to me, but we both know the Seiko-kai wouldn't bend a knee to a—let me guess—Class 2 AI? Which means they don't *know* what you are. Did your Oyabun?"

"He had me created. And he wanted me to take over the Seiko-kai."

"Did Okamoto know that?"

"I don't know," she said slowly. "I don't think so."

"You're probably right. He'd have turned the Seiko-kai against you already, if he did." I stared at her for a few seconds, my face expressionless. "We need to go. *Now*. But I have a few questions once we're in the clear."

She got a curious look on her face, surprised at my reaction no doubt, and then she nodded. I helped her to her feet, and she slapped the flex-blade around her waist where it became her belt once again.

"A deal's a deal," I said. "I don't want that thing. It should be destroyed."

"That was always the plan," Buki said as she took it. "Creating this was the only thing I ever disagreed with Satō-san about. I wasn't even supposed to know about it, so I couldn't say anything. It was a mistake."

She stepped over to where the statue had fallen and touched the mask to it. In a flash, the mask molded itself around the statue, turning it white and adding a good deal of mass in both height and width. The perfect camouflage.

I peeled off my raincoat and handed it to her. "You should cover up." With a nod, she put it on and secured the front so nobody would see her slashed artiflesh or the android chassis beneath.

I picked up the briefcase and opened it. There was about a million yen inside. Closing it, I turned and headed for the front door. "Let's get the hell out of—" I started but froze just as I turned the corner.

A shadow filled the doorway—a Shadow Warrior, to be more precise. And he had a blaster in his hand and a small bag under his arm.

* * *

The Shadow

I stared at Nakano Junichiro, a blank expression on my face. My life, such as it was, had come to a close. I would be taken before the Emperor, condemned, and executed.

I wasn't all that surprised to see a Kage No Gundan barring our path. The mask had been created specifically for Shadow Warriors, which meant someone in their ranks had commissioned it. I *was*, however, surprised that it was Junichiro-san standing in the doorway.

He was a decade younger than me, with iron-hard eyes and chiseled features. He'd been my protégé once upon a time, and the best I'd ever trained. I'd watched him surpass me in ambition and rank. He'd been making a bee-line for Station-Chief of Neo-Kyoto as fast as his manipulations could carry him. Yet, here he was, in the field, aiming a blaster at me.

"*Someone* at the Shadow Corps ordered this fucking thing from the Seiko-kai so they could kill Kage No Gundan," I said.

There's something I need to clarify. I left the Shadow Corps because I was tired of hunting people—of killing them without due process simply because I was ordered to and paid well for the trouble. Make no mistake, they were all guilty, and their deaths saved innocent lives. For all our ruthlessness, the Kage No Gundan are not only necessary, they're actually the good guys—well, mostly. I just couldn't do it anymore.

The idea of someone within that organization building a weapon specifically designed to kill Shadow Warriors was a tyrant's play—someone wanted Shadow Warriors out of the way so they could do terrible things. It was the only possibility.

Junichiro smiled. "Sharp as ever, Moto-san." He had the good grace not to use my old name.

"Was it you?" I asked. "Did you order Satō to have it made?"

"No," he replied flatly. A straight answer actually surprised me. It wasn't his style. Never had been. "The Station Chief for Neo-Kyoto—Fukuda Rai—put this operation in motion. I'm cleaning up his mess."

Like a lightning bolt, I understood what had happened. It wasn't Buki that found me dying in that alley. It was Junichiro, and he'd scanned my DNA when he found me. He got me to Buki. He'd given her my file. And he was the one who got us Koda's address.

"And you used me as the mop"

He smiled again. "Like I said… sharp as ever." He held out an open palm. "My hands are clean. The Shadow Corps is clean. Fukuda has been… *retired*, and his association with Seiko-kai erased. That means I can create an association all my own." He turned to Buki. The gun never moved. "Fukuda worked with the Seiko-kai for years, and for a reason. You're thieves, but you're honorable ones. I believe continuing that association—a subtle and secret one—would be of value to both of us. Fukuda was a lot of things, but he was no fool."

"I can't lead the Seiko-kai," she said. "The moment they try and hand the reins over to me, my Ident-Scan will show them what I am."

"We both know you've been the brains behind Satō's throne for a very long time." Junichiro glanced at me and then gave her a smile. "I suspect you'll be able to figure something out. *Both* of you, if you have the balls." He tossed the bag and it landed at my feet. "That's the thirty-thousand from the crap game... plus a little extra to get you off-world if that's the play you want to make. But you should consider: your identity is clean, thanks to the device she used to re-initialize your system. Nobody at the Shadow Corps knows you exist. Your DNA records will now scan as Moto Kosuke wherever you go. And I *trust* you."

"Why are you doing this, Junichiro-san?" I asked. "You'd make your career by dragging me before the Emperor in binders."

His head cocked to the side, and he looked at me for a long time.

"Because I have to believe what you did is possible, old man," he finally replied. "And that there might be a place for me someday besides a plaque on a wall in a dark basement somewhere. You're the only one who ever got out on your feet—" he gave me a wry grin "—with a little help. Who knows, someday I might want to disappear into the fog of Shinjuku and start a new life. I have to know it's possible."

"Thanks, old friend," I said.

"Maybe you'll have a chance to pay me back someday," he said. His eyes shifted to Buki, who held the white kitsune statue clutched to her chest.

"Buki-sama, lock that thing away..." he said. "Save it for a rainy day." The use of the honorific surprised me. It was meant for individuals of a higher rank or those deserving of the utmost respect. "Getting caught with it will carry the death penalty, but if your back is against the wall…" He gave a slight bow. "You might need it if you truly intend to take over the Seiko-kai, just as Satō-sama wanted."

"Why would you trust anyone with this?"

"Because I suspect you'll be sticking around. And who better to hide it away than the one man who knows what it's capable of and still wants it destroyed?" Junichiro drew in a deep breath and let it out. "There's something happening at the Shadow Corps. I don't yet know if I nipped it in the bud. It worries me. You're my insurance policy, Moto-san."

"So… what? You'll just call me up if you need me. A sort of break glass in case of emergency kind of thing?"

Junichiro smiled. "Something like that." He bowed to both of us and then stepped back through the doorway as sirens blared in the street below. He was gone in an instant.

* * *

The Oyabun

"You keep what you kill," Buki said, shifting a genuine Masamune katana from one hand to the other as the holo faded from view. The holo had shown everything my bug had recorded, from entering Koda's apartment right up until I picked up the briefcase. The room around us was hidden in deep shadows. The conference table—a wide circle of obsidian, gleamed beneath the holo-image. Buki let her gaze flow over our audience of seventeen *shateigashira*. "You all know the code." They were the regional bosses of the Seiko-kai, and they stared at me—sitting at the head of the table—with cold, calculating eyes. The image changed to Satō's will, and the clause leaving his throne to Buki was highlighted. "And Sato-sama's intentions were clear. Although I can't own property, you've all known me for years. You know I've always ensured this organization ran smoothly with as little interference in your regions as possible. We have all profited, and it is my intention to ensure that continues. I choose this man, Moto-sama, to hold the reins of the Seiko-kai. He is both intelligent and deadly. He helped me take down a traitor who had sworn his allegiance to our Oyabun—an Oyabun who always treated each one of you with fairness and respect. Whether you embrace the old traditions or the new rules, Moto-sama has more right to sit at the head of this table than any of us. I give him my support and my loyalty, without hesitation."

The whole thing had been her idea. To be perfectly honest, I had mixed feelings about it. There was a fair chance I would be dead in the next few minutes, but I'd cheated death twice in as many days. Three's the charm. Isn't that what people say?

Become the Oyabun of the Seiko-kai? Let an AI run the organization while I play figurehead?

Why the hell not?

"Thank you Buki-san." I pulled a pack of cigarettes from inside my suit coat and slid one out. Like I had only a few days earlier, I propped it into the corner of my mouth to dangle like an unfinished thought. I don't talk to Yakuza without a cigarette in my mouth, and I never would. Rising to my feet, I held out my hand. She placed the katana in it with a good deal of reverence. "I know what you're probably thinking. Who is this pretender? He hasn't bled with us. He hasn't paid his dues or proven himself. It would be wise of you to think these things." I drew in a deep breath and let it out slowly, meeting the hard gaze of each one of them. With my implants active, and despite their encryption, I was able to pull up everything the Shadow Corps had on each one of them. Their histories were sordid, to be sure, but each one of them was known to follow the bushido code in service to the Seiko-kai. Ten men and seven women, each one committed to Seiko-kai business above all else, and without drenching the streets in innocent blood. "I give you this pledge—this oath. Give me the opportunity to earn your respect. Give me one year to prove to each one of you that I can be the Oyabun you both need and want. In exchange, I vow to keep the Shadow Corps from interfering in our business. I vow to eliminate any rival clan that seeks to take what we have worked so hard for. I vow to serve each of you as much as you serve me. Together, we can extend the reach of the Seiko-kai beyond Shinjuku. Beyond Neo-Kyoto. Even beyond the Kagoshima Hegemony." I placed the katana on the table in front of me. "If I fail, even once in any of these things, then my life is forfeit and you may take it with this. It will remain here until you are certain I am worthy." Murmurs and whispers circled the room as I sat back down. "I have only one condition, and it is one that you have already met."

"What is that, Moto-sama?" the burly older man on my left asked. He was Suzuki Kuma—the Bear—and the next in line for the position of saiko-kommon. Buki had said that if he agreed, the rest probably would too.

"Only this: that the Seiko-kai never shed the blood of the innocent. Know that any failure there will bring down my wrath."

"Everything else also stays the same?" Suzuki asked. "Our tribute? Our territories? Our endeavors?"

"Everything," I replied.

Suzuki let out a long breath with a sound like a waking bear. He rose to his feet, reached out, and picked up the Masamune. He pulled the blade a few centimeters out of its *saya* and then eyed me.

I gave him no reaction at all.

"I will abide," he finally said. "I will hold to your condition—as I have always done—and I will hold you to yours."

I stood again and bowed respectfully at the waist. "Arigatou, Suzuki-san."

The big man looked around the table, meeting the gaze of the *shateigashira* and nodded once.

In one motion, the sixteen regional bosses of the Seiko-kai stood slowly.

One-by-one, they bowed respectfully to their new Oyabun.

* * * * *

Quincy J. Allen Bio

National Bestselling Author Quincy J. Allen is a cross-genre author with a wide assortment of publications under his belt. His media tie-in novel *Colt the Outlander: Shadow of Ruin* was a Scribe Award finalist in 2019, and his noir sci-fi novel *Chemical Burn* was a Colorado Gold Award finalist in 2010.

He's actively working on his fantasy steampunk series the Blood War Chronicles, and he just wrapped up book three in the fantasy series "The Way of Legend" with Marc Alan Edelheit. He and Kevin Ikenberry are working on *Scourge*, the sequel to *Enforcer*, and he's also working on *Cradle and All*, a novel in Jamie Ibson's Contractor Wars universe. Most importantly, he is a founding member of the "Eldros Legacy," and his debut novel *Seeds of Dominion* kicks off a ten-book series entitled the Legacy of Deceit.

In short, he's going in eight directions at once and is loving every minute of it. He works out of his home in Charlotte, North Carolina, and hopes to one day be a *New York Times* bestselling author.

For more information about his ongoing efforts, check him out at:

http://www.quincyallen.com

https://www.eldroslegacy.com/the-founders/quincy-j-allen

# # # # #

Running Free by A.K. DuBoff

A Cadicle Universe Story

R*un.*

The mantra had become a way of life for Lexi Karis. She'd been running for so long that remaining in one place for more than a night or two felt like she'd given up on survival. Stay on the move, stay free. There was no choice.

Her current temporary refuge was the crawlspace under an air processing system exhaust vent. Though noisy, it had enough room for her to stretch out, and it was warm, which was more than could be said for other secluded areas in most space stations.

"I can't believe no one else has claimed this spot," Lexi's sole travel companion, Greta, said as she positioned her bedroll on the metal grating. She'd taken the nicer blanket when Lexi had won them in a game of Fastara at their previous stop.

Lexi arranged her own ragged blanket next to Greta's, kicking up a little plume of dust as it flopped down. She held back a sneeze while she positioned her backpack as a makeshift pillow. "This station is bigger than most. Room enough for everyone, I guess."

The older woman gave her a sad smile. "For a time."

Lexi nodded her understanding. This place, like all others, was merely a stopover.

She'd given up on the idea of having any location be "home." Greta's company was her only constant—as close to a mother as she'd ever have and her protector for the last eighteen years.

"I'll go find us some dinner," Lexi offered.

Greta's brows drew together, decades of fatigue and weariness showing in the lines of her face. "No," she stated flatly, without giving a reason. The older woman had long ago lost the desire to come up with excuses.

Lexi resisted the urge to sigh. Lately, this had become the routine.

And it keeps us from fussing about it. The bioluminescent glow in Lexi's irises was getting more pronounced every day, and soon others would take notice. If the wrong people singled her out, all their running would be for nothing.

"What if I wear the glasses?" Lexi hopefully withdrew the tinted lenses from the top pocket of her backpack.

Greta grunted disapprovingly.

"You were just lecturing me about how I need to be more independent." Lexi slipped on the glasses. "How am I supposed to do that when I can't even feed myself?"

They stood there, eyes locked, each willing the other to surrender.

Finally, Greta broke off the contact and waved a weathered hand back the way they had come.

Lexi darted off before the woman could change her mind.

The tinted glasses were a temporary fix, and it was poor cover, at that. It's not like Lexi was the only Gifted person around—Greta herself was, too—but the glowing eyes were a beacon inviting trouble. All anyone would need was a simple genetic test to confirm her identity. The bounty on her was old, but any tracker who sorted by contract value would happily brush the hand of every young woman her age with glowing blue eyes on the off-chance they might get a nice payday.

Lexi donned a pair of maroon gloves to complete her outfit. Covering her hands and eyes made a statement, but she'd rather be taken as a potential criminal than be recognizable in other ways. One could never be too careful. Plus, she needed this to be a successful outing. Any trouble, and the argument for keeping her tucked away would become insurmountable.

Lexi slinked through the maintenance tunnel back toward where she and Greta had entered the secluded area. There were no doubt occupancy sensors around, but Outer Colonies space stations like this didn't have a large enough Enforcer presence for anyone to care about a couple of rogue travelers venturing into the non-critical service corridors.

The maintenance tunnel terminated at a swinging door with a centered lock wheel. It was designed to be hand-operated, but she knew from her recent entry that it was stiff from years of disuse. Instead, she reached out telekinetically to loosen the wheel.

An awful, griding groan filled the confined space as the lock began to spin under her touchless instruction. Greta wouldn't be happy about Lexi using her Gifts so close to an inhabited area, but at least back here she was out of sight.

With a final clang, the lock slid open. Lexi gripped the wheel and tugged it toward her, leaning back to use her body weight to get the large, heavy door moving. She cracked it a couple of centimeters and then peeked outside.

The side passageway was empty, but Lexi could hear the din of space station life in the distance. With a confirmation glance in both directions, she crept out and pulled the door closed behind her, only partially locking it with a half-turn.

Just passing through. I'm no one interesting. She took on her most unassuming stride, keeping her gaze downcast and maintaining enough tension in her shoulders to show she was on guard without looking for a fight.

Though it was Lexi's first time to the Gallos Station, a large transit hub, it may as well have been one of the dozens of other places she'd passed through over the years. A concourse or two full of nice accommodations for those with sufficient means to afford them, shops and services for working spacefarers, and enough dark corners for the less desirable members of society to hide out. Lexi wasn't rich and didn't even have a stable income, so the dregs were her only option. Unfortunately, the people who were after her also gravitated toward those same places.

She kept a watchful eye as she made her way down the commercial concourse toward where she and Greta had noticed food vendors on the way in, knowing all too well that pickpockets lurked in crowds like this. Though few people carried physical currency chips, there were plenty of valuable items to be found in a pocket. Lexi had learned that early on under Greta's guidance.

Those lessons had evolved over time, elevated from quick fingers to using her Gifts to covertly levitate an object from its owner's care. She didn't like stealing, but she hated being hungry more.

An enticing, savory aroma caught her attention. She set her path to its source, a freestanding cart a short way up the corridor.

I think I've found our dinner! Lexi eagerly approached the cart, looking for a menu. To her pleasure, the meals were affordable and the written descriptions sounded as good as the scents indicated.

"Two of the number threes, please," she requested from the vendor.

"All right, that will be eleven credits. I'll have it right out to you," he acknowledged.

She handed over the credit chips from her pocket, and he got to work.

Lexi stepped off to the side while she waited for the order, taking in the passersby. The occupants were typical enough for these kinds of ports, showcasing the diversity of people from across the expansive Taran Empire. Most were somewhat rough around the edges, as one expected in the Outer Colonies as opposed to the affluent Central Worlds, but she spotted the occasional high-quality garments indicative of wealthy merchants.

A stern-looking man across the corridor stood out from the rest. There was nothing visually remarkable about him, but her enhanced senses caught an aura of ill-intent. Greta referred to it as "instinct" in her lessons. Lexi preferred to call it 'vibes.' Either way, she got the clear impression the guy was up to no good.

Lexi glanced inside the food cart to check on the status of the meals. The vendor appeared to be packing them up. *Come on! I need to get out of here.*

The creepy man across the corridor wasn't looking directly at her, but Lexi nonetheless felt like she was being watched. She resisted the urge to dance from foot-to-foot while she silently urged the vendor to finish faster.

"Here you go. Enjoy." He placed a bag on a little counter at the serving window.

"Thanks." She snatched it, keeping a peripheral view of the creepy man.

Hoping he wasn't actually watching her, she stayed on the far side of the corridor while moving away from him, covertly glancing behind her to see if he followed. Her stomach dropped when he stepped into the flow of traffic and started heading in her direction.

Shite! She picked up her pace, looking ahead for any potential cover.

Unfortunately, the corridor was lined with open storefronts so the only refuge would leave her exposed and at a high risk of someone pestering her with the hope of making a sale. That kind of engagement might be enough to dissuade a casual pursuer, but she didn't know what sort of person she might be dealing with here. Escape was her best option.

She quickened her stride again and began weaving through the crowd. Though she was rapidly approaching the turnoff to the maintenance tunnel, she had no intention of leading him back to her hiding spot.

Lexi dashed through the spaceport, darting around people and objects whenever possible to mask herself from view. She used her enhanced senses to feel for her pursuer, finding that he was keeping pace.

Stars! Where can I go?

She spotted a large throng of people ahead, more densely packed than the other places. They were standing next to a market area, which was set up with vendor stalls in tight rows.

Lexi dove into the crowd and quickly normalized her pace to match with the other people, falling into step next to a large man. She kept close to him as she entered the market, then ducked down at her earliest opportunity to crawl inside the narrow space between the fabric wrapping of two stalls.

The canvas was musty and rough against her face, but there was enough room for her to wedge herself out of view.

Where am I? With a lurch of her stomach, she realized that she'd lost track of her position within the spaceport relative to the service tunnel where Greta was waiting. It couldn't be too far.

After five minutes in hiding, Lexi wiggled her way through to the other aisle between vendor stalls, opposite from where she'd entered. She risked poking her head out to get her bearings. To her relief, she spotted a sign indicating the location of a landmark she recognized and could use to orient toward her safe haven.

There was no immediate sign of the man who'd been pursuing her. While she doubted he'd give up easily, she hoped he'd run past her and had yet to circle back around to search here.

Better get away while I can. Using other people for cover, she wove her way back in the direction she'd come from.

The high volume of traffic in the port worked to her advantage, allowing her to blend in when viewed from a distance. She kept her hands in her pockets, with the food bag looped over one arm, head tilted down and her dark-brown hair hanging forward to hide her face from the side.

At last, she backtracked to the side corridor containing the access tunnel entrance. She stopped next to the turnoff and leaned against the wall, pretending to wait for someone while she checked around her to make sure no one was watching. She didn't see anyone out of place.

Before that changed, she ducked into the side corridor. After one final check, she opened the door and then quickly pulled it shut behind her, spinning the wheel a full three turns to lock it.

Stars, that was too close. Lexi leaned against the cool metal, sucking in deep breaths. Her heart pounded in her ears. She willed her heartrate to slow and her skin to stop burning.

After a minute, she felt calm enough to return to the camp.

Greta was seated cross-legged on her bedroll when Lexi arrived. Her lips were pressed into a firm line and her eyes were slightly narrowed. "What happened?"

Lexi swallowed. She thought about spinning some story but rejected the idea almost immediately. It would do no good; Greta could sniff out a lie as easily as Lexi had tracked down their dinner. "I was chased. Don't know why."

"Who?"

"A man." She tossed down the food bag in front of Greta. "I ditched him."

Greta shook her head, making her trademark exasperated grunt at the back of her throat.

Lexi threw up her arms. "I'm sorry! I'll try to be more careful."

"You'll get both of us caught."

"I spotted him, and I got away. Case closed." Heat burned her cheeks. It was a risk every time she set foot in public, but she couldn't stay hidden in service passageways forever. What good was it to stay alive if she couldn't *live*?

Greta met Lexi's stern gaze. "I know it's not fair how we have to scrape by."

Lexi swallowed her frustration. "Maybe they'll give up on the bounty eventually, and it won't have to be like this."

She knew it was wishful thinking, but she could dream. The powers that be on Cytera would never let one of their precious Gifted run free, not when there were so many uses for them as conscripted servants. From mind-reading to enhanced combat, there was no better way to retain power than by cultivating an army of fighters with specialized skills. Lexi's parents had tried to break free, and they'd paid the ultimate price. Greta had helped Lexi escape, though she was too young at the time to remember it. In the time since, Lexi had learned that "freedom" was a relative concept. She lived in constant fear, with a bounty on her head to be returned to her home-world, where she would be forced into servitude.

Greta grabbed the dinner bag and started to open it. "We have to be realistic."

"Yeah." Lexi took her meal from Geta.

They ate in silence for several minutes. The food had started to get cold from Lexi's circuitous path back, but it was still warm enough to be enjoyable. The flavor also lived up to the promise of the aroma, making it one of the most satisfying meals Lexi had had in a long time.

She sat back with contentment when she'd finished scarfing it down. "Mmm. I could get used to eating this well all the time!"

Greta looked down, her expression twisting as if she had bitten into spoiled food. "A lot would have to change for that."

"I know. Just gotta stay alive for there to be any tomorrow, right?" Lexi had heard it a thousand times. She had long since given up on false hope for a better future.

Greta set down her empty food container. "No, Lexi, it's time we start thinking long-term."

"How?" That was new. Greta had never discussed long-term goals. Each day was about survival. Run. Avoid capture at all costs. Lexi couldn't even recall the last time they had discussed plans more than a day or two out. The proposition of *something* beyond this animalistic existence was tantalizing.

Greta pursed her lips in thought. "For starters, you can't keep wearing those glasses to hide your eyes."

Lexi looked away reflexively. "Can't I just get contacts like yours?"

"It's not the best solution. They itch like mad and show up in security scans."

"What other options are there?"

Greta looped her arms around her upright knee. "I've heard about a practitioner here in Gallos. He has a procedure."

"What kind?"

"He can take away the glow."

The statement struck Lexi like a physical slap across her face. All of Greta's teachings had been about how lucky she was to be Gifted and how she should be proud of her abilities. "How could you suggest that?"

"Because it's a chance for a normal life." Tears welled in Greta's eyes. "I can't keep running like this."

Lexi dove forward, wrapping her arms around the other woman. "I'm sorry." She knew it was her fault. Greta had saved her as a baby, and she'd been saddled with the responsibility ever since. Lexi tried to pull her weight, but she could sense Greta's resentment mounting with each stopover.

Greta took a shaky breath. "I'm just so tired."

Could there really be a way out? Lexi rocked back on her heels, considering Greta's suggestion from a more objective vantage. "Would the procedure blind me?"

"Oh, no, no." Greta clicked her tongue against her teeth. "It only takes away the bioluminescence. Your eyes would be like they were before your Awakening."

A cosmetic change. It won't change me… right? Lexi took an uneven breath. "Do you really think this is what's best?"

She hesitated. "At this point, I don't see another way."

Lexi thought for a moment. "Wait, how can we afford this?"

"Let me worry about that."

"Is it even worth the cost?" Lexi had lived in fear, knowing a brief touch of her hand, or swabbing a glass she'd used, was all it would take for a DNA scan. Though not having her Gifts be obvious from across the room would be helpful, it wouldn't be lifechanging.

"Trust me." Greta reached over and took her hand. "You do trust me, don't you, Lexi?"

The question took her aback. Greta was the *only* person she could trust. If not for her… well, best not to finish that line of thinking. "Of course."

"Then please believe me when I say I've found an answer. A chance for a fresh start."

"Okay. What do I have to do?"

* * *

The storefront didn't look like a place in the business of changing lives, but Lexi had learned better than to judge anything by its outward appearance.

"I've made all the arrangements," Greta said. "There's nothing to worry about."

"Who is it?" Lexi asked. It seemed like a prudent question to inquire about her surgeon's credentials.

"I got a referral. They'll take good care of you."

Greta had an aura of nervous energy around her, unlike behavior Lexi had seen before from the other woman. Her tone had a business edge she normally employed when negotiating shuttle fare with pirates or haggling over meager supplies from vendors. Never had she used it with Lexi. Not once had Greta tried to *manage* her.

Something's not right. Lexi stood her ground, her eyes pleading for a straight response from her friend. "What was the deal?"

"We'll talk inside." Greta took her arm and tugged her in the direction of the entry door.

Lexi resisted. "Tell me."

She relaxed her grip. "The cost of the procedure will be covered in exchange for us doing a job."

"That kind of deal is never as good as it sounds. Forget it." Lexi turned to walk away.

"Not this time."

Lexi spun back toward her. "If it's so great, then why aren't you having the procedure done, too?"

"We can only go so far into debt, and the payoff for you is much better. My service in exchange for your eyes. That's a good deal to me." She brushed her fingers along Lexi's hairline.

The words were comforting Lexi, though the voice in her head still shouted that something wasn't right. Nonetheless, she didn't have a lot of options. Greta had been her guardian for most of her life, and if she couldn't trust her, there wasn't a person in the universe who'd have her back.

What choice do I have? She's right; we can't keep running and hiding like this. Reluctantly, she allowed Greta to escort her into the building.

The entry room was equipped like a convenience store at first glance, but the inventory was too sparse for a functional business. It was a front, by Lexi's estimation. Such establishments weren't uncommon at large ports like this—maintaining just enough of a legitimate appearance out front to keep the Enforcers from snooping around, but the real business was handled in back rooms. That wasn't a surprise, given that the procedure Lexi was there to receive wasn't exactly mainstream.

A large man stood behind the counter, his hands resting on the back edge with his fingers curved over the top. He watched them approach with an intense gaze, the muscles in his bare arms tensed for action.

"We're here to see Lazlo," Greta told him.

He gave a single nod, making no other movement.

A moment later, a door along the back wall popped open with a low screech of stiff hinges. Another formidable man, nearly the size of the first, stepped out. "Which one?" he asked.

Greta motioned to Lexi. "Her."

"Come with me." He held the door open for Lexi.

"Can't she come back, too?" Lexi asked.

"Only you."

Greta nodded. "It's okay. I'll see you soon."

"Um…" Before Lexi could form a proper protest, the man had nudged her through and closed the door.

Lexi plodded down the dim corridor to an open doorway at the end. A reclining single chair stood in the center of the room with a contraption mounted to the floor behind it, equipped with a long arm and an electronic device on the end. A man and a woman, both dressed in surgical gowns, were standing on either side of the chair.

"Have a seat," the man said.

Lexi hesitated in the doorway. *This doesn't feel right.*

"Sit down," he repeated.

"You know, I've changed my mind." Lexi turned around. "I'm gonna go—"

The man who'd escorted her down the hallway gripped her arm, halting her retreat. "A deal's a deal."

Lexi fought against his grasp. "The terms have changed."

He tossed her into the room. "Sit!"

She caught herself from stumbling, whipping around to face the escort at the door. "No! Greta!" She started to bring up a telekinetic shield around herself.

A cool tingle spread from the side of her neck, numbing her as it spread outward.

I should have been faster. The world faded around her as she slumped toward the chair.

* * *

Lexi became aware of an ache behind her eyes as her senses slowly returned. The room stank of cleaning products and a mechanical whir overshadowed the mumble of conversation in the distance. Yet, there was only black-ness.

She tried to open her eyes, only to find that something was hold-ing them closed.

Shite! The final seconds before she'd fallen unconscious came back to her with a sickening lurch in her gut.

The procedure was complete, whatever it was. Putting up a fight now wouldn't change anything, so she lay still. "Is anyone there?" she asked as calmly as she could. Her voice quavered a little but not enough to give away her true fear.

"It's okay, Lexi. It's over." Greta's voice had none of the comfort it'd once offered Lexi. She'd betrayed her trust.

"I can't see," Lexi said, making no effort to keep the bitter des-pair from her tone.

"It's temporary," Greta replied. "You don't need your eyes to find your way. Use your Gifts."

Lexi reached out with her other senses. She began to put together a mental image of the space around her, listening and sending out telekinetic probes to feel for objects. Her breathing began to normal-ize as her surroundings took shape in her mind. By her estimation, she was still in the same room as when she'd been knocked uncon-scious, reclined in the center chair.

"There you go," Greta soothed, placing a gentle hand on Lexi's shoulder.

"I'd changed my mind," Lexi choked out. "I didn't want to do this. I tried to stop them, but—"

"Shh, stay calm."

Lexi swallowed a sob. "Where were you? Why didn't you stop them when I called out?"

"I'm here now," she said.

That's not an answer. Lexi tried to sit up but felt straps preventing her movement. "What's going on? Greta!"

Greta strengthened her grip on Lexi's shoulder. "You're safe. It's okay. Once you're calm, I'll remove the restraints."

"Why am I tied down?"

"Standard procedure." There was a clinical detachment to her tone. All the relative warmth was gone.

A tingle of fear crept up Lexi's spine. This wasn't anything like the woman she knew and loved. Where was the care and compassion?

Lexi made a conscious effort to still her movements. The only way out of this situation was to play along. "When can the bandages come off?"

"I think it's been long enough. You slept through the night."

It's been a whole day? She didn't feel rested.

"Let me help you."

As Greta peeled off the bandages, cool air touched Lexi's close lids. Her eyes ached more without the pressure of the wrapping over them.

"Slowly now," Great said. "Your vision may be a little blurry at first."

Lexi cracked open her eyes. The lights in the room were thankfully dimmed, but those that were present cast blinding stars in the corners of her vision. She winced.

Greta began undoing the chair's restraints. "The doctor said your dilation response might take some time to normalize." When the final strap was released, she handed Lexi her old pair of tinted glasses.

"I thought the point was to be done with these?"

"Do as you please."

Begrudgingly, Lexi put on the tinted glasses to offer temporary relief from the light glare. Right now, being able to see would help her think more clearly, and she needed to figure out what in the stars was going on. *Has Greta turned against me, or is this all just a misunderstanding?*

Lexi swung her legs off the chair and tried to stand up, using the seatback for support. Her legs were wobbly, but she was able to support her weight.

"I want to see it," she said. "Where's a mirror?"

"There's a washroom through there." Greta indicated a metal door in the back right of the room.

Lexi stumbled toward it, reaching inside to find a light switch before thinking better of it. There was just enough light streaming in from the main room for her to make out her reflection.

She took off the tinted glasses and stared into the mirror. The glow was completely gone from her eyes—they were just the pale blue of her youth, from before her abilities emerged. She'd spent most of her life with her eyes like that, but she couldn't help feeling like she'd lost an important part of herself. Tears threatened to fill her eyes, but the immediate stinging prompted her to suppress the wave of emotion.

What's done is done. I can blend in better now, and that's what matters. She took a steadying breath.

Now, standing and feeling less woozy, she remembered that she'd been unconscious for the better part of a day. She took the opportunity to use the toilet and wash her face; she was unlikely to get those facilities back in the maintenance tunnel.

When Lexi emerged from the washroom, Greta was standing next to the exit door. She held out Lexi's backpack to her.

"Come on," the older woman said.

Yes, let's get out of this awful place. She took the backpack and slung it over her shoulders.

Greta opened the door and led Lexi down the hallway toward the storefront. Only, rather than walking straight out to the spaceport, they were stopped by the large man who'd first escorted her in.

"What is this?" Lexi asked when he didn't move out of their way.

A look passed between the two of them then. His was mild curiosity punctuated with a lopsided grin, while hers was all nervous hand-wringing desperation. The moment drew out to an uncomfortable length.

Lexi inhaled sharply, preparing a rather acidic demand.

"We have an opportunity," Greta explained, rushing to fill the silence.

Alarms went off again in Lexi's mind. *When will this nightmare end?*

"I've been waiting for the right chance to come along," Greta continued. "I didn't want to get your hopes up, but all the pieces are in place now. We only have to do one simple task and then we'll have the money we need to pay off the bounty on both of us. We can finally be free."

Lexi swallowed. "What kind of task?"

"A certain businessman will be passing through the port in a few days, carrying a valuable piece of merchandise. He enjoys the company of young women but is wary of Gifted. Now you, though, could get close without raising suspicion."

The plan became clear in Lexi's mind. "You mean you want me to steal something from him?"

"All you need to do is telepathically compel him to give the device to you. He always keeps it with him."

Pickpocketing and general theft wasn't new to Lexi, and she was adept at using her telekinetic abilities to support those activities. Positioning herself as someone's plaything while invading their mind was another matter. "Sounds risky."

"No more than anything else we do. He can afford to lose it."

"That's not the point." She glanced at the man guarding the door, who was standing impassively like the two women didn't exist.

"Since when are you so touchy about theft?" Greta asked. "We've done it almost every day for your whole life."

"This is different. Mind control is a slippery slope," Lexi insisted. "Besides, we only ever took what we need in order to survive. Stealing was never a *job*."

"There are times to set principles aside. If we get this device, then they'll get us the credits needed to get our bounties canceled in the central database."

"The contract will just get re-upped. It's a temporary fix, at best. Not worth it." Lexi started to walk away.

"Except, there *isn't* anyone to renew it," Greta blurted out.

Lexi stopped cold. "Wait, what?"

"I've learned that the original issuers aren't around anymore. If we can get it canceled, we'll be free. I found us the big payday we need to get out from under this for good."

"Hold on, what are you saying? You mean, those families aren't in control on Cytera anymore?"

Greta hesitated. "Yes, things are different now."

Why didn't she say anything sooner? Lexi staggered backward. "So, I have a price on my head but the person who put it there is dead or gone? I've been hunted my whole life because of a *ghost?*"

"It's more complicated than that."

"I don't know, it sounds pretty bomaxed simple to me." Lexi's chest burned. *I don't know what to believe. I thought I was running from the people who killed my family, but could they really be gone?* She glanced between Greta and the man blocking her path. "If we can pay off the bounty and go free, then what does it matter what my eyes look like?"

"We still need to get that money to get out from under the bounty. With a little sacrifice, this one job is all it will take."

What is this device that's valuable enough to offset a surgery and two bounties? Nothing. It was too good to be true, plain and simple. The real value was having a trained, Gifted thief who didn't look like one. Reality snapped into focus.

"You bartered for your own bounty to be paid off in exchange for me, didn't you?" Lexi's stomach twisted with the awful realization that she'd been sold into servitude.

The muscular guard at the door tensed, taking a step closer.

Greta motioned for him to stay out of it. "Alexandra, don't make a scene."

All this time, she's treated me like her daughter, but was I really just a useful tool? She thought back to Greta's lessons and tactics over the years. In hindsight, those skills doubled as valuable preparation for conducting specialized crime. Though the training had been administered under the guise of learning to survive, somewhere along the way that must have shifted. Maybe that hadn't been the original intention when Greta had saved her on Cytera, but desperation changed people—obligation degraded into resentment, and that bitterness could fester until even the unthinkable became possible.

Perhaps Lexi had been so blindly faithful to Greta, the one constant in her life, that she had ignored the warning signs of their deteriorating relationship. Now, though, she saw the situation clearly. Whatever trust had once existed between them was gone. She was truly on her own.

Lexi backed away, for the first time in her life, fearful of her mentor. Tears flooded her eyes; she didn't mind that it stung. "I won't do it."

"Lexi, come on." Greta dropped her shoulders disarmingly, stepping slowly toward her. The love was still there deep in her gaze; despite her horrific intentions, she genuinely believed she was helping. "It won't take long for your debt to be paid off, too, and then—"

Lexi brought up a telekinetic shield around herself, not making the same mistake again by waiting too long. "No."

Greta's face darkened. "This isn't a game, girl. Drop your shield."

At that, the guard lunged for Lexi.

Lexi halted him telekinetically, drawing on her training to hold him in place without hurting him. Greta's lip curled up with a hint of approval.

"You'll have to clean up this mess on your own," Lexi said, stepping toward the door.

Greta lashed out with the telekinetic net to snare her, but Lexi deflected it with her shield. Doing so without letting the man go tested Lexi's limits. The older woman was more skilled, but Lexi was innately stronger. She'd need every bit of that ability to get free.

Lexi kept her hold on the man and her shield as she backed away. *I never thought our time together would end like this.*

Though she hated the idea of being on her own, staying with Greta was now a worse prospect. After how much faith she'd placed in their relationship, Lexi's heart ached with the knowledge that Greta ultimately thought of her as disposable. Her parents had died on Cytera so she could break free from servitude to others. She couldn't give up on that dream of a free future they had envisioned for her.

"It's just one job!" Greta tried to telekinetically ensnare her again.

Lexi was ready with a counter-move. She gripped Greta in a telekinetic vise and forced her arms to her sides, sliding her back across the floor to stand next to the guard.

"We both know it never is." Her chest tight, Lexi walked away.

She held onto the telekinetic restraints for as long as she could. Eventually, it was too great a distance, and she released her grasp on Greta and the man. She broke into a run.

Lexi dashed through the station, not caring about her path so much as putting as great a distance as possible between herself and her pursuers, content to never see them again.

Where can I go? She didn't have anyone else to turn to and had no possessions other than what fit in her backpack. No options, yet infinite potential.

One thing was certain: she had to keep moving. Ultimately, it didn't matter what things were like now on Cytera or who was in power. The fact remained that there was still a bounty on her head—logged in the interstellar database—and it would remain active until someone licensed closed it out. No one was going to do that unless they got a worthwhile payday, and she wasn't in a position to offer those kinds of funds. Whatever "solution" Greta thought she had found certainly wasn't the way to get her name cleared.

She kept up her pace, paying little attention to her surroundings aside from not running into anyone standing in her way. The sprawling port had plenty of places where a person could disappear; she just needed to find the right quiet corner to regroup.

After fifteen minutes of blind running, she decided it was time to get her bearings. Her stomach lurched when she realized that she'd wandered straight into the part of the port where she'd been chased two days before. *Shite, I should have been paying more attention.*

She looked for the nearest station map so she could figure out a path away.

There was a directory a hundred meters from her, and she jogged toward it. When she arrived at the map, she was dismayed to find that it could only be accessed from the side facing the corridor, meaning she'd need to have her back to the foot-traffic.

And they wonder why so many people get pickpocketed. Arranging herself as best she could to maintain a view of her surroundings, she brought up the map and began searching for a good place to hole up for the night.

Something cool pressed against her neck. Before she could react, strong hands gripped her arms from behind. "Where did you run off to?"

Lexi instinctively reached out for a telekinetic defense, but she found her abilities were blocked. *What the...* Her legs felt unsteady under her. *Shite! They found me.*

Lexi fought against the man's firm grip. "I won't work for you!"

"Work for me?" The man sounded genuinely surprised.

"You're here to enforce Greta's deal, aren't you?" She couldn't get a look at the man holding her, but he felt the right size for the goon from the shop.

"Who? No. I've been tracking your bounty, and now I finally get my payday."

Lexi's stomach dropped. *No! This is so much worse.*

Whether it was the same man who'd spotted her two days prior or someone else, she'd been caught. For almost two decades she'd evaded people just like this man. She'd lost her one friend in the world to stay free, and now her life was over all the same.

Even as fear and despair threatened to consume her, determination for freedom burned within. *I have to get away.* She didn't know *how* yet, but she'd wait for the right moment.

She allowed the man to half-carry her through the port. Her legs weren't working right—numb, but just mobile enough to keep her from falling flat on her face. Far more concerning was that she couldn't access her Gifts.

"What did you give me?" she asked.

"Oh, just a dash of a special helper to make things easier."

Her mind raced. She'd heard about certain sedative drugs inhibiting abilities—not by actually dampening them, but by altering brain chemistry in a way that made it difficult to focus. If that was the case, she could beat this. Her abilities were a part of her, not something that could be shut off with the flip of a switch.

I'm in control. It didn't feel like it at the moment, but maybe if she said it enough times it would become true.

The man directed her toward one of the nearby concourses berthing small transport vessels.

Okay, so he's trying to get me off-station. That much was clear to Lexi.

The moment that ship took off, however, she'd be stranded on board. Her best bet was to break free before then.

Putting up a fuss now while there were still people around was an option. Someone might come to her aid, but more likely the Enforcers would get called in, and they'd probably arrest her. Though she'd never seen her official rap sheet, she knew she'd racked up a number of petty crime offenses and maybe a couple more serious infractions—nothing to land her major time in a lockup, but *any* time would be counterproductive to her ambitions.

That left one option: wait until she was somewhere private with the guy and try to make an opportunistic escape. One shot to get it right.

You can do this. She did her best to psych herself up, using every bit of strength she could muster to fight the effects of the subduing drug in her system. With conscious effort, she could almost access her Gifts. A little more, and she'd have enough.

The bounty hunter made a sudden right turn away from the concourse lined with ship gangways. He dragged her down a short side corridor with three large airlock doors, each facing a different direction at the end. He placed his hand against the biometric scanner for the door on the left. It flashed blue for approval and then hissed open.

The inner door of the airlock cycled simultaneously, retracting upward to reveal a shuttle bay containing four small vessels.

Ah, he's just got a little puddle-jumper. Relief flooded through Lexi, giving her the extra energy boost she needed. This was the perfect venue to make her escape.

Lexi allowed him to keep leading her toward his ship, an older-model transport about thirty meters long with sleek lines suitable for atmospheric entry. The bounty hunter approached it on the starboard side, placing his hand on the hull near the midpoint of the ship. A doorway appeared in the side, which slid upward, and an entry ramp extended to the deck.

"Say your goodbyes," he said to Lexi.

She grunted weakly in response, playing along that she didn't have her faculties about her.

"In you go." He shoved her up the ramp.

Lexi stumbled into what appeared to be a lounge room adjacent to a galley. The bounty hunter released his grip on her to access the controls.

Now.

Lexi put up a telekinetic shield around herself. She gave it a couple seconds to confirm it was stable. It was as solid as it was going to get.

"I'm leaving now," she stated, heading for the ramp.

"Shite! How…" He pulled a sidearm and pointed it at her. "Stop!"

"I'd rather you shoot me than end up wherever it is you're taking me." She continued walking down the ramp.

"Last warning. Your bounty is dead or alive, but they pay more for living. Better deal for both of us."

"No, thanks." Lexi braced for the impending impact on her shield.

The shot struck, deflecting harmlessly from the invisible telekinetic bubble around her, but causing an uncomfortable hum of pressure in her head as she drew more energy to maintain the protective cover.

"Unauthorized weapons fire in Bay G-247," a synthesized voice announced over the intercom.

"Shite!" the bounty hunter shouted, making a run for Lexi. He fired another blast.

She ducked to the side just in time. The blast passed her by and struck an oxygen line of the exposed station mechanical systems. It didn't ignite, but Lexi heard the hiss of a leak.

They'll keep coming after me. I need to end this. She knew what she needed to do.

Lexi sent a telekinetic spark. The oxygen ignited in a brilliant flash. At the last second, Lexi expanded her personal shield to encompass the bounty hunter. He dropped to the floor, reflexively diving for cover.

The flames licked the outer confines of the bubble, passing over them harmlessly.

The area was bathed in pulsing red light as a siren sounded. Simultaneously, the inner airlock door snapped shut.

"I could have let you die," Lexi told the bounty hunter. Her hand trembled sightly; she wasn't sure if it was from the drugs in her system or the exertion, but it was taking all of her focus to maintain the shield. "You owe me your life, so I want mine in return."

He squinted at her in the red light, seemingly caught between surprise and confusion. "It doesn't work like that."

No, it doesn't. But there is a way. Lexi hated herself for what she was about to do, but this *was* a matter of survival, unlike Greta's "job." If ever there was a time to break her code of ethics, it was now. *No more running.*

She dove into the bounty hunter's mind, accessing his innermost thoughts. *"Board your ship,"* she instructed him.

He twitched, resisting her. "N-No," he stammered.

Despair flooded through her. *He's been trained in mental guards.* She hadn't expected that. Nor had she accounted for the effects of the drugs still causing fuzziness in her mind. She might be able to break through, but there wasn't time. The area would be swarming with Enforcers at any second.

Lexi only had one play left. She released her hold on the bounty hunter and dropped the shield. "Have you read my file?"

"Of course."

"Then why are you bringing me in?"

He shrugged one shoulder sheepishly. "I need the money."

"Even knowing I didn't do anything wrong?"

He tilted his head. "It said you're in possession of valuable stolen property."

She'd often wondered what her file said—how the price on her head had been justified. Circumstances of birth hardly seemed like it would make a compelling case to an outsider. She motioned to herself. "Does it look like I have anything of value? I *am* the property. I was born to essentially be a slave, and I got free. If you turn me in, there's no one to pay out; they're gone." She looked into his eyes, laying it all on the line. "Will you help me?"

It was a weak case, she knew it. Yet, she didn't know what else to do. Aside from trying to run—and stars knew where that had gotten her—she had no other options.

"Is it because you're Gifted?" he asked, his expression too flat to read.

She nodded.

He swallowed hard. "Your file didn't say that."

"I was just a kid then, no abilities yet." She took a step toward him. "I've been running for my whole life. I have nothing left to lose."

"Lady, look—"

The tone of it was a preamble to disappointment. She couldn't let him get those words out. If he finished that sentence, it would all be over.

"Listen to me," she cut in. "Today you have the opportunity to grant someone a chance to live a free life. I know you have no reason to agree to help me, but I have to ask all the same."

His gaze shifted between her and the sealed airlock where Enforcers would no doubt bust through. "Fine, but first I'll need to verify your story. If it checks out, we can discuss this further. If it doesn't, the time for talking will be over. Do you understand?"

She did, far better than most people. It took every ounce of restraint she had to resist looking at the tools of the bounty hunter's trade arrayed across his person. "Fine."

"Wait on my ship."

Between taking her chances with the bounty hunter and dealing with the Enforcers, Lexi was stuck between two terrible options. However, the hunter was open to a conversation, which was more than could be said for the other group. She was in so deep now, she needed to go for it.

She ran back to his shuttle and up the entry ramp a moment before the bay's airlock opened. As expected, Enforcers dressed in rapid response armor stormed in.

"This has all been a misunderstanding," she overheard the bounty hunter say. "I was going after a charge, and she slipped me."

The response was indistinct. Lexi remained huddled just inside the hatch to the hunter's ship, willing the Enforcers to forego a search of the vessel's interior. She didn't fully understand the relationship between Guild bounty hunters and the Enforcers, but she could only imagine the police force had the ultimate authority.

After what felt like an eternity, she heard footfalls approaching the ship. She brought up a shield around herself again, not knowing what to expect.

The bounty hunter came into view up the ramp. Without saying anything, he closed the hatch.

"What happened?" Lexi asked.

"We're getting out of here."

"The Enforcers let you go? What about the—"

"Easier to send a problem away than keep it around," he replied, heading toward the front of the ship.

She wasn't entirely sure what he meant by that, but it sounded favorable. "What now?" Lexi followed him into the cockpit. She hated that she had to trust this person—especially after what had just happened with Greta. If she had a better option at the moment, she would've taken it.

"We get far away enough from here that they can't shoot at the ship if they change their mind about letting me off with a warning." He went through the process of powering up his craft with practiced ease.

Instinctually, Lexi watched and committed the startup sequence to memory. One could never be too careful.

She needed to keep him talking. Needed him to see her for who she was—not just some paycheck waiting to be collected.

"How did you pull that off?" Lexi had never really had any *friends*, but she took on the tone she'd heard others use. It was maybe a little awkward, but so was she, so hopefully it worked well enough.

"A big favor and a lot of sweet talk." He fired up the ship's engines with a final flip of a switch. "Name's Kieran, by the way."

Lexi took the empty seat next to him and strapped in. "Thank you, Kieran, for helping me."

He looked at her then. A long, measuring look, like that of a butcher weighing a prized piece of meat post-slaughter and trying to decide if he was being screwed or not.

Then he grunted and looked away.

"Here's the thing," he told the air between him and the front viewport, "I haven't decided if I am or not."

Shite!

"You didn't let them arrest me." Fear clawed at the back of her throat. This wasn't working. She needed a Plan B.

Kieran chuckled. "That's true. But then you would have been in their custody and not mine. Less than helpful for me."

Her heart sank. "So you're going to take me to Cytera?"

"No," he said, clipped and matter of fact. "I'm going to verify your story, like I said I would."

There's still a chance, then. After the day she'd had, Lexi didn't dare to hope—but she held onto the glimmer of possibility all the same.

With the push of a button, he turned the ship's controls over to the station for guided exit from the bay.

Lexi watched as he leaned back in his chair and rubbed at his eyes. "You know, us Guild members aren't actually bad people. Most people with bounties on their head are terrible, and we do this job to keep lowlifes off the streets. If you really do have an unjustified price on your head, it's my duty to clear it."

"It... is?"

He cracked a smile. "What, you think we're only in this for the profit?"

"Yeah, isn't that kinda the deal?"

"Common misconception."

"Oh." She swallowed. "Are you saying that if I'd talked with a Guild member sooner, they would have heard my case?"

He laughed. It had been so long since she'd heard genuine mirth, the sound made her lips twitch up into a smile, despite herself.

After he regained his composure somewhat, he said, "Depends on who you talked to. Some of the newbies are too eager for stats to care. You're lucky I tracked you down and not someone else."

She sank back in her seat. "Guess so."

Kieran took over the controls again once the station released its remote pilot. "I'm just going to get us away from here, then we'll talk."

He initiated a short spatial jump. The area around the ship was momentarily enveloped in ribbons of blue-green light and the starscape began to fade. Time appeared to elongate, and then for a few seconds, the ship was surrounded fully by the light. Soon, the starscape returned, solidifying outside the front viewport.

Lexi released a long breath as the ship dropped back into normal reality. There was no sign of Gallos Station or anything else but the distant stars.

"All right, let's have a look at this file," Kieran said. He brought it up on the holoprojector above the front controls.

Lexi's stomach knotted as she read over all the accounts of her wrongdoings. The Enforcers had been keeping tabs on her, it seemed, though none of the offenses had triggered new bounties. The only Guild-authorized offense was her original count of "stolen valuables." She scoffed.

Kieran frowned at the readout. "I can't believe I missed it. Your birthdate and the bounty issue date are only a year apart. My stars…"

"Told you."

He ran his hand over his close-cropped hair. "These old bounties get sold off to third-parties and details are lost in the shuffle. I can't tell you what happened with your case, but I can try to set it right. Let me run it up the chain."

Kieran made several entries on the touchscreen in front of him.

"How long will this take?" Lexi asked.

"Should know shortly."

They sat in silence, watching the screen.

"I'm sorry that happened to you," Kieran said after a few minutes. "Don't give up on everyone. There are some good people out there."

"I don't know if I believe that."

His handheld chirped, and he pulled out the device to check it. A smile spread across his face. "Well, now you have proof." He passed the handheld to her.

The text stood at the center of the screen: "Bounty: Cleared."

She met his gaze. "I…" There were no words. Her throat closed as emotion welled within her. Relief. Gratitude. Anger. All this time, Greta could have just *asked* for the bounty's validity to be challenged, but instead they'd been running, racking up other offenses. For what? Nothing more than the ghostly orders of toppled psychopaths.

Lexi wiped the tears starting to form in her eyes.

Kieran gave her a sympathetic smile. "Hey, life isn't fair, but sometimes things have a way of balancing out."

Still unable to speak, Lexi only nodded in response.

"I'll drop you at the Aldria Station," he said while plotting a jump course.

"Thank you." Lexi crossed her arms around herself, taking in a slow, deep breath to ease the knot in her chest. She was on her own now. No more Greta. But also, no more running. In that moment, she vowed to never look back.

I'm free now. It was a fresh start, and nothing else mattered.

* * * * *

A.K. DuBoff Bio

Amy (A.K.) DuBoff has always loved science fiction in all its forms, including books, movies, shows, and games. If it involves outer space, even better! She is an award-winning and USA Today bestselling indie author specializing in space-based science fiction and fantasy. Dubbed the modern "Queen of Space Opera" by her readers, she is most known for her acclaimed Cadicle Universe. Amy's short fiction has been published by NewCon Press, Seventh Seal Press, and in numerous indie publications. When she's not writing, she enjoys travel, wine tasting, binge-watching TV series, and playing epic strategy board games.

# # # # #

Hard Bounty by Jason Cordova

A Quintus Fox Story

Getting bounties in this day and age is pretty simple. You enter a system, plug in your creds, and some government lackey confirms everything. After a few moments they send you an info packet with all of the open bounties in the area. You go hunting some poor idiots who crossed the law, make some credits, and leave for greener pastures once you've bilked the system for all its worth, all the while leaving the impression you're the best in the business.

Easy peasey. Usually.

"I hate to be the bearer of bad news, Mister Fox, but there just aren't any active bounties for you currently in the Gab'adai System," the reedy voice insisted over the comms. He didn't sound like he hated being the bearer of anything which would make my life miserable. There was something nasally and whiny about the man's voice which drove me to distraction. Being a famous bounty hunter meant I had to have patience in order to catch my quarry. Said patience did not extend to flunkies, though. Or Comptrollers who thought they were a bounty hunter's equal simply because they controlled the bounties.

Comptrollers were worse than flunkies. They were *bureaucrats*.

"You gotta be kidding me," I drawled, letting the last syllable hang in the air for a moment. Quantum communications allowed for instantaneous transmissions throughout the system, so the pause was clearly deliberate. I needed to remind him who he was dealing with without being obtuse or overbearing. He had to know by now who I was. He'd run my creds, for crying out loud.

Which made his response even more irritating.

"I'm sorry, Sly Fox, but there simply aren't any bounties in this system at the moment. They've all been collected."

I snorted. *Bullshit*, I didn't say. "Nobody's that good. Outside of me, that is, and since I'm asking about bounties, we know it wasn't me. Ergo, the bounties haven't all been claimed."

"We had fifteen active bounties eight days ago, sir," the squalid-sounding man confirmed. *"They've all been claimed and dockets closed in the past thirty hours."*

I opened my mouth to argue further but felt a tug at my boot. I jerked away before Lazarus could chew another tassel off my pa's boots. The damned quantum wolf pup was the most annoying of the terrible trio. None of them were full grown yet, but they were all still larger than your typical dog. This limited what they could do, though. Instead of being able to phase through solid matter, the trio were all protected by some sort of diamond pelt. It made them impossible to kill. Or, more importantly, to get things out of their mouths, which weren't supposed to be there, like the tassels off my boot.

Of the three, Lazarus seemed to be their leader. He was tenacious, fearless, and smart as a whip, which made me more inclined to like him. However, some lines were sacred, and he continued to cross the one involving my pa's boots and their tassels.

I'd acquired him, along with his two siblings, on my last job when I'd been forced to hunt down their mother on Deep Eleven Space Station months before. An accident, actually, since I hadn't known what she was at the time. I thought I'd been hunting criminals for criminals. Instead, I killed a nursing mother of an endangered species. It was only after I killed the beast did I realize she had pups. My pa would have been disappointed in me.

"Always be certain of your quarry," he'd always say. I shook my head fondly. *Sorry, Pa. I screwed the pooch on this one. Literally.*

"What, you got a team of bounty hunters patrolling your system or something?" I asked as I freed the stray tassel from the pup's mouth. Lazarus was undeterred and went after another. Suddenly, what had been a standard call to a Collections' Comptroller had turned into a fight for the life of my boot's tassels. Lazarus dodged around my hand and attacked from another angle, which earned him a cuff on the shoulder. However, it did more damage to me than anything else. "Ow! Damn it, Laz! Stop!"

"Say again, Sly Fox. What was your last?"

"Nothing. Talking to, ah, one of my crew."

"As to your previous query, all bounties were paid to a single individual," the Comptroller continued in his patented nasally voice. I could hear the condescending tone from five million miles away and the desire to shoot someone—preferably the system's Comptroller— blossomed in my guts. I pushed the sensation down, shoved Laz away from another damned tassel, and frowned. There weren't many bounty hunters in the business as good as I was. None were better. At least, that's what I'd always believed. Fifteen bounties in eight days, though? I wasn't sure if I could pull it off. Not without help, and I hated help.

They always wanted a share of the cut. Greedy little buggers.

"May I ask who?"

"*You may, but our standard NDA dictates you will be disappointed with my non-answer.*"

Oh, I wanted to kill the man right then and there, burn everything to the ground, then piss on the ashes for good measure. Gab'adai was one of those secretive systems where the government insisted on everything be out in the open for the public—unless it was protected by their Official Secrets Act. Since they made you sign a non-disclosure agreement for everything you did for the government while in-system, though, nothing was out in the open. Transparency with a blindfold, legally binding and completely aboveboard.

Governments... am I right?

"*However, most bounty hunters in the system tend to congregate at Leo's Bar on Vasa Station,*" the Comptroller relented slightly. I raised an eyebrow. This was unexpected. Most government officials were so full of themselves they wouldn't even throw a starving dog a bone. I revised my opinion of the man. Slightly. He was still a bureaucrat, and a man can only give so much leeway. "*I can forward your credentials to the station for berthing purposes, Sly Fox.*"

I had no idea why the man suddenly decided he would be nice, but my pa always said to never look a gift horse in the mouth. I had no idea what a horse was, but it sounded like solid advice. "Copy that, Comptroller. Thank you kindly."

"*It's the least I could do for Quintus Fox,*" came the reply. I smiled inwardly as Lazarus finally gave up on my tassels and moved to the toe of my boot. My creds must have been delayed originally, and finally gone through. He recognized my name and must have gotten a little starstruck. Couldn't blame him, really. I'm fairly famous, even in these parts.

"*Sly Fox*, out." I killed the comms and picked Lazarus up by the scruff of his neck before he could chew a hole in my boots. It took quite a bit of effort but I got him up. A pup, sure, but he and his siblings had gained fifty pounds each since I got them. Holding him up, I kept him just out of range and looked at his face. The little diamond-coated wolf's teeth were wickedly sharp, though he seemed more inclined to eat my pa's boots than me. So far. Since quantum wolves weren't known for their temperament, one never knew when they would snap and eat your face. "Laz, why you gotta try to hurt Pa's boots? I love these boots."

Lazarus growled and whined, desperately trying to lick my face. Bright red eyes met mine. He was a good pup, all things considered. I relented and set him down on my lap. Sharp claws dug into my thigh as he balanced. He put his paws up on my chest and immediately tried licking my face again. Chuckling, I tugged gently on his ears. Lazarus seemed to enjoy it, and his back leg began twitching.

"Well, let's get on over to Vasa Station and find out who's been claiming all the bounties here," I said and punched in the coordinates given by the Comptroller. Leaning back, I scratched Laz's ears. His tail thumped painfully into my thigh. More licking commenced. There was no point in trying to stop him now. When he was happy, he was determined to make everyone else happy was well. After a moment, though, I sat back up and stared him straight in the eye. He tried to look innocent but I was catching on to his ways. Pa didn't raise no fool, and apparently I wasn't raising foolish pups.

"Wait... you're distracting me, aren't you? Oh hell... what are your siblings up to?"

* * *

Don't ever let anyone tell you that quantum wolves are stupid critters who can't work together.

I stared in dismay at my bed. While Lazarus had been distracting me up in the cockpit of the *Sly Fox*, his sisters, Naomi and Ruth, had chewed through the zero-g mattress of my bed and pulled the stuffing out. All of it. My bedroom looked like a Zarkasian blizzard had exploded inside it. All three wolf pups stared up at me, their tails wagging. They had no shame. In fact, they looked damn proud of their work.

Too proud. I sighed. I didn't have children for a reason. If this were any indication of what my progeny might be like, I never would.

"Do y'all know how much this bed cost?" I asked rhetorically as I tried to pick up the bed's ruined innards, to no avail. Zero-g beds were filled with some sort of fiber that made them conform perfectly to your body when you lay in them, but the moment the stuffing broke containment it turned almost powdery. It also was damn near impossible to clean up without some sort of vacuum system—which the *Sly Fox* lacked. I'd been meaning to get one, but since the pups didn't shed like normal animals, I hadn't gotten around to it. I sighed. "Confounded mutts."

All three tails started wagging at this. For some reason, they seemed to think the insult "mutts" was a form of endearment. I didn't understand it. Frowning, I opened my mouth to admonish them further but the ship's berthing alarm sounded. The pups yipped loudly to match the siren's sound. I rolled my eyes at the racket but didn't try to stop them. In my short time with them, I'd quickly learned there was little I could do to stop them from their barking once all three got going.

"Damn it all."

Ten minutes and the beginnings of a headache later, we docked on one of the many tethering connectors to Vasa Station. Unlike most space stations I'd dealt with, Vasa Station did not have artificial gravity in their connectors. Since the station was a shipping center, it made some sense. After all, loading and unloading goods in zero-g meant a lesser workload. Granted, there were other dangers to worry about. An improperly strapped load could disrupt the traffic of a tethering connector for hours, maybe longer, if it came loose. Idiot barge captains who sometimes tried to disembark too quickly and crashed into incoming traffic were also a common threat. There are pros and cons to everything in the universe.

Before departing from the ship, however, I needed to make a choice. I could leave the pups behind on the *Sly Fox*, which was… not the best option. I hadn't left them alone on the ship since I got them. If they panicked—or worse, grew bored—the amount of damage they could cause gave me nightmares. On the other hand, they'd never been around people before.

Correction: they'd never been around *living* people before. The memory of the partially-digested human finger Lazarus had vomited up the first day I'd gotten him was something I tried not to dwell upon too often.

Potential destruction of my ship, or possible attacks on the citizenry of Vasa Station. In the end the decision was pretty easy.

Watching the pups navigate zero-g was a joy. They were far more graceful than I'd expected. They used the various handholds as launch points. They would twist their bodies in mid-flight, bounce off a wall or handhold, and zip away, playing tag with one another. Ruth and Naomi were more agile than their brother, who moved with the grace of a million-ton barge augering into an asteroid. I usually ended up being the asteroid.

The tethering tube was empty, thank the stars. Ruth, the smallest of the three, dodged me every time. She stayed just out of reach of her siblings. Naomi was better at making me believe she was about to run me over before she'd flip, get a paw on a handhold that looked out of reach, and fly off in a new direction.

Laz? Not so much. Each impact felt like a solid blow to the ribs delivered by a prize fighter. If not for my Algravian silk body armor, I'd be covered in bruises. Still, we managed to get across the zero-g zone with only a few bumps. Once gravity returned, the three pups all settled down and began sniffing the air. Their bodies stiffened, and their ears flicked forward. It was as if someone had flipped a switch on my demonic pooches. One second they were rambunctious puppies. The next? Stone cold killers.

Perhaps keeping them isn't such a bad idea…

I quickly talked myself out of the thought. There were far too many variables. Plus, I was supposed to take them back to Jax where they could be raised amongst their own kind by the Royal Game Warden until they matured. Nobody was supposed to have a quantum wolf off-planet, even if it were by accident. Having a quantum wolf and not returning it—never mind three pups—was liable to get me on a government list or three.

Without a customs agent to check my ID at the tether's entry hatch, there was no way anyone could grouch at me for bringing the pups with me if they spotted me later. I mean, it wasn't *my* fault nobody was there. The lack of security was a bit disconcerting, but it was also very refreshing. The last time I'd stopped at a space station for a job I'd been betrayed by the men I was working with. If not for the deceased mother of the pups, I would have been turned over to the Duke brothers and murdered. Or worse still, forced to marry the cousin of theirs whose honor I'd allegedly "besmirched." I'd rather be killed, slowly and as painfully as possible. I mentally snorted. Marrying her *would* be the worst form of death they could inflict upon me. Marriage was the slowest of deaths possible.

I came back to the present. The pups were attentively staring off into the distance, their sensitive ears clearly picking up the noises on the other side of the hatch. I'd had no one watching my back on the last job, and I'd almost been shot for my troubles. They were smart, but could they understand?

"Hey," I said and all three heads whipped around simultaneously to look up at me. Vague memories of my pa training a dog tickled the edges of my mind. I held a hand up. "I need your attention. Sit. *Sit.*"

All three rear ends hit the deck. Bright red eyes locked on mine.

Not bad, considering I haven't really worked with you on training yet.

"This could be dangerous," I told them. All three started wagging their tails. "Dangerous means someone could get hurt." Their tails started wagging harder. "*I* could get hurt." The tails stopped. A deep, throaty growl emanated from Lazarus. It was hard, not smiling. "Keep an eye out. If I yell, come running. If someone tries to hurt one of you, or me, kill. Do you understand?"

Tails started wagging again. Either I was the luckiest son of a gun in the universe, and they understood every word, or I was a delusional crackpot who was probably going to die.

I took a deep breath and opened the tether hatch. With a hiss, the airtight door slid open. Metallic air blasted us in the face. I took a deep breath, gave my body a moment to adjust to the change in air pressure, then the four of us strode onto Vasa Station proper like we owned the place.

One thing about being a famous bounty hunter is that you get used to the stares. What I wasn't prepared for were the way people were ignoring me. Their gazes were in my direction, true, but each and every one of them were staring at the wolf pups around me. A few local toughs who looked the type to try something found other places to be. Even the constabulary, a rotund man with dangerous eyes tipped his hat toward me as we passed by.

Hot damn, I thought and tried not to smile. The trio were walking in stride with me, their eyes constantly scanning our surroundings as we moved further into the station. Their pelts sparkled under the ultraviolet lights of the station, and their eyes bore the telltale signs of keen intelligence. I'd grown used to their child-like shenanigans on board the *Sly Fox*. In doing so, though, I'd forgotten what they were at the core of their being. These were Jaxian Quantum Wolf pups, and it would be wise of me to always remember that. They were the most dangerous entourage this side of Teegarden's Star, and, for the time being, they were following my lead.

It took a few minutes of searching the station's promenade before I found the bar the Comptroller told me about. I wasn't disappointed by its exterior. Holographic neon lights offered all forms of alcohol and other drinks, while more graphic images promised more enticing wares for the discerning clientele upstairs. Leo's Bar was the sort of dive I'd come to expect on stations like Vasa—seedy, yet struggling to maintain a semblance of respectability in the face of entropy.

There wasn't really a front door to the bar but a pair of swinging half-doors. Painted red, they were a quaint reminder of the world from whence we came, a history time has almost forgotten. The doors were on hinges, which allowed for movement in both directions. They even squeaked loudly, though I think this was a feature and not a bug. Laz had to duck to avoid the door, but neither of the girls had a problem following me inside.

As my eyes adjusted to the lighting, I quickly noticed my previous expectation was shattered by the cleanliness and modernity of the place. Instead of a rough and tumble Wild West knock-off saloon, I was greeted by very chic, modern furniture and seating arrangements. Screens lined the walls, offering the clientele various forms of entertainment not of the carnal kind. The room was filled with all sorts of customers, men and women alike, who were clearly here for the atmosphere. You can always tell by what they're drinking. In truly seedy bars, the clientele would be sipping watered-down whiskey from dirty glasses. Here at Leo's, the glasses were clear and the beverages had little decorative umbrellas in them. The people here were a higher class of citizenry than what I was used to dealing with.

I'd grown too used to dealing with the dregs of society. Polite company was rare out here in the Striderlands.

On a far wall was a screen with a long list of names and numbers next to them. Nobody seemed to be paying attention to it, save for a strange-looking alien with pink and black hair atop its head. It was clearly a bounty board, though I'd never seen one with so many red checks next to their names. If they'd been green, it meant the bounty was active. Red meant closed, bounty paid. I scoffed at the list. Either they'd been small time chumps or somebody was very, very good at their job.

"Barkeep! Another round of Djenlivet for everyone, on me," the pink haired alien called out in a high-pitched voice. She turned in my direction and hoisted an empty old-fashioned glass into the air. I got a better look and had the shock of my life.

Oops, nope, that's a little girl, I corrected. To be fair, she looked very out of place here. Most of the other clientele were dressed in their finery, and the worst dressed of the place—not counting her, at least—was myself. Besides her pink hair, her face was half-covered with a holographic tattoo which seemed to shift colors in the light. She had two short metal bars through one eyebrow and a ring piercing her lower lip.

I couldn't believe someone would let their child do that. Then I remembered she'd ordered the Djenlivet, and the bartender hadn't batted an eye. The little girl was probably old enough to be out on her own. However, her penchant for buying everyone in Leo's the most expensive whiskey in the sector made me wonder just whose rich kid I'd stumbled upon.

She's not a Lythano, I thought and accepted a proffered glass filled with amber-colored liquor from the passing server bot. The Lythano Cartel was *very* particular about who saw their daughters in public, and I'd never come across one without at least a platoon of heavily armed security guards present. Or one of their people with any sort of facial adornment.

I gave the glass a delicate sniff. The twin subtle aromas of apricot and chocolate made my eyes go wide. There was only one planet in the known universe where chocolate could be reliably made, and it cost a fortune to merely buy an ounce of it. I gave it a sip and my eyes rolled back.

Oh my… that's some damn fine whiskey.

Laz whined at me. His eyes were locked on the pink haired girl. I tried not to smile as I finished the drink. It burned pleasantly the entire way down. Faint notes of chocolate filled my senses, then apricots. It was the most exquisite thing I'd tasted in years, possibly ever.

"C'mon gang," I muttered as Laz bumped against my thigh, "let's go and thank our hostess for the drink."

I ambled over to where the pink-haired girl was seated, carefully avoiding the serving bots along the way. Laz stayed on my left, his gaze sweeping continuously across the room as we approached. His sisters stayed on my right, their shoulders pressing against one another's as they moved in sync. A few of the bar's patrons had finally noticed the pups and their gasps were clearly audible. These were gentle folk, not used to dealing with the vagrants of the universe. Or if they were, they'd never seen anything like the pups before. To be fair, not many people had.

The pink-haired girl noticed my approach as well. She tried to feign disinterest but I could see her eyes on Lazarus. Not that I could blame her. He was a hefty boy.

"Thanks for the drink," I said once I was close. She snorted and rolled her eyes dramatically.

"Just 'cause I bought a round for the house doesn't mean I'm looking for company, old man," she said as she gave me an old-fashioned once-over. "Besides, I'd probably break a dandy like you."

"*Excuse me?*" I sputtered with indignancy. Laz, the traitorous little beast, started wagging his tail. He seemed to be enjoying himself. "Me? Old? Listen here you little shit…"

"I've reached the end of my patience, old man," she stated and casually dropped her free hand to her hip. I let my eyes track her obvious intimidation attempt and spotted a laser pistol. It was brand new, just like her holster. Narrowing my eyes, I looked back at her face. The tattoo shifted color to a deep red color as she smiled. Transmorphic tattoos were even more expensive, though not as much as the whiskey she'd just casually given away. Clearly she wanted to send a message. What she meant and what she said, though, were two entirely different things altogether. "I'm celebrating my bounties, if you catch my drift."

I raised an eyebrow. "Your bounties?"

"That's right." Her smile grew bigger. "Fifteen bounties pays for a girl's more *refined* habits."

No way.

"You're a bounty hunter?"

"Yep."

"You."

"Uh, I said yes already."

"Really?"

"Yes!"

"Sure you are," I chuckled and shook my head. Her smile quickly disappeared.

"These bounties I collected suggest I'm right, old man," she growled in what was supposed to be an intimidating tone. It wasn't, but I had to give her marks for trying. "You dandy-looking, tassel-wearing pretty boy trying to say I'm not a bounty hunter? You doubting my words?"

"Don't talk about my tassels," I warned her. "You ain't earned the right."

"I'm Tara, and I can talk about whatever I want. This here piece on my side backs me up."

"Okay." I tried not to roll my eyes. The girl had one hell of an act going, but it was time to deflate her ego just a tad. "So, Miss 'bounty hunter.' Let me explain where you done gone and screwed up. That holster on your side is brand new, not worn or broken in yet. That means when you draw your shiny new pistol—which, by the way, isn't even at full capacity for charges—it'll get stuck on the lip of the holster until time and use wears it down. The Magrave Five tactical hip holster is made for larger pistols with big grips, see. Your tiny laser pistol is too deep in the holster. It's going to be difficult for you to pull it in a hurry, or even grab it cleanly by the grip."

I looked her over again and smirked. "You're leaning back in the chair, which means your backup piece is on your ankle and not the small of your back. Smart, but you put a table between yourself and your backup. Anyone with an ankle piece knows in potentially dangerous situations they sit with one leg crossed upon their lap for easier access. Your body armor is good, but obvious. Weak points up at the collarbones and the throat. It ain't rated for knives or lasers, just low caliber projectiles. You got ripped off there. Plus, your back is to the door, where anyone can sneak up on you. No, you're too new at this to have earned fifteen bounties in eight days, which tells me that not only are you a liar, but that you have no idea how far in over your head you truly are. Worst of all is that someone else is going to be wanting you dead in short order for stealing their bounties."

"Uh…"

"Before you die, though, I have a question. How'd you do it?"

She tried to speak but nothing came out. It was easy to see I'd struck a nerve. Her tattoo shifted from the bright, angry red to some shade of deep blue within the span of a half-dozen heartbeats. Coughing twice to clear her throat, the young "bounty hunter" finally found her voice.

"Who *are* you?"

"You!" a voice thundered from the entrance to the bar. "I warned you three times, you little bitch. *Three times!* I gave you every opportunity to stop your runnin' on my bounties. You didn't listen. Now? Now you're dead."

"Oh shit," the young girl breathed. I tried not to smile.

"Friends of yours?" I asked pleasantly.

"*Fuck.*"

"That's not going to help you in this situation, Miss Tara," I pointed out as I felt the presence of four men approach me from behind. None of the pups had moved, though Naomi's gaze was locked on their leader. Laz was keeping an eye on Tara. Poor Ruth was clearly caught between following her brother's lead and watching her sister's back.

"She with you?" the gruff voice asked.

"The pups are mine," I commented and side-stepped out of the way. "Don't mess with them, and we'll be all right. The girl? Just met. No dog in that fight."

"Smart man," the speaker grunted. "I was about—wait a second, I know that voice. Well I'll be. Quintus? Quintus Fox? What in the nine hells are you doing way out here?"

I glanced over my shoulder and sized up the man. He looked vaguely familiar, but I couldn't place him. Taller than me, massive shoulders and the build of someone who either had serious mod work done or a heavy lifter. He sported a wicked scar which ran across his forehead and curled down toward his left eye, which had been replaced by a cybernetically enhanced upgrade. The man wore his sandy-colored hair short, save for a narrow single braid which was tucked behind his left ear. I did a double-take as the scar triggered a memory.

"Barney Jones? Damn, boy. You grew up on me. How's your daddy?"

"Wait… you know him?" the girl asked incredulously.

"Barney? Oh, his daddy and I go way back," I smiled. "Used to be one of the best bounty hunters in the business until he retired. Not as good as me, mind you, but good enough."

"It's Barnabas now. I ain't been called Barney in years, sir," Barnabas said with a nod. "Let me deal with this problem and we can go grab a drink, catch up on old times. I heard you were down at Deep Eleven. Old Boss Herzog pays well, rumor has it. Ain't that place haunted?"

"It was," I said and eyed the girl curiously. It was obvious to me she was terrified. Of whom was up for debate. I do, after all, have a reputation. "How'd she get your bounty, Barney?"

"Barnabas, if you please, sir. She was able to steal my bounty because she's a Runner."

My eyes may have widened a fraction of an inch. Runners were a weird bunch of humans who existed in a nebulous state between the artificial and the real. They were formally known as Coderunners but people, as wont to do, shortened it to the simple "Runner" moniker. Normally, Runners were in the employ of criminal bosses who ran the underworld. Coderunners could splice into any I/O port on a station and hack it with their mind. Genetically modified from birth to become psychically linked with any and all computer operating systems, they were what we bounty hunters liked to call a walking gold mine. You see one out in public, like Tara, and you slap her in irons and find out who's missing a Runner, then get paid enough to retire when they come to collect. They were always escapees and never lost, though. *Nobody* loses a Runner. Not with what it costs to raise one.

"You don't say," I murmured. "Didn't see a tag."

"She doesn't have one, sir," Barnabas replied. "It's why I've been easy on her for a while now. Just a kid who got thrown out of the creche for not being good enough. Tried to warn her off. Many times."

I'd never heard of a teenager being thrown out of a Coderunner creche before. Usually, a child who doesn't show enough potential is identified early, usually before they turned six, and tossed out onto the streets. It shames me to admit I didn't usually pay them any mind. They weren't my problem, after all. I'm a bounty hunter. Raising children—especially children like failed Runners—were for other people. They had homes for them, I heard.

"So what are you going to do with her now?" I asked. There were many ways this could go, and only a few ended up with the girl living. Of those, none would lead to a pleasant existence. Barnabas' father, Cornelius, had been a crotchety old bastard who'd been a tenacious bounty hunter. However, he adhered to a code very similar to my own. It's why he and I got on so well. Cornie was, and forever will be, a right honorable prick. He would have either killed the girl and been done with it, or given her a chance to pay him back—with interest, of course.

His son, though? I didn't know just yet. Time would tell.

"I'm going to get my money," Barnabas stated firmly, "one way or the other."

"No you're not!" Tara said and yanked her laser pistol from its holster. Well, she tried, at least. As I'd warned her not five minutes before, the lip of the brand-new holster snagged her pistol, causing her to nearly drop the weapon. She recovered nicely, and it was almost smooth enough to make one think she'd done it on purpose, but I could see it had been a bumbling newbie mistake. Despite her claims, this girl was not a bounty hunter in any sense of the word.

All four men started reaching for their pistols as well. I had to do something before it became a bloodbath. Someone could get hurt—notably, me.

"Peace!" I shouted. "Hold up! The girl isn't going to hurt anyone!"

"She pulled her damned weapon!" Barnabas countered angrily. I could tell he was moments away from losing his cool. Looks like the receding hairline wasn't the only thing he inherited from his daddy. "She's lucky I have good trigger discipline!"

"No, you're lucky!" I reminded him. "Otherwise, you wouldn't get your money!"

"Back away!" Tara shouted. I could hear the fear in her tone and knew we were mere seconds away from a complete and utter disaster. Fortunately for us all, she wasn't pointing the laser pistol in any particular direction. I knew, though, the moment it came up and the barrel was pointing in the direction of either Barnabas or his men, she was probably going to die.

I would probably go as well. What a horrible way to meet my maker. I needed to put a pin in this delicate situation without it blowing up in my face.

"Let's just all calm down here," I tried, keeping my voice in a soothing tone. "Tara, holster your pistol. You three? I suggest you do the same. Let's talk this over like reasonable men."

"Who the hell you think you are? I'll plug you full of holes, old man," the bounty hunter on Barney's left growled. I could tell by the look in his eye he was spoiling for a fight. "You ain't nothing. You're wearing *tassels* on your boots. Stupid old man. What can you do besides go take a nap?"

"I invite you to test that assumption at your earliest convenience," I replied in a cool, calm voice. "Perchance when this ends, you'll come to regret such hasty words."

"The hell you say to me, old man?" the tough asked, taking a half-step forward. His hand dropped to his piece and his palm touched iron. His eyes dropped ever so slightly.

It was all I needed. He didn't even get his hand wrapped fully around the grip of his gun before my six shooter had cleared its holster and was pressed directly into his chest. I gave him the coldest smile I could.

"That means, you stupid young punk, that if you fuck around, you *will* find out. And don't talk about my tassels. These are my pa's boots. Comfy. I love 'em. All I have left of him."

"Hold up there, sir." Barnabas held his hands up placatingly. "He meant nothing bad about the tassels, or your boots. He's new. Meant no harm. I only want the girl. Don't shoot him. I have no beef with—"

The hunter who'd been on the verge of doing something stupid completed the journey and slapped my six shooter away. His buddy, who'd clearly been waiting for this opportunity, reached for his gun at the same moment. I took a step back, lashed out with my boot and connected solidly with the first man's shin. He yowled in pain and hopped back. I kicked him again in the gut and he doubled over, gasping. His buddy tried to keep him upright while grabbing for his gun.

"Aw hell," Barnabas said as the third hunter pulled his weapon as well. I flipped the table next to me over and slipped behind it just as Barney's trio began shooting wildly in our direction.

Tara screamed in fear and ducked behind a nearby table. Patrons still in the bar—those stupid enough to have hung around when Barnabas and company strode in looking for a fight—cried out in alarm and quickly vacated the premises as fast as they could. My pups, who had been sitting nearby and watching everything play out with no sign of interest, had belly crawled toward me and taken up positions behind two fallen chairs. Laz gave me a doggy grin, and his tail started to wag. A chunk of wood from the wall fell onto the floor near his head, and he immediately started chewing on it. It was clear the idiot was having a grand old time.

"We talked about this," I scolded them all as I pressed my back against the thick table. All three tails started to wag. Lazarus, bless his heart, had started crawling away from us. Either he was getting into a position to flank the bounty hunters, or he was abandoning us. The odds on which were pretty even, if I had to be honest with myself.

While it seemed my luck with the pups was going nowhere, I'd gotten lucky when I chose this one table to flip. It had a steel under-liner, which gave it extra support for drinks—and provided an anchor for magnetic drinking mugs in case of a sudden loss of gravity. Conveniently, it was thick enough with the falsewood on top to protect me from any shots. I wasn't as confident about Tara's table, however.

Ruth began crawling after her brother and my hopes sank just a bit. Lady Luck was not on my side, it seemed.

"Get down!" I shouted at Tara as a shot caromed wildly off the table and into the wall. Splinters of real wood showered her head as she quickly ducked back behind the makeshift barrier. Not at the possibility of her being injured by the wood, but the damage to the wall. Real hardwood was almost impossible to come by out here. The damage we were doing to these gorgeous walls might very well bankrupt the owner of Leo's Bar. Another large gouge was taken out of the wall. I winced sympathetically. "Damn! That sounded expensive."

"What do we do?" Tara cried out. I could see the poor girl was terrified. Not that I blamed her one bit. Being in the middle of a gunfight was the last place I wanted to be. A firefight in a fancy bar, where they were probably going to hit me with legal reparation requests afterwards for the damage? Assuming I survived, this was going to take a large chunk out of my savings.

"Not sure what this 'we' stuff is, miss," I called back. "You got yourself into this mess by drawing on a group of hardened bounty hunters. You're lucky, though."

"Lucky?" Her tone was incredulous. "How am I lucky?"

"Barney over there is aiming to wound, not kill. So yeah. Lucky. His lackeys, though…"

"I don't feel very lucky."

"Laz! Ruth! Gunman, door!" I called out, hoping like hell they understood what I was trying to say in the midst of the gunfire. Naomi was still by my side, protecting my left from any stray gunfire. Her fur apparently was just as effective against gunfire as it was against knives and lasers. With the exception of the loud reports from the gunfire, she seemed to be enjoying herself. Life simply wasn't fair sometimes. "Naomi, stay."

"Woof!" she agreed. I patted her head with my free hand before pulling out the semi-automatic pistol on my other hip. Wielding two guns in the middle of a firefight was risky and usually failed in combat. It was difficult at best to truly have what some of the greats called "two gun mojo." However, I had an ace up my sleeve. Barney wasn't the only one who was biometrically enhanced. Closing my eyes, I delved into the enhancements implanted into my brain. The activation sequence kicked in. My dopamine receptors were flooded with stimuli. Highly-evolved nanites, oxygen, and only a chemist knew what else was quickly dumped into my bloodstream. The nanites activated the synthetic blood cells I'd had injected into my body years before. My pupils dilated, and my sense of smell heightened dramatically. I could feel the individual hairs on my arm. Everything was clear now. I was more capable, better, stronger than anyone else in the room. Time slowed to a crawl, and, suddenly, I could almost see the individual rounds cutting through the air.

I hate the enhancements I had done in my impetuous youth. Sometimes, though, they sure were handy.

Meanwhile, the pups were moving. Apparently they either understood my intentions or were simply in a killing mood. Hard to say. Lazarus bounded over a table and grabbed one of Barney's henchmen by the arm. The pup wasn't quite heavy enough to bring the shooter down on his own, though. His teeth, however, were sharp enough to cut through the ballistic cloth of the long sleeve. The man cried out in pain as Laz began to try and rip the man's arm off at the elbow. The two crashed to the floor behind one of the overturned tables. Ruth, seeing Laz drop the man, rushed in from the side and began ripping into the downed gunman's face. There were a lot of wet, disturbing sounds from where the two pups were busy trying to kill one of Barnabas' henchmen.

"What now?" Tara asked fearfully. I shrugged my shoulders.

"No clue. It's up to young Barnabas over there."

"He wants me dead."

"He does seem pretty committed to that course of action, yes," I agreed with her. "Perhaps we might be able to change his mind."

"How?"

"Working on that," I muttered under my breath. Truth be told, I was running out of ideas. Gunfights weren't something I particularly enjoyed. No real bounty hunter wanted a gunfight. We want a quick, clean capture and an even faster payout. A hard bounty meant the risk of injury and death. Sure, the young ones in the business always said they were eager to shoot it out with a hard bounty. Until the actual bullets started to fly, at least. Then their tune quickly changes, or they die young and stupid.

Bullets flying... It wasn't much of an idea, but it was better than sitting there and waiting for a stray round to hit the girl. Or worse, me.

"Hey!" I hissed over at the girl. Tara blinked and looked at me. "Yeah, I'm talking to you. We were just conversing, remember? Get your head in the game. You're a Runner, right? How good are you?"

"Uh... good enough to rip them off?"

"But not good enough to do it and not get caught," I finished for her. She scowled but nodded, albeit reluctantly. "Can you get into this station's systems?"

"Why?" she asked. "Everything here is so old."

I tried not to roll my eyes in exasperation, but it was hard. "That's the point. Can you?"

"I guess," she said as her eyes unfocused. It was creepy as hell. One minute she seemed fully engaged, the next it was as though nothing existed in the universe except what was in her mind. Even her voice sounded changed. "I'm in. There are no defense points in this bar. The nearest defense point is five units—"

"Not interested in defense points," I cut her off. I'd heard Runners became *something* else during a hack, and she sounded as if she was ready to start listing everything about the station in a slow, monotone voice. It was quicker to direct the girl to what I needed. "Environmental controls?"

"I have access."

"Art-grav?" I asked. Artificial gravity was a mainstay on every modern ship and station in the known universe. You could find a few stations which relied on centrifugal force but those were exceedingly rare. Artificial gravity, or "art-grav" as most people called it, was the best way to go. My boots had magnetic locks on the heels, but they were old fashioned. Most people didn't bother anymore.

I was counting on this.

"I have access," she repeated. I shivered. The tone in her voice would probably give me nightmares for weeks.

"Kill all art-grav for this sector."

"Warning: artificial gravity in this sector is tied into life support. Do you wish to continue?"

Aw, damn it. Hopefully nobody innocent would get hurt.

"Yes."

"Confirmed. Artificial gravity and life support are now offline. Environmental controls have been disabled. Hard reboot in fifteen seconds."

Being in zero-g is weird. Your sense of up and down immediately disappears. The head feels fuzzy and, if someone doesn't have a strong stomach, their lunch is always threatening to come up. Unless one was prepared, like I was, it could get very uncomfortable in a hurry.

Everything around me started drifting upwards. Debris, tables, grown men… Without gravity, gunfire became erratic as the recoil pushed the shooters wildly around the room. I could hear the confused shouts from the bounty hunters as they struggled to regain control. It wasn't much of an opening, but it was all I had. My only hope was that somehow I wouldn't have Cornelius coming for my head after this was all over with.

"Naomi! Go!" I shouted. The wolf pup was already moving, using the objects floating around the room as launching points. She skillfully bounced off one wall and was flying at the throat of an unsuspecting bounty hunter before the man had even noticed the diamond-coated missile flying at him. She latched onto his throat and tore the poor bastard's throat open to the trachea. Blood flew everywhere in a horrific red spray. The bounty hunter never had a chance. Two down.

"*What the hell?*" Barnabas shouted as Naomi, using the dying man as a new launching point, rocketed back across the room toward us. He squeezed off a few rounds at the retreating pup but none of them penetrated her thick diamond coat. I grinned and activated the maglocks in my pa's boots. I *thunked* back down onto the floor and whipped out my six shooter. Taking careful aim, I squeezed off a round at Barnabas.

Shooting in zero-g is tricky. Rifles actually work better than pistols when gravity is not around due to the barrel's rifling. A semi-automatic pistol isn't bad, either. A six shooter, though? Hard as hell to use one without the benefit of gravity and rifling. Sure, there was some threading, but not much. It didn't matter, though. The enhancements I'd activated ensured my vision was better than normal, my hand was steady, my aim true. I pulled the trigger.

It broke cleanly. Revolvers are wonderful that way. The bullet flew in a somewhat flat trajectory toward the intended target. Zero-g made it a difficult shot, but not impossible. The shot was perfect. All I could do in my enhanced state of mind was wait and see how Barnabas would react.

The bullet hit Barnabas square in the chest, roughly four inches to the left of his breastbone—right where his heart was. However, instead of a spray of blood, Barnabas was tossed backwards due to the impact. I smiled and ducked back down behind the floating table. As I'd expected, he was wearing ballistic armor. However, the message had been sent. It was time for gravity to return.

"Tara! Gravity, now!"

The girl slowly nodded, her eyes still looking into a far away place where the universe was nothing but letters, numbers, and symbols. Gravity returned rather abruptly and everything in the bar crashed back down. Bottles, glasses, and fine dishware shattered upon impact. Men and women alike were rudely returned to the station's deck. Barnabas, the fortunate young man, landed comfortably on an overturned lounge chair and rolled onto his back. The only damage was to his ego. The same couldn't be said for the final survivor of his clique, though. The last remaining member of Barnabas' bounty hunter team landed awkwardly and his leg snapped. The subsequent screech of pain made my stomach turn.

The one Ruth and Lazarus had tag-teamed was ripped to pieces. Somewhere along the way, Laz had chewed through the man's ballistic chest armor and had gone to town on every single vital organ in the chest cavity. It was… disturbing wasn't the right word, but it would suffice.

Naomi's target was missing his head. I… wasn't sure how she'd done that. Last I had seen, she'd only torn the man's throat out. Pa always said one needed to maintain situational awareness while in battle, but you can't keep track of everything. What's a mysteriously severed head in the grand scheme of things?

"Walk away, Barney!" I shouted out. "You're down two men already, probably a third. I still got my pups, my guns, and this psychotic Runner. Odds looking pretty good for me right about now."

"*Psychotic?*" Tara screeched. I held a finger up to my lips.

"Hush up, now. You caused this. Reap the benefits."

"I ain't gonna walk. Hell, sir. If I wanted you dead, I would have started tossing grenades!" Barnabas shouted back at me. Frowning, I quickly reloaded the six shooter and checked the ammo status on the semi. Once satisfied with both, I risked another look at Tara. She was breathing heavily but the panicky fear which had frozen her before was gone now, replaced by a steely determination. I smirked a little. If the girl survived this, she might make something of herself in this universe yet.

"What sort of idiot brings grenades to a gunfight on a space station?" I called back as I reached down to my belt. Clipped to my belt and looking rather innocuous to the naked eye were two tiny popper grenades. They were more for small, confined spaces than an open layout like the bar.

"If you don't have a grenade or two on you, everything I remember about you from when I was a kid is wrong and you're just too old to be in this business any longer," Barnabas replied loudly. I snorted. He had a point. "Always bring some sort of surprise to every situation" could have been my motto long enough it could have been on our family crest. "I don't have any issues with you, sir. I just want the girl."

"I killed your men," I reminded him.

"Local hired guns. They knew the risks. Don't bother me none."

"Cold."

"But reasonable. Besides, they were stupid. I warned them to let me do the talking and to not make any rash moves."

"You should only want your money," I countered. "You're making this personal, Barnabas. Never make a bounty personal."

"She stole from me, damn it! Not once or twice, but fifteen times! Enough is enough!"

"I'll make her pay you back, with interest!" I said loudly. Killing Barnabas would be a bad idea. I *really* didn't want Cornelius coming after me. He was one of the few men in the galaxy not related to me who I trusted, and he knew my habits as well as I did. Besides, Barnabas was a good kid. Well, compared to most bounty hunters at least. He hadn't really been trying to kill me. Not really. Plus, he'd been polite the entire time. That had to count for something, right? "Hell, I'll pay you some of it now, and she can pay the rest with what she has left! Then she'll owe *me*."

This got his attention. "You don't say?"

"We can end this now, the easy way, where everyone walks away and—except for little miss Runner here—with money in their pockets. Well, everyone who is still alive, I mean."

"Hellfire," Barnabas grunted. It felt like forever before he responded to my proposal. "Fine. You got a deal, sir. I was almost out of ammo anyway."

I risked a peek and saw Barnabas with both hands in the air. The pistol was in one, but I could see the magazine had been removed. His accomplice wasn't going to be doing much, not with his leg bent in such an unnatural direction. The other two? The less said, the better.

"I'll pay you everything I got left," Tara added. "I'm sorry. I just—"

"Stow it," Barnabas cut her off. "I've heard your prattling whine of an apology already. A dozen times, if I remember right. I want confirmation now, in my account, of the money you still have that you stole. You have two minutes."

It took but a second. I had to hand it to her. The girl might not be a good-enough Runner for the crime lords, but she wasn't half-bad at it. A shame, really. At the rate she was going, it would only be a matter of time before she crossed the wrong person and ended up as a human icicle in space.

"Mister Fox?" Barnabas holstered his weapon and gave me a nod. He waved vaguely at the damaged bar. "Since you and my daddy go back a long ways, I'll cover the damages here, sir. But if that girl ever comes near me or mine again, I won't negotiate with her. I won't even give her the chance. It's going to be a bullet right between the eyes from two hundred yards. She'll never know it's coming"

Tara's face paled. Barnabas was dead serious. She stammered a bit before finally spitting out the words, "You'll never see me again."

"Good," the young bounty hunter nodded. He looked over at Laz, who was covered in the blood of the dead local bounty hunter. Ruth was licking her paw and wagging her tail. If not for the corpses it would have been a humorous sight to behold. Barnabas shook his head and sighed. "Sir, can I ask where in the hell I can get one of them?"

* * *

"You owe me a lot of money," I told her once Barnabas was satisfied and had walked off. His surviving local hired gun, it turned out, was not so local after all and had a bounty on him in another system. Tara, bless her little heart, had forwarded the bounty information to Barney and he'd immediately slapped the injured man in irons. The amount he'd earn from the lackey, plus what Tara had paid him, almost covered all the money she'd stolen. I covered the last twenty thousand, and we settled up nicely.

He's a good kid. Hopefully he'll learn to not let little girls rip him off so easily in the future. Judging by who his daddy is, though, I had my doubts.

"I can work it off," Tara said as we slowly walked toward the berthing tethers where the *Sly Fox* was docked. All three of the pups were having a grand old time at all the attention they were receiving.

It'd taken me awhile to clean the blood and random fluids from their hides. Turned out while their fur was impenetrable, it was a pain in the ass to clean when blood dried on it. It took two trips through the scrubbers before I finally managed to get all of the blood off Lazarus. Ruth was easier, since she was fastidious about keeping her own fur clean, while Naomi had somehow managed to behead a grown man without spilling a single drop of blood on her. If she could talk, I'd really like to know how she pulled that off.

"Doing what?" I asked Tara as we slowed our pace. "A Runner, on my ship? It'd be a waste of your abilities. I'll call it a wash and be done with it. It's only twenty thousand."

"*Only?!*"

"I don't get out of bed for bounties less than one hundred large, little girl."

"That's… I don't…"

"Besides which, I don't trust you. You're a thief."

"But a good one."

"Middling at best."

"How rude!"

"Am I wrong?"

"Then teach me to be good at what I do?" she pleaded with me. "Please? I need to get off this station. The owner of Leo's said if he ever saw me around again he'd beat me to death with a broken chair leg."

"I can't believe all the wood in there was real," I commented, remembering back to the man's purplish face as he'd screamed at Tara. I chuckled. "I thought he was about to have a stroke."

"What do you say, sir?" Tara stuck out her hand. I looked at it suspiciously before checking the other hand. Just because I couldn't see a blade didn't mean one wouldn't be plunged into my back at a later date. She's already proven just how ambitious and cutthroat she could be. Young bounty hunters had no sense of honor these days. For them, it was all about getting paid, and damn anyone who got in their way. "Teach me your ways. I'll do odd jobs for you to help pay you back. I'll earn my way. Promise."

Then again, she had risked a lot to pull my irons out of the fire. She'd put her money where her mouth is. Granted, my irons had been hot because of her own foolishness, but she tried to make things right. Remorse is almost as good as being honorable, in its own perverted and twisted way. Tara had already proven herself once. Laz whined at me. Glancing down, I saw him and his sisters staring up at me. All three of their tails were wagging, and they wore their stupid, grinning, happy faces.

I sighed.

"I'm not that old. I'm in my prime. But you on board my ship... gotta ask my crew," I told her gruffly. She gave me a strange look.

"Crew? I thought the famous Quintus Fox worked solo?"

"Oh, so you *have* heard of me," I snorted, amused. "I do have a crew. Laz? Ruth? Naomi? What say you, loyal crew? Do we bring on this tempestuous, irritating, pain in the ass little girl as part of the crew?"

"You're asking the *dogs?!*"

"These aren't just any dogs," I replied as all three of the pups' tails began to wag even harder. She'd seen them in action, working as a unit, and yet she still underestimated them. Just like I had, once. Tara would either learn, or she'd move on. "These are Jaxian Quantum Wolf pups. They're smarter than your average bounty hunter, as you should have figured out already. I trust their survival instincts. They seem to like you, Miss Tara, for some strange and mysterious reason, so I'm inclined to accept your proposal—on a probationary status."

"Thanks Mister Fox!" she practically gushed, clapping her hands together. Her smile could have lit up a room. I inwardly sighed and remembered being that young, once. "You won't regret it."

"I hope I don't." I already was, but there was no need to let her know. Then again, she was going to have to clean the old aft berthing space, not me. Karma always makes me smile, just a tad.

She paused, looking down at the deck. Laz bumped his nose against her shin and she scratched his ear just how he liked it. Ruth and Naomi stayed close to me, their eyes locked on their traitorous brother. I foresaw many non-verbal pup arguments in the near future about pettings and scratchings.

"Since I'm part of the team now, sir, can I ask a delicate question?"

Oh boy, here we go, I thought as I gave her a short nod. "Sure."

"What's up with the boot tassels, old man?"

* * * * *

Jason Cordova Bio

Author Jason Cordova is both a John W. Campbell Award and Dragon Award finalist. The author of over a dozen novels and thirty short stories, he has dabbled in everything from science fiction to urban fantasy. He is a Navy veteran and former middle school teacher. Jason currently lives at an undisclosed location in North Carolina but you can find him at www.jasoncordova.com.

# # # # #

On Cloud Nine by
Hinkley Correia

hat is it about sapient life that it manages to make everything unfun?

When Callahan was a little kid the idea of space travel had been the stuff of adventurers and heroes. Unfortunately, she struggled to maintain the same kind of idealism while being squished between a Daeldis, a fat alien with a large nose, and a Zidis, a cybernetic lifeform that might as well have been a small tank. The tank's name was Tirraks, and he was the more annoying of the two because every time they bumped into each other they clanked.

That was exactly why she had bought a little speeder, something only big enough for her and maybe one other human if they squeezed. Unfortunately for her, the man in charge of this hunt opted to be cheap and had made them all travel to his station together. He couldn't even be bothered to pay for a nice transport.

White dust filled the windows. The buzzing started against her feet, and she immediately braced. It grew into a tremor, before the entire ship wildly shook. And then, as quickly as it started, it ended. Callahan adjusted the straps holding her into her seat and tried to shove the Daeldis off her. He only snorted at her.

Yet another reason she preferred to work alone. She could deal with the limited space, but she was getting sick of all of the side glances from the rest of the group. Humans were still new to the Galactic Confederation, only making first contact about a hundred years ago, and very few made it this far out of their system. When compared to other species that could live up to a thousand years, or that could absorb a hundred rounds of solid ammunition without even blinking, or that could take one look at a computer and list all of the parts used in alphabetical order, humans were considered young, weak, and foolish. It was the young and weak part that made her being a bounty hunter surprising, it was the foolish part that made it not impossible.

Callahan could also tell that they were looking at her helmet, trying to see through it, but she didn't see why that was so weird. Plenty of species constantly wore armor, for plenty of reasons. Some cultural , some religious, and some, like her, who just had no interest in showing her face. *Excuse me for protecting my privacy.* She ignored the looks. It wasn't like she was one of their marks, anyway. Hopefully.

A holographic projection flickered to life right in the middle of the transport. The picture itself was grainy, and the colors were way too neon, meaning the holo was either second-hand or just a piece of junk to begin with. Callahan could still make out what was shown without much difficulty, so it was good enough. Besides, it was kind of difficult to not recognize the… unique face of Cormac Rackham, her current employer. She'd only ever met the guy once in person, and, in all honesty, she couldn't tell if he was a human or not. He looked the part, but his skin was too smooth, completely lacking in scars, wrinkles, or even pores. His eyes were just a bit too big, and his smile stretched too wide and firmly into Uncanny Valley. Not many things could set her fight or flight response off, but the eccentric businessman sent her reaching for her pulse rifle.

"Welcome, weary travelers! Thank you all for coming on such short notice! I take it you all had a pleasant trip?" The transport remained dead quiet in response. "Perfect!"

"Now, I'm sure you all know why I hired you, but let's have a little refresher, yes?" The hologram flickered again and the image was replaced by a space station, and Callahan could only hope that all the gaudy lights and colors were from the broken projector. "Years ago, I founded Cloud Nine as a pillar of luxury and comfort on the edge of the galaxy, and a monument to human ingenuity. It is an oasis for all great explorers before taking the plunge into the unknown."

Callahan rolled her eyes. *Human ingenuity, my ass.* It used Iktoid-designed anti-gravity, like most everything these days.

"Disaster struck us last year when we were hit by an asteroid, which collided with the left wing and forced us to close it down until we could complete repairs. Unfortunately, during that time, an... *uninvited guest* made its home in the abandoned wing." The picture changed yet again, to a model of a huge, bipedal monster with half-foot long blades for teeth and claws the size of Callahan's forearms. Razaks were the stuff of nightmares, told to children to make sure they didn't wander too far from their parents. Few had ever survived an encounter with one, and even fewer had managed to bag one. Those that had, though, were set up for life. The standing bounty the Galactic Confederation had on them was the only thing keeping them from spreading further into the system, and the only thing that made the casualty rate worth it.

Very few people had seen one in person, which did raise a very good question. Rex, a Yeeze that looked like one of those old-school werewolves, asked it. "How exactly did a Razak get onto a luxury resort?"

"What the patrons of Cloud Nine do is between me and them, and this particular matter has already been taken care of. Now, since the West Wing has been completely sealed off, we've been able to keep everything under wraps. However, we've taken a massive hit to revenue since we haven't been able to rent out nearly a quarter of the hotel. And now, because of the inconsistencies in that revenue, we've had law enforcement poking around. We'd rather not have that, which is where you come in. You have all been hired to take care of this little problem while keeping the situation quiet. If you can do that, you will receive a bonus straight from me, and you will be allowed to keep the rest of the bounty from the Confederation. Are there any questions?"

Nobody said anything in response, so Rackham merely smiled. "Alrighty, then. I'm excited to see your results."

The projection flicked off, leaving the bounty hunters to their own devices. One of the two lizard-like Iktoids, Raizen, stood up in the holo's place. "Alright, let's go over the plan one more time. We'll be arriving at the station right before the night cycle starts, but since Razak are completely nocturnal, we're going to wait until the day cycle starts so that we can get the drop on it. Our tracker is going to get the location of its nest, and then the rest of us are going to kill it. After that, we'll contact the Confederation, and they'll pick up the body, and then we can collect the bonus from Rackham."

All the other aliens side-eyed her again, but this time with less judgment and more appraisal. A squishy little human wasn't going to stand a chance against a fully grown Razak, but all she had to do was act as the tracker and let all the much bigger aliens take care of the fighting.

It was a decent plan. Unfortunately for the rest of them, Callahan had a different finale in mind. When the Confederation arrived and they turned the Razak over, it wouldn't be a real patrolman, it would be her good friend and partner in crime, Walker. His ship had Holographic Camouflage, which used light to change its appearance, from the paint job, to the model, and she knew for a fact that he had managed to modify it to make it nearly invisible. While the hunting group would be celebrating a job well done and awaiting payment, Walker would be taking it to an actual patrol, and transferring the reward to his and her accounts. By the time any of the bounty hunters figured it out, the two of them would long gone.

The ship changed directions, bringing Cloud Nine into sight.

Wow, it somehow looks even worse than in the video.

Lights flashed up the side in a rainbow of colors until it reached up to a bright neon sign proudly shining the name. A massive cloud of glittery debris gathered at the bottom, in a way that did look kind of neat until she realized that they would have to go straight through it in order to dock. Landing was already the worst part of flying, and somehow their cheap transport managed to make it worse. Laughter of all different kinds bubbled up from the aliens when they noticed her clutch her rifle closer and brace herself, only for it to quickly die out when they hit the cloud, and the transport started to violently shake. For a couple of seconds, she thought they were all going to die in the stupidest way possible, but they leveled out at the last possible moment and smoothly slid into the docking port.

The hatch hissed open as the pressure between the shuttle and the port hit equilibrium. Echoing footsteps filled the cold air, bringing attention to the fact that she couldn't see another ship in the large port. Callahan couldn't even make out the slight shimmer of her backup ship's Holo-Cam, which meant that Walker either wasn't there yet, or he parked somewhere else. Disappointment started to creep in, but she squashed it as quickly as it rose.

Oh well. I'll just have to see him afterward when we're rolling in cash.

Even the docking port was fancier than it needed to be. Marble tiles lined the floor, and the edge looked out over the cloud of dust. Only a thin energy shield separated them from the vacuum of space. The main lobby was through a huge marble archway, and, beyond that, was the rest of the hotel. A little robot waddled out of the archway to greet them. "Welcome to Cloud Nine, where every day you're on cloud nine! Your assigned rooms have been added to your ID chips, which will also serve as your key. Please follow me!"

The interior of the hotel was a little better, but not by much. She was expecting everything to be covered in gold-leaf, so the gaudy paint and the lights were a relief. Whoever had to work the front desk in the lobby had her genuine condolences. Construction equipment still littered the ground, leftover from when the crew had to evacuate, and the entire thing felt unfinished. The little robot led them past it and into a large dining room, complete with a huge, sparkly chandelier and a wall covered entirely in windows to show off the view.

"This is the West Wing's main dining room, where we serve breakfast, lunch, and dinner all day! We also provide full room service. Your rooms are just down the hall. Thank you for choosing Cloud Nine, and please enjoy your stay!" With that, the robot wandered off, leaving the group of bounty hunters to their own devices.

Ghux, the large Ukinit with spiked, armadillo-like armor and a gun that was half Callahan's height, began to laugh. "It seems that the hunt is on! Let us begin and let the feast be glorious!"

The cockroach man, Vrolti, clicked his mandibles at him. "Yes, and we're going to just run head first into a Razak's nest without any preparations. The feast will be glorious indeed, at least for the Razak."

Ghux started to pull in his shoulder armor and pace toward Vrolti, who extended his wings to look bigger, but Oxo, the green Iktoid with a long, scaly tail, stepped between them and stared down the overgrown armadillo. "My friend, I understand that you are excited to fight, but please understand that we are supposed to be working together. If you wait just one more evening, we will be much more effective."

"Yeah man, just chill out," Scaldheart, the Zidis, jumped in, only to jump right back out when Ghux rounded on him. Despite the fact that Scaldheart was a little bit bigger, he visibly drooped back.

"Pull it together! We made a plan, and we need to stick to it!" Raizen, the other, red, Iktoid, tried to take charge, to no avail. Ghux's armor was full up, and he wasn't going to back down, which wasn't helped by Vrolti poking at him with his insect leg.

Honestly, there was nothing she could do to de-escalate the situation, so she didn't bother. It wasn't like she knew him or had enough of Ghux's respect to talk him down, and he was two feet taller than her with two inch thick skin, so there was no way she'd be of any help if things got physical. After carefully weighing her options, she decided to just leave.

Unfortunately, Raizen's red tail wrapped around her wrist before she could slip out the door. "And where do you think you're going?"

What is he, my dad?

"Bed. We've got a long day tomorrow, and I'd rather be fully conscious for it."

He pinched the bridge of his nasal scale, which she hadn't known was a universal thing, and sighed. "Fine. Just be back first thing in the morning. We need to get started as soon as possible."

Callahan gave a mock salute and headed down the hallway the guide robot showed them earlier and continued on until she found her room. The lock was top of the line, designed to only open with the owner's ID. Otherwise, the three inches of Illathium steel was electromagnetically sealed shut.

Her room was drab in comparison to the rest of the resort, but it was still nicer than anything she had stayed in since she became a bounty hunter. While it was only a bedroom and a bathroom, there was still a lot of space. Other than that, it seemed like a fairly normal hotel room. Cream-colored walls, a desk with empty drawers, an overly fluffy bed, and little travel soaps. All the necessities. One of the walls had a television on it that she was going to ignore. The window had another screen in it in case someone got bored of looking at space on their vacation to space. She flipped through a couple views, settling on a pretty sunset of a private beach.

She finally took off her helmet and took a deep breath, only to get a lungful of stale, recycled air. Maybe her senses were too highly tuned from training all her life, or maybe it was who she was as a person, but she always preferred real fresh air over the sterilized stuff they used for space travel. It was one of the few things Scott saw in her, back when he first took her in.

A pang of anxiety hit when she thought about the old man. Scott Callahan was her mentor and father figure. Almost everybody in this business knew his name. After her family had been killed, he raised her and taught her everything about tracking. He was one of the few people she respected, and, without him, she would never have made it this far. At best, she'd be a criminal, and, at worst, she'd be long dead. He was a good man, and she wondered how pissed he would be that she was pulling this scheme on other bounty hunters. Considering how much of a hardass he was, she'd be lucky if he was only angry. At best he'd give her a lecture and make her run through her exercises until her hands bled, but even worse, he'd be disappointed.

In her defense, she needed the money. Out of habit, she flipped her ID out and went to the Confederation's official bounty board. She'd stayed on the same old bounty for years now. The image and all the details had long since been burned into her mind, but she still liked the visual reminder every once in a while.

Iria Winslett. Wanted, dead or alive for destruction of property, fraud, and manslaughter. Reward was five million credits, an astronomical sum for a fourteen-year-old with no place to run. The rest of the Winslett family had been hunted down and slaughtered, their name and reputation dragged through the mud. The Alaric group had seized most of their assets and treated it like a charity while refusing any aid to the teenager that had nothing to do with it.

If Callahan managed to pull this scheme off, she would have enough credits to pay off the old bounty, and by Confederation law, nobody would be allowed to hunt her anymore unless she committed any more crimes. Since no one had seen her or managed to track her down yet, it should be pretty easy for her.

Rage boiled in the pit of her stomach, felled only by the cold helplessness that surrounded it. An entire family was murdered for the sake of a few credits and some blueprints, and the Confederation couldn't even be bothered to look too hard into the incident. There genuinely wasn't anything she could do about it though. At least, if everything went according to plan, she could get on with her life and never have to take another bounty again. Maybe then she'd be able to take a break, get some rest. Tomorrow couldn't come soon enough.

* * *

After what felt like an eternity without sleep, a fake sun rose over a fake ocean, and the station's day cycle finally kicked on. Callahan got up, stretched as much as she could in her armor, and headed down to breakfast. Since it was right after sunrise, she had no idea if anyone would be down there or not, but she was pleasantly surprised to see that Raizen the red Iktoid, Tarraks the Zidis, and Vrolti the cockroach, were all there and eating already. For a human-based resort, the robot chefs were programmed with a wide variety of food from around the galaxy.

Raizen ate something vaguely insectoid that had too many legs for her liking, Tarraks was pouring soup into his mouth receptacle, and Vrolti was idly nibbling at what looked like a salad. Callahan had coffee and whatever scrambled eggs she could fit under her helmet.

It took about an hour for the rest of the group to file in and get situated. Ienied stumbled in with matted fur and loaded a plate full of breakfast meats. Oxo was the last one in, and, as far as she could tell from his slitted eyes, he was also tired. Guess he was also nervous about the whole thing.

Wait, no.

They were missing a certain overgrown armadillo. Ghux still hadn't shown his face yet, much to Raizen's poorly hidden annoyance, but as long as he got there eventually, then it didn't really matter. Unfortunately, that point stretched on for nearly an hour, before Raizen finally stood up.

"I'm going to go get him."

Vrolti made a chittering sound that was probably supposed to be laughter. "The Uknit? Why? Maybe he was so eager to hunt that he forgot that we are supposed to be a pack. Or maybe he thinks he can wrestle it and take it home!"

Raizen's pupils narrowed and his posture got a little bit straighter. "Then we should all go. Unless you'd like for him to get all of the reward?"

Ienied's tail perked up at that, and Callahan almost thought it was going to wag. Raizen scanned the group, and it felt like his gaze hung on to Callahan for just a moment longer than anyone else, but it was fine; she was just being paranoid, and she played it cool. Just as quickly, it ended, and he marched out the door and back up to the rooms. With a myriad of grumbling and complaining, the rest of the group followed.

The door was already halfway open when they got there. Callahan didn't get a glimpse of the interior of the room, however, because as soon as it was fully open, she was shoved to the back of the group. It was more than a little irritating, but she supposed that if she was also given a shot to just off the beast and go home, she'd take it, too. She was stuck against the door, so she got a clear look at the locking mechanism. It was glitching out.

Eventually, enough of the hunting party filtered out of the doorway enough that she could squeeze through. It wasn't much, but it was enough to see…

Yikes. No wonder Ghux never made it to breakfast.

Callahan felt herself go numb at the sight, years of training and experience taking over. She's seen more than her fair share of bodies over her lifetime, but rarely anything dismembered like this was. Fluorescent green spattered the wall and soaked into the carpet. She heard the rumors that Uknit blood glowed in the dark, and, now that she'd seen it in person, she kind of believed it. The rest of the suite didn't look much better, like someone went through and flung around everything that wasn't nailed down, but the walls looked fine. Outside of the door itself, and Ghux, obviously, nothing in the room actually seemed too damaged.

Oxo, looking even greener around the gills, was the first one to remember that she was there. "Callahan. You are a tracker, yes?"

"That's what they hired me for."

"Is there anything you can tell us about what killed him?"

She shrugged and took her cue to start working, starting with the body. Ghux had been popped open like a crab leg. His head was mostly intact, if you ignored the fact that the rest of the body was two feet away. Plates of his armor had been wrenched off and scattered. His torso was ripped into, and while she was no expert in Uknit biology, she was pretty sure he was missing some organs. Two of his limbs, an arm and a leg, were gone as well. Like the remains of an animal that got eaten by a predator, and then picked over by a flock of Kwakles. Whatever got to him was big, bigger than the average Razak, but she didn't know what else could leave marks like that. The good news was that since the remains were still there, there was probably only one.

Next up was the room. All the drawers were opened, and whatever had been inside had been taken and dumped all over the floor. *Huh.* There was blood on the insides of the drawers, in similar patterns to the splatters around the rest of the room, meaning they had to have already been open when the attack happened. She moved around the room, picking up other objects on the ground. Green covered the top of all of them, but there wasn't a drop underneath.

The murder had to have happened after the mess was made. Either there was a struggle that somehow none of them had heard, or the room had been searched and then Ghux murdered, but, either way, the place was ransacked before the death. But, if it really was a Razak, why would it search the room? They were supposed to be fairly intelligent, but she had never heard of them doing something like that. Maybe it was supposed to be a message. Marking their territory by showing what kind of destruction it could bring?

Callahan continued her sweep of the room, checking drawers and cabinets. Almost everything was empty, naturally, since they were only there for one night. Anything in them was courtesy of the resort and matched everyone else's. One thing she noticed, though, was that she couldn't find any kind of money or communicator. Now that she thought about it, she hadn't seen his ID chip anywhere, either. A Razak wouldn't have done that, but none of the other aliens on the station had the strength to rip Ghux apart like that. This had to have been two separate events. Someone came into the room while he wasn't there and robbed the place, taking his ID chip with them. Then, sometime after he came back to his room, the Razak ambushed and killed him.

She probably should have been more surprised, but she really wasn't. She wasn't in any position to judge. The line between bounty hunter and bandit got really thin in the outer reaches of the galaxy. It was why she always kept anything actually important directly on her. The real question was should she say anything? If she did, the entire group was going to be even more suspicious of each other, and the last thing Callahan needed right now was everybody paying extra attention to her right as she was about to rob them, so she leaned toward no.

Almost everyone here is armed to the teeth. If they can't protect themselves from someone going through their stuff, that's not my problem.

"Well?" Raizen's tail flicked back and forth, and he tapped his feet.

Especially if he's going to be condescending about it.

"If I had to guess, we're dealing with a fully grown Razak, probably on the bigger side. Just the one, because if it had a nest it would have taken all the remains with it. Everything's still fresh, so it can't have gotten far."

Oxo's pupils dilated, and his rifle made a slight hum as it charged. "We should hurry up and get a move on, then. We're all going to stick together and watch each other's backs, and we'll kill this thing in no time. Let's go."

Something big like a Razak couldn't have fit through the air vents, and the windows led straight into the vacuum of space, so it had to go back through the door. But where did it go exactly? Maybe the security cameras caught something. She didn't know anything about electronics, but she did know someone who did. It was time to phone a friend.

Callahan reached out with her mind and established a Connection. *"Hey, Walker?"*

"What's up?" Only a few seconds passed, and then Walker was standing right in front of her. His projection looked solid, so he must have arrived and gotten into position. No one beside her could see or hear him, but she still muted the microphone in her helmet for good measure. She usually forgot that she didn't have to talk out loud with a Connection Link.

"Is there any way you can get into the security cameras for me? We've got a pretty good starting place, and I want to make sure we're headed in the right direction."

"You mean that the great tracker Callahan needs me to hunt down a quarry for her? I'm honored."

"Oh, shut up. The longer it takes to find this thing, the longer you have to sit there. Unless, of course, you can't do it?"

"*You think so lowly of me. Hold on.*" Walker shimmered out of view for a few moments before reappearing. "*Aren't you in the west wing, right outside the dining hall?*"

"*Yeah?*" Where else were they supposed to have been?

"*I'm not getting anything. Looks like all the cameras have been off since the asteroid hit. I can try to turn them back on, but you're SOL for anything before that. Sorry.*"

"*Don't be. Just means that I'll have to do things traditionally. All I need you to do is pick him up after we take care of him.*"

"*Alright, if you say so. I'm going to keep trying to get the system up and running, and I'm going to keep listening in on our Connection, if you don't mind.*" He didn't wait for a response before disappearing.

Old fashioned way it was. Smooth industrial carpet lined the hall. No one had been on it yet, so it still looked brand new, no wear and tear at all. She dropped to the floor. It was slight, but she saw long, thin, scratches where it was torn up, like someone took a knife and dragged it. *Bingo.* Callahan started to follow the lines, and once everyone else noticed what she was doing, followed after. It was quick work. Now that she saw it, the trail was obvious, and it didn't seem to deviate. It never went into any of the rooms that lined the long, winding hallways, though some of the door handles had claw marks on them.

Guess the locks were too complex for it.

But if they were, it only furthered her suspicions of foul play. They traveled along in tense silence for a while before the path hit a junction.

Hm. The hallway split off in two different directions. Both paths had the torn carpet, meaning it had to have gone down both at some point in time. The real question was which one had it taken more recently. They still had plenty of time before the night cycle started and all the lights turned off, but that meant at least one more night at the mercy of a killer, and who knew where it would be tomorrow. But now that they knew what they were dealing with, it should've been fine.

She didn't care, so she let the group decide. "The trail breaks off in both directions. I don't know which one it went down last, but the nest is probably in one of them. Which one do you guys want to go down?"

Tarraks' mouth lit up. "We could always split up."

"I'm sorry, what?"

"We should split into two groups. We'll be able to cover more ground that way. If we run into the beast, we'll radio you, and we can take it down."

"That is the worst idea I think I've ever heard. Have you ever seen one of those things? You might be made of metal, but it'd tear through you like paper."

"Even if we do find it, it's still daytime. It should still be asleep. All of us have more than enough ordinance to take it down when it's out like that. Besides, everybody knows that Razak can barely see when it's light out; what's it going to do to us?"

Surprisingly enough, Rainen took her side, making it the first pleasant interaction she's had with the red lizard. "I agree with the tracker. The most efficient way to deal with this creature is to stick together and hit it with all of our firepower at once."

Oxo jumped in. "I don't know; if they really want to split up and form their own group, maybe we should let them? Tarraks does have a point. Razak are nocturnal, and Ghux died right before the sun came up, so it probably went back to its nest and went inactive. If either group finds the nest, they can contact the other, and we can all take it by surprise."

"Yeah, man. The sooner we can get out of here the better. This place gives me the heeby-jeebies." Scaldheart shivered, and all his fat jiggled. Ienid nodded and sniffed at the air.

Vrolti put his insect hand on Callahan's shoulder. "I don't care what the rest of you do, but I'm going with the human. In our culture, a good tracker is to be listened to, even if they are weak and scrawny."

Was that supposed to be a compliment? "Thanks?"

Raizen sighed. "Alright, fine. We can split up. But if you run into the Razak, do not engage. Wait for the rest of us. Who's going with Tarraks, and who's going with Callahan and I?"

After a few moments of deliberation, Scaldheart and Ienied both decided to go with Tarraks, while Raizen, Oxo, and Vrolti would be with her. She still thought it was a horrible idea, but there wasn't anything she could do about it, unless…

Callahan fished through her pockets before she found three little devices. "Take one of these. It's a tracking device. If something happens, we'll all be able to tell where everyone is and get to each other's location as soon as possible. Unless we find anything, we'll meet back at the dining hall before the night cycle starts."

"Sounds reasonable enough." The other group all took one before they headed down the hallway. All she could do now was pray that they found it before it found them.

Well, nothing left to do but keep following the trail.

Time slowed to a crawl as they made their way through the hotel hallways in complete silence. None of them tried to make conversation, and anytime anyone did, Raizen glared a hole into them. Oxo was the only one really making any noise, as he absentmindedly flipped a switch on his forearm back and forth, but he seemed oblivious to the nasty looks he got from the other Iktoid. Even their footsteps were silent; they were ready to hide at any moment. The hallways looked exactly the same, though, and the trail went forward without deviation. The trek quickly shifted from scary to boring. As dull as watching three little dots move across a screen was, it still beat looking at nothing.

Three dots, everyone was still fine. They had a little bit of time before the hallway was supposed to split off again, so she cleared her head and linked with Walker. The entire room faded away, leaving her in a sea of soft blue. A lone figure sat before her, watching a wall of screens taller than she was. Each showed new information or an error screen. Walker didn't notice her right away, so she spoke up first.

"You got all that, right?"

Walker jumped about three feet out of his chair. Sometimes she wondered how focused he had to be on his work to not notice her establish a Connection Link. The two-way psionic connection was easily the most secure way of communication, allowing things like sight, sound, and even touch to be transmitted at a distance, but it wasn't exactly subtle. It wasn't the first time it had happened, either.

"Jeez, Cal! You scared the shit out of me!" He clutched at his chest like an actress in one of those super-old black and white movies, but he

was grinning from ear to ear, so clearly his heart was in no real danger. *"Yeah, I got all that, and I got something else."*

With a click, one of the screens switched to one of the popular bounty boards, right on Iria Winslett's wanted poster.

"Walker, you realize that I've seen this before, right?"

"You're not the only one. Turns out that there have been at least three other inquiries about this particular bounty within the past week, all from different IDs."

"That's... weird." And also really bad. *"Can you tell who it was exactly?"*

"Second and third one have been hard to pin down, but I'm pretty sure they were both from planet Sonovis. Which narrows it down to only a couple billion people. But, I do think that given the timing, the two might have been communicating with each other."

"So you think they might be a team?"

"Would make sense to me." Walker turned back to the computer, fingers dancing across the keyboard. *"The really interesting one is the first one. Our old friend Mr. Cormac Rackham, from right here on Cloud Nine."*

"What? Why?" What would Rackham possibly have to gain from something like that? He had plenty of money, and Callahan knew exactly who set the bounty, so unless he had something to do with them, she couldn't see any reason why he would even be looking something like that up.

"I don't know, but I really don't like it. Don't know about you, but this all screams bad news to me."

Leave it to Walker to be the voice of caution. Unfortunately for both of them, the plan was already underway. *"I think we can still pull this off. Worst case scenario, you show up to grab the Razak early, while I bounce and collect the money once I'm out of the system."* It would be way more suspicious, but as long as she kept the attention off Walker, he should still be able to make a clean getaway, and they would only be going after her.

"If you say so."

"Now, if you'll excuse me, I've got an alien to catch."

"Cal, wait."

Uh oh. She knew that voice. When it got all soft and careful, it was more emotional than she could deal with. It meant he was about to say something heartfelt and sincere, and she was probably going to have to lie to him again. Just like that time a couple of missions ago, when he was a little tipsy, and he told her how much she meant to him, and she was only able to respond with complete obliviousness. Callahan wasn't stupid. She knew exactly what he meant, and what he was trying to convey, but she didn't know how to respond. It wasn't like she could never feel that way about him. If push came to shove, she could probably imagine a life together, but she never really thought about life in general before he brought it up. To be honest, she probably wouldn't have thought about it until well after the mission was over, and she was getting paid.

The smart thing to do was pretend she hadn't heard him and sign off, but instead she looked back over her shoulder at him, like an idiot. *"What is it?"*

"You know you don't have to do this, right?"

"We've already been over this. If we manage to pull this off, this is the last bounty we have to take."

Walker sighed and ran his hand through his hair. *"I know, but what's going to happen if we don't?"*

"Don't jinx it! As long as we stay calm and stick to the plan, everything is going to be fine!" Walker still didn't look convinced, so she moved closer and threw her arm around him. *"Besides, you and I? We're awesome! Whatever happens, whatever life throws at us, I know for a fact we can handle it."*

He only gave her a look, a way too familiar one that could only mean that he knew she was lying, and suddenly she felt awful. Lying was easier than breathing sometimes, but every time she tried it on Walker, her gut twisted. The truth was, she didn't know what she was going to do if this failed. She'd thought this through hundreds of times, but there were always ways it could go catastrophically wrong, but she wasn't lying when she said that the two of them could handle it.

Walker grabbed her shoulder and looked her dead in the eye. *"I know that money and pride are both important to you, but neither of them are worth anything if you're dead. Just be careful, okay?"*

She rolled her eyes. *"Fine, I'll be careful. Just for you."* The artificial world started fading around them. *"Trust me."*

The blue completely faded before she could hear whatever exasperated response he had for her. Walker meant well, but she could do without the negativity. Nothing had changed in the real world. Same looking hallway, same silence. Time to check in on the others.

Wait a second. There was only one light on the screen! She zoomed out as far as she could, but she still couldn't find the other two who had split off. Did the trackers get destroyed? She made all her devices sturdy, so whatever broke them had to have been really strong. Callahan flipped her radio on and tried to contact them, but she got nothing but static. "Scaldheart, Tarraks, Ienied. Can anyone hear me? I repeat, does anyone copy?"

Vrolti twisted his head completely around to look at her. "What are you doing?"

"I've lost two of the trackers. See if you can get a hold of any of them."

Everyone fiddled with their radios, but only got more interference. An eternity passed before a shaky, nasally voice finally filtered through. It was Scaldheart, and he was losing his mind "—oh please, Spirits, watch over my souls that I may pass into the Void—"

Oxo raised his wrist communicator closer to his face. "Scaldheart! Can you hear us? What happened?"

"I don't know! The power kept turning on and off, and one of the times it came back, Ienied was just gone! Then it happened again, and Tarraks was smashed to pieces! I can't do this! I want to go home!"

The three hadn't gotten far from where the path diverged. It wouldn't take them long to backtrack. "Stay on the line," Callahan ordered. "We're going to head your way and provide backup. Try to double back and meet with us, if you can."

Raizen stopped her before she got very far. "And who put you in charge? They knew what they were getting into when they decided to split up."

"Quite frankly, it sounds like we're out of our depth. Between the two of our groups, they had the better firepower. We have an approximate location, and we could really use the strength in numbers."

He huffed. "Typical human. Just a coward who needs to hide in a crowd."

"Well, you're free to go if you're so confident in your abilities."

That struck a nerve, and Raizen stomped toward her, though with his flat feet, it sounded more like slaps. "Listen here—"

Screaming filled the coms, echoing from several radios and off the walls, before it abruptly cut off, leaving the rest of the group in tense silence. Callahan checked the tracking device again.

No signal.

Oxo tried to reestablish contact. "What happened? Can you hear us? Scaldheart, come in!"

"I think he's dead." Two sets of slitted eyes flicked over to her, but it needed to be said. She wasn't happy about it. The fat Daedlis was pretty chill and would have made a good shield, but there was no way he could take on a Razak by himself.

Vrolti's antennae twitched. "Now what?"

"I hate to say it, but we should fall back for now. Try to get some reinforcements." Raizen snarled. "Stay close and keep an eye on all angles. We don't know where it'll strike from next."

They made it a little over a hundred feet before the lights started to flicker and then darkness completely enveloped them. Callahan couldn't see her hand in front of her face. The dark vision in her helmet glitched out, so she barely made out the outlines of anything around her while she punched it to get it working properly. She felt the brush of someone slipping past her, but she couldn't tell who was who. Lines flickered across her sight as the dark vision rebooted, just in time to see the Razak rip Vrolti's head straight from his body.

Instinct took over, and her pulse rifle was in her hands and firing before she took the size of the monster in. It was at least three feet taller than her, with claws to match. There were at least two rows of teeth, and those were only the ones she saw. Oxo and Raizen were also shooting. The noise of the gunfire was deafening.

It ignored the gunfire and strode toward them.

Guns aren't working. Time to go to Plan B. "Run!"

Callahan took off down the hallway. Only the sound of the slap-slap of their weird lizard feet against the floor told her the two Iktoids were following her. *Dammit.*

What are we supposed to do now? None of our weapons were enough to pierce it's skin. What we need is a bigger gun, but all of them are long gone with the other group, all of whom are dead. No more options, unless—

"Walker! Your ship has a laser cannon, right?"

"Huh? Yeah, but it could take a minute to charge."

"Great! I need you to meet us at the port and be ready to fire! It's coming right for us, and it's pissed!"

"Copy that."

"Who was that?" Oxo looked confused, and Callahan mentally cursed. She'd forgotten to turn off her external mic, so they heard the entire thing.

Raizen, however, sounded angry. "Probably her little sidekick. She's been planning on betraying us the entire time."

So he might have figured me out. "Okay, I understand you're mad, but we have other things to worry about right now! You can yell at me later!"

He growled, but otherwise stayed silent as they sprinted down to the port. The Razak stopped trying to be quiet, and she heard it rampaging down the hallway, knocking stuff over. A couple of times it sounded like it was right behind her, but she didn't dare look back to check. If it got her, it got her, and she was scared enough already. They passed the dining room, then the front lobby, then finally, *finally*, they made it through the massive granite archway and into the port.

Where was Walker? She didn't see him anywhere, but she didn't really get a chance to look before the Razak stalked into the port after them.

"Get down!" Callahan didn't think, just dropped to the floor and covered her head. A bright white light passed over her like a shooting star and hit the Razak directly. The energy discharge caused Walker's ship to shimmer into view. She used her rifle to push herself back up and took aim at the smoking mass that was previously a Razak. There would be time to be relieved later.

Unfortunately, the Razak twitched and started to rise. The panic in her chest rose even faster. If a laser cannon couldn't take it down, what was she supposed to do? She wasn't supposed to be fighting in the first place! Its skin was just too thick! At this rate, the only way they'd be able to get rid of it was if they somehow killed it from the inside. From the inside?

"Walker! On my signal, I need you to put a bunch of energy into your Holo-Cam. Let's flashbang this bastard!"

"What's the signal!?"

"Trust me, you'll know!" She held her rifle as tight as she could and sprinted toward the Razak. "Hey asshole! Look at me!"

The Razak whipped its head around, eyes trained on her, and only her. It took the bait, charging straight at her while she just braced for impact. It pounced on her like a truck. It knocked her to the floor, and time slowed to a crawl. For a long half second, they stared each other in the eyes. The Razak's mouth unhinged, impossibly wide, until it could swallow her whole. It exhaled, and the stench permeated her oxygen filters, foul enough to choke her.

I'm going to die.

A blinding light glowed from behind her. Walker put so much energy into the Holo-Cam that his ship turned into a spotlight. It was too much for the Razak's sensitive eyes, and it reeled back just enough for her to wedge the muzzle of her pulse rifle right into its soft palate. She fired. Then she fired again and again, until her gun's power core started to overheat and burned her hands.

Silence.

Then, "Is it—is it dead?"

Oxo sounded breathless, and the weight of the now limp Razak was starting to squeeze the air out of her lungs. It took all her strength to heave the body off of her. Maybe it was just the adrenaline, but it wasn't nearly as scary when it just flopped over. She pushed herself up on shaky legs and felt a grin crack on her lips. One of the biggest, deadliest monsters in the galaxy, and now it was a smoking, bullet riddled corpse. "Yup. Looks like it."

"Huh. Not bad for a human." Even after killing a massive monster, Raizen still wasn't impressed. "So what should we do with Miss Traitor now that the mission's over?"

Right. She forgot about that. "We could split the bounty three ways and forget this ever happened?"

Raizen jabbed his gun into her forehead. "No. Hands behind your head."

She complied. "Yeah, didn't think so."

"Cal!" Walker couldn't fire the cannon without hitting her.

Raizen's tail wrapped around her neck, and he dragged her into the lobby and out of sight. Then he shoved her to the ground. The blaster was pointed right between her eyes, close enough that she could see it charging.

Oxo looked panicked. "Whoa, whoa, whoa, there's no need for that! We won't gain anything by killing her."

"She tried to betray us. Who knows what she'd do if we let her go free?"

Oxo sighed and flipped the switch on his gauntlet again. The world turned weightless; everything, including Callahan and Raizen, drifted upwards, away from the deck. Raizen managed to grab the front desk with two digits, but lost his blaster in the process.

No, not *everything* floated free. Oxo remained stuck to the floor and calmly pulled out his blaster. With no hesitation, he shot Raizen right in the head.

Callahan hadn't expected that. "Uh, thanks dude."

He smiled, before slipping his tail between her helmet and her armor, then he stabbed her in the neck. Her vision started to blur and darken. "You're welcome."

She passed out.

* * *

Everything hurt.

It reminded her of stupid Scott Callahan and his stupid training regimen. She didn't even want to be a bounty hunter. It wasn't her fault that he wasn't paying enough attention to his wallet. Walking the backstreets of Torscapa with that amount of money was just asking for it to get pick pocketed.

Ugh.

She tried to wipe her eyes, only to find that she could barely move and was floating in anti-gravity.

The events of the day hit her like a brick.

Oxo murdered Raizen. He drugged her.

She took in her surroundings and was surprised she recognized them. They were back in the dining room. The air was stale and cold, which meant her helmet had disappeared at some point. She barely made out Walker's ship jinking back and forth in front of the wall of windows, but he couldn't fire without venting her into space. Oxo paced back and forth while messing with his wrist communicator, flicking the lights on and off. It must have been a remote control, the same one that turned the gravity off.

Of course. He was the one screwing with the gravity.

Iktoids had little hairs on the bottoms of their feet that let them stick to walls, so he still had mobility. Everything else, from plates to chairs to anything that hadn't been nailed down drifted around.

Even the massive chandelier was floating. Was it always that flimsy looking? Especially the wire, which looked like it might snap if enough force was applied to it. Like, say, if she managed to get the gravity back on. But how was she going to do that? Walker was still locked out of the station's systems, and, even if he wasn't, she couldn't contact him. Whatever Oxo had drugged her with blocked her ability to form the Connection, and he hadn't passed the window in the past few minutes so she couldn't give him any visual signal.

She eyed the gauntlet again. If she could get close enough, she could lift it. She hadn't pickpocketed in a long time, but she didn't have to be subtle. All she needed to do was get it away from him long enough that she could drop the chandelier on him or shoot him. But the only way she could get it was if he came to her. Oxo didn't strike her as nearly hot-headed as some of her other marks, so she had to play this super carefully.

"Hey shithead."

Eh, it definitely got his attention, so, good enough.

"I see the venom is starting to wear off. Don't worry, it only induces a temporary paralysis. It will pass, but by the time it does you'll be in stasis on your way to my employer. Normally I would leave the gravity on, but you've become quite infamous for dodging the authorities, Ms. Callahan. Or would you prefer Iria Winslett?"

"I'd prefer if you left me alone. Probably be less slippery, too, if you didn't stab your allies in the back, you coward."

He lightly chuckled. "I'm afraid you don't have much room to talk, Ms. Winslett. After all, we wouldn't be here without your partner, now would we? What was his name again? Burton Walker?"

"At least I never planned on anyone dying. You're just a murderer and a thief that got lucky. Aren't your people supposed to be leaders and strategists?"

His mouth curled into a snarl before he grabbed her by the front of her armor. *Bingo.* Oxo didn't realize the mistake until she smirked at him. In one fluid motion, she grabbed the gauntlet and kicked him solidly in the chest. The force was enough to send him stumbling back, and her gliding across the room and bumping into the window wall. Which button was the one that controlled the gravity? Screw it, she had nothing left to lose and no more time to think. Lights blinked on and off as she wiped her hand across the gauntlet and pressed all of them.

Everything happened at once. Callahan hit the ground at full force, knocking all the air out of her lungs. Before she could get any of her bearings back, there was a loud snap followed by a deafening crash. There was no time to think about that, however, because she needed to move before Oxo shot her in the back.

He never got a chance to. With the screech of mangled metal and twinkle of shattered crystal, he disappeared beneath the chandelier.

A second passed. Two. More. All her muscles were still sore and she could barely lift her own bodyweight, but she still rose back to her feet. Oxo wasn't dead—but his lower half was crushed. He strained against the weight of the chandelier that pinned his body to the floor. His fingers just barely brushed against his blaster. Stumbling over, Callahan plucked it out of his reach. Exhausted, she slid down with her back to the wall so she could look him in the eye.

"How'd you figure it out? Have you been looking for me or did you just get lucky?"

"Why would I tell a rat like you?"

"How long do you think it'll take for someone to find you? Right now, we're the only ones that know what happened here, and nobody's coming until we give the all clear. With how dangerous a Razak infestation is, who knows when that could be? What do you think will happen first? Will you starve to death? Or will your wounds get you? I'm going to be too busy spending all my money to find out. Of course, Mr. Rackham does want this cleared up as soon as possible, and, knowing him, he could probably have someone here within the hour. Either way, I'm going to be long gone. Tell me, is this really the hill you want to die on?"

Oxo grit his teeth. "Fine. The Alaric group contacted me. Offered a bonus to take you straight to them alive. More than the Confederation was willing to pay for you."

The Alaric group was a business conglomerate with its nose stuck in every nook and cranny in the galaxy. After the rest of her family was killed, they bought out most of the company and took all of their employees. Callahan had long since had her suspicions, but it didn't give her any ease to have it confirmed by a glorified assassin.

"Why do they want me brought back alive?"

"Hell if I know. Human infighting isn't my problem. Any more questions, *princess?*"

"Yeah, just one more. What was the deal with Ghux? You were the one who searched his room, right?"

"Ghux was a Confederate dog. Was doing it all for the honor of it, wasn't even going to collect the bounty on you, just turn you in, but he had connections to figure you out. He was helping me until he figured out that I had no intention of turning you over to the authorities, even after I offered to split what the Alaric group was willing to pay me. Unfortunately, he still had all the files, so I had to search his room for them. Didn't expect the Razak, though. Now hurry up and get someone over here."

"Sure thing."

Oxo smiled, until she leveled her blaster at his head and pulled the trigger.

Was it the most moral thing she's done? No, but she wasn't about to take any chances. The last thing she needed was Oxo spill-

ing that she was still alive or coming after her again. Besides, she had
people she needed to protect.

"Cal!"

Speak of the devil.

Walker ran toward her, clearly out of breath, with a pulse rifle
cradled in his arms. "Are you okay? What happened?"

"Yeah, just a little sore." She gestured to the dead Iktoid. "Oxo
knew who I was. He was going to turn me in, so I had to take care of
him. And... I think I know who killed my parents."

Walker froze at that, and his voice was hesitant. "So, what are we
going to do now?"

"Well, I don't know what you want to do, but I vote that we go
get paid and get some food. I'm starving."

He laughed, and she couldn't help but smile along. He pulled her
to her feet, and she sagged against him. "Fine, but you're paying."

"Fair enough."

* * * * *

Hinkley Correia Bio

Hinkley Correia has written two other short stories, appearing in the Target Rich Environment and Noir Fatale anthologies. She is a full-time student, and is currently working on her first full-length novel.

# # # # #

Vocational Rehab by Casey Moores

A Contractor Wars Story

A Veteran's Lament

Let me be blunt.

Recruiters lie.

Some might say that's harsh, but face it—they're salesmen. Their whole purpose is to convince you to risk life and limb for a pittance of a wage and some combat training. Once upon a time, they'd appeal to your sense of patriotism, pride, nationalism, or whatever, but that train sailed long ago. No one has pride in planetary defense forces and even less so in MegaCorps. Maybe if they weren't so corrupt, but I digress.

Said *combat training* is a wide open gray area. If you show the aptitude—i.e. you're big, strong, and weak-minded—combat training entails forging you into a hard-core killing machine, complete with cybernetic mods. Let's be honest, if that were the case, odds are some MegaCorp recruited you before you knew any better.

If you're average, as most of us are, it's the luck of the draw. You might wind up a CorpSec goon, cannon fodder (I'm not kidding, that's an actual specialty code), or maybe a deskie. Some lucky bastards, usually those who already have the skills, get something techie-oriented and score decent paying gigs when they get out.

If you're not a muscle freak or nerd, it's a crap shoot. In fact, it's worse. As I said, recruiters lie, and they're highly skilled in the bait and switch. Whether they're recruiting fodder for a Gov PDF or MegaCorp staffers, it doesn't matter. They have random algorithms paired with sadism that decides where new hires go that are diametrically opposed to your wishes. The belief is they judge your aptitude, but I'm convinced the whole system is designed to screw with you because someone, somewhere, thinks it's funny.

Case in point—I joined the Yorkshire Five Lions Guard to be a hardcore killer. As I didn't have the body type, I would've been okay with any shooter-type job. Instead, they made me a rigger—a pilot who's hardwired straight into a vehicle. A lot of you might dream about being pilots, but I didn't. I'm afraid of heights, and I get motion sick. *Got* motion sick, I should say. It took a lot of vomit to cure that, but they were pretty determined.

Basic flight school was miserable. I spent weeks trying a million different methods to control my nausea. I earned the nickname "Witch Doctor" for all my multi-faceted homeopathy. Somehow, I survived the initial screening—the basic, un-augmented flights that prove you have any kind of ability. Reason told me to flunk out so they'd put me somewhere else, but I was too stubborn to fail.

After I'd proven myself, they wired me up with the implants. It would've been nice if they'd at least knocked me out before slicing into my arms, legs, spine, neck, brain, but no. They hit me with a neural block, and I got to watch as they cut into meat, nerves, and bones to insert new parts. It was intrusive in the same manner that a hurricane is breezy. I still get nightmares.

I got a few weeks of simulators while my body healed up, which helped me learn checklists and procedures and the like without the constant illness.

Then... when the docs signed off that the implants had taken, and I was healthy enough to try it... they plugged me in for the first time.

I've never known a greater ecstasy. Alcohol can be fun, sex is pretty cool, and some drugs are kind of neat. None of that came anywhere close to the feeling of plugging in. The hum of the electronics in my ears... the close, intimate connection with every single wire... the warmth and the raw power of the engines... the freedom and exhilaration of soaring through the air, the wind pressing up against my wings and body... giving gravity the finger. Every aspect of it ran deep and satisfied my soul.

It's the high I've been chasing ever since.

From that moment on, every aspect of my job was bliss. When I flew a gunship, I was the God of Death. Those muscle-bound freaks and the WarBorgs, even with all their combat mods, they might as well have been china dolls once I'd pumped 30mm tungsten beads through their titanium skulls. When I flew medevac, I was a mighty Valkyrie swooping down to the battlefield to rescue the wounded and weary.

The time I spent disconnected—in between jobs, sleeping, eating, etc.—was torture. I was only alive when I was on the job.

This brings me to the last bit they don't tell you. No matter how well it actually works out for you, no matter how much you might eventually come to love whatever job they ask you to do... it's all going to end.

Abruptly. With a kick in the ass when they shove you out the door. Sometimes that's literal. The life you had, the things you were issued, the things you were provided—like shitty food that you grew to enjoy, crappy billeting that eventually felt like home, friends you'd die for, all of it—gone in an instant. As much as they used you for all you were worth, they also provided for you in their own sick, twisted way... and it became your life. You walk out the door, happy to be free, dreaming of the endless possibilities that await you... and all you find is an abyss of emptiness.

For a rigger like me, withdrawal was hell. In fact, I might've preferred hell. Without my mechanical body, I was nothing. My pitiful hands and scrawny human legs were bugger all next to the raw power I'd plugged into every day for years.

With my training and mods, you'd think I could've gotten a job. However, turns out it's all a big pay-to-play scam. The contras and PMC's require a buy-in. Without five digits to invest, you're shut out of the contractor market.

I might've started my own biz, been a taxi driver or transporter or something, but buying a ride and surviving until you develop a rep and clientele takes even more credit. I briefly scored a bus driving gig, but let's just say people are stupid.

Booze, women, drugs... none of it made me feel anywhere close to how I'd felt flying my ZP-28 Havoc. My mind, spirit, body, and wallet dwindled further into a death spiral, with no way out in sight.

* * *

Rock Bottom

So that's how things were when this story begins. I sat along sniffer's row at the Rock Bottom gentlemen's establishment. The virtual places never really did it for me, so I found one of the few flesh and blood spots. I had a choice—spend my last few credits on a drink, or tip Jazzy, the busty brunette who wriggled about in front of me. Maintaining a hazy buzz was just as important as maintaining the fantasy that gorgeous, sexy dancing women liked me, so it was a tough call.

If I'd stopped tipping, the bouncers would've made me move, so I chose Jazzy. She sidled to me with a convincing smile and jutted her hip out. I stared into those sparkly, amber eyes. As if in a dream, I eased my credit stick into her slot. A healthy tip transferred over and my funds were drained. I'd have to hold onto this moment. Milk it for all it was worth. (*The pun was intended, please forgive me*).

With a dramatic spin and bow, Jazzy stalked off the stage. I tried to slow my brain, to drink in every curve, the flex of every muscle, the jiggle of every jiggly bit, and the flow of every strand of hair. I wanted to preserve it all in my memory to stretch every ounce of value out of those last credits. I swear she gave me one last, personal wink... then, she was gone.

"Howzit, Doc?" a familiar voice said. Someone smacked me so hard on the back that glitter puffed out of my clothes.

I turned and found a muscle-bound blonde man. Beaufort Maseru had been an exchange pilot from New Rhodesia, another system in the Windsor Cluster. He brushed a hand across his mustache while gazing from me to the stage. His characteristic look of smug superiority flashed over his face.

"Beau, the hell you doing here?" I asked. "I figured you were happily back in Botswana Bay. Didn't I hear you separated?"

And can you spare a few credits?

"Oh, I'll be on the job, just now," he said. "Figured I'd grab a chot and have a jol before I got to it."

Between the New Rhodesian slang and the thick accent, I tried to process his words. I came up blank. I noticed a good number of augmentations that hadn't been there before. *Interesting.*

"Sorry, you still don't understand a word I say, do you?" he asked. "I'm gonna grab a girl and have some fun before I go to work."

"Sounds wonderful," I said. "What's the job?"

"Oh, nothing big," he said. "Rounding up miscreants for money."

He shifted, which revealed a large holster on his hip. The Tsionni Industries insignia was unmistakable. Judging by the size of the holster, I guessed it was meant to hold a Tavor-14, one of the finest gauss pistols on the market.

"You mean, like a bounty hunter?" I asked.

"That term's offensive. I'm more of a collector."

"And now, on the center stage, Bin Krarxk!" the DJ said.

A diminutive Asian woman launched herself onto the pole in the middle of the stage and swung around it with reckless abandon. I called her the Flying Squirrel due to her anger and... stage presence.

"What've you been up to, Doc?" Beau asked.

"Oh, this and that... you know how it is," I replied.

The Flying Squirrel flew at someone on the other side of the stage. In a flash, she'd knocked the man down and started jumping on his chest. He laughed and tossed credit chits toward the stage.

"Still looking?" Beau said with a hint of pity. "Any interest in the bounty hunter business?"

"Does the job come with a gunship?" I asked.

"Sadly, no," he said. "Not until you earn enough to buy your own. I only got one small, humble grav car, and she's mine."

"Then I appreciate it, but doesn't really sound my speed," I replied. "Let's keep in touch, though."

"Yeah, let's," he said. His head jerked up and he waved an arm. "Hey, Jazzy, let's have a dance, girl!"

At the call, I turned my head and found Jazzy re-entering the room. Beau was on her in an instant. She smiled, grabbed his elbow, and led him to some dark corner to do expensive things. Jealousy boiled up inside me as I watched them disappear into the shadows.

I took my last drink and stood to leave.

The Flying Squirrel must've taken offense to this because she leaped across the stage, grabbed my neck and spun me around. She pressed the back of my head against the stage and ground her—well, *herself*—against my face. The crowd went wild.

It could've been worse. I'd seen her whip people with their own belts and stick beer bottles into their backsides.

As easy as she was going on me, I was still freaking out. A tip was expected for this sort of service... a *big* tip. Her temper was not something to mess with. After an eternity of having mango and coconut-covered goosebumps smeared across my face—which I have to admit, was pretty nice—she grew bored and let me up. As one would expect, the Flying Squirrel's credit reader was on the inside of her thighs, so she remained squatting in front of me as I recovered. The patrons hooted and hollered.

Having no better ideas, I nervously slid in my credit stick. Sadly, I was broke as the tooth fairy in a meth house.

She shrieked in some strange language. A moment later, a heavy mechanical hand grabbed my collar and lifted me up. I snatched my credit stick back and relaxed. Knowing this would be my last time in the Rock Bottom, I snatched someone's drink and downed it. Jack, the head bouncer, cuffed the back of my head as I swallowed.

Jack threw the front door open and, like some sort of Kagoshima anime character, tossed me a dozen meters across the street. I curled into a ball and accepted my fate. The pain of slamming against the adamancrete stole my buzz.

I didn't even bother to get up as pedestrians and vehicles swerved to avoid me. I couldn't go back to my tiny, empty apartment as I was very late on rent. Without a credit to my name, I wasn't going to another bar or anything.

There was nowhere else for me to go, so I just sat there. I tried—and failed—not to dwell on how pathetic I'd become.

* * *

Faustian Bargain

Time had no meaning as I sat there on the street, not bothering to move.

A message pinged inside my brain. I had some serious filters to keep out the porn, male enhancement, extended vehicle warranty, and generic scam messages, so the sender must've had my specific identity code. The message was from the Selection Service for Skilled Separatees, which sounded enough like all the other worthless employment organizations that I figured it *might* be legitimate. I wanted ignore it, but didn't have the mental discipline to avoid opening it.

<<*To the Witch Doctor. Job opening for CVI-augmented driver with the JG Corporation. If interested, respond to this message within the next sixty seconds.*>>

There was a substantial credit offer attached.

It was probably my severe depression talking, but starting a new job was the last thing I wanted to do. A brief search told me only that the JG Corporation had something to do with shipping, construction, and waste management. Sounded horrible. Plus, use of my nickname and the time component were big red flags that it was illegal or a scam.

Even if it was legitimate, it didn't actually say what the job was and the list of things I didn't want to do was pretty long. However, there's that saying about beggars and choosers and whatever. I'd been begging for months and was in no position to choose much of anything.

A request for a Cybernetic Vehicle Interface augmented driver got my attention. It meant they wanted someone who could plug in. In the state I was in, I would've plugged into a skateboard just to feel *something*.

Beyond all that, the pay offer was life changing.

Before I could talk myself out of it, I replied that I was interested.

With a lot of grumbling, I stood, stretched, rubbed my temples, and wondered how long it would be before I got a response. After several minutes of standing around, I wondered if I'd imagined the whole thing and checked the message. Then, I started to assume it'd been some sort of scam to get information from me or something. Joke was on them—I had nothing worth stealing.

A whirring sound echoed down the street. I searched the wide open street as it got louder and resolved into high frequency chopping. A small, two person vertol, a TLA 11 Wyvern, swung out around a corner a block away and swooped straight toward me. Dirt, scum, and trash flew into the air. When the rotors were close enough that I feared they might chop me up all over the sidewalk, it rotated hard and settled perpendicular to me. A goggle-eyed woman stared at me from the pilot's seat. The goggles magnified her crystal blue eyes, and dirty blonde curls spilled out from an anachronistic leather cap. After a moment, she jerked a finger to indicate the single passenger seat.

I climbed aboard, and my heart leapt as I looked for a connection. Dejected when I found none, I put on a headset. Envy bit me when I saw *she* had a connection. I stared at the port the way an addict stares at pills.

"Hello?" I said.

"Got you," she answered. "You got me?"

"Five by five," I said.

"What in the bloody hell's that mean?" I'd missed it in her first words, but now I picked up a strong Yorkie accent.

What are they teaching kids these days?

"Good strength, good clarity… never mind. What's the job? Where we going?"

"Whaddya mean? I saw a pathetic little man standing around, figured no one'd miss him, so I picked you up. Figure I'll have my way with you and toss you into a pit when I'm done."

Right about then, I realized I'd assumed she was my ride with zero proof. Contrary to my mother's warnings, I'd hopped into a vehicle with a stranger. *Oops.*

"You're hilarious," I said dryly. "Seriously, what's the job? Do I get to fly one of these?"

"You don't care what the job is, do you? Just want to stick your plug into whatever they'll give you, don't you? Anyway, I'm just your taxi driver. We'll be there in a bit."

That, at least, gave me confidence she was my pickup. We cleared the nasty slums of Wembley and headed north.

"Okay. Can I get your name?"

"Kristina Littlewood. Nice to meet you. I hope you survive the day."

What?

Before I could respond, I noticed her lips moving. Deducing she was on some other channel, to which I was not privy, I let her be.

I bit my tongue and focused on our route. I got my hopes up when she wandered close to the opulent high rises of Ratcliffe—where the Uber-wealthy of Yorkshire Prime lived. Sadly, we continued on toward one of the industrial areas.

Ten minutes later, she set down in an open parking lot in the Longsight District of New Manchester. I looked for a sign of what I might be flying but found none. Undeterred, I resolved to fly whatever they offered, like an alcoholic who'd eat deodorant just to taste the ethanol. Not that I've done that, of course.

As the vertol settled, my pilot turned and stared at me again. When I made eye contact, she waved her hand outward. Taking the cue, I removed the headset and stepped out. The small vertol lifted away before I'd set my other foot down, so I stumbled forward and narrowly avoided falling. I took one last glance before she left. She craned forward and scanned the skies as if expecting Zeus to toss a lightning bolt. Flying just a few feet off the ground, she threaded her way down a narrow alleyway.

"The Witch Doctor, I presume?"

I spun to find the caricature of a snooty, Windsorian butler walking toward me. He gestured me through a door into the warehouse, and I stuck out a hand in greeting.

"One Witch Doctor, pilot extraordinaire, at your service."

"Rupert Pemberton, at *your* service, sir," he said. "If you'll excuse me, we're in a bit of tight spot. I'll need you to come this way if you would, please."

As I stepped through the door, my attention went to a Julia Ostland JO167 Hyacinth Macaw parked off to my right. I knew the model as the crème de la crème of luxurious vertols. Only the heads of corporations flew in birds like that. It looked beautifully maintained, fueled up, and ready to go. I literally started drooling at the thought of plugging myself into that gorgeous, perfect piece of machinery. The music we would make together would be the envy of the gods. Two men sat inside doing pre-flight checks to prepare it for me.

"Are you familiar with this model?"

Suddenly self-conscious, I wiped the spittle off my chin and glanced to see if he'd noticed. He wasn't looking at me.

Nor was he looking at the orgasmic Julia Ostland JO167 Hyacinth Macaw.

He was facing a grav limousine parked well off to the left. Not a stretched job, just a simple, four-door Wolfgang Cricklewood Nightstalker town car. Not the highest end in luxury grav cars, but still decent. Shiny and pretty, sure, but I wasn't the grav car kind of guy. They're super fast and hella expensive, but I disliked them on principle because in the Guard they were used as staff cars for snooty high-ranking officers.

Rupert "Stickuptheass" Pemberton cleared his throat and glared.

"Um, yeah, sure, I can drive it," I said. My hopes and dreams shrank three sizes as the words came out.

"Excellent," he said. "The destination has been loaded. The route is up to you. If necessary, you'll find weaponry in the center compartment. It's the same model for which you earned a marksmanship badge."

I nodded.

Weaponry? What kind of job is this?

"We will charge you for any ammunition expended, but there will also be a substantial bonus in the event such becomes necessary. Please." He motioned toward the vehicle.

I strolled around the perimeter to give it a once over. While I perused the exterior, Rupert opened the driver's side door and cleared his throat.

"If you would, sir, time is of the essence."

With a shrug, I continued around and hopped into the seat. Just off to my right side was the connection port. I tried not to stare, but every fiber of my being begged to plug in immediately. As I got my bearings, Rupert cleared his throat again.

"Can I ask what the hurry is?" I asked.

"We're about to be raided by a combined effort by the New Manchester Police and the Yorkshire Five Lions Guard. Sources estimate two minutes before their first surveillance asset arrives overhead."

My sphincter tightened so much I feared I might suck up my seat cushion. Just a few months prior, I'd been flying for the Five Lions Guard.

The warehouse door rolled up in front of me.

"Off you go then," Rupert said. "I'd suggest a low profile until you're well clear of the area."

My military-honed instincts kicked in, and I forced myself to calm.

"One quick question," I said while I flipped switches and fired the car up.

"Do make it quick," he replied.

"I'm just moving a car? That's it? It stolen or something?"

Rupert rolled his eyes and guffawed.

"Of course not," he said. With a glance to my rear, he said, "You're moving her, of course."

* * *

The Client

Glancing into the back, I discovered a skinny, young, red-headed woman. I guessed her the child of whoever owned this soon-to-be-raided warehouse.

Great, I'm a chauffeur for some entitled little princess.

She was buried in her tablet—probably messaging everyone she'd ever met about her idiotic new driver who was covered in glitter and smelled like a mix of body odor, coconut, mango, and alcohol.

"Please show her all due respect," Rupert repeated. "Now you have less than one minute."

I got the impression he meant *all due respect* literally and not as a punch line, as we veterans used it. He slammed the door.

Feeling the pinch, I tapped a few more commands and verified the system was ready to receive me.

Ready to receive me!

It was the first time a system had been ready to receive me since my one brief foray into the world of bus driving.

The thought of plugging into this vehicle, snooty luxury grav car though it might be, flooded me with excitement. I won't go into all the ways in which I got excited—I'll leave that to your imagination. Suffice to say, I was in heaven as I pulled the connection wire out and slid it into the socket on the side of my neck.

It. Was. Ecstasy.

It was everything I'd hoped it would be and more. It was the high I'd only dreamed of for months. My nervous system merged with the exquisite Wolfgang Cricklewood circuitry. I don't know how it actually works, but I imagine my blood intermeshing itself with the electrons. I revved my engine up and discovered my heart was turbocharged.

In a flood of euphoria, I became the Nightstalker, one of the finest machines ever crafted by sentient beings.

With a soft pulse of energy, I got a feel for my grav sled and eased off the ground.

"Go!" Rupert shouted.

"Um, can we get going already?" the snarky brat asked.

Smooth as an ice skater floating on a single blade, I slid out of the warehouse. The sun felt good on my shiny, chrome body. I looked through a multitude of eyes and absorbed my surroundings. My new chassis had an impressive sensor suite.

Based on Rupert's excitement level, I gunned it and steered into an alleyway. Juicing the throttle might've bent the warehouse doorframe a touch, and my grav drive definitely warped the walls of the alley as I shot down it. Normally, a grav car shouldn't be used in such tight spaces at anything but minimum power levels, to avoid damaging property with the gravity field, but time was of the essence. It seemed prudent to get away, yet stay low.

Looking through my rear cameras, I watched the roof of the warehouse blow open. That gorgeous vertol lifted up moments later, barely clearing the warehouse's walls before ducking down over the low income housing.

A Yorkshire Five Lions Guard vertol swooped overhead and chased after the JO167. From my experience, I knew the Five Lions' air assets were prioritizing higher value targets. It didn't mean they hadn't seen me, just that they'd judged me a smaller fish. That meant they'd dropped their coverage, which gave me a window to disappear. I eased off the acceleration and coasted forward.

If the Five Lions had just arrived on station, it meant the NMPD was still moving in on major roadways to surround the area. My sled's grav field left a trail of noticeable damage in the narrow alley. I'd stick out until I reached a roadway.

My new database had detailed high-resolution 3D imagery of the entire planet that updated twice a day from satellite imagery. Since I was wired straight into the database, I could manipulate it in my mind without losing focus on my driving.

I slowed as I approached the first actual street. Cameras on my front corner bumpers told me the road was clear enough for me to rush across it, so I did. I continued along the alley until the next open street. Smooth as butter, I turned left onto the street, in the same direction any inbound police vehicles would be going. Cutting straight to the other side, I came to a rapid halt as if parking.

In any normal vehicle, the swing and deceleration would've tossed my passenger and likely gotten me fired. However, my elegant Nightstalker had remarkable inertial dampening.

For the first time, I considered whether I should've had second thoughts about a job that would put me at odds with the authorities. However, I'd already plugged into the machine. The idea of disconnecting... I'd rather have died.

Switching into reverse, I glided backwards down the street. I casually moved two blocks that way before I received warning about several units of the NMPD heading toward me. I eased myself into a parking spot and settled down.

"What the hell are you doing?" Snarky asked. "This isn't where we're supposed to go."

"Good to see you're paying attention," I replied. After a moment, I added, "Ma'am."

"Look, you're getting paid to—"

"I'm just... waiting for something."

"And that is..."

I drew in a deep breath to suppress the urge to spin around and smack the sneer off her face.

"Excuse me, I asked you a question!"

I threw a hand up, which only upset her even more.

Motion drew my attention to my rear cameras. The whine of klaxons announced the approach of three NMPD squad cars. Adrenaline surged and I had to consciously stop my engine from revving in concert.

They flew past, lights flashing, without giving me the slightest bit of attention. The klaxons grew, peaked, and receded as they raced away from us. As soon as they'd gone by, I lifted up, cranked myself around, and headed up the street in the opposite direction. My heart was pounding, but I kept my acceleration slow and controlled.

"Huh, I guess you're not completely worthless," Snarky said. "I suppose I won't have you killed just yet."

A chill ran down the back of my neck. She sounded more matter of fact than sarcastic.

In my rear cameras, I saw a squad car stop to inspect the busted-up alleyway I'd used to enter the street. Thinking fast, I turned at the next intersection. If the cops recognized the damage had come from a grav car, hopefully I'd disappeared before they started looking for one.

"Okay, genius, but what are you going to do about the flyers?" the brat asked.

Instead of responding, I hooked a hard right onto the ramp to the M17. Almost immediately, we descended into the underpass to Mancunia. It was the only underpass in the entire city which was large enough to allow grav cars. Shadows flashed over the road behind us just as we escaped into the wide-mouthed tunnel.

"Slick," she said.

In my time with the Five Lions, I'd been a part of countless exercises and actual operations. They weren't too imaginative in their practices. Plenty of times, while bored and waiting for a chance to do anything worthwhile, I'd mused about how easy it would've been to elude them.

"How else may I be of service, madame?" I asked. A stream of snide follow-ups flooded my mind, but I elected not to use any of them.

"Well, you could stop dicking around and actually take me *toward* where you're supposed to," she replied.

"As madame wishes," I said.

We cleared the underpass, and I maneuvered over a couple lanes. Shortly thereafter, I took an exit into the sled lanes, the designated air corridors where a grav car could hit the really high speeds. The cleaner air above the city tasted sweet. I'd forgotten how sweet it tasted.

Through my passenger camera, I watched my client open a drawer, retrieve a glass, and place it against my beverage dispenser. As the dispenser was part of the car and the car was a part of the me, I knew that a martini poured into her glass.

"Are you old enough to drink?" I asked.

She chuckled, shook her head, and took a sip. Her attention returned to her tablet.

A call rang in my ear. I hesitated for three rings. Then, I answered.

"*Howzit, Doc? Hear you found yourself a job, eh?*"

It was Beau. Half a click back, I found a re-furbed Musk Alacorn, bucking left and right to pass the traffic behind me.

How the hell did he find me?

"*Look, bra, I know you needed this, and I'll guess you're getting good boodle for it. But look, bra, the bint's worth far more than they're paying, even if we split it between us. Turn her over to me, and we'll both be rich men.*"

Through my passenger camera, I glanced back at the girl. Sure, she was a snotty little teenager, but whatever the hell her mom or dad—or both—had done shouldn't be cause to make her a target for bounty hunters. Even with her rampant bitchiness, I just couldn't get past the idea she didn't deserve this.

What can I say? Despite the shit hand the world dealt me, morality is still my fatal flaw. Besides, there was no way in hell I was unplugging from that fine automobile.

"Give me a moment, Beau, I'm thinking it over."

The possibilities of how he'd tracked me ran through my head. My connection was untraceable—planetary defense tech that I'd spent decent coin to re-enable after I'd separated. Odds were, that wasn't it.

"Don't think too long, bra. I'm right on you. Make up your mind quick, and I'll give you seventy-thirty. Make me wait, I'll smack you so hard your teeth'll vibrate for months and the deal becomes hundred-zero. Tick tock."

The most obvious way to track me came front and center. It wasn't me, it was the bounty. She was still heads down in that damn tablet. I wanted to reach back and throw it out the window.

Now, how do I put this?

"Um, Miss? Is there any chance they're tracking you by that tablet? It's something, and I think that's the most likely."

"It's not my tablet. Now leave me alone and do your job."

Well, that went well.

With no other ideas, all I could do was run. "Sure thing, Beau. Tell you what, I'll head over to McCarthy Park and hand her over. You buy me an ice cream while you're waiting, and I'll be right there. Salted caramel, if you would."

As he closed in behind me, I settled my nerves, evaluated my location, and developed a plan.

"Ma'am, you might want to either finish that drink or dump it. Apologies, but it's gonna get bumpy for a bit."

She took a casual sip, placed her hand over the top of her glass as if that would save it, and raised a disappointed eyebrow—the kind of look I used to get from my mum when I'd done something stupid. The corner of her lip gave the slightest hint of a smile. Deep down, she was digging this.

"You're making a big mistake, Doc. This could've changed your life. Now, it'll be the last nail in your coffin."

I ended the call, cut out of the airway, and dove toward an on ramp to the nearest M road.

On the way down, I checked on my passenger. I have to give it to Snarky—she didn't spill a drop.

* * *

The Chase

I f you've never been in a high speed grav car chase before, don't. It's a horrible idea that causes tons of destruction and is best left to the professionals.

As I cleared the grav airways, a slug bit my rear bumper. A glance in my rear camera told me the New Rhodesian was racing toward me, arm out the window and blasting his Tavor-14 indiscriminately. Must've had some real expensive mods to shoot me through grav fields at those speeds.

A rigger feels every one of those bullets. It's toned down, more like a needle jab, so we're not overwhelmed in a gunfight. Still, it'll add up over time.

I dove toward an M road, hoping he wouldn't shoot into ground traffic. The rate of fire slowed but didn't stop. I took a few more rounds before I broke off into the high rises to put some buildings between us. On my first turn, I cut a little too close to one of those high level gyms. I caught sight of a gorgeous, athletic woman in tight spandex, with black hair tied back in a bun—just before my gravity field shattered the aliglass and sent her diving for cover.

Crossing to the next building, I edged away enough from an office floor to simply crack the exterior. The glass shattered anyway when Beau's gauss pistol clipped some poor staffer. I ducked and turned into another street that was even narrower.

A NMPD vertol hovered in my way. Judging by the pilot's look of surprise, he hadn't been waiting for me. I dropped underneath him and then popped back up to make it harder on Beau. The vertol pilot wobbled and headed upward. Beau tried to go over him and nearly crashed into it. The lift fans on the vertol warped and it dove. Beau, however, stayed tight on my tail.

Trying to shake the bastard, I made a hard left and a right turn which took me down the middle of King Street. It's a wide-open street with lots of good shopping. I gunned my engine and accelerated the way only a grav car can. Checking the back seat, Snarky had a full-on look of amusement. With one big gulp, she finished her drink and set the empty glass down.

Watching her, I almost hit the big arching King Street banner. Thinking fast, I ducked under it. That would've been bad—that sign is iconic. Even so, I'm pretty sure I bent it a little. A moment later, Beau put a round clean through the "N", which is why people now joke about it being Kirg Street.

Just past that, I hopped over the "Purdy's" sign that ran down the side of the legendary toy store. I missed it, but Beau ran smack through it. Sparks and glass showered down while wide-eyed kids and parents stared at the spectacle.

There wasn't anywhere to hide on the wide street and speed wasn't doing the job, so I juked right through a gap into a parking garage. My grav fields mangled a whole slew of cars as I raced through the narrow confines until I burst out the other side. For the record, there's no evidence that *all* the damage was mine since Beau followed me through it.

I emerged into the Crowne Plaza and slid hard around the massive advertisement obelisk that stands in the center. Some ad was blasting an awesome guitar riff as I flew through. As I swung around, I warped the middle of one of the screens, widening the midsection of a giant Lora Darsen lingerie model. Beau led me and went inside my turn, getting close enough to pop a couple more rounds into my tail.

From there, I was stuck on High Street longer than I would've wanted to be, but it led me to my goal—the Magic Roundabout of Churchillton. It's named for the fact that it's the only roundabout in the city where sled lanes and ground streets merge. This creates a nerve-wracking flow issue as cars and grav cars swerve all over the place in a dizzying chaotic mess. Like all roundabouts, you have to slow and yield to any traffic on the circle itself. For a grav car, this means you have to slow to a hover to enter to avoid cutting off the other vehicles.

I didn't slow in the slightest until I'd already cut into the roundabout itself. My intent was to cut to the inside of the circle, where I could slow and hug such a tight turn that he wouldn't be able to shoot at me, especially with all the other vehicles around. I cut off some poor bloke in a small, two-seat Aphid Roadster, and my deceleration was such that my grav field almost threw him into the adjacent car. He shook a fist and shouted something.

With some brilliant flying and a smidge of luck, I buried myself in the middle of the Magic Roundabout. Beau slowed and entered further back.

To my left, I saw the corner of Big Pen, the largest penitentiary in all of New Manchester. It's a tall, dreary block of a building that stands thirty stories tall.

On the opposite side of the roundabout, I swung past Parliament, a legendary four-story bar frequented by celebrities and the wealthiest entrepreneurs. I wondered if some billion-credit deal or perhaps rights to the next blockbuster movie were being negotiated inside.

Focus.

Once I was buried deep inside the roundabout, I meant to make a few quick loops and hop out when I judged Beau was blocked by other vehicles. However, as soon as I tried to cut back out, a bloody grav lorry cut me off. Fearing Beau had seen me, I pulled two more loops before trying again.

"Excuse me, are we staying here all night?" Snarky asked. "If so, I have a dinner booking I need to cancel."

"No, Miss, just giving you a tour. That's Big Pen over there. And there's Parliament, which, if you didn't know, is the name for a group of owls."

"Ah," she said. "Big Pen. Parliament. Brilliant. Well, thanks for that."

"Glad to be of service, Miss."

Clenching my teeth, I cut underneath an expensive sedan and jinked up over one of those big red tour buses. I can only hope I didn't flatten any tourists.

I broke out into Harrison Road, which bends around the major stadiums of New Manchester. It was the bend I was going for—I could accelerate and keep the stadiums between us. I checked for Beau and smiled when I didn't see any sign of him.

All too late, I discovered a Five Lions' Havoc gunship waiting around the bend. It blared the standard legalese warning that I'd given dozens of times. I hadn't considered that my time in the roundabout would give the authorities time to catch up. Slugs rained across my windshield and cracked spiderweb patterns all around, but I was surprised to find that none punched through. Snarky laughed when she saw me ducking as low as my seat would let me.

"You didn't think this thing was armored?" she asked with a sneer.

Two thoughts passed through my mind in a millisecond—since that's all the time I had. One, armored is fine, but the gunship had been firing a 6mm rotary gauss cannon. I'd never met a luxury grav car with *that* kind of armor. The other thought was that she was remarkably calm for the situation. I didn't dwell on either issue.

On reflex, I wrenched myself up to put my belly toward the gunship. More rounds stitched me up and a few found some vulnerable spots. I passed in front of the vertol's fan disc by a few feet, close enough to crack the fan housing and bend its blades all to hell. That hadn't been my intention, but it did a nice job of solving that problem. As the gunship wobbled and dropped, I hoped it hadn't been anyone I knew.

I continued to pull hard over the top and rolled out going back the way I'd come. Beau was heading right for me, tossing gauss rounds like they were cheap. With a newfound confidence in my tough skin, I charged straight for him. A few more impacts cracked against my windshield as we closed at a blinding speed.

When gravity fields intersect, it's like two positive magnetic fields pressing against each other. There's resistance and then it pops when both gravity fields fail. There's a safety feature to prevent grav cars from getting close enough to each other for that to happen. I overrode it.

"Wait, what are you playing at?" Snarky asked. The sneer was gone—for the first time, I saw fear on her face.

"Trust me, I know what I'm doing."

Her rush to buckle into an emergency restraint told me she didn't trust me.

As I got close enough to see a crazed smile on his face, I bunted my nose down and cranked it right back up into his grav coils.

We slammed hard against each other and bounced apart. In my rear view, I saw his nose drop as the coils went offline. My plan had worked. I set straight to re-engage my grav fields—no easy feat in free fall. While they spooled up, I felt fluid draining from my under-carriage. One of my coolant lines had been clipped by the gunship and a grav coil capacitor failed.

Just ten meters above ground, the gravity field re-engaged, but weaker than it should have been. Losing that capacitor cost me. I took a quick turn took me down a tighter alley where I wreaked more havoc on the windows in passing. At the next intersection, I realized we were back in Wembley and made two more turns on instinct while I reviewed my system's status.

In pilot terms, I only had enough power left to get us to the crash site.

With my heart on fire, I settled us back to terra firma and shut myself down seconds before our charred remains would've become graffiti. Across the street, the line outside Rock Bottom watched us with apathy. Of all the places in the city I could've crashed, I found myself outside the same exotic dance club. I'd come full circle, inad-vertently ending up within a few dozen meters of where the Wyvern had picked me up.

"You know, we're still quite a ways from our destination," Snarky said.

"Yes, Miss, I'll see what I can do about that, Miss."

The car was already shut down, but it still caused me great misery to pull the plug out. A crushing sense of being small, weak, slow, and generally *pathetic* washed through me. The door behind me opened as Snarky decided it was time to get out.

I popped the center compartment open and found a Yorkshire standard issue McCormick K18 6.9mm pistol—built by the lowest bidder to be usable by the lowest common denominator. I grabbed it and the three spare magazines underneath it. Finally, I kicked my door open to chase after Snarky. As I stepped out, a gauss round cracked into the door and knocked it back into me. I bounced, fell to my knees, and looked up the street. Beau was on foot with his Tavor-14 out, two blocks away and closing fast.

I struggled back to my feet, grabbed Snarky by the elbow, and dragged her toward Rock Bottom. I knew that bringing the daughter of some rich crime lords into a strip club might not have been the best idea ever, but it was the only idea I had.

* * *

Gunfight at Rock Bottom

In the movies, the round always clips the hero's shoulder when they're running away. I should've been so lucky. Beau's hand cannon caught me on the side. Must've grazed me or gone clean through, because it didn't kill me outright. I elbowed past the first asshole in line to reach Jack, the same giant wall of a bouncer who'd thrown my broke ass out less than an hour earlier. I hadn't had time to form a decent story—and I had a gun in my hand.

"The hell, Doc? Am I gonna have to crush your bloody skull? Daft bastard, go on and—"

The angry Yorkie facade evaporated the moment he spotted Snarky.

"Bloody hell, sorry mum," he said.

Confusion smacked me in the face for somewhere between half a second and three thousand years. The pain in my side snapped me back to reality. Then, the first patron in line's head exploded. Brain and skull splattered all over Jack, who drew his own piece with one hand while gently guiding my client though the door. He was too busy returning fire to stop me from following. Belatedly, I registered the screams and chaos erupting from the rest of the line. As we entered, the ear-splitting music and drastic change in lighting left me deaf and blind for a few moments. Snarky and I came to a halt as I let my eyes adjust to the dim red light and smoky haze.

Once inside, the patrons and employees alike remained oblivious to the events outside. Girls meandered through the clientele offering their services, while the patrons gawked at them or stared at the stage. Diamond was up at the moment, rapidly bouncing some of her finer features in gravity-defying ways.

While I shuffled forward, I heard a loud smack against the wall outside. I swiveled my head back to find Jack crumpling sideways to block the door. He was still shooting feebly but twitching from the impact of gauss rounds.

"Hey, Doc!" Lisa said in her characteristic high-pitched, bubbly voice. She smiled and arched her back. "Get you something? Or your girl, maybe?"

"Lisa!" Eddy, the weaselly manager of the place, stepped between Lisa and Snarky.

He whispered something to Lisa, who put a hand to her mouth and blushed in embarrassment. While he spoke, Diamond finished her set and started collecting her credits. When the music died down, I expected to hear gunfire, but didn't. A pounding bass shook the place as the DJ put on some interim music.

Eddy turned back to Snarky with a look of remorse.

"My great apologies, madame," he shouted. "Lisa's new here."

Though I was unclear why he'd apologized to my underage client and not kicked my ass for bringing her in, I had bigger concerns. Clutching my side with my left hand and grimacing, I twisted back to look for Beau. The big New Rhodesian stood at the door behind Jack's crumpled form. Beau raised his Tavor-14 in slow motion toward me.

Some lucky suit was getting a dance from a limber woman with blue hair on a velvet couch. I knocked Snarky down behind it. The gauss pistol cracked a round our way. As we hit the floor, it occurred to me it had taken more to move Snarky than I would've guessed. She had mods I hadn't noticed.

I looked up as Eddy fell against our feet, his head a bloody mess of brain and bone. At the entrance, Jack fought Beau with his last ounce of strength. Beau cursed, jerked his pistol free, and put one last round into Jack's forehead.

"Next on stage, please give it up for Misty!"

A powerful, synthesized riff blasted through the room to announce her entrance.

Due to the loud music and flashing lights, only a single customer noticed the gunfight. He nervously looked at everyone else in bewilderment, as if wondering if it was his imagination. I pulled Snarky back up, trying to get out before anyone else noticed. I staggered at the pain of my wound and found my left hand soaked in blood.

Misty, a leggy, skinny blonde, stalked out onto the stage on crazy tall heels as if she owned the room. She paused six steps in, pointed at the bloody mess Eddy'd made, and screamed.

A mad panic grabbed all the patrons. Rich, poor, married, lonely, bachelor, pervert, rock star... all the patrons were equal as the fear ripped through the room. To my great bewilderment, most everyone flooded out through the front door. They stumbled and piled over the slumped form of Jack, oblivious to the very danger that had killed the poor, faithful bouncer. Beau disappeared behind the mass.

I steered Snarky toward the dressing room. Most of the club's dancers shrieked and ran that way as well, A few of the patrons tried to follow them, but Dutch, a muscular Caledonian bouncer with sleeves of tattoos, bloodied his knuckles holding them back.

"Dutch, he's after us, you gotta let us through!" I shouted as we approached.

The bouncer dropped an unconscious staffer in Orinoco orange to the floor. He waved us past, drew his piece, and scanned the room.

The lights and mirrors in the dressing area dazzled me again, but I fought through it and herded Snarky toward the exit. Halfway down, I noticed most of the girls, Jazzy included, were hiding under their cheap vanities. The exit door was open and a shadow stood in the way. Realization struck just as light glinted off that damn gauss pistol. Though gripped by terror, I fired a few shots in his direction without even thinking about it. One clipped the door frame and he flinched.

A screeching battle cry stole my attention. The Flying Squirrel, it seemed, wasn't the sort to hide under a table. In a flash, she was on him, stabbing away with a knife in each hand.

I used the distraction to pull Snarky up and back the other way. Two of the other dancers got up and ran ahead of us, clacking loudly on their platform heels.

Glancing back, I saw Beau throw up a defensive arm while he brought his gun to bear. It clicked empty. The Squirrel laughed, danced around, and stabbed until Beau backhanded her across the face. She flew into a vanity, smashed the mirror, and crumpled.

I fired another wild shot toward the big man, which pinged off the ceiling. As we ducked back into the main area, I heard Beau slap in a fresh magazine.

"Dutch, he's in there!" I shouted as we ran back out. A round cracked against the wall as we passed by. The bouncer spun, took a knee, and aimed.

While the two exchanged rounds, I tried to herd Snarky back to the entrance. My foot snagged on the unconscious Orinoco staffer, and I tumbled to the floor. Dutch grunted and fell backward as Snarky helped me to my feet. The dancers who ran to the entrance had to climb over Jack and two other immobile bodies. As the first one jumped clear, red blossomed on the other's back. She cried out and slumped on top of the others.

I yanked Snarky down below the line of the stage and we crawled under cover. If you've never had to crawl on your hands and knees on the floor of an exotic dance club, count yourself lucky. I can't describe the kind of nasty, sticky things we came across.

The DJ's booth was the best cover we could get to, but we'd still be vulnerable for a few steps until we got there.

"Get ready," I told Snarky. She nodded.

I kicked one of the sniffer's row chairs as hard away as I could.

"Go!"

Snarky ran for the booth, and I followed as Beau shot the chair to hell. We piled into the black plywood structure and crouched low. When a piece of sound equipment exploded in a shower of sparks, I decided I'd picked a poor piece of cover. Concealment—yes. Cover—meh.

Feeling a touch dizzy, I realized I should do something about my injury. To staunch the bleeding, I grabbed a hoodie laying next to the sound board and tied it around my waist.

"How the hell did he find us?" I asked out loud, though I meant it rhetorically.

Snarky looked at my back, raised an eyebrow, and plucked a tiny metal button off my shirt. I flashed back to the hard slap Beau had given me earlier.

"I wonder," she said.

How'd he know I was about to get this job?

"Hey Doc!" Beau shouted. "I'll give you one last chance at ninety—ten. Hand her over, all is forgiven."

I'm not sure what it was that made me so stubborn over the issue—aside from my natural predilection to recalcitrance. Spite, maybe? Whatever it was, it was as if I was saying no simply because he demanded that I say yes. I gave a glance at Snarky, who looked back at me with what I'm pretty sure was boredom.

"Ten percent of not a whole lot doesn't sound worth losing my job over," I shouted. "She's just some teenage brat, after all. How much can she be worth?"

I was expecting Snarky to frown or get pissy, but she looked amused. I searched in desperation for anything useful. I had my pea shooter, but there was no telling what mods he'd gotten since I'd last served with him. For all I knew, my pathetic little bullets would bounce off him.

"You really don't know who you got there, do you?" he said. From his voice, he'd come all the way around the stage. I guessed he was two quick bounds from closing the distance and killing me.

When I scanned over the DJ's console, ideas leapt out at me.

"What?" I shouted. "Is she royalty or something? Princess of Windsor? Miss Teen Mobile?"

"No, bra, this chot's the damn—"

I flipped every switch on the DJ's panel as fast as I could. Lasers, smoke, spotlights, and puffs of glitter exploded from every corner of the room. A heavy beat reverberated through the room with bass so strong everything shook. Taking the chance he'd be at least momentarily distracted—a big gamble since most vision mods can gain down for bright flashes of light—I took off across the room and ducked behind a chair. I looked back at Snarky, who gave me a look of casual consternation.

When I peeked over the chair, I found Beau blinking and waving away the smoke—but his attention was still on the DJ booth. As he took another step forward, I eased my pistol up, slow as molasses, and took aim. He caught sight of me just as I pulled the trigger. His head jerked back, but he remained standing. Calm and collected, I readjusted my aim after each shot and fired over and over as he stumbled further back and eventually dropped. The pistol clicked empty.

As I'd been trained, I dumped the empty magazine, dug another one out, and reloaded while stalking toward him. Taking no chances,

I kept whatever furniture I could between us until I was right on him. He didn't move as I walked up, but I'd seen enough action vids to know that—

At blinding speed, he twisted and kicked his leg further than I thought he could reach. It broke my wrist and I dropped the pistol. Before the pain even registered, he'd rolled forward and gotten a hand on my throat. His face was bloody mess. One of his eyes sparked and smoked, his nose was cracked, his jaw didn't line up, and flesh was torn away to reveal metal in a few spots. I'd been afraid of that.

"Thtupid thon of a... Dammit. Can't thalk right, bathtard."

Slowly, the hand clenched tighter. My head felt like it was going to pop. I tried to gasp for air, but it had nowhere to go. I kicked and punched and tried to wrestle with him, but he wouldn't budge.

With better stealth and composure than some professionals I've seen, Snarky strolled up beside Beau and slid a knife into his neck joints. My old flying buddy gurgled, released his grip on my neck, and lay back like he was taking a nap. He wasn't going to wake up.

Snarky drew the blade out and wiped it off on my shoulder.

"I'll have to say, this isn't quite how I pictured my day going," she said. "But, I'm not one to second guess the actions of my employees. I'm in one piece and well clear of that debacle at my warehouse, so I suppose I'm at least a little bit in your debt."

A touch confused, but no wanting to show it, I returned my attention to Beau. "And I suppose I'm in for debt for that. Thank you."

Her gaze wandered through the devastation all around us. "Yes, this *will* be coming out of your paycheck. In case you didn't know, I own this place."

Looking back up at her, I frowned and narrowed my eyes. "Miss, I don't know who you are, but Tessa Napier owns this place. You know, the notorious crime queen of New Manchester?"

With a raised eyebrow and smirk, she extended a hand.

"Yes, but you can call me Madame Napier, seeing as you're now my personal chauffeur."

"You're… no, no, Miss, that can't be right. Tessa Napier was old when I was a kid. You're a teenager."

At this, she rolled her eyes and sighed. Then, she shook her head and pointed at Beau's corpse. "Do I really need to explain to you that appearances mean almost nothing these days?" She tapped a knuckle against her own head to reveal the augmentations. "I'm stupid wealthy and, as you said, I've had decades to alter everything about myself."

I couldn't help but release a flustered chuckle.

"You really had no idea who I was, did you?" she asked.

I shrugged. "I figured you for some br—, um, rich child of… someone."

"And yet, you went to all this trouble to keep me safe. Even if it meant dragging me in here." Her eyes brightened, and she broke into laughter.

The reverberating beat of a vertol announced itself outside. Her attention went to the entrance and she shook her head. "That'll be my ride. I hope you don't mind, but I had Miss Littlewood shadow us at a healthy distance just in case something like this—" she waved her hands around the room "—happened. Apologies, but there's only room for one."

"Miss, er—*Madame* Napier?"

"Yes?"

"What was this all about, then? Why would you choose an unknown someone like me to get you away from a raid?"

"Oh, I only needed you to get me out from the perimeter they were setting. I didn't much expect you to survive much further, yet somehow you did. For that, you've got yourself a job. Of immediate concern, I'll make sure my best surgeon finds you. After that, keep clear of the authorities, and I'll have Rupert send for you when this has all blown over. Don't think of saying no… you'll be paying this off for a while, at least."

The beat of the vertol's fans was getting louder fast. A light popped and sparked to my right. I flinched and looked at it reflexively. When I looked back, she'd gotten to the door and stood over Jack. She placed a gentle hand at his cheek.

"Shame. He was one of the better ones."

Past her, out the entrance, the same Wyvern that had picked me up earlier settled down in the street. Dazed and dumbfounded, I walked to the door as Miss Tessa Napier, Crime Queen of New Manchester—and my new boss—walked to her backup ride. The cute blue-eyed pilot hopped out, ran to the wrecked grav limo, and tossed something in. The grav limo exploded in a bright shower of sparks. The pilot waved a cheery goodbye as the Wyvern lifted off. As I numbly waved back, they disappeared around a corner.

"Did..did you just save Tess Napier's life?"

I turned to find Jazzy a few feet away, gawking at me. She pulled a silk robe tight as she clacked up in her heels. Wide-eyed, Jazzy reached toward my side.

"And you're bleeding!"

"Uh-huh," I said, mustering a facade of nonchalance. "Think I broke my wrist, too. All in a day's work."

"Oh, poor baby," she said. She gave me a hug and kiss on the cheek that made all the pain go away. "Here, I'll get you back to my place and have a look. You're way more badass than I ever would've guessed, Doc."

I'll venture to say I love my new job. The pay, like I said, was life-changing. But the perks... well, let's just say they're *super* perky.

* * * * *

Casey Moores Bio

Casey Moores was a USAF rescue/special ops C-130 pilot for over 17 years—airdropping, air refueling, and flying into tiny blacked-out dirt airstrips in bad places using night vision goggles. He's been to *those* places and done *those* things with *those* people. Now he lives a quieter life, translating those experiences to military science fiction, fantasy, alternate history, and post-apocalyptic fiction. His biggest challenge is focusing on any one genre. Or focusing on anything at all, really.

For Chris Kennedy Publishing, he has written in the Four Horsemen universe with stories in numerous anthologies, several novels about Bull and his black ops rescue company, and much more to come. He's recently expanded into the Salvage System and Fallen World as well.

Casey has joined Three Ravens Publishing's JTF-13 series with Witch Hunt, a story about monster-hunting marines in the Civil War. He also writes in Cannon Publishing's Fallen Empire series.

Finally, he has several stories out in his Deathmage War fantasy series, one of which—*A Quaint Pastime*—was a finalist in the FantaSci fantasy story contest.

This is his first foray into the We Dare series and the Contractor Wars universe in particular.

A Colorado native and Air Force Academy graduate, he is now semi-retired in New Mexico.

Find him at www.caseymoores.net

# # # # #

You Will Not Go Breathing Into That Long Night by William Alan Webb

A Last Brigade Universe Story

Introduction

On April 15, 2025, terrorists set off a nuclear device on top of the New Madrid Fault Line in Northwest Tennessee. The subsequent earthquakes were historic in size and destructive power, damaging or destroying bridges across the center of the United States and wiping out everything south of St. Louis along the Mississippi River. Instead of leaping into action to help stabilize the country, power brokers who cared only about their own agenda steered the Federal Government onto a course of using the chaos to destroy their political enemies. Thus began the years of what later came to be called The Collapse.

* * *

Prologue

Hennepin County District Court
Minneapolis, Minnesota
May 25, 2025

The bail verdict by Judge William Smith stunned even the defense counsel for accused murderer and child rapist Michael Roenell.

"After due consideration, bail is set at five thousand dollars."

Taciturn until that moment, Assistant District Attorney Leticia Avery took half a step back, stunned.

"Your Honor, with all due respect, the defendant—"

"Save your breath Ms. Avery. I've heard your arguments and made my decision. I do not consider the evidence compelling, so be glad that I did not grant the defense motion to dismiss the charges in their entirety, or release the accused OOR. Five thousand dollars should be enough to guarantee that he shows up for trial. Court is adjourned."

"All rise," called the bailiff.

As an experience bounty hunter, Dani Colton had sat through dozens of bail hearings, arraignments, and trials without ever saying a word in court, except on the handful of occasions when she'd been called as a witness. Under other circumstances she would simply have shaken her head in disgust at one more judge who put their own agenda above public safety. But that day was different, and her interest in Michael Roenell was personal.

"That son of a bitch killed my sister and raped my niece!" she yelled, standing and pointing at the wiry man behind the defense table. Roenell craned his neck, spotted her, and smiled. "He's a pedophile and you're letting him go? What the fuck is wrong with you?"

Already halfway across the dais toward the Judge's Chambers, Smith whirled to see who had spoken. Bailiffs moved forward toward her. Others in the courtroom began chattering too, the clamor echoing from the room's hard-paneled walls.

"Order!" Smith said, then louder, "Order in my courtroom. Bailiff, I want order!"

Colton tightened her lips and stared at Roenell. She had to get out of there before they arrested her for contempt, but she wanted Roenell to know that she was going to get him, one way or the other. Grabbing her phone, she violated another rule of the court to video him as she made threatening faces. Her scowl had the opposite effect, however. Even as the Deputies pushed toward Colton, her sister's murderer puckered, held up his hand and blew a kiss.

Whirling, she slid through the milling spectators and onto the street outside the courthouse. Traffic was light. Like the rest of the country, high absenteeism left the streets mostly empty as the city shut down, little by little. News commentators compared it to a slow death from organ failure. Colton crossed the street and trotted toward her car, doubting anybody would chase her. She was right.

Stopping beside a beat-to-hell black Trans-Am, she stared down some punks eyeing it from a distance. Unlocking the vehicle, she reached into the center console, retrieved the Glock 22 inside, and slid it into the holster on her belt, turning to ensure they saw her weapon. Loaded with Remington 180 grain Ultimate Defense rounds, Colton was so angry from the Judge's bail amount that she hoped the thugs would try to carjack her. Two had started crossing the street; when they saw the handgun, they turned and walked the other direction.

Once safely away, she immediately started planning. If Roenell took off like her Bounty Hunter's instincts told her he would, Colton was going after him. Wherever he went, whoever tried to hide him, she would dig him out. And once she'd caught up with him, which she would, his need for bail would be cancelled with extreme prejudice.

* * *

Bad Leroy Brown made Roenell's bond, which Colton considered a good sign. She'd done a lot of work for Bad Leroy over the years, and he hated bail-jumpers with a passion, much more than most Bail Bondsmen. Leroy considered it personal disrespect.

Although Colton lived in the most dangerous section of Minnetonka, Minnesota, the public services still worked most of the time, including power, water, internet, TV, and cell phone service. She was lucky and knew it; utilities were shutting down across the country as the value of money plummeted and workers stayed home, fearing the increasingly violent streets.

Colton got the call at 11:08 PM, while watching a special on the destruction of Arlington National Cemetery by a tidal wave of *Antikapitalista* 'protestors.' Apparently, the President ordered the military to stand down and not resist, but twenty armed forces members ignored her order and stood fast at the gate. A gun battle ensued, in which all the armed forces died, along with more than 100 of the red-scarved *Antikap* rioters. One of the fallen was a general named Sam Cannon, which she thought sounded made up.

Colton answered on the second ring, and Leroy began talking before she could say 'hello.'

"He gone, just like you spoke the word," Leroy said in the strange parlance that was unique to him. "Boy done gone flyaway on me. You want the hunt?"

"You're talking about Michael Roenell?"

"Who else I be calling you about this time o' night?"

"You make a lot of bonds Leroy."

"Not even about the money," he went on, failing to verify that it was Roenell who had skipped. "Pride, sister, that's all we got, and it goeth before the fall."

Rather than ask what that meant, she asked, "Any leads on where he went?"

"Know where he's goin', not where he went."

"What about a co-signer?"

"David Patrick Duffy."

"Address?"

"The wind in the willows."

"Uh-huh, so the address is bogus. Anything else?"

"Ain't more."

"Can you scan the bond application and email it to me?"

"Power's been out for hours. The Lord seen fit to leave us in the dark to await the light of His word."

"Sure, sure. So David Patrick Duffy, right? I'll find Roenell, Leroy, make bank on it."

Brown paused a moment then continued in a softer tone. "This is the evil man that killed your sister, Dani?"

"This is him, Leroy. He left my ten-year-old niece in a coma, brain dead. The doctors say she won't ever wake up."

"Men such as he defile God's Earth. Smite him Dani, do you hear old Leroy? Smite him like the Sword of the Lord. Leroy gonna pay your fee like they did in the old days, dead or alive, but if I can express a preference, that preference would be dead."

She spent the next half hour with legs tucked under her on the couch, replaying the video of Roenell in the courtroom over and over again, fantasizing how he would look with a bullet hole between his eyes.

* * *

Outskirts of Minnetonka, Minnesota
May 31, 2025
6:44 PM

Columns of oily black smoke towered over the burning strip mall. Hundreds *Antikapitalista* members, marked by their red scarves, gyrated in the parking lot like acolytes of an ancient fire god. Some threw bricks into the flames, others through flammable liquids, but all seemed mesmerized by the destruction, particularly of the gun shop.

Dani Colton hung near the back of the crowd, her own scarf wrapped tightly around her nose and mouth to filter out the smoke. Like all the others she screamed and waved a fist, exulting in destroying businesses built on capitalism. What nobody noticed was her eyes roving over the crowd itself, looking for one particular face, round, with a scraggly beard and an impressive turkey neck for one so young, the face of David Patrick Duffy.

Recognizing him should have been much easier now than two months earlier, before the president mass deputized the *Antikapitalista* organization. Then, *Antikap* members all wore black masks to avoid being recognized. Now that the federal government officially sanctioned *Antikap* and membership was a badge of honor, the black masks had been replaced by red scarves, leaving their faces revealed even amidst the day's destruction.

Even so, drifting smoke made it hard for Colton to make out faces in the mob. As part of her bounty hunting business, Colton had long since infiltrated many of the dark web forums dedicated to illegal activities. Although said to not have a formal organization, *Antikap* had long used the forums to plan attacks and coordinate with professional agitators bussed in from other parts of the country. Sponsored by the Billionaire Györgi Rosos, they weren't simply organized, they were *very* organized. Over a number of years, Colton developed a presence among the *Antikap* posters, against the day when she might need it. Today was that day.

Tracking Duffy wasn't hard once she figured out that he was a 'Junior.' Hacking his computer took longer than she'd expected because the internet kept crashing, but once she got into his browser history, she found links to a number of forums. He'd deleted the links without bothering to scrub them, a lazy mistake. Most were to legitimate gaming sites, but not all.

Once she had access to his history, she understood how Roenell and Duffy knew each other; they both belonged to a fantasy forum that centered around underage girls. Some of the bond jumpers she'd tracked down had used those types of forums, so Colton knew that they were like. Previously, she'd tried to remain distant from the reality they represented, because she was there as a huntress, not an avenger. Now that had changed, and she paid attention in a way she'd never done before. Sickened by what she saw, Colton kept plowing through link after link to similar forums and, when those ran out, more links to some radical political movements, from Nazis to Anarchists to radical Communists, and finally the one for *Antikap*.

Bingo!

David P. Duffy went by the username DDuf, one she recognized. When word went out on the forum about wrecking the gun store, DDuf said he'd be there, using five exclamation points to indicate his excitement.

Colton showed up two hours early to select the best vantage point to look for Duffy, map out escape routes, and ask around if anybody knew him, all while showing her excitement at wiping out the gun store. She didn't think that the original intent had been to burn the place down, but instead to loot the store of any remaining firearms, knives, ammunition, and anything else that could be used as a weapon, sold, or bartered. She held back as the crowd smashed its way inside, thinking how stupid it was to invade a store that sells guns. Apparently, none of them had thought of that, and only when shots from inside chased away the intruders were Molotov cocktails thrown through the windows. The fact that a sandwich joint, hairstylist, and nail salon were also in the strip mall didn't seem to matter; capitalism was capitalism.

Skirting the back edge of the crowd, Colton had to sometimes stop and stand on a bus bench or car bumper to see over the crowd. The wind picked up and thinned out the smoke hanging close to the ground, affording her a clear view. With the sun low in the west, shadows bisected the mob.

The fourth time Colton swept her gaze over the crowd, she spotted her quarry up front and off to her right. Even at 50 feet she recognized the fat face with its patchy beard. Now the trick was to get Duffy alone somewhere. With that in mind, Colton had worn a tight black T-shirt and no bra, which, combined with her tightest black jeans was guaranteed to get the attention of any heterosexual male, regardless of his politics. The trick was going to be not lashing out as she moved through the crowd, because *Antikap* members were not known for having manners or self-control. Her instinct would be to cut the hand off the first man who grabbed her breast, but that wasn't what she had come for, and it would take willpower, real willpower, not to do it. What focused Colton on her objective was the grinning face of Michael Roenell, which never quite left her mind's eye.

In the small of her back and covered by her shirt, two sheaths attached to a leather belt held wooden-handle push daggers. Looking around to ensure nobody saw her, Colton drew the knives in case someone threatened her. She didn't care if someone grabbed her ass, because that would not prevent her from carrying out her mission, but if it went any farther, they would regret it. *Antikap* internet tough guys talked about washing the streets in blood, until that blood was their own. Colton doubted they would like that as much.

As she made her way to the far edge of the mob, a section of the flaming roof fell in, showering sparks and burning wood into the parking lot. A young woman with rainbow-colored hair darted to pick up something that fell onto the sidewalk, dancing away with green bottles of expensive shampoo. The rest of the mob ran backward 30 or 40 feet until out of range of the embers and debris. Duffy pushed people out of the way while running to the back of the crowd. Once there and bent over with hands on knees, he gulped air, while others yelled at him for shoving them around. It couldn't have worked out more perfectly for Colton.

The mob wasn't as densely packed after they moved back, so Colton had to weave her way among the people in the rear. That was when she felt a hand slide down the back of her pants. He missed the empty dagger sheaths as his fingers cupped one butt cheek. Normally Colton would have struck him in the Adam's Apple, but with so many witnesses around she instead was going to politely ask the man to stop... until he started dragging her backward by grabbing her jeans.

Aside from trying to physically manhandle or rape her, now he was interfering with what she'd come to do, and so, keeping the knife in her left hand low, without turning she laid its tip against his groin. Although taller than her, he was thin to the point of being emaciated, and she could tell he was addicted to something.

"If you don't back off right now, I'll cut off your balls and shove 'em down your throat."

"I... I... hey, I mean—"

The man backed away and held up his hands in surrender.

"We are all in this together, sister. I just thought..."

"I don't give a fuck what you thought, I'm here for the cause, not some piece of shit crackhead."

Rather than reply, the man turned around and fled into the crowd. She saw his shoulders scrunched together as if expecting her to throw a knife into his back. It didn't sound like a bad idea, but the puckered lips of Michael Roenell made her instantly forget the encounter.

It took a moment to relocate Duffy, who had retreated behind a car on the far side of an adjoining parking lot, in front of a looted and abandoned pharmacy. He was by himself, smoking a cigarette, and either eating something or shoving drugs up his nose. With no one else around there was no point in trying to approach without being seen, so instead she made a beeline for the car, first re-sheathing the daggers in the small of her back.

Colton changed her gait so that her breasts bounced when she walked, for all the good it did. Duffy was bent over, too absorbed with his nostrils to notice her coming.

"Hey brother," she said, getting close enough that when he looked up, the first thing he would see was her chest. His eyes lingered for two full seconds. Colton pointed at his smoke. "Share a hit?"

"It's not weed," he said, stammering a little. "I smoked it all."

She doubted he'd ever been so close to a female over the age of 12, but her face reflected only affection. One skill a good bounty hunter needed was acting. She grinned and held out her right hand, separating the middle and forefinger as if to grip the smoke. Held low and behind her back, her left hand slid one of the daggers out of its sheath.

"That's cool," she said, "smoke is smoke, yeah?"

"I guess so," he said.

Colton knew better than to try and overpower him. Regardless of what they showed in those ridiculous action movies, where 100-pound women beat the hell out of men the size of a horse, physics didn't work that way. Duffy weighed at least 300 pounds, and, while it all appeared to be flab, it was still a huge mass of flesh. Colton was half his weight; she'd have to use speed over power.

Duffy took a drag and held the cigarette out butt first in his right hand. Their eyes met. Hers were blue, his yellow, the surrounding pupils so dilated that his eyes appeared black. Instead of grabbing the proffered cigarette, she reached across her body and grabbed his right wrist. Instead of pulling him toward her, though, she used the grip to pull herself in close, until the point of the knife touched the side of his neck.

"Kneel," she said.

"Hey, that hurts!"

"Kneel, you sick son of a bitch."

"You can't—"

The tip of the dagger drew a single drop of blood. "One more word, asswipe, one more word..."

Leveraging his thumb with her right hand, Colton forced Duffy to his knees. Sweat made his skin slippery, so she crouched and increased the pressure, forcing him all the way down and not stopping until his nose touched the asphalt.

"I didn't do anything," Duffy said, whimpering. "Why are you doing this to me?"

"Is that what all those little girls said?"

"What are you talking about, I've never hurt a girl!"

"No, you only bought pictures from those who did. So, here's the deal, *David*. You tell me where to find Michael Roenell, and I let you go. I don't hurt you, I don't say anything about what's on your computer, you go away and never see me again."

"But—"

"Wrong answer."

Peering over the car's hood, Colton looked to make sure no one had seen them, but the crowd was too busy yelling and throwing stuff into the dying flames to see them behind the car. Keeping the dagger at his neck, she sat on his back. Using the heel of her left hand, she pushed on the back of his head, grinding his nose, lips, and teeth against the asphalt.

"Let's try this again."

Duffy squirmed until the point of the knife drew a trickle of blood. The pavement muffled his frantic screams. After a few more seconds, Colton grabbed a handful of hair and raised his head. A roar from the crowd accompanied one wall caving in, so she leaned forward.

"Ten seconds to talk," she whispered into his ear.

"I don't know anybody named Roenell!"

"Wrong answer again." She smashed his face into the pavement, and pulled it back up using his hair. "You bought photos from him, a lot of photos. Five seconds."

"No, I didn't!"

"Three, two—"

"Texas!"

With her face close to his, Colton could see bloody bubbles dripping from his nostrils.

"Nice try. One."

"Cross-something, I swear, it's in Texas. Near Dallas, that's all I know, I swear."

"Not enough. Zero."

"Some writer lived there!"

"Rider? You mean like horses?"

"No, writer, some famous dude, I can't remember his name. Roenell said he had a cousin there, I think… maybe his mother, I wasn't listening."

"You're sure about this?"

"I am, I swear to god. Can I go now?"

"Yes, you can go now." Colton grabbed the second dagger and put it against his neck, shoved both blades in up to their hilts, then jerked them back out. Blood spurted from the wounds, covering her hands and pouring onto the pavement. Duffy convulsed and floundered, which only made him bleed out faster. Within twenty seconds, he stopped moving. Wiping her hands on his clothes, Colton sheathed the daggers and strode to her car without looking back. "Straight to hell."

* * *

Minnetonka, Minnesota
June 1, 2025, 2:02 PM

If anyone noticed or cared about David P. Duffy's corpse, Dani Colton never heard about it. The few news services still broadcasting never mentioned much more than the worsening international situation, the latest major catastrophe in the nation, or some particularly awful local situation. One dead *Antikap* member likely wasn't even reported to the police, assuming there were still police on the job to respond.

But, although David P. Duffy was the worst sort of predator and deserved a cruel death, Colton couldn't shake off her depression at having killed him. All that night, she sat on the couch with a bottle of vodka, mixing it with whatever sodas she had left, at first Fresca, and later Diet Orange Fanta, staring at the TV and getting progressively drunker. Never in 19 years of bounty hunting had she ever inflicted more than bruises on someone, much less killed them on purpose. Did it make her a murderer? The face of Michael Roenell laughed at the question before answering it.

"When you kill someone who isn't threatening your life, yeah Dani, that makes you a murderer. Welcome to the club! But be careful, something this much fun can be addictive."

"Fuck it," she answered him. *"The shit deserved it, and I'd do it all over again."*

Roenell laughed again, pointing at her. *"The Righteous Avenger, a classic excuse."*

"I'm going to kill you too, Roenell. I'm going to do it slow, and I'm going to enjoy it."

"It makes me so happy to give your life meaning, Dani. I can't wait 'til we meet again."

Awakening the next afternoon around two, Colton chased four aspirin with glass after glass of cold water, thanking God the whole time that the power and water still worked. Expecting to revisit the depressed guilt of the night before, she found it hard to even remember what Duffy had looked like. Did that make her a sociopath? *If so, then fuck that, too.*

With grocery store shelves even more bare than usual, she made lunch out of whatever was left in her refrigerator, combining a 4-egg omelet with Gouda cheese, some stuffed Manzanilla olives and half a can of leftover Spam, all of it heaped over three slices of toasted gluten-free bread she'd bought for a friend and stuck in the freezer. It tasted like glue. Slathering the bread with the last of the butter helped some, but not enough. Regardless, it was food, and if her alcohol-abused stomach was able to digest it, the calories would offset some of her hangover.

As she ate, Colton powered up her tablet. The cable internet was down, and, on a local app, a neighbor said it had been all day. Calls to Customer Service went unanswered, which likely meant that service was gone for good. Fortunately, her cell phone still worked, so Colton used it as a hotspot to look up Cross-something, Texas, home of a famous writer. It didn't take long to find her destination:

Cross Plains, Texas, home of Robert E. Howard, the creator of Conan the Barbarian. She'd heard of the character, but Colton didn't like science fiction or fantasy; her reality was gritty enough without adding made-up layers of somebody else's nightmares.

The direct route to Cross Plains down I-35 came in at 1,070 miles, something like 15 hours of driving time. With stops for gas, food, and bathroom breaks, call it 18 hours, she calculated. A long day, but doable. She'd done longer, but not for a few years. And, if the highways really were barren of cops, as some people said they were, she could make it in twelve or thirteen hours. The problem came up when she shifted to a driving app that accounted for road conditions such as wrecks, construction, and bridges closed. Only then did Colton start to process the full damage done to the nation's infrastructure.

When the nuke detonated in Northwest Tennessee in April, triggering the New Madrid Fault, the subsequent earthquakes compromised bridges up to at least 500 miles on either side of the Mississippi River, and, in places, bridges fell up to 1,000 miles from the epicenter. Instead of taking I-35 south all the way to Dallas, according to the app, the safest route took her through South Dakota, then Nebraska and Central Kansas, the Oklahoma panhandle to Midland, then east to Cross Plains. Very little of the suggested route was over Interstates, or even four lane state highways, and the estimated drive time was 51 hours, 34 minutes.

Shit.

That would require at least two sleep stops, and she would have to count on finding increasingly scarce gasoline in quantities great enough to get her to Texas. Oil companies were concentrating their resources along the major highways, at the expense of lower volume stations in smaller cities and minor roads. Worse, what little news coverage still existed featured increasing reports of in-motion car-jackings, where multiple cars would surround an isolated vehicle and force it to pull over at gunpoint. In response, truckers were organizing convoys with 'guard cars' filled with armed men.

Colton had no such protection, nor would she have maintained the slower speed that was inevitable for convoys. Whatever direction she went, she would have to be her own guardian angel. Belching, she was relieved that her food stayed in her stomach and didn't come back up, a good omen. There was no way she could take the backroads for more than detours; she'd simply have to take her chances on the interstate.

Success would require careful planning. Colton's apartment came with its own enclosed garage, which made packing easier. Cars parked in the open might as well be left unlocked, since thieves would smash out the windows if they weren't, and her apartment had been broken into more times than she could count. But she'd lived a spartan lifestyle and owned nothing worth stealing, and eventually word got around. Rather than buy material things, Colton put all available funds into the tools of her trade, which included keeping stacks of cash on hand. Friends told her to invest in this and that, mostly virtual currencies, but that was a step too far for her.

Instead, she kept $10,000 on hand at all times, hidden in top-quality safes under flooring and in the walls. The garden variety thieves in her neighborhood never found them, which for them was a good thing. As an added security measure, if they had dialed in the wrong combination and grabbed the lever to open the safe, it would have resulted in a nasty electric shock. Over her career, Colton learned many skills, from how to electrify things using store-bought batteries or by tapping into electric circuits, to working on her car.

She drove a 2008 Pontiac Trans-Am, which might have attracted too much attention had it not been beat to hell. The once-red paint job had long since faded to a mottled, brownish purple, chipped and dented across the entire body. A visible rope held down the wrinkled hood, while a peek inside showed holes in the seat and strands of headliner hanging from the ceiling. The roof had a dent. The car appeared to be a wreck.

It was anything but. Instead of the standard engine, a friend helped her install an LSX-454 engine, one which developed 840 horsepower. Everything else behind the façade of a junker was upgraded around the monster engine, including drive train, braking system, racing transmission, tires, and even the dents in the body, which an engineer designed to look random, but actually provided streamlining to lower wind resistance.

Next, she took it to an ex-boyfriend who ran a company known for providing security cars for politicians and celebrities around the world. He installed titanium steel armor plates in the doors and behind the grill, and a reinforced titanium box inside the trunk, with bullet proof glass all around. At her suggestion, he put a small triangular window inside the larger driver's side window, which could be opened using a separate switch. The ex asked her why she wanted that, and when she explained it was for shooting through, he incorporated the feature in all future designs. Lastly, she had a sound system installed with 4 sub-woofers behind the back seat, 12 other speakers scattered throughout the interior, and 4 amplifiers, all powered by two deep-cycle marine batteries. Colton liked classic rock, and she liked it *loud*.

Every weapon she owned had its own hidden place inside the car, held there by custom-made clamps. The Glock went into the center console, which had been enlarged to hold it. A compartment inside the driver's door held a Sig Sauer P320 XCompact, with a 15-round magazine. Yet a third handgun was clipped to the underside of the driver's seat, another Sig, only this time a full-sized P320 loaded with the highly illegal Russian 7N31 military-grade, armor-piercing 9mm round. Colton had once confiscated two boxes of the cartridges from a bounty and never reported them, although the possession of them was a federal felony. She'd never fired such a round, but they might prove invaluable during the upcoming trip.

Like most of her law enforcement and bounty hunter friends, Colton had loaded up on MREs long before the first terrorist attacks hit the country in 2024. Food being the top priority after guns, ammo, and gas, she took them all, which didn't leave too much room for clothes, toiletries, and basic first aid supplies. One other thing she had collected over the years were 5-gallon gas cans, since chasing fugitives had occasionally resulted in long car chases through desolate territory. Ten of them fit into the trunk, held in place by knapsacks and gym bags filled with blankets and underwear. The problem was finding fuel to put into them. Only one local station remained open, at triple the price of the previous month, cash only, and they had a ten-gallon limit. The owner only let her fill up two days earlier because she promised him a blowjob, which meant she could never go to that place again.

A call to the ex-boyfriend who ran the armored car business resulted in him grudgingly admitting that he did still have some gasoline on hand in the tank out back, and, after extensive wheedling, he agreed to meet her early next morning so she could fill up. He extracted a promise of a dinner date when she got back, and Colton readily agreed. He still thought the country would recover and things like dinner dates would again be possible, but she knew better. Once she left Minnetonka, the chances of her ever returning were slim, but, if she was wrong, dinner sounded good.

"You are such a little slut," said Michael Roenell as she crammed stuff into her car. *"Like all girls."*

"How do you want to die, Michael? I'll give you your choice, as long as its slow, and hurts a lot."

Sleep came easily, as it always did the night before she embarked on a bounty hunt. David Duffy's dead face didn't haunt her, as she'd feared it might. Instead, all she saw was Michael Roenell, although he didn't speak to her. She dreamed of slicing open his mouth so that his jaw hung slack in a Joker's grin, after which she sawed off his feet and hands, and dropped him in the middle of a busy Interstate at rush hour. The next morning, she woke up refreshed and ready.

* * *

Minnetonka, Minnesota
June 2, 2025, 7:39 A.M.

After meeting the ex at his business, Dani Colton made one final visit to her sister's grave. Janenora Perry Colton had the best marble grave marker that Dani Colton could reasonably afford. Standing beside the grave, looking down at the bright summer grass, she'd spoken to her sister in a low voice.

"I'm heading out, Jane. I don't know if I'll be back or not. The country's pretty fucked up right now. I really hope you're in Heaven. I know you believed it's a real place, and I want to believe it too. Maybe it's kind of blasphemous to say so, but I'm asking God to give you buckets of lighter fluid to pour on Michael Roenell as he burns in Hell. Seriously, watching him dance around for the rest of time, burning while you keep pouring. Don't worry that he's not there yet, I'm gonna take care of that real soon. I love you forever, sis."

One more stop, and she could hit the road. Situated on ten waterfront acres, the early morning sunlight reflecting off Lake Minnetonka bathed the Ave Maria Home in shades of gold and silver. Built of red brick during the 1950s, the order of Catholic Nuns that ran the facility had repeatedly turned down lucrative offers to sell the property, and for that Dani Colton was glad. There was something comforting about her niece being cared for by the Sisters in such a tranquil environment, even if the girl was in a deep coma. Pushing through the front doors, Colton saw none of the usual staff in their blue scrubs, or the receptionist manning the front counter, only an aged woman in the full habit of a Dominican nun.

"Good morning, Sister," she said. "We haven't met. I'm Danielle Colton, here to see my niece, Calliope Kelly Colton."

"Good morning to you, Ms. Colton." The nun's voice had a thin hoarseness that comes with age. "I am Sister Agnes."

"Did the staff bug out on you?"

"Most, yes. I cannot blame them in the current circumstances, although it does make caring for the patients difficult. Do you know the way to your niece's room?"

"Yes Sister, I do. Umm… there's one more thing. I'm going away, and I don't know if I'll be able to get back. I don't want Cally to suffer, so… it's hard to talk about…"

"You wish to sign a do not resuscitate order?"

"I do. Does that violate the rules?"

"No, my dear. If God decides it is our time, then it is our time. A DNR does not change that."

Cally Colton had been a typical ten-year-old girl, all arms and legs, reminding her aunt of a young colt just breaking away from its mother. She had been one of those lucky pre-teens who could wolf down insanely huge amounts of junk food and never gain an ounce, with a smile so pretty and friendly that she was about two years away from driving her mother crazy with worry. And then Roenell got her.

Colton heard the details from a cop friend. Roenell had been watching Cally's elementary school from across the street for weeks, singling her out as a potential target. He followed them home and discovered the address. Sometimes her bio-dad picked her up, sometimes Jane did. On the day in question, it was Jane. Since Roenell already knew where they lived, he beat them home and hid in the bushes. When Jane paused to open the front door, Roenell slammed a hammer into the base of her skull, grabbed Cally and dragged her inside. Brandishing a gun, he told her to shut up while he got Jane's body out of the doorway. Then he got down to business with the girl.

The crime happened before the nuke went off, when the country still more or less functioned as normal. Colton knew the grim details from reading notes of the police investigation. The upshot was that because of the severity of Cally's brain damage, her doctors gave her no chance of ever regaining consciousness.

"This is exciting!" Michael Roenell said as he matched her stride for stride down the hallway. "I just love looking at my work."

Colton stopped, closed her eyes, and forced the image from her mind. Despite him being an illusion generated by her imagination, she would not allow Roenell near Cally ever again.

"Be patient, Michael," she said out loud, "soon you'll get to see *my* work."

Outside the open window a bird sang, unaware of how badly humans were fucking up their world. Colton admired the bird's blissful ignorance. Sitting on her bed, Colton spoke to the girl as she stroked her hair. The overwhelmed Sisters were doing their best, but, from the smell, she knew they hadn't bathed Cally for a few days.

Water in the bathroom still worked, though, and even got reasonably warm, so Colton used a washcloth to wipe down her niece's face and neck, afterward emptying her bed pan. Without help she couldn't change the bed sheets, although she did tuck them in better and removed a crimp in the feeding tube. Finally, having done all she could, Colton kissed the girl on the forehead and left.

"Good news, Michael, I'm on my way."

* * *

Getting out of the city meant taking backroads until well south of Burnsville, where she got onto I-35. With traffic light and no cops in evidence, she edged her speed ever closer to 100 mph. Ominously though, once into the sparsely settled countryside north of Des Moines, Colton began seeing burned out passenger vehicles and slowed down, about the same time as she bumped over large cracks in the road. The earthquakes hadn't only destroyed bridges; in places, they had also left huge cracks in the pavement.

In Des Moines, Iowa, a long bridge over the Des Moines River flood plain had partially caved in along the center divider wall. Signs warned cars not to enter, although the large barrels meant to block traffic had all been shoved aside. No police were on hand to prevent cars from crossing, so Colton followed a minivan along the shoulder, keeping enough distance so that if it fell into a hole, she would have time to stop.

They made it safely across, unlike at least two dozen other vehicles that had fallen into gaping holes. Breathing easier, 20 miles south, she pulled over at a Truck Stop that claimed to have gasoline for sale. To Colton's surprise, it did, although at five times the price of two months earlier.

On the station's marquee was the message 'Antikap not welcome,' a direct challenge to the president's elevation of the group to the status of a deputized federal militia. Moreover, every person either openly wore a holstered firearm or carried a rifle, in defiance of the recently issued Executive Order outlawing personal ownership of guns. Sliding the Glock into a belt-holster, she retrieved the Compact Sig P320 and tucked it into the front of her jeans. After counting out 220 dollars, the amount needed to fill up the Trans Am, she went inside to pay.

On high alert for danger, she noticed that eyes from several different directions followed her. Off to one side were several SUVs and minivans, with families milling around outside, and, the instant she left her car, two men and a woman trotted toward her. From thirty feet away, they began begging for money and kept talking as they got closer. Finally, Colton stopped, turned, and laid a hand on the Glock.

"Please help us!"

"We're trying to get to—"

"Ignore him, my kids haven't eaten in three days!"

"Whose fault is that you stupid—"

"Shut up, all of you," Colton yelled, her expression leaving no room for argument. "I can't help any of you, do you hear me? Leave me alone."

The young mother bent over and made a begging gesture. "But my kids!"

"Are *your* kids, not mine. Now go away!"

"But—"

"I don't want to hurt you, lady, but I will. I'm going inside now. If I see one of you touching my car, or even getting near it, I will shoot you dead, family or no family."

Colton waited until they slunk back to their cars, grumbling things she couldn't hear. Watching them go, behind her sunglasses, she blinked away tears. If there had only been one of them, and nobody else watching... but the world was collapsing around her and there was nothing she could do about it. A lot of people were already dead, millions along the lower Mississippi alone, and millions more were likely going to die. Her sole purpose in life had become making sure that Michael Roenell was among the dead. Until that happened, she doubted his face would ever disappear from her every waking thought.

A huge man wearing denim stood watch by the double front doors. Holding a shotgun in the crook of one arm, he nodded as she drew near.

"That was smart," he said. "But it sucks, too."

She looked up, said "yeah," and pushed through the left door. Other armed men stood guard inside. All the customers were men who eyed her like street dogs drooling over the same piece of meat. As a bounty hunter, Colton was used to that. She had learned to walk the fine line between letting men know she was dangerous without directly challenging them. Her expression didn't waver when they locked eyes, with her reading them as much as they read her. None of them triggered her internal alarms... except for one snake-eyed guy wearing an Iowa State ball cap near the bathrooms. He could be trouble.

After paying for what she thought would fill the tank, Colton still had seven dollars left. The store shelves were mostly empty, but they still had cigarettes behind the counter. Even though she didn't smoke, she'd read somewhere that cigarettes had always been a currency during bad times. For a measly seven dollars all she could buy was a pack of generic menthols, which didn't matter to Colton. Someone desperate for a nicotine fix wouldn't give two shits about that. Pushing back through the front door, she stopped beside the guy in denim.

"Anybody mess with my car?"

"Not with me here."

"Thanks. If that guy in the ISU cap follows me, warn him that I can blow out his kneecaps from thirty feet."

"We don't like gunfire," the guard said. "That's dangerous around all this gas."

"Only if you miss."

"Kneecap's a small target."

"Speak for yourself. But let's avoid the whole situation, just don't let him follow me to my car. I need to conserve ammo."

The guard smiled. "Will do."

Returning to the Trans-Am, Colton walked slow enough that she could react in any direction, should someone want a piece of her. Nobody did. Snake-Eye had obviously wanted to, but the guard at the door had the shotgun stuck into Snake-Eye's stomach. With the other hand he waved at her as she pulled out.

The driving app showed blockages ahead in Kansas City, so at Omaha she diverted west onto I-80. A number of bridges had 'Cross At Your Own Risk' signs, but somewhere along the way she'd quit caring about dying. The only reason not to take dangerous risks was that a wreck might derail her mission. Once Roenell was dead... she had no idea what came next. Maybe nothing.

By mid-afternoon, she was hungry, tired, and her eyes burned. After turning left at York onto US Highway 81, Colton pulled onto the shoulder in a straight stretch of road running through endless corn fields, somewhere past Burning, Nebraska. She left the car running and got out. Stretching, she made sure nobody was in sight, climbed into a roadside ditch to pee, and fished her solar powered thermal flask from the backseat. Filling it with water, she laid it in the passenger seat, where afternoon sunlight would heat up the water for some coffee, and maybe an MRE.

The roadbed didn't appear to have any earthquake damage, but also hadn't been resurfaced in a long time, as evidenced by the faded color of the asphalt. It was only two lanes, and cracks ran through it that went from side to side. Parts of the shoulder had crumbled away. She'd have to keep her speed down until joining I-335 north of Wichita.

Cresting a low hill, her eyes caught a dust cloud in the rear-view mirror. That someone else used the road was no shock, it *was* a highway, likely the main artery for towns in the area, but when it reappeared, the vehicle was much closer than it had been. She looked at the speedometer, which indicated she was going 61 mph. The car behind had to be doing at least 90.

Well, shit.

There was no time to fret or regret, there was only time to get ready. Carefully, Colton laid the Glock within reach so the chambered round wouldn't accidentally go off. Next, she reached under the seat and unclamped the Sig with the armor piercing rounds, putting that pistol in her lap. Finally, she opened the compartment in the door that held the third handgun, leaving it in place for the time being, but within easy reach. Visibility ahead showed a clear road for at least a mile, so Colton slowed down a little. Choosing the battlefield was critical.

Gulping deep breaths, she prepared for what might be her final minutes. Despite living a dangerous lifestyle for nearly two decades, she'd never been in a shootout, much less one involving moving cars. Driving with her left hand, she opened the small, triangular window and reached across her body to hold the nose of the Sig out into the wind. She wouldn't fire the first shot, but if it came to a fight, she fully intended to fire the last one.

What materialized in her left side mirror was a black Ford pickup speeding the wrong way in the other lane. The boiling wake of dust made it hard to distinguish anything clearly, until a man hung out the passenger side window holding a gun… a shotgun, from what Colton could tell.

Good luck with that.

The truck slowed to match her speed. Two men rose in the bed, each holding a rifle. Counting the driver, that made four. There wasn't time to think or plan, there was only time to react. When the truck pulled even, the passenger aimed the shotgun at her and motioned for Colton to pull over. Wind turned one side of his face bright red, and he looked angry.

"Let's get this over with," she said. Letting go of the wheel for one second, she held up the middle finger on her left hand.

With no more than four feet between their vehicles, the man fired. Large caliber pellets struck her door and window, while the men in the pickup's rear bed also opened fire. Metallic *thunks* rippled across the car's body, peppering it with holes but doing no real damage. Double-ought buckshot might rip a deer apart, but, against titanium steel armor places and bullet-proof glass, it had no effect.

"My turn, asshole."

Colton fired once. The recoil pushed the barrel backwards out of the tiny window, and several seconds passed until she could line up a second shot. When she looked across at the pickup, the passenger had withdrawn back into the cab, his face twisted in pain. With bullets still hitting the Trans-Am from the men in the pickup's bed, she fired again, this time aiming slightly higher. The armor-piercing round hit the wounded man in his right ear, blew out the other side of his head, went through the driver's head and shattered the far window.

The pickup veered hard right and would have hit the Trans-Am, except Colton floored it the instant she fired, and the massive 840-horsepower engine rocketed the car ahead. Watching in her rear-view mirror, she saw the pickup flip and roll over four or five times. Braking, she cautiously backed up as dust settled over the wreck.

Colton waited for something to happen, for the distant scream of a police siren, or someone to crawl out of the wreckage, but after several minutes of nothing she got out of the Trans-Am. Swapping the Sig for the Glock, she approached with gun at the high ready. At a *pop*, by reflex she dropped to the hot pavement. It smelled like dirt and oil. Lying flat on her belly, Colton searched for a target as more gunshots came from the smoking truck, until she realized it was ammo cooking off. Somewhere inside there had to be a fire.

It stopped after five *pops*. Seeing no evidence of fire or smoke, she cautiously rose to one knee, sweeping the pistol back and forth over the truck. Once it became clear that it was safe to stand, Colton inspected the pickup to see if anybody had survived, or if maybe there was something to salvage.

With the Ford lying on its side, there was no practical way to siphon any remaining gas out of the tank. She only found two of the guns, both 20-gauge shotguns, which were damaged beyond repair. Three of the men were dead, but the last, an older guy with a gut, lay moaning in some weeds beyond the shoulder. Semi-conscious, he squinted up at her and held up one hand.

"Help me, call my wife, tell her that Lucas… please help me."

"Help you? You tried to kill me."

Her words had no impact on him, and Colton saw why. Blood streamed from a four-inch hole in his forehead, where scraped-away skin revealed white bone and brain matter. Maybe immediate transport to a trauma center could save him, and maybe not. Either way, it didn't matter, and she wheeled to leave. Nothing she could say or do would make any difference. The man yelled at her, alternately cursing, and pleading for help. Colton looked at her watch. Fourteen minutes had passed since the wreck, and still no indication anyone had noticed. Overhead, the first vulture circled. Time to go.

* * *

Once out of Nebraska, Colton pulled over and made coffee using water from the solar powered thermal flask, along with a spaghetti and meatballs MRE. The coffee was freeze-dried, which she mixed extra strong in a travel cup, and bitter, but she wasn't drinking it for pleasure. Eventually, somebody would notice the mess she'd left behind and come looking for whoever did it, and with such sparse traffic, a beat-up Trans-Am with dozens of holes in the body would attract attention. But her body wasn't cooperating, as hunger and fatigue made her risk the ten minutes it took to prepare and eat the MRE, washing it down with the coffee.

With the gas gauge nearing *Empty*, Colton took ten minutes to refill it from the cans in the trunk. She counted holes from more than thirty shotgun pellets in the trunk hood and rear fenders, yet none got past the armor plates. Using up most of three fuel containers, once back on the road she calculated that if all went well, she *should* have enough gas to get to Cross Plains, with maybe a little left over.

Unable to use the air conditioning because it increased fuel consumption, by the end of the day, Colton felt sticky with sweat. The setting sun cast long shadows by the time she reached Wichita, and it took her a moment to realize what was wrong; all the lights were out. In the distance, she spotted headlights on a parallel road, but, other than that, all was dark. Turning on the radio, she tried to find a station on FM or AM, with only a faint voice coming through on a very weak signal. It might have been from Amarillo.

Taking the I-235 loop west of the city, only then did she remember a brief news story about cities being hit with EMPs. No details came to mind, as it was simply one more bit of bad news in a long litany of terrible events. Had Wichita been among the cities hit with an EMP? If so, that would explain the total power outage.

By the time she reached the city's south side, people had seen her headlights and blocked the interstate, waving for her to stop. Some had pushed derelict cars into the pass-through lanes. Some brandished long, straight objects, maybe guns, maybe metal rods, while others held up what Colton assumed were babies wrapped in blankets. None of it mattered. Only watching Michael Roenell die mattered.

"I'm turning you into me," he said, "and it's delightful to watch."

Concentrating, she blinked until his face disappeared.

Judging there was enough room to pass between the blocking cars and the guard rail, Colton shifted into high gear and accelerated past 80 mph. People scattered and dove for cover, and someone might have fired a shot, but Colton had measured things well. She slipped by with inches to spare on both sides. Someone slammed a steel pole into the passenger window, doing no damage to the thick glass, and others threw rocks or bottles. Then she was through and speeding away, their images lost in the gathering darkness.

* * *

Under a cloudless night sky, the waxing crescent moon lit the highway north of Oklahoma City well enough to see for miles. On a desolate stretch, with no houses or cars in sight, she once again pulled over. Sleep was like a seductive lover whispering in her ear, and, without realizing it, Colton's head began to droop...

"I knew you couldn't do it," Roenell said, shaking his head with a bemused smile. "You're like all the other bitches, you talk tough but then lay down and take what a man gives you."

Her head snapped up, to see Michael Roenell staring back at her from the windshield.

"You know I'm coming to kill you, right?" she said.

"No," he said, *laughter choking off additional words, until he coughed and got himself back under control. "I don't know that. It sure doesn't look like it."*

Infuriated at his mocking, Colton forgot that she was arguing with a figment of her imagination. "I'm not going again until you are dead, Roenell. Not captured, dead. Three days earlier I had never killed anyone in my life, but I've killed five people just so I can kill you, and I'm going to do exactly that."

"It comes so easy now, doesn't it? Hate will do that, but when someone's needs to die, they need to die. Like your sister, and your sweet little niece. Sally, wasn't that her name? They both needed to die. If you think about it, I did them a favor."

"Hours, Roenell, that's all you've got left. Hours."

She drank the last of the sun-heated coffee, now lukewarm, and she made more coffee and ate another MRE, grabbing one at random. It was a Chili Mac. Next Colton filled the gas tank, using up the last drop. While holding the container against the car, she heard coyote calls from much closer than she liked. It made her feel less safe.

Hypnotized by the monotonous drive, Colton occasionally passed other cars, all of which pulled over as she rocketed by, exceeding 100 mph. Approaching the Cimarron River, north of Oklahoma City, she spotted headlights crossing the median and heading back the way they'd come. Why did they turn around? Warnings flashed in her brain, and she braked, not hard, but enough not to go flying into the river when she saw the bridge lying in the water. At her previous speed she could never have stopped in time. As it was, Colton was able to follow the other car and backtrack.

Taking the first exit, she wound driving west up on Highway 77 in a sparsely populated area. The road led into Guthrie, where, on the outskirts, she saw something unexpected: lights. Guthrie had power. What's more, a pink neon sign advertised Molly's Donut

Shop, open all night. Slowing to a crawl, she wondered if they had any real coffee, even the sludge all-night diners were known for.

People at tables inside saw her creeping by and pointed. Colton pulled into the gravel parking lot. Without committing to a space, she stopped near the street, squinting to make out details. The layout had display cases for donuts near the register, although she didn't see any of the pastries. Four or five tables were clustered near the windows. More worrisome, none of those inside were females, not even behind the counter.

She had decided not to go in when several men rose and pushed through the front doors, heading toward the Trans-Am. Colton floored it back onto the highway, spraying gravel in her wake. If they wanted to chase her... good luck. Blowing past a school on her left and a closed convenience store on the right, followed by long rows of clapboard houses, Colton left Guthrie doing 70 mph, heading for Oklahoma City.

* * *

Cross Plains, Texas
June 3, 2025, 7:39 a.m.

Twenty-four hours to the minute after she arrived at Ave Maria Home in Minnetonka, Dani Colton shaded her eyes against the rising sun in north-central Texas. Staring east toward Cross Plains, the Trans-Am idled like a hungry lion warning others away from its kill. Unfortunately, the gas gauge showed maybe four gallons left in the tank. Restarting the car would burn more fuel than leaving it running for a few minutes. A green sign on the right shoulder read 'Cross Plains 1, Comanche 40.'

Finally. Like every bounty she had ever tracked, Colton could feel Roenell's proximity. Like a predator tasting the air, she *knew* he was close. Except now something stood in her way, something she couldn't outrun or blast through, a police checkpoint.

Flat fields on either side exposed the Trans-Am like a low-slung dinosaur. She couldn't avoid the police position, couldn't get around it, couldn't run it, and if she turned around, they might pursue to find out what she was hiding. Under normal circumstances she'd take her chances outrunning the police, but the fuel tank was too low for that. Seeing no other choice except passing the checkpoint, Colton reached into the console for her driver's license, bounty hunter badge, registration, and insurance card. Then she moved forward at slow speed.

Guard rails on either side marked the beginning of a water course. Two Sheriff's Department SUVs blocked the highway. The SUVs were painted black at the front and rear, and white in-between. The one closest to Colton was in the west-bound lane, and fifty feet further on another one blocked the east-bound lane, so to get by you would have to slow down and weave between them. Beyond those two was a third parked along the shoulder, likely for pursuit if someone ran the roadblock. As she drew closer, Colton noted that all of them stiffened at the sight of her car, no doubt from the dents and bullet holes. Several men and women in khaki Stetsons waved her to a stop.

Two deputies stood on the right shoulder, hands on pistol grips, another flanked her on the left holding a shotgun, and a man in his forties with a close-cropped Van Dyke beard stood ten feet away from the driver's door. Without awaiting instructions, Colton rolled down the window and held out both hands.

"Please turn off the car and exit the vehicle, ma'am," said the man nearest her. A patch reading 'Denton' was stitched above the pocket on the left breast of his uniform shirt.

"Would you like my license, registration, and proof of insurance?" she said.

"In a minute, ma'am."

Colton turned off the Trans-Am. The clicks of the hot engine sounded loud in the sudden silence. Standing on the bleached asphalt, she held up both hands, palms out, like a prisoner of war. The man waved her to lower his arms. By training she inspected him for jewelry, tattoos, or other identifiable body marks, and noted that he didn't wear a wedding ring.

"I'm a—"

"Hold on there, ma'am. First, may I please have your name?"

"Danielle Colton... Dani."

"Are there any illegal drugs, open containers of alcohol, or firearms in the car?"

"No, no and yes, Deputy."

"I'm *Sheriff* Dennis Denton, ma'am, and since you want to smart off to me, which is it in the car?"

"Firearms, *Sheriff*."

"How many?"

"Not enough."

"Anything else that might injure one of my deputies?" he said. She read his expression as irritated, but also... something else. What was it?

"Just the car itself," she said, "if you try to open it wrong."

"I don't know what that means ma'am, but the president has out-lawed possession of all firearms by private citizens. Please turn around."

"When did that happen?"

"Word came down yesterday."

"Can she do that?"

"Ma'am, I'm not going to tell you again, turn around."

"If you want to look at my ass, Sheriff Denton, just ask. If you're meaning to handcuff me, you might want to rethink that. I'm a bounty hunter. Besides being unconstitutional, I question whether the President's order even applies to me."

Denton had one of those taut-skinned faces that made it impos-sible to hide his emotions. A spray of wrinkles spread out from the corner of each eye as he squinted, and slight creases in his cheeks vanished at the tightening of his jaw. Of the two deputies in Colton's line of vision, a young male looked stunned by the way she'd spoken to the Sheriff, while an older female had a lopsided grin.

"Maybe you'd best get that ID now," he said. "Slowly."

Colton handed over her credentials, folded her arms, and leaned against the Trans-Am's front left fender near the wheel well as one of the deputies ran her plates and license number. In the meantime, she and Denton stared at each other, him trying to hide what he was thinking, her smiling because he was doing such a bad job of it. After what seemed like half an hour, the deputy handed Denton her IDs and whispered in his ear. The Sheriff nodded and handed the cards back to Colton.

"You're supposed to contact my office before operating in my county," he said, trying to sound irritated.

"I called the other day, and nobody answered," she lied. "Six or seven times."

"Yeah, alright. So what brings you to Callahan County, Mrs. Colton?"

"No misses, no miss, just Dani."

"Good to know," he said, blushing. "I'll keep that in mind."

"I hope you do."

"Are you here on a bounty?"

"Yes," she said. "I've tracked a bond jumper to Cross Plains, and I'm here to bring him back. Unless I get lucky, and he gives me a legal reason to kill him. The warrant's on the net."

That sobered the deputies, who all glanced back and forth. The younger one touched his pistol.

"I'd rather you didn't do that," Denton said, "I don't need the extra paperwork. What'd this guy do?"

Colton's upper lip curled. "He killed my only sister, raped my ten-year-old niece, and left her brain dead."

"Oh," Denton said.

Nobody spoke for a while.

"I'm sorry for your loss," the female deputy finally said from the edge of the road.

"Yeah," Denton said. "We all are. Doesn't seem like there's much comfort to be had there, but whatever we've got, its' yours. Does this scumbag have a name?"

One of the deputies called out from the other side of the road. "I'll bet it's the same guy." Denton held up his hand to let her speak.

"Michael Roenell."

The deputy hooted. "Told ya."

"That's enough, Lloyd."

"What's he talking about?" Colton said, nodding toward the deputy behind her.

"Rather than tell you, Ms. Colton—"

"I told you, call me Dani."

"Alright, Dani, follow me into town, and I'll show you."

"Will do, Dennis," she said.

"That's Sheriff, Ms. Colton... Dani."

"Fair enough. Lead the way, Sheriff Dennis." The female deputy couldn't stifle a giggle, even after Denton gave her a stern glance. "But I'm almost out of gas, is there a station open somewhere?"

"Follow me into town, I'll show you where you can park your car and then you can ride with me."

Denton took the SUV parked behind the roadblock. Weaving between the parked SUVs on the highway, Colton followed him past farm fields and a row of low buildings with window-unit air-conditioners. Barns and picket-fences came next, until they passed a diner made up to look like an old Texaco station. Beyond a large electric sub-station and some abandoned buildings, Denton turned left into a grocery store with gas pumps out front. Next door was a boarded up Dairy Queen, leaving Colton with a sudden craving for a chocolate-dipped ice cream cone or anything that was not another MRE.

Denton parked, and she slid in beside him. Twirling his finger for her to roll down the passenger side window, he said to hold tight until he returned. Two minutes later, he came out with two cups of coffee, handing her one.

"I hope you don't take anything in it," he said.

"Oh, hell no." Taking a sip, she closed her eyes and leaned her head back. "Okay, Sheriff, you can take me now, I'm all yours."

Denton cleared his throat. "Uh, Royce is the proprietor here, and what with the supply being unreliable these days, he only sells gas to locals. I asked him to make an exception in your case, and he agreed. Fifty dollars to fill up, no matter how many gallons it takes."

"I paid more than twice that up in Nebraska."

"Let's just say I called in a favor. Go ahead and fill up, then you leave your... *car*... here. I doubt anybody will bother it, but if they do, Royce is a volunteer deputy..."

With the time approaching 9 a.m., the Texas sun warned of a hot day to come. Convection inside the SUV heated the passenger seat so that when Colton sat beside the Sheriff, she squirmed until it cooled down.

"Bring me up to speed, Dennis. You seem familiar with Michael Roenell, like there's something you know that I don't."

"You know I never told you to call me Dennis, right?"

"Yeah, I know."

"Okay, just making sure."

"Roenell?"

"Michael Roenell made a serious mistake by attacking Maggie Castro. I've known Maggie since she was born. Her daddy Miguel and I used to hunt together until he got bit by a Diamondback rattlesnake. Yep, very dangerous. They dump a lot of venom into your system."

"Dennis... *Sheriff*... Michael Roenell? I've driven straight through seeing nothing but his face in my windshield; he's haunting me. Can you please get to him? Where is he?"

"That's what I was doing, *Dani*. So anyway, Miguel lost his left leg below the knee. He couldn't hunt with me anymore, but asked me to take Maggie along sometime, so I did. I taught her to hunt and handle firearms—"

"The point?"

"Damnation you're impatient. The point is, Maggie learned not to ever leave home without a weapon. A few days ago, she and her 12-year-old daughter Marisa had been out swapping crops at the local market, tomatoes for some strawberries and lettuce. When they got home, Michael Roenell crawled out from under Maggie's trailer as she was fumbling with the house key. He tried to hit her with a hammer, but Marisa pushed him, so he hit Maggie in the shoulder, not the back of the head. They fell in a heap, and Maggie dropped her purse. Marisa knew she kept a Smith &Wesson revolver in there. The girl dug it out and shot Roenell in the back, near the base of the spine. Maggie got her girl inside and called me."

"The shot was fatal?" Colton said.

"Let's just say he died and leave it at that."

"Michael Roenell is dead?"

"Two… no, three days ago."

Colton looked out the passenger window with seeing the countryside beyond. That was it? Roenell was dead without her being involved? If true, it left her feeling empty. What was the point of going on, what would she do now? But then suspicion flared. What if the Sheriff was covering for him? What if he was another David Patrick Duffy? Her tone changed, and she turned in her seat.

"Where is he?"

"In a hole, where he belongs."

"I want to see him."

"That means digging him up. You good with a shovel?"

Could he be luring her to someplace alone, to kill and bury her there? Would Colton be digging her own grave? He hadn't frisked her for an ankle holster, even though she wasn't wearing one, but that could be to put her at ease. Suddenly everything seemed like a plot to entrap her.

"I've used one a time or two."

"Good. We've got a stop to make first."

"Why?"

"Damn lady, what're you thinking that's got your hackles up? People around here don't tolerate Michael Roenell's kind. Men like him have been known to disappear, never to be seen again, so whatever you're thinking, stop thinking it. All I want is for you to see *why* Michael Roenell turned out the way he did, to understand there's a reason."

"I don't give a goddamn why he hurt my family."

"I don't blame you," Denton said, pulling into a narrow gravel driveway that led to a tiny frame house. "But we're here now, you might as well take a look."

"We're where?"

"Michael Roenell's mother's house."

The yard had tufts of weeds growing between patches of muddy-brown soil. In places, the siding had fallen off, revealing soggy insulation that oozed out of the holes in tangled strands of pink. A faded blue tarp covered most of the roof. Stacked cinder blocks acted as front porch steps. Still wary, Colton followed Denton to the front door, noting a white sheet over one of the front windows being pulled back, and then released. Denton pounded on the door with his fist, rattling the frame.

"Beulah, open up, it's the Sheriff."

"Unless you arrested that slut what killed my boy, you get out of here, Dennis Denton. You hear me? I got no call to open the door for you, and you ain't got no other business here."

"You're right, Beulah, I can't make you open the door. This is a courtesy call to let you know we're digging Michael up, in case you visit the gravesite. We'll be going now."

Denton didn't bother turning away. Seconds later, a deadbolt shifted with a metallic *clunk* and the door swung open. Backdropped by a dark interior was the face of a woman in a shapeless robe, who could have been 90 or 100 years old. Dirty gray hair stuck up like straws from a scalp riddled with sores. More lesions covered the left side of her face. All of her front teeth were gone, with only a few others remaining in either jaw. She squinted against the morning sunshine, further deepening the ruts cut into her cheeks.

"You cain't dig my boy up without my permission," she said in a voice that sounded like a screech, even at low volume. "You cain't do it, Dennis Denton. Sheriff or no Sheriff, you cain't do it. I know my rights. I know my boy's rights, too, 'cept that don't matter without a law man who respects the law. Michael was a good boy, and you're letting that slut who murdered him get off Scott free." Leaning against the door, Beulah Roenell's pointed her jaw at Colton. "Who's this, your newest whore?"

"She's from—"

"My name's Colton," she said, pushing past him to face the woman. "Your 'good boy' murdered my sister and her little girl, and I drove here to put a bullet in his brain. I'm only sorry somebody else did it first. Your son was a coward and a pedophile, and now I see where he got like that. Why don't you do us all a favor and shove a pitchfork up your ass?"

With that she stalked away, heading back to the SUV, glad that Denton hadn't let her bring a weapon.

"Did you hear that, Sheriff? She threatened me! Do your duty and arrest this piece of shit bitch, right now."

"Arrest her for what, Beulah? Telling the truth?"

Wheeling, he followed Colton back to the SUV. With gas too scarce to use the air conditioner, Denton had the windows down as they turned around in the yard. Dust plumes drifted through the front seat. Colton heard the old woman screaming after them.

"Don't you touch my boy, you hear me Sheriff? You got no right! He's a good boy, you leave him alone, hear me, leave him alone!"

Neither of them spoke. There was no need. Colton had seen plenty of long-term meth addicts in her life, she knew its effects, how it ate away at brain and soul until there was nothing left. As they drove, she stared straight ahead, hands clasped around one knee, until Denton began to slow down at a cemetery.

"Don't," she said.

"Don't? I thought you wanted to see his body."

"It's not important now."

"You don't want to see for yourself that he's dead?"

Colton shook her head. "No, not anymore. It's not important now. He was never really alive anyway. Take me back to my car. Please."

Once back at the convenience store, she turned to him and forced a smile. "Thanks for your help, Sheriff."

"What happened to Dennis?"

"I thought you didn't like that."

"I said that I didn't give you permission to call me Dennis, I never said I didn't like it."

That brought a tiny smile. "Then thank you, Dennis, I appreciate your help."

"It's not an excuse for what he did, you know. A lot of people grow up with terrible parents and turn out just fine. Michael Roenell had it rough, sure, after his daddy left; his mama used to bring her tricks over to the house, but that didn't give him license to turn bad. Evil doesn't excuse evil."

"No, I know. It's just that, I've got this hole in my soul, and I thought killing Roenell might fill it. I've spent most of the last week thinking about what I would do when I got my hands on him, how I'd find a lonely corn field up in Kansas or Iowa and... well, somehow I thought there would be satisfaction in watching him scream, beg for mercy. Now I'll never know."

"It wouldn't have. It never does."

"You know that for a fact, do you?"

He paused. "Maybe."

For half a minute she bit her thumbnail, staring at a point on the dashboard.

"Did I tell you that he's been taunting me? All the way from Minnesota, non-stop, sitting in the passenger seat, grinning that evil grin... telling me details about what he did to my sister and niece, like he was doing it all over again, *enjoying* it all over again. Do you believe in ghosts, Dennis?"

"You mean, do I think Roenell's ghost was haunting you? No, Dani, I don't. I've seen some weird stuff in my time, sure, but Roenell is dead. What you saw was just a figment of your imagination. I'm betting that now you know he's dead, that stuff will stop."

"I'm sure you're right. Once again, Dennis, thank you."

"What are you going to do now? Go back home to Minnesota? That car looks like it's been to Hell and back, and I'm guessing it wasn't like that when you left."

"It was a rough trip."

"Stay here," he blurted. "At least for a few days. You'll be safe, and it'll give you time to think about things."

"I don't know anybody in Texas. Where would I stay? What would I do?"

"Stay here, I'll find you a room, maybe with Carol. She was out at the roadblock. As for what you could do... hell, at the rate I've got deputies quitting, you could work for me. Bad times are coming, Dani, very bad times, times like we've never seen. They've been coming for years now, but I don't think we're going to pull out of this. Stay here, give it a few days. Callahan County might grow on you."

"Just Callahan County?" she asked, with a faint upturn at one corner of her mouth.

"Maybe one of the elected officials too. You never can tell. Royce had some homemade sausage and biscuits; I told him to save some for us. Why don't we eat and talk about it?"

"Real food? Count me in."

"For staying?"

"Maybe," she said, staring out the windshield. She waited for Michael Roenell to appear and mock her, but he didn't have anything left to say. "Everybody's gotta be somewhere."

* * *

Colton had never been inside a double-wide trailer before, much less slept in one, but, when Carol offered her couch for the night, Colton didn't hesitate to accept. Typically one to stay up late, she drifted off around nine p.m., waking for the first time when Carol's Spaniel-mix, Dolly, licked her hand around midnight. The second time, her wind-up alarm clock read 3:41 a.m., and she was not alone. No more than three inches from the top of her head, Michael Roenell sat cross-legged on the couch smoking a cigarette.

"Hello Sleepyhead," he said. "Miss me?"

Lying on her back, she stared up as he blew a smoke ring into her face. Hallucination or not, she choked on the acrid tobacco smell.

"You're not real," she said. "You only in my mind."

Even in the darkened room she could see his features clearly. "You wound me," Roenell said, pouting, "deeply, deeply wound me, Dani. And here I thought we were friends. I *was* your niece's first lover, you know."

"You're dead, Roenell; you're not real."

"Your sister's dead too, which gives us all of eternity to play together."

"Go away, dead man."

"I'll never go away, girlfriend. Never. I'll be with you always, like a forever marriage. I hope you don't mind if there are others, your sister for one. She's stalking me."

The cackle that followed seemed practiced for maximum irritation. Colton sat up and threw off the blanket Carol had given her. Standing, she crossed the room looking for her jeans, clad only in sports bra and panties.

"Not bad for those who like 'em old, but I'll bet you were hot back in the day," Roenell said, "twenty-five, maybe thirty years ago."

She didn't respond, concentrating instead of getting dressed. Roenell kept talking as she tied her shoes, jabbing and prodding, but Colton had mind up her mind how to get rid of him, once and for always. Knocking on Carol's bedroom door, Colton stuck her head inside and called out softly.

"What, what?" Carol said, waking instantly with a cop's reflexes.

"Dani? What's the matter?"

"I need directions to the Sheriff's house."

"Now? It's three-thirty in the morning."

"I know, I'm sorry, but yeah, now."

Then Carol's tone changed. "Oh, it's like that."

I've gotten you all hot, haven't I? Roenell said.

"Huh?" Dani said, realizing what Carol meant without Roenell's help. "No! Not like that, it's… I need him to show me where Michael Roenell is buried."

"Can't it wait until morning?"

Roenell stood next to her, still smoking, but his smile had faded some.

"No, it can't wait," Colton said.

Carol clicked on the bedside lamp and drew a crude map. Cross Plains was a small town and Denton only lived a few minutes away.

"You want me to go with you?" Carol said.

"Thanks, go back to sleep. I'll find it."

"Be careful."

"Tell that to anybody who gets in my way."

Roenell sat in the passenger seat on the drive across town, his knee bouncing up and down as he chain-smoked. *It's so cute you think this will work.* The grin came back, only it seemed forced.

"Yes, it will," she said out loud.

Like small town Sheriffs the world over, a pre-dawn knock on his front door brought Dennis Denton within seconds. The porch light switched on, followed by an eye at the peep hole, then the door opened.

"Dani, what's wrong?"

"I'm sorry to bother you Dennis, but I need you to show me Michael Roenell's grave."

Rather than say 'how' or 'why,' Denton only nodded. "Wait here." Ducking back inside, he was back in less than two minutes in full uniform. "You didn't bring any coffee, did you?"

"No, sorry. Do you still have those shovels in the back of your car?"

"Yeah…"

"Good," Colton said, "you drive then."

"Where are we going?"

"To dig up Michael Roenell."

What are you doing? Roenell shouted in her ear as she waited for Denton to return. He laughed. *Do you think you can get rid of me that easy? Not happening girlie, not happening, it's you and me forever.*

Roenell kept talking after Denton came back, brought the car around and drove them to the site. Sitting in the backseat, his words came faster and his voice became shrill as the Sheriff turned off of a paved road, and onto a dirt one. With dawn barely a hint on the horizon, the SUV's headlights cut the darkness through a flat, featureless landscape. Finally, he turned into a field that was remarkable only for the closed horse-gate blocking its gravel driveway. Getting out, Denton opened a padlock and unwound a chain. Once through, he parked near the entrance.

Stupid, stupid, stupid bitch, this is a fucking waste of time. You're like all the rest, a total nothing burger. I don't know what you're hoping to accomplish, but I can't wait to say I told you so.

His patter never stopped. Colton ignored him.

"This is our Potter's field," Denton said. "Callahan County buries those who can't afford a burial, or were criminals, unknowns, you get it."

"I do, yeah. Let's get digging."

Using flashlights, Denton led them to a spot of recently disturbed soil with no headstone or official marker. Somebody had nailed two pieces of plywood into the shape of a cross, and written Roenell's name in black marker, but, otherwise, the grave was anonymous. It took less than half an hour to find the corpse. Instead of being six feet down in a coffin, Roenell's grave wasn't more than three feet deep, and had been tossed into the hole like a rotting deer carcass.

See what they did to me? he yelled from behind Colton. *These people are inhumane; they're un-Christian. They ought to be the ones locked up, they've the criminals, they're—*

Denton shined his flashlight across Roenell's body. "That what you wanted to see?"

"Yes," Colton said.

Worms and ants crawled over the bloated remains. Roenell's face and hands were a dark red, and the reek of decomposition was strong.

"Are you done?" Denton said, covering his mouth with a cloth. "Seen what you needed to see?"

"Not yet," she answered, not even noticing the smell. Instead, she was fixated on the dead face, the same one she'd seen since that day in court, only twisted in death.

Live fast, die young, and leave a good-looking corpse, Roenell said, the grin back on his face. *You can't say I didn't accomplish all three.*

Colton stood at the far end of the open pit. Along with holding her flashlight, she drew the big Glock from its holster on her belt. Denton hadn't seen it earlier but didn't said nothing as she aimed at the body.

Hey, what are you doing? That's not going to—

"This is for Jane and Cally," she said.

Crack!

The Glock recoiled up and slightly back as the first shot echoed over the field, startling a flock of birds. The big forty-caliber slug exploded Roenell's forehead like a pumpkin. Adjusting her grip, Colton fired five more times, slowly, carefully, making certain of putting her bullets into anything not yet destroyed. Brains and bones shards flew up and out, as if the bullets shattered eggs instead of human flesh. Taking a moment to glance up, she saw Michael Roenell with a stricken look on his face, a man who knew with certainty that he would never again walk the Earth. Then she put one last round into what remained of his skull.

Panting, she looked around. Roenell was gone. Holstering the Glock, Colton grabbed the shovel and began refilling the grave.

"You done?" Denton said.

"Yeah," Colton said, still breathless. "I'm done."

"Get what you came for?"

Using the back of her hand, Colton wiped hair away from her face.

"I don't know. I'm not sure I'll ever know, but I think I got what I needed. Thanks for helping, Dennis."

"Anytime."

"You think Royce has any sausage and biscuits?"

"Only one way I know to find out."

* * * * *

William Alan Webb Bio

A successful DNA splice in early 1955 led to Bill's birth later that year, which led his mother to trying an old Greek and Roman custom she'd read about: exposure. When the neighbor called the cops, she quickly brought him back inside and raised him to be a fine, upstanding young man, well-educated, polite, and ambitious. That it didn't work was not her fault.

After using his high school years to best advantage by playing chess and reading X-Men, chiefly during Spanish class, college found him searching for the right major. Entering the University of Tennessee at Knoxville, Forestry came first among the fields of study, until he discovered that science courses had a lot of negative requirements, like work, so, by a process of elimination he wound up majoring in Creative Writing. Then his parents gave him some sage advice, "You can flunk out closer to home for a lot less money." Thus began his career at the University of Memphis. The rest is history, messy, complicated history, with marriage, kids, jobs, and stuff like that, but history, nonetheless.

He still likes X-Men.

# # # # #

The Bounty Hunter's Creed
by Rachel Aukes

A Bounty Hunter Origins Story

"Which one's the boss?" Joe Ballast asked a man tossing bits of steel into a bin.

The worker in greasy coveralls pointed to a thin fellow with thinning white hair who was working on a machine at the far end of the building.

"Thanks." Joe walked through the metal reclamation plant, the clanging of metals ringing in his ears.

The man noticed Joe approach and asked, "What do you want?"

Joe tucked his hands into his pockets. "I'm here for the job, sir."

"Which one?"

"Any of them."

The owner of the metal reclamation plant looked Joe up and down. Joe noticed the slight scowl. Something set off the owner.

"I'm a hard worker," Joe said in a rush. "I'll always get the job done, no matter how long it takes."

The owner narrowed his eyes. "You got the look of a soldier about you. What side did you fight on in the Revolution?"

Talk about a loaded question. If Joe told him he'd fought with the rebels, this guy was definitely a Zenith State supporter. If Joe told him he'd fought for the government, then this guy was, without a doubt, patriot. The trick was Joe had fought on *both* sides.

"I'm here for a job. You can count on me for getting the job done and not causing you any headache," Joe answered.

The owner's eyes narrowed even more before he shook his head.

"Sorry, I don't have no openings."

"Your sign outside says otherwise," Joe said.

"I forgot to take it down."

"Please, sir. I've got a wife and kid to feed," Joe begged. It was true, even if Sara and Little Nick weren't *his* wife and kid.

"No openings." The owner went back to his work.

Joe waited a full minute without the owner looking up once, before Joe said finally, "Okay. Well, thank you for your time."

He trudged back through the plant and to his cutter. The metal reclamation plant had been his fourth stop of the day. Joe had stayed in the Revolution too long. All the good jobs had been taken by the time he'd returned to Cavil, not that any of the jobs had been very good to begin with. The war had been hard on an economy that was in the toilet before the first shots were fired. After the war, things were even worse.

He'd try again tomorrow and the day after that until he found a gig that paid. He had to. While Sara had managed to get by while her husband, Nick, was fighting alongside Joe, she was struggling to find food. Back during the war, Joe had promised Nick that he'd look after his buddy's family should the worst happen, and sure enough, the worst had happened. After the war, Joe had returned to Cavil, bringing with him only a dog tag and a *Dear Sara* letter to give to a young widow and her son who'd never meet his father.

Joe started to drive toward Sara's house to check in on her, but instead parked at a pub. Sara didn't need to see him in his current mood. He headed inside and took a seat at the bar.

The place was busy—at least a dozen other (likely) unemployed patrons sat around drinking. A few of them looked rough—the sort that thrived on picking fights—and Joe was careful not to give his back to them.

"What'll ya have?" the bartender asked. She was young, with the voice of a lifelong smoker.

"A glass of whatever beer you got on tap," Joe replied.

"That'd be our home brew." She went about pouring him a glass of what promised to be some of the worst-tasting beer he'd ever tasted by the looks of the greenish-brown liquid pouring from the tap.

He slid a coin across the bar when she set the glass down. He took a drink and winced. He was right. That beer was some of the worst he'd ever tasted, but he drank it anyway. Neither side paid for his time in the war, so that made his funds more than a little tight. He wasn't going to let a beer he paid for go to waste, even if it tasted like donkey piss.

As he went to take another drink, a man burst through the door. He had wild eyes and had a rougher look to him than most Joe had seen. The man scanned the bar in a rush and then ran for the bar. Joe didn't carry a gun anymore, so he discreetly pulled out a knife and held it on his lap.

The man was just reaching the bar when a bounty hunter entered the bar, though this guy didn't seem to be in much of a hurry. It was obvious this newcomer was a bounty hunter because he wore an exoshield—as all professional hunters did—and he held a blaster in his hand. The exoshield was full body armor, covering the hunter from head to toe, and the blaster was something the MRC had outlawed for everyone except for those with special authorization. This hunter had been around the block: his exoshield's green paint was chipped and worn off in places. On his chest plate read the callsign, *T-REX.*

"Arnie, Arnie, Arnie," the hunter tutted. "Why'd you have to go and try to run? You know I hate running after you guys."

The man called Arnie had made it behind the bar and now held a switchblade to the bartender's throat. "Go screw yourself, hunter," he said.

"Don't make me shoot her to get to you, Arnie," T-Rex said. "Because if you make me do that, I promise you, I'm going to kill you, and it's going to hurt you a whole lot more than it'll hurt me."

Arnie's eyes seemed to grow wilder as he furtively looked for a way out. Seeing none, he jerked the bartender closer. "One more step, and she's dead."

The bartender sucked in a breath, and a trickle of blood ran down her throat.

The bounty hunter tsked and started to raise his gun higher. Even without seeing the hunter's expression, Joe knew T-Rex was going to shoot the woman to get to his target. Still in his seat, Joe drew back his knife and threw it. The blade hit Arnie's hand that held his knife. He yelped, dropping his own blade. The bartender leapt away the split-second before the bounty hunter shot his target dead-center in the chest.

Arnie bore a look of surprise, then he collapsed to the floor.

T-Rex approached the body and fired a second shot at near point-blank range through the man's skull. Then he raised his armlet computer wrapped around his left forearm and snapped a picture. He bent, pulled out the knife, stood, and held it out for Joe. "Thanks for the help, partner," T-Rex said.

Joe took the knife and wiped the blade on a bar towel within his reach. "I wasn't helping you. I was helping her."

"Help's help. The why's don't matter." He leaned onto the bar to get closer. "Ya know, I think everyone in here pissed themselves except you. You have the kind of look that a person who's seen their share of trouble and then had fun mud-wrestling that trouble. Tell ya what... the agency I work for just went through a change in management, and we're trying to rebuild. We could use another hunter. The money's the best you'll find for honest work in these parts. What d'ya say, partner?"

"Thanks for the offer, friend, but I'm done with violence."

The hunter looked down at the body and then back at Joe. "I'd disagree. But I ain't gonna try to convince you. I'd rather save my breath for breathing if you get my meaning." He pulled out a business card and slid it across the bar. "In case you change your mind."

With that, the bounty hunter departed.

The bartender scowled, holding a towel to her neck, as she took tentative steps toward the bar. "At least he could've taken out the garbage." She kicked the dead man.

Joe shrugged. "I'll drag it out of here for you, for ten credits."

"Five."

"Deal."

* * *

Five credits wasn't enough to buy meat, but it was enough to buy two loaves of bread and bones for broth. He drove into Far Town, which was the seediest, poorest side of Cavil, and parked behind a dirt-colored, dome-shaped house that looked identical to every other dome in that row. Each dome held only the entrances and small sitting rooms to enjoy the one cool hour of the day just before sunrise. Humans had spent centuries living in underground silos due to the intolerable surface conditions. The surface still wasn't pleasant, but it was at least survivable—if you didn't count the deadly radioactive storms that randomly passed through the Midlands.

He jogged inside, carrying the food, and took the stairs down to the main living area where he found Sara and Little Nick on the floor, building things with little colored blocks. They glanced up as soon as they heard him.

The two-year-old beamed and ran to greet him. "Ja Joe!"

Joe picked up the toddler and held out the sack to Sara. "It's not much, but it'll cover us for tonight and into tomorrow."

She examined the contents. "These bones look fresh. I'll get them on the stove right away. Have you eaten?"

"I had something on the way." He set Little Nick down.

Her brow rose. "Beer?"

"Something." His stomach growled then, betraying him.

WANTED, DEAD OR ALIVE | 289

"You need to eat. I think you've lost ten pounds since coming here. No one's going to hire a skeleton. Speaking of which, how'd the job hunt go?"

"I've got a few leads that I'll run down tomorrow," he replied.

He took a seat on the worn couch. The neighbors assumed Joe had taken over Nick's family, but it wasn't like that at all. Sara was gorgeous, sure, but things had never been more than platonic between them. It didn't help that Joe could see Nick in Little Nick's eyes.

An hour later, they ate the bread.

The next morning, they had bone broth and stale bread.

The next night, they went hungry.

Joe sat on the couch as Sara tucked Little Nick in. As he sat there, he kept flipping a business card in his fingers. Hope was a stubborn idea that if a guy did the right thing, everything would turn out. But things didn't work that way, at least not in Joe's experience. Before he could change his mind, he called the number on the card.

* * *

When T-Rex said the Haft Agency was looking to add hunters to its payroll, Joe had expected it to be more than one hunter and the owner, Reuben Tally. It had the infrastructure for something bigger with a heavily secured office in the back of Harry Haft's Bar.

The owner, on the other hand, didn't inspire as much confidence. Reuben was scrawny for being twenty-one and fidgeted constantly. He was the exact opposite of what Joe thought a bounty hunter should look like. Reuben sat across from Joe and T-Rex at his desk. Behind him was another metal door, likely to a basement, and the agency's logo—a single fist—in faded paint on the wall.

"See? I knew you had the look of a hunter about you," T-Rex said.

Or the look of desperation, Joe thought, but didn't voice the words.

Reuben was looking at a computer screen rather than at the two men before him. "Let's see. Your profile's got some gaps, Mr. Ballast. Looks like you fought for the MRC in the Revolution. It says you were on the Raven squad. What's that?"

"That means our boy here was an assassin," T-Rex answered for Joe. With his helmet off, he was no less intimidating with his shaved head and hard eyes.

"The Ravens were spec ops, *not* assassins," Joe clarified.

"Tomato, tomahto," T-Rex said.

"The MRC listed you as going AWOL and cut from their payroll near the end of the Revolution. Everything's blank until you showed up in Cavil last month," Reuben said.

"I moved around a bit. Did some odd jobs here and there," Joe said.

T-Rex chortled. "Odd jobs. That's a nice way of putting it. I heard the Ravens switched teams and joined with the *new* rebels once the MRC showed they were no different from Zenith State. Ain't that so?"

"You seem to hear a lot," Joe said.

"Keeping my ears open is how I stay alive."

Reuben leaned forward, focusing on Joe then. "Listen, I don't have any problems with what you did or whose side you fought on. What I care about is if you've got what it takes to be a bounty hunter. This job's not for the faint of heart. Some of the targets you go after are the worst of the worst. And the public ain't fond of hunters, either. You gotta have eyes on the back of your head to make sure you don't get stabbed in the back. With what you'll see out there, an exoshield isn't a nice to have. It's a downright necessity to have full body armor. Now, I offer the same payment plan that any agency would. I can get you an exoshield and deduct from your payouts in return to having you sign on for a ten-year stint with the agency."

"I still have my exoshield from the war," Joe said. He could've sold it to be scrapped, but he hadn't been able to part with it yet.

"You do? I'm surprised the MRC didn't put out a warrant to get it back," Reuben said.

"I guess they thought I'd earned it." The MRC had let all the Ravens keep their exoshields, likely because they didn't want to send anyone to retrieve the body armor.

"Well, it works out good for you. No payment plan. Though, I'd still like you to sign on for a tenure contract. That's standard for any agency."

"I don't sign contracts," Joe said.

Reuben frowned. "But then what's keeping you from bringing in the bounty and taking the full payout for yourself?"

"My word."

"What?"

"I give you my word that any job you give me will be delivered through you," Joe said.

T-Rex chuckled. "I learned by the age of four that people can't be taken at their word."

"Then you haven't been around the right crowd," Joe said. "Besides, I know better than to bite the hand that's feedin' me."

Reuben thought for a length, then pulled out an armlet and slid it across the desk. "All right. Let's try you out. I'll send the details on the job to you. Go home and get your armor—"

"I have it in my cutter," Joe said.

"Good. All right. Grab it and I'll get you authorized for a blaster. Rex will go with you on your first ticket to help you get the hang of it," Reuben said. "He'll make sure you don't get yourself killed out there."

Joe gave a simple nod, made his way to his cutter, and put on his exoshield. Each exoshield was customized to its owner's body. Joe had added patches to his armor during the Revolution and the two short wars that followed for improved protection against blasters and knives. His helmet was simple, with eye slots that had night vision capabilities, hearing enhancement ear cuffs, and a breathing mask. There was housing for darts on his forearm, but he'd long since run out of his inventory. Everything on his exoshield was functional except for the three crimson stripes painted on his helmet and the crimson cape he wore. Those items represented who he was and where he'd come from: three stripes for three wars, and the cape was the tattered banner every Raven carried.

His chest plate read *HAVOC*.

Rex approached him then. "Well, look at you. You look like you could pass as a bona fide bounty hunter. Now, let's go tag ourselves a baddie."

* * *

The pair of hunters made their way deep into Far Town. As Rex drove, Joe read the details on their target. "I don't get it. This guy doesn't sound any worse than anybody scraping to get by in Far Town."

"He's a baddie. Otherwise, he wouldn't have a bounty on his head," Rex said.

"His crime is listed as assault, first offense, but we're supposed to bring him to the labor camp. That's a bit harsh, don't you think?" Joe asked.

"He's a baddie. They're all baddies. If you think otherwise, you won't last long as a bounty hunter."

"Even if they're innocent?"

Rex chuckled as he pulled up and parked at brothel with a sign that read *Madame Bovary's*. "There ain't no innocents in this world, Josey. Listen, this guy probably stole from the wrong person— probably stole from the nephew of a local MRC administrator or something like that. That would've upped his crime from petty larceny to getting a bounty on his head and getting tagged for the labor camp. It ain't fair, but that's the way of the world, and we ain't changing it. So you can either go hungry trying to buck the system, or you can make some bucks off how the system works. What'll it be? Buck or bucks?"

Joe ignored the comment, and the pair exited the cutter and entered the hotel. Plush velvet couches sat around the wide-open space, and a large spiral stairway in the center of everything led below ground to where Joe surmised were the brothel's rooms. With how the girls waved at Rex, he'd been there a time or twenty. He was surprised to see how busy it was for that time of day, though he supposed sex made for a pleasant distraction at any time of day.

A woman came strolling over—the madame with how the girls deferred to her. She was older than most of the girls, with strands of gray in her dark hair. But she was easily as beautiful, if not more so, than any of the other working women there.

She approached Rex and kissed both his cheeks, even though he was wearing a helmet. "Rex, dear, please tell me you're here to introduce your new friend and that you're not here to cause trouble with the clientele."

"Business before pleasure, unfortunately, my darlin' Layni," Rex said.

She wrinkled her nose. "Well, I hope who you're looking for isn't here."

"Oh, I'd bet a week's worth of tickets that he's here. According to the camera feeds, he's been here every day this week from eight until nine AM. He works the late shift and comes here to wind down," he said.

"What's his name?" she asked.

"Gregor Kaminsky," Joe replied.

She wrinkled her nose. "Oh, Gregor. He needs to learn that baths aren't the devil's work. Well, in any case, you'll find him in room 3A. Please be careful to not hurt Veronica."

"I'd never hurt one of your girls," Rex said, and then motioned for Joe to accompany him.

They descended the stairs. The brothel looked like any other hotel except that there were scantily clad women out and about. One woman who squeezed between them wore nothing above her waist.

"Excuse me, Rex," she said with a sly grin.

"Any time, Mona. Any time."

When they reached room 3A, Rex pulled out his blaster, and Joe did the same.

"It's not a knockout ticket, so don't kill him," Rex said.

"Knockout?"

"K-O. Kill Order. We only get paid if we bring him in alive."

"Then we'd better bring them in alive."

"And that means relatively uninjured. We get docked for injures that can hinder their productivity at the labor camp."

"*Relatively* uninjured?"

"Yeah, you know. It's all relative."

Joe paused. "Wait. Since you're with me, are we splitting this bounty?"

"Of course. Sixty-forty."

"You mean, I get sixty, you get forty, right?" Joe asked.

Rex slapped Joe's shoulder. "You're a funny guy. I like you."

Rex went to knock on the door, but movement to their left caused them to both turn. Strolling out of one of the floor's communal toilets was Gregor Kaminsky, who was smiling and chatting with another fellow. Both looked like the ass-end of bad luck.

"Hey, you, ugly," Rex called out. "No, not you. The other ugly. Yeah, you."

Gregor's eyes went wide.

"Don't do it!" Rex yelled.

Gregor did it. He spun on his heel and took off running.

"Damn it, I *hate* it when they run," Rex said. "You chase him down, will ya?"

"Fifty-fifty," Joe said.

"What? Oh, fine. Fifty-fifty. Now you'd better get going, Josey, before he gets too much head start on ya." Rex reached out for the nearest prostitute. "I'm just going to hang out here for a bit."

Joe sprinted through the hallway, dodging prostitutes and their patrons. The man who'd been chatting with Gregor stuck out his leg to trip Joe, but Joe saw the movement. Without slowing down, Joe hurdled while simultaneously punching the man.

Gregor yanked open a door and disappeared beyond the other side. Joe considered firing for a second until the door slammed closed. He ran as fast as he could to catch up, but he was well over ten meters behind.

Joe grabbed the door and jerked it open, exposing his head for only a split-second as he scanned the stairway for Gregor, finding him two levels below.

"Stop, Gregor. Don't make me shoot you," Joe called out.

The man didn't slow.

Rather than running down the steps, Joe slid down the railing, shaving seconds off each flight, as they descended underground. They were reaching the public walkways and trains, and Joe ran a fair chance at losing Gregor in the crowd if he made it out of the stairwell.

Gregor had his hand on the door handle when Joe slid down the last flight and slammed into his target. Gregor fell in a heap and wheezed to suck in air.

"Gregor Kaminsky, I've got a warrant for your arrest," Joe said.

Gregor waved weakly with one hand while the other was wrapped around his chest. "Pl-please. I was framed."

"A magistrate reviewed your case already and assigned a guilty verdict. Sorry, buddy, but you're coming with me."

"I was framed! I bumped into an MRC officer by accident. That's all. I didn't mean to. You know how bad those trains jolt. It was busy, and I got pushed into him. I didn't attack nobody."

"You can ask for a second review."

"You know the magistrates always side with the murcs. *Please*, mister. My family will starve without me. I got three kids with another on the way. I'm all they got."

Joe considered what Sara and Little Nick would have to do without him chipping in. The economy was in the crapper before the Revolution. After the Revolution, things were ten times worse. Joe needed the money, but he knew what Gregor's future held if Joe brought him in. No one ever left the labor camp after they were sent there. No one.

Joe had survived this long by going with his gut. He'd find another way to get money.

"Keep your head down and stay out of the brothel," Joe said.

Gregor's face brightened. "Really?"

"Go. Before I change my mind."

Gregor's feet slipped on the floor as he scrambled to stand, but within seconds, he was on his feet and through the door to the public walkway.

Joe waited for the door to close completely before he made his way back to Rex, who was, surprisingly, still waiting in the hallway rather than having absconded to a room. Though, he'd removed his helmet and was kissing a woman who wasn't the one who'd been with Rex when Joe left him the first time.

Rex pushed her away when Joe approached. "Where's Kaminsky?"

"He got away."

Rex scowled, then did a three-sixty, kicking the wall while cursing. When he turned to face Joe, he pulled on his helmet. "Well, there goes our paycheck, not to mention a big fat black mark against Haft. Maybe I overestimated you."

"Maybe you did."

* * *

Joe spent the rest of the day cleaning Sara's place. It was after dark when he settled onto the couch and turned on the TV to watch the news when Sara returned, carrying a sleeping Little Nick in her arms.

"How was your day?" she asked.

"Same old, same old," he replied.

"I need to tuck him in. Then you can tell me about it." She carried the toddler into his bedroom.

He turned back to the news. What he saw made him lean closer, bracing his elbows on his knees.

There, on the news, was none other than Gregor Kaminsky, caught on video, as he stabbed to death a local MRC captain less than three hours ago.

Joe glared. "Son of a bitch."

* * *

The following morning, Joe was back in front of Reuben. "Give me another chance. I'll bring Gregor Kaminsky."

Reuben shook his head. "Too late. Rex clipped that ticket nearly an hour ago. The bounty went up once it became a knockout ticket, so it worked out for us. I mean, it worked out for the me and Rex. It didn't work out so well for you, obviously."

Obviously.

"Then give me another ticket. I'll see it done."

Reuben scrutinized him for a length and then held up a finger. "I have something you can work." He tapped on his computer, and Joe's armlet chimed. "I just sent the ticket and all known details on this guy: Marcus Alder. He's had a ticket out on him for over a month now. Wanted for murder. He's as bad and as tough as they come. He's already killed two hunters."

"I'll take it."

"It's a knockout ticket, which means he doesn't need to come in with a heartbeat. But if you kill him, I need proof of death. Think you can stomach it?"

"I can manage."

"All right. You take him out, and you've got a job at Haft Agency, but you're going to have to sign a contract."

Joe clenched his jaw and nodded.

"And you're going in alone. Rex isn't going to be there to cover your back this time. You can take another weapon or two, but you've got to do this on your own."

Joe nodded. "I'll be back once it's finished."

* * *

It took Joe three days to track down his target. Marcus Alder was sneaky about staying off the grid, but he had a vice: gambling. On the first day, Joe had covered every casino in Cavil. The second day, he'd covered all the surrounding holes in the walls. The third day, he started hitting places within a fifty-mile radius of Cavil, and he found Alder in a gritty casino in an even grittier trading post called, appropriately enough, Smith's Trading Post.

Joe strolled into the casino, not expecting to find Alder—he'd strolled through twenty-six casinos before that one—so he was surprised to find his target sitting at a table near the bar, facing the door. Marcus Alder noticed Joe as he entered but then glanced away too quickly while the other patrons threw hearty glares his way.

"Damn bounty hunters," someone muttered to Joe's right.

"My pops always told me to keep skunks, lawyers, and bounty hunters at a fair distance. They all stink something fierce," someone else said, accompanied by several chuckles.

Joe ignored them and instead kept his focus on Alder while continually scanning for any additional trouble. Joe casually pulled out both his blasters as he made his way to the poker table. He stopped when he was a bare four feet from Alder.

"Can't you see we're in the middle of a hand, hunter?" Alder said.

"I hear that a pair of blasters beat a pair of aces," Joe said. "Marcus Alder, I've got a ticket for your arrest."

Alder tossed his cards on the table. "Aw, and I had a good game going, too."

He then looked Joe up and down. "There are some folks out there who wouldn't take kindly to a hunter wearing their crimson banner to try and intimidate folks. That's what they call stolen valor, my friend."

Joe raised the blaster in his dominant hand to be better aimed at Alder while the other blaster he kept leveled at the bar area, where the men seemed the most angsty. "It's not stolen valor in this case, and I'm not your friend. Now, you're coming with me. Whether you walk out on your own or are carried out is up to you."

Alder nodded toward Joe's weapon. "You should be careful where you point those. It might be illegal for us regular folks to carry blasters nowadays, but I can promise you there are still a few around."

As soon as Alder said it, a blaster shot deflected off Joe's back. He spun around, but whoever had fired the shot was hiding his blaster, and no one was looking in the culprit's direction. Movement sounded just as Alder plowed through Joe, knocking him off his feet. Joe jumped up, grabbed his weapons, holstering one, and took off after Alder, who was disappearing through the door by the bar. Joe fired, but the shot hit the closing door instead.

Joe took off after him. He shoved the swinging door open and sprinted through. He'd expected Alder to keep running. He hadn't expected Alder to stop and spring a booby trap, which all came to a startling reality when Joe found himself ensnared in a net, hanging a few feet above the floor.

The net was slowly rotating around, and Joe, crammed tight, tried to poke his blaster through the netting to aim it at Alder, only to hear the clink of a blaster pressed against his helmet.

"Nuh-uh," came Alder's voice. "I wouldn't do that if I were you. This spark shooter may not pack much of a punch, but it doesn't have to at this distance. It'll cut right through your skull and fry up your brain like an egg. If you don't drop your blaster—*both* of your blasters—in the next second, you'll find out what it feels like to have your brain fried."

Joe dropped the blaster in his hand, then cautiously unholstered his other blaster and dropped it. He still had three knives tucked away, and he planned to use them the first chance he got.

Alder kept his blaster leveled on Joe as he nodded to someone behind Joe, who reached in and pulled off Joe's helmet. Alder smiled as he pulled the blaster away, only to raise a canister in his other hand.

Joe tried to kick away. "No, don't—"

Alder sprayed the bitter contents directly in Joe's face.

Joe didn't remember anything after that.

* * *

Joe came awake to find himself in a rather precarious predicament. He was out of his exoshield, wearing nothing but his underwear, hands tied behind his back, and hanging upside down from a chain wrapped painfully tight around his ankles. Blood pounded in his head, making the headache from the sedative spray even worse.

He took in the room, which looked to be a storeroom.

"You've reached the end of your rope, my friend," Alder said from behind him.

Joe tried to turn to see the other man walk into view, holding Joe's blaster. "When that's the case, I tie a knot and hold on tight," Joe said wryly despite the pounding headache and his awkward position.

"You do, huh? Well then, you've only got to hold on for a little longer. I've got a nice shallow grave all picked out for you outside. I just have to wait for the sun to set. Some things don't need to be seen by bystanders; don't you agree? What's wrong? Cat got your tongue when you know I'm about to do what you were going to do to me?"

"I wasn't planning on killing you," Joe replied.

"If you don't kill me, I guarantee the MRC will finish the job once you deliver me." He took a casual lap around Joe. "We're more alike than you know. I also fought for the MRC. And, like your Ravens, I switched to fight against the MRC when they started beating down the very people they'd promised to help."

"That was then. We helped some and failed others. The MRC won. There isn't much either of us can do about it now," Joe said.

"You're wrong. We can keep fighting," Alder said.

"This isn't war, not anymore. Any killing you do now is a crime."

"What the MRC is doing is the real crime. They're starving the innocents and stockpiling the food to be given to only the select few."

"And you think you can bring down the MRC all on your own?" Joe asked.

"Not on my own, no. But that doesn't mean I can't try."

"And then you'll keep getting bounty hunters coming after you."

Alder scowled. "I have a strong dislike for bounty hunters. They keep trying to kill me."

"I don't like bounty hunters either."

"Then why are you a hunter?"

"Turns out, I don't seem to be a fit for anything else. A man's gotta make a living, and there's not a lot of jobs out there for men like us."

"You don't have to kill for a living," Alder said.

"I'm not the one talking about killing someone today. In case you haven't noticed, I'm the victim here," Joe said.

Alder belted out a laugh. "You're no victim. You're just muscle for the murcs."

"I don't work for the MRC, and I won't ever work for them again."

"Who do you think assigns all those tickets you chase down? The only reason bounty hunters exist is to take care of anyone causing trouble for the MRC."

"So you didn't murder someone in cold blood?"

"I killed a murc, all right, but it wasn't in cold blood. He had it coming. You've seen them. Those murcs take whatever they want from whoever they want. The people need someone to help them," Alder said.

"Be still my heart. I'm in the room with Robin Hood himself," Joe quipped.

"Joke as much as you want. It doesn't change the fact that you're helping the wrong side."

"I'm just doing a job for a paycheck," Joe said, then winced. "Can you at least set me right side up? Hanging upside down is hell on my head."

"Don't worry. You won't be hanging there much longer. The sun's about to set."

* * *

The moment the door closed behind Marcus Alder, Joe rushed into motion. Having his hands tied behind him was a challenge. If they'd been tied in front, he'd have himself out of his restraints in a few seconds flat. Instead, as Joe crunched his head to his feet, he had to shimmy to get his fingers around the chain. Relieving the pressure on his head provided immediate relief, and he allowed himself a quick breather as soon as he grabbed onto the chain holding his ankles.

It was an awkward grip, with his hands restrained behind him, but he was still in good shape, despite it being a month since returning to Cavil. He adjusted his grip to give a little slack between the chain and his ankles before he wiggled to squeeze his butt and hips through his arms. Some guys were born with long arms—Joe wished he was one of them. Instead, he had to squeeze through, bringing pain to his wrists. As soon as his hips were through, it was easy to get his hands in front of him.

He could now get a better grip on the chain and began tugging himself up it in earnest. As he did so, he jostled his feet to loosen the links wrapped tightly around his ankles. Link by link, the chain loosened. His feet, numbed by the chain, began tingling terribly when the blood flow returned. Another few links, and the chain was loose enough to slide his feet through.

Joe let himself fall to the floor, twisting in midair, to land on his feet. But his feet were still too numb, causing an excruciating jolt through his soles when he touched down. His ankles were still too weak, and they rolled, leaving Joe in a heap on the floor. He came up on his knees and searched the room for something to cut the rope, but the shelves were lined with basic pantry staples. Nothing sharp.

"Well, aren't you a spry fellow?" Joe jerked around to see Alder enter, with Joe's blaster leveled at Joe's head. "I thought I heard something back here. The other bounty hunters that came for me were drunken old fools who couldn't do a sit-up to save their life. Color me surprised. I guess there's still a hint of Raven in you."

"Put down that gun, and I'll show you," Joe challenged.

Alder grinned. "Tempting, but only a fool has to prove himself to anyone."

"Damn," Joe muttered to himself.

"To your feet. The sun's still setting, but it'll do. You know, you might be the first man I've ever met who's in a rush to meet his maker."

"I'm rather mindful of dying and certainly not in a hurry to do so," Joe said as he struggled to his feet. He swayed, but after a couple of seconds, he could stand relatively decent.

Alder motioned to the back door with the blaster. "After you, my friend."

Joe sighed as he wobbled his way toward the door. "I told you…" Joe feigned falling and grabbed a shelf for support. "You're not my friend." He grabbed a bag of flour and swung it around at the same time he tried to dive out of the blaster's line of fire. He mostly succeeded.

Alder fired just before the flour hit him in the face, bursting into a cloud of white powder. An icy burn went through Joe's left shoulder. He'd been shot a number of times in his life. It never became easier. He tried to ignore the stab of agony that was rapidly spreading out from the cauterized wound and launched an attack at Alder, who was firing randomly while trying to wipe flour from his eyes.

Joe grabbed Alder's hand that held the blaster as he tackled the man. They tumbled, with Alder landing hard on his back and thumping his head on the hard floor, causing him to loosen his grip on the blaster. Joe's wrists were bound, his feet were still weak, and he'd been shot, but he was a Raven. He'd been trained in hand-to-hand combat more than the average soldier. He compartmentalized the pain, focusing purely on his opponent. Joe swatted the blaster away and head butted the other man.

Alder was both taller and bigger, which was often a detriment when wrestling. Joe twisted around Alder, using his bound wrists to his advantage by sliding them over Alder's head to choke him. Joe poured his strength into choking Alder. The larger man swung out, connecting two solid blows against Joe's temples. But Joe held on, fighting through the tunnel vision and through the writhing man. Alder passed out faster than Joe expected. He continued choking the man for several more seconds to make sure Alder wasn't feigning before relaxing his grip.

Joe checked Alder's pulse and frowned. Marcus Alder was dead. He must've had a bad ticker because Joe had choked him only long enough to knock him unconscious. Joe pushed away from the body and retrieved his blaster. The pair had made plenty of noise, so he was more than a little surprised that no one had come to check on things. Evidently, Alder didn't have friends helping him here.

Joe found his exoshield and other weapons stuffed in a potato sack in the corner, where he cut his restraints and hastily redressed, all the while keeping the blaster in easy reach to take out anyone who came through either door.

Once he was fully dressed, he checked Alder's pulse again for good measure. He was disappointed that Alder was dead, but he also didn't feel guilty as that man had been about to kill Joe.

He used his armlet to take a picture of Alder and submitted it to Reuben. He glanced at Alder one final time before turning and heading out the back of Smith's Trading Post.

* * *

Rex patted Joe's sore shoulder, bringing out a grunt of pain. "I'm kinda glad to see you lived, Josey. Things are too quiet around here with just me and the kid."

"Just *kinda* glad?"

"Don't get cocky. You made me put in extra time to close that Kaminsky ticket." With that, Rex winked at Joe and then walked over to a side table and poured himself a drink.

Joe turned back to Reuben, who was still busily tapping at his computer. "Just about done, Joe. Takes a few seconds for the funds to transfer... and there." He tapped a key. "You're all set. Check your armlet. You should have the payout in your account."

Joe accessed the screen on his armlet. Since he wore that computer on his left forearm, he was careful to not move his injured arm as he opened his banking account. What had fewer than ten credits left in it yesterday now displayed five thousand credits.

He must've shown his surprised because Reuben said, "Nice, isn't it? The knockout tickets pay better."

That money would decently feed Sara and Little Nick for months. Plus, Joe could finally get his own place and quit squatting at Sara's.

"I say, all's well that ends with a paycheck," Rex said before taking a drink of an amber liquid.

"The money's nice, but if I'm going to work for you, I need one thing from you," Joe said.

Reuben's brows shot up. "What's that?"

"I get to review any ticket before I accept it. I gotta believe they're at least somewhat guilty if I'm going to go after them."

"You don't think Alder was guilty?" Reuben asked.

"Oh, he was guilty, all right. He was the worst kind of guilty. He thought he was being heroic in killing. There's never anything heroic in killing," Joe replied. "I just want to lay my cards on the table. I'll be a bounty hunter, all right, but I also need to be able to look myself in the mirror."

"Aw, that's cute. We got ourselves a Goldilocks," Rex said. "Only wants tickets that are just right."

Joe ignored him and instead stayed focused on Reuben. "Is that good for you?"

Reuben shrugged. "Sure. Whatever you gotta do to make it feel right. Any tickets I give to you, I'll give you whatever I've got on 'em."

Joe gave a nod, then held out a hand. "You've got yourself another bounty hunter."

Reuben smiled and shook his hand. "Welcome to the Haft Agency."

Joe found himself smiling. He had a job, and it was a job he could live with.

Rex downed his drink and set the glass down. "Give it time. A year, three, ten. You won't want to read the tickets and instead will just want to close them. Trust me."

"We'll see."

* * * * *

Rachel Aukes Bio

Rachel Aukes is the bestselling author of over thirty books, including 100 Days in Deadland, which made Suspense Magazine's Best of the Year list. She is also a Wattpad Star, her stories having over seven million reads. When not writing, Rachel can be found flying old airplanes with an incredibly spoiled dog over the Midwest United States.

# # # # #

Open Ended Contracts by Josh Hayes

A Weaponized Universe Story

L ucas Hawkins recognized the woman almost immediately, but, for the life of him, couldn't place where from. She didn't strike him as the underworld type, but, then again, neither was he, and he actually looked the part. She moved like someone who knew she was being followed, but it was more than a little obvious she wasn't a pro. She kept glancing over her shoulder, head and eyes sweeping the crowd.

"I'm up here," he whispered to himself.

The holographic optical overlay floating in his vision listed all the relevant account information, and, despite Verona Hackl's normal, mundane appearance, the premium was one of the highest he'd seen in a few months. Especially around these parts. The account holder was listed as Prodigy Transtellar Systems, a shipping conglomerate out of the Gustavas System, six light years away. She'd stolen classified corporate documents to sell on the black market, and Prodigy desperately wanted to prevent that. But why did she look so familiar? He initiated a scan program and left it running in the background; if there was anything else to find, his i3's AI would track it down.

Hawkins adjusted his stance at the building's edge, his cybernetic legs clinking against the metal roof. Six stories below, Hackl continued to make her way through the crowd. She seemed to be on a mission, maybe on her way to meet her buyer, and, if that was the case, that meant that Hawkins needed to move quickly if he was going to fulfill the contract as written.

He scanned the street ahead of her, zooming in with his cybernetically enhanced eye, working through all the faces he could see, trying to identify anyone else of interest. Each face was filtered through his internal database of known facilitators and cross-referenced with any known contacts to the R and D world.

Corporate espionage and theft weren't all that uncommon, and, while some of those cases were indeed picked up by law enforcement, more often than not those agencies were too busy to fully man their corporate crimes divisions. Thus, a fair majority of said cases were farmed out to private security companies, and, when very special attention was needed, they were handed over to the Commission for... clearance.

And that's where Hawkins came in.

With a thought, a map appeared in his optics, which he manipulated, turning the three-dimensional image around to get a better view of the area. Nonsong's old-town district was laid out in a basic grid pattern, filled with unremarkable buildings common to most backwater worlds like Sayoko Prime. Holographic signs hovered in the air above doorways, neon lights pulsed and flashed, bots floated aimless through the sea of humanity, announcing special events and splashing "exclusive" deals on the optics of everyone that passed by.

The street—out in the open—wasn't the best place to make the snatch, but sometimes it was the only option. The work he did bordered on illegal, but with the Commission supported by the majority of big-name corporations—and, by extension, most of the bureaucrats and politicians—the work was more or less sanctioned. Among other things, it paid his bills, and, for the most part, he only brought in commissions that were legit. He'd never taken a kill order.

Up until recently, he'd been working by himself; although, working with Jevin was pretty much the same thing. He was a decent pilot, but, other than that, the man was pretty much worthless, and that meant most of the commissions Hawkins took on needed to be handled with a fair bit of finesse. So far, it had worked out in his favor, and he'd managed to stay under everyone's radar, Commission included. There were dozens, if not hundreds, of hunters who lived in the spotlight, men like Berkay Langrial—the Duke—who managed a flotilla of mercenaries and rarely went anywhere without drawing a lot of attention. Of course, when he didn't want to be found, he was a ghost.

Hawkins pinned an alley three blocks away that appeared to lead to one of the many parking garages in the district, then turned his attention back to Hackl. She'd stopped and was talking with someone at a street-side bar, still making furtive glances over her shoulder, still obviously afraid she was being followed.

"Found a friend, huh?" Hawkins whispered to himself.

His optics drew an orange outline around the man's face, enhanced it, and immediately started running it. The man's demeanor and hand movements suggested he was attempting to calm Hackl, but she didn't seem to be buying it. A new panel appeared in his optics displaying the man's pertinent information: Joel Summerer, freighter pilot, freelancer. A handful of run-ins with law enforcement, no convictions. Relatively clear, given the local color.

"Looking for a ride out of here?"

A panel on his cybernetic thigh opened. He plucked two microbots from their housings, tapped them awake, then tossed them into the air. They spiraled around each other as they swooped down toward the street before pulling up and zipping over the heads of the oblivious crowd. They two tiny machines weren't anything unusual, just two more in a sea of hundreds. Absolutely nothing special about them at all.

"*... no, you're wrong.*" Hackl as saying, her words growing louder as the bots closed in to orbit over her and the man. As much as she tried, there was no way to cover her thick German accent.

"*I'm telling you; you don't want to do this. I can't be involved any more, I just can't. I'm sorry.*"

"*You promised me, damn it.*"

"*I know, and I'm sorry. I just can't... I can't do it.*"

"*You son of a bitch, I came a long way for this. Do you have any idea what they're doing?*"

"*Yes, and you can't say I didn't warn you. Look, I know what you're going through, but I've got a family. I can't risk pissing these people off. Not out here.*"

"Go against the Commission at your own risk," Hawkins said. The registry didn't have any open contracts on Summerer, but he was obviously opposed to do anything that might get his name added to the list. "No love lost among the wicked."

"*You're a real son of a bitch, you know that?*" Hackl said.

"*Hey, I'm sorry.*"

"*Yeah, sure you are. You all will be.*"

Summerer reached out to stop Hackl as she turned away, and she shrugged him off, slipping away from the bar and into the flow of people. The pilot hesitated for a moment, appearing almost like he was going to chase her down, then shook his and looked away.

Hawkins was just about to recall the bots when Summerer's i3 flashed, sending a burst transmission that Hawkins' i3 traced to one of the local nodes. The bot's upgraded sensor suites were definitely not standard make, and Hawkins had been more than a little surprised when his supplier had offered them up. Never one to look a gift horse in the mouth, he'd taken them along with several other toys. Out here, you could never be too careful.

The flash traffic message reached the local node where it was scrambled and forwarded through the network. He could've gone further into the node's server but didn't want to risk anyone seeing him snooping around. It was unlikely anyone would even be looking, but out here you didn't take anything for granted. There were only a few people Summerer could've been reaching out to anyway, and none of them were good for business.

* * *

Hawkins ran along the row of prefabricated buildings, all of them in the process of falling to pieces after years of misuse and neglect. Thick power cables dropped from steel pylons and brackets attached to the edges of the taller structures. Water pipes and air conditioning ducts snaked over and around buildings, flanked by metal walkways that provided access for techs to inspect and make repairs, though, it didn't appear as though anyone had bothered to do any kind of work there in years.

Small heel thrusters launched him over a wide gap between buildings, his i3—intrinsic internal integrator—calculating optimal flight angles, landing positions, and possible structural issues. He landed lightly on his cybernetic feet and continued across the roof, ducking cables and hopping over conduits. His implants and prosthetics gave him superhuman speed, agility, and balance. The i3 wasn't quite AI level, like some of the super computers that ran the League's warships, but it was damn close.

He didn't slow as he passed Hackl, wanting to get enough space between them to plan out his next move. The snatch was always the more difficult part of any contract. That and the extraction, but he had that covered.

With a thought, his i3 connected him to Jevin. The pilot's voice came through his cochlear implant anxious as ever. *"You got her?"*

"Not yet, but I'm close. Where are you?"

"Ten klicks out, circling an old, abandoned warehouse district. They really have let this place go to shit."

"This place has always been shit," Hawkins said. "I'll let you know when I have her."

"You got it."

Hawkins dropped down two levels, landing on an external structural support that spanned the alley between two of the taller buildings. It creaked slightly under his weight, and dust puffed up from several places, but it held. A handful of vagrants and druggies mingled in the shadows below, but otherwise, the alley was dark and quiet; a perfect place for a snatch.

He slipped the shockbolt from a pocket and tapped the activator. The palm-sized inhibitor came to life, glowing blue, instantly connecting to his i3 and displaying active status on his optics. Technology had done wonders for humanity over the centuries, but with every advancement, someone inevitably found a way to turn it against the masses. Almost every person in the galaxy had an i3 implant; granted, some were more advanced than others, but they all basically did the same thing. The relative AIs had become essential parts of society, but they'd also exposed their users to more than a few security issues.

Hackl looked over her shoulder again as she approached the alley, seemingly focused more on who or what was behind her, rather than possible threats in front of her. She completely missed the microbot hovering ten meters above her. Well, she wasn't a seasoned operator; that was obvious, which left Hawkins to wonder how she'd managed to steal such high-level documents.

Almost as if in answer to his question, his i3 beeped and a new panel appeared at the edge of his optics. The search program he'd all but forgotten about had found something, and Hawkins was more than a little surprised at the results. Hackl's face looked back at him from the panel, but someone else's name appeared underneath, along with a long list of accolades, employment history, and awards. The recognition he'd felt when he'd first seen her coming back to him now as he shook his head, not quite believing what he was seeing.

"You've got to be kidding me," Hawkins muttered to himself.

Verona Hackl was actually *Estelle Wernicke*, an investigative reporter for the Galactic Times Interstellar, one of the biggest news organizations in the League. Or, at least, she had been until a few days ago. According to the file, she'd been terminated for insubordination. None of this information had been available on the open net, of course; GTI kept a tight lid on its employment records. Luckily for Hawkins, he had access to more than one secured databank.

On a hunch, Hawkins checked the origination date on the contract. He didn't know whether he should be surprised, or not, that the date coincided exactly with her termination from GTI.

"So, how did a nice little girl like you get a Black Card?" Hawkins asked aloud, turning his attention back to the woman he now knew as Wernicke.

Black cards fell along the same lines as kill orders for Hawkins, shady, usually on the other side of the line he was willing to cross. They paid extremely well to ensure the contractors kept their silence and the issuers kept their anonymity. There were no records, save for the actual contract, which, once it was fulfilled, would be wiped from the database, along with any trace of the principle or the contractor who'd worked it. Some in Hawkins' line of work wouldn't have had any problems with it, but, for Hawkins, there were some things he just wasn't prepared to do.

In his optics, Wernicke froze, her attention focused on someone in the crowd ahead. The river of people broke around her, some oblivious, others irritated she was inhibiting the normal flow of traffic. Hawkins followed her gaze to a small group of men standing ten meters in front of her. An alert panel opened, and Hawkins muttered a curse as the face of Nicolai Jonker appeared, complete with his intricate, multi-colored nantoos running from just above his right eye to the left side of his neck. Jonker's Commission ID and name glowed underneath his image.

This is who Summerer had sent his encrypted message to, and it meant that this contract had just become a lot more interesting.

* * *

The Commission, as a rule, didn't have anything resembling a rank structure, but there was a definite hierarchy, with men like Berkay Langrial at the top. Langrial hadn't actually operated for years, at least, not on contracts like this, preferring to send his underlings out to haul in the big prizes, underlings like Nicolai Jonker. Hawkins' heart pounded in his chest, and he considered the multiple directions this thing could go. Before he'd landed on a course of action, Wernicke made he decision for him. She took off at a full run away from Jonker and his men.

Her abrupt move sent several people sprawling to the ground, eliciting several angry shouts and more than a few curses from the surrounding crowd as they struggled to get out of the way. Where Hawkins preferred to operate strategically, Jonker and his men favored brute force tactics. They shouted for Hackl/Wernicke to stop as they shoved their way through the crowd.

Hawkins launched himself up three stories to the adjacent roof, landing at a full sprint, deftly navigating each the buildings' exostructure. His i3 mapped out his route ahead of him, identifying obstacles as he ran, allowing him to traverse the roof without slowing to figure out the most effective route to take.

The bots zipped through the air above Wernicke, effortlessly tracking her through the sea of humanity. She was pushing her way through groups who were just now becoming aware that something was wrong. She knocked a woman to the ground, then tripped over the kid she'd had in tow. The people around her spread apart as Wernicke picked herself up and took a moment to get her bearings.

* * *

Estelle Wernicke cursed as she picked herself up, pausing briefly to check on the kid, then quickly glanced over her shoulder, looking for her pursuers. She didn't know who they were, but she had no doubt as to what they wanted.

The balding man with glowing face nantoos was gaining. The fury in his face turned her stomach.

"I'm sorry," she muttered before pushing through onlookers. "Move! Please!"

Panic pumped through her veins as she frantically searched for a way out of this place. Several side streets led away from the main concourse, but if whoever was behind her had managed to track her here, she had no doubt they'd be able to follow her down any alley she chose. But she'd been careful, she'd paid attention, she hadn't told anyone where she was going, not even her handlers at GTI; there wasn't any way anyone could know where she was.

Except for that pilot, Summerer, but he was part of GTI's network. He'd come highly recommended; he'd been vetted. He couldn't have. But it was the only thing that made sense. She's known the backstabbing was going to come, she just hadn't realized it was going to happen this quickly. She should've expected it, however, with this much power and money involved; it was no wonder two of her colleagues had gone missing trying to cover the story. And soon to be three if she couldn't get away.

Her lungs burned as she made her way through the concourse, doing her best to weave through the people without knocking any more over. She caught sight of an alley to her right and abruptly veered toward it, almost losing her balance in the process. A couple shouted in surprise as she cut them off, cursing her for a druggie.

The alley was considerably narrower than the main road behind her but contained fewer travelers, giving her room to run full out, something she hadn't done since college. She hadn't been the best athlete on campus, not by a long chalk, but she'd put in the hours. Now, however, she wished she'd at least maintained that training, but her life had become filled with so much more now, it made time for anything else almost nonexistent.

Over her shoulder, she caught a glimpse of the nantooed man turning into the alley, his companions right on his heels. They were going to catch her; there wasn't anything she could do about it. She pulled the small, pulser from her jacket pocket and gripped it tight. It wouldn't stop all of them; hell, it might not stop any of them, but she had to try. She'd already invested too much of herself in this thing to stop now.

She turned left, into another smaller alley, and her heart sank. Twenty meters ahead, a ceramacrete wall blocked her path. She was trapped. She slowed to a stop at the end and turned to face her pursuers, bringing the pulser up in shaky hands.

The nantooed thug appeared around the corner, then skidded to a stop, his eyes locked on Wernicke's pulser. His three friends stopped just short of bumping into him, all of them winded on some level or another.

Wernicke's heart pounded in her chest, her lungs burned, and now her muscles were beginning to ache. She managed a weak, "Stay back!" and felt immediately silly for saying it. Nothing she said or did would convince these monsters to leave her alone and go back to wherever they came from.

"Put that damn thing down," the nantooed man said, the colorful fractal patterns on his face shifting as he spoke.

"Leave me alone!"

"Can't do that, Missy. You must've pissed off some pretty powerful people." Slowly, he reached behind his back.

"Stop!" Wernicke screamed. She tensed against the recoil and squeezed the trigger.

Nothing happened.

Rage melted to confusion as she glanced down at the weapon in her hands, trying to understand what had happened. In the split second her eyes were averted, however, the nantooed man produced his own pulser and leveled it Wernicke's face.

"Now, why don't you be a good girl and put that thing aw—"

A brilliant flash of light filled the dark alley, accompanied by an earsplitting bang. Reflexively, Wernicke dropped her pulser, her hands covering her eyes as she stumbled away from the explosion. Her ears rang and time slowed. She opened her eyes to a blurry, white haze. The world spun around her as her equilibrium struggled to right itself.

A dark shape appeared in front of her, and, as she registered a person standing there, something folded itself around her torso. She brought her hands up to resist, slapping at the figure, shouting at him to get away, her words sounding like she was underwater, the incessant ringing drowning everything else out.

There was a sudden jolt as she was lifted off the ground and into the air. Wind buffeted her as she and the figure rose out of the alley, dark shapes of the street and buildings around her slowly coming into focus as they gained altitude.

Someone was shouting over the din. She squeezed her eyes shut, trying to clear them, then opened them to a matte black and grey helmet coming into focus centimeters from her face. A digitized male voice was saying speaking, but she couldn't understand the words. She thought he said something about it being okay.

* * *

"It's going to be okay," Hawkins shouted, even though the woman was clearly disoriented and probably wasn't comprehending anything going on around her.

He adjusted course, the thrusters housed in his cybernetic legs pushing them both over downtown, east into one of the residential districts. Two panels opened on either thigh and six decoy drones launched from their racks, each shooting off in separate directions, spewing false signature codes meant to confuse any pursuer. Jonker was good, but Hawkins didn't think he was that good. In fact, he was counting on it.

Location icons appeared over the building he'd targeted minutes before. His i3 adjusted their flightpath automatically, bringing them in on a low arc, least-time course for the building's roof. The extra weight and reduced aerodynamics caused by Wernicke and the counter-grav harness he'd strapped to her forced him to keep his speed lower and angle gentler than he would've preferred, especially with Jonker more than likely on his trail.

The dazzler should've kept them out of commission for a few seconds, but they were also professionals—well, competent at least—and it wouldn't take them very long to figure out what had happened. They hadn't emerged from the alley yet, which probably meant they weren't sporting gravpacks, but Hawkins wasn't so much worried about being followed as being identified. He'd spent far too much time getting to where he was now, and part of him was kicking himself for making such a rash decision, but what else could he do?

Sixty seconds later, he touched down on the roof of a ten-story tenement, cut his thrusters and deactivated the gravharness. Blue light faded from the emitters attached to the harness as it detached and unfolded from Wernicke's body. She immediately backed away from him, confusion and fear plastered across her face.

"You all right?" Hawkins said, slipping the harness—now the size of his hand—back into his pack.

She opened her mouth to respond, but no words came out. She shook her head, eyes flicking over his shoulder, then back to him, questioning. "I don't… I don't understand."

"Well, like Jonker said, apparently you've pissed off some pretty powerful people."

"Jonker?"

"That ass back there with the big gun. The merc that was going to haul you in."

"Haul me… I don't understand."

"Lady, you've got one of the biggest Black Cards I've ever seen for someone that doesn't exist. Estelle Wernicke."

Surprise flashed across her face. "How…"

Hawkins smiled, then remembered his helmet was still covering his face. With a thought, the faceplate unlocked, then the entire unit began folding back into its storage position in a small compartment at the base of his neck.

"Let's just say, I've got connections. And, apparently, you do as well if you were able to set up such a convincing alias. I had to dig deep to find it."

"You shouldn't've been able to find it at all," Wernicke said, moving around him to look over the edge of the roof. "That ID has been buried for years."

"Yeah."

"You're not a merc."

It was a statement, not a question.

"What makes you say that?"

"No merc that I've ever known could've possibly accessed the databases needed to uncover my name."

"What, you think working for GTI makes you some kind of a spy?"

"I've been out here, doing this kind of work for two years. I've never been ID'd once."

Hawkins shrugged. "All it takes is once. Come on, we need to get off this roof."

He started for the building access door at the center of the roof, then hesitated when Wernicke didn't follow. He raised an eyebrow. "You'd rather those jackwagons back there catch up to you? I guarantee they've got plans for you, plans you won't like."

"And I'm just supposed to go with you? To trust you? I don't know anything about you. As far as I know, you're just another bounty hunter, looking to make a quick buck. And how the hell do you know my real name?"

"Don't know that you're in any kind of position to argue, but hey, feel free to take your chances." Hawkins accessed the building's security node, unlocked the door and stepped inside. He held the door and waited, until finally Wernicke reluctantly followed him in.

"So, what now?" She turned to face him as he shut the door behind them. "You going to 'haul me in' now?"

Hawkins looked at her for a moment, considering his next words carefully. "I guess that depends on whether or not you stole Prodigy's docs like the contract says you did."

"Prodigy? I've never even heard of Prodigy. And I definitely did not steal anything from them. I'm not a thief."

"Yeah, well, three-hundred thousand credits says otherwise."

"Three hundred thou—I don't understand."

"For being as deep as you are, you sure don't understand a lot." Hawkins started down the stairs. He opened the contract on his HUD and read, "You—well, Verona Hackl—have an open contract out right now for three hundred thousand, five hundred credits. Alive, if possible, dead if necessary. Fulfilled by Prodigy Transtellar out of Gustavas." He stopped at the landing and looked back at Wernicke who was still standing just inside the roof access door. "That's a lot of money to put up for nothing."

Wernicke frowned as she started down the stairs after Hawkins. "I told you, I'm not a thief. Whoever this Prodigy is, they're lying."

Hawkins chuckled. "You know, it's ironic how many people say that, but in your case, I'm inclined to believe you. What I'm really interested in is why someone would go to so much trouble to put out a Black Card on you. That shit doesn't just happen, especially at three-hundred K. If you didn't steal anything, you must have done something else to piss them off, and knowing who you actually are… Let me guess, you saw something you weren't supposed to see. Maybe took some pictures? What was it, some business exec sleeping with his mistress or something?"

"What do you care? You're just another merc, right? How do I know you're not working for them, playing some good cop routine to get me to talk?"

Hawkins laughed. "If I was another merc, I wouldn't be interested in anything you had to say. I'd be hauling you in as fast as I could for that cash."

"So," Wernicke said, "who are you?"

Before he could answer, Jevin's tag appeared on his optics, his voice coming through his i3. *"Hawk, what the hell is going on, man? The network just lit up like a damn Christmas tree!"*

"Just stand by where you're at, I'll call you."

"You'll call me?"

Hawkins killed the link. "Sorry about that, our ride's getting a bit anxious."

"Our?"

"That's right. Look, I can help you, but I really need to know why you've got such a big target on your back."

"Help me? You don't know anything about me. Why do you want to even *want* to help me? I don't know who you are."

He extended his hand. "Lucas Hawkins. Friends call me Hawk. I can't really say much more than that. But I can tell you, I don't work for the Commission, and I have pretty good connections. Depending on what kind of information you have in storage up there." He tapped his head.

"So, you want me to trust you, when you don't trust me enough to tell me anything about yourself? Doesn't sound very fair."

"Hey, life's not fair, is it?" She gave him a doubtful look. He started down the stairs again, and continued, "I can tell you I work for some pretty powerful people, much more powerful than the people after you. We make things happen all over the galaxy, and we're involved in more than a few interstellar operations that you, or anyone else for that matter, will never, ever, hear about."

She didn't respond right away but followed him anyway. After a few moments, she said, "You're a spy."

He smiled, but otherwise, didn't answer.

"You're a spy working as a merc?"

"You should really tell me what you know."

* * *

Wernicke sighed, but what other options did she have? She'd made a living convincing people to trust her, and she'd never once broken that trust. Sure, there were people after her, but hadn't there always been? That kind of thing was a mathematical certainty in her line of work. If she didn't have anyone pissed at her, she wasn't doing her job.

Only this time, it felt different. Maybe that's because it was. This wasn't some business exec stepping out on his wife or a priest abusing a parish member, if she was right—and there wasn't any chance she was wrong—this thing involved some of the most important people in the League, and that put her in a very dangerous position. Anyone, from the President to this man standing in front of her, could be involved, and that terrified her.

"Look, Estelle," Hawkins said, "I get it, the Commission is a scary bunch of bastards, but you can trust me. I'm on your side."

He'd known her real name, something not many outside a few select people at GTI knew. She'd had almost all traces of her real life scrubbed, effectively erasing Estelle Wernicke from existence to protect her family. No one had spoken her first name aloud to her since her mother had said goodbye almost seven years ago. The name sounded strange, felt wrong almost. Especially for someone to throw around so causally.

But if he had the resources to uncover her true identity, he was at least telling the truth about one thing; he wasn't an ordinary merc. If there were traces of her old self still lingering around somewhere, it would have to be an intelligence service that had them, but, spy or not, it didn't mean she could trust him. In fact, it put her more on the defensive than ever.

"You're a spy," she said, finally, "and you expect me to trust you? For all I know, you're in on this whole thing. Everyone else is."

"Hard to know if I'm in on it unless you tell me what *it* is," Hawkins said without turning around.

"Where are you going?"

"I would've thought that'd be obvious; away from those pricks back there." He jerked a thumb over his shoulder.

"Okay, but what then? You're not really a merc, so you're not going to turn me in?"

"Oh, I didn't say I wasn't a merc; I said I didn't work for the Commission."

"There's a difference?"

Hawkins laughed. "The Commission isn't the only game in town, sweetheart; they just happen to be the biggest."

"So why the hell should I trust you then? You're all alike. In it for the money and shit else."

Hawkins turned to face her again, a calm but serious expression on his face. He almost looked respectable, if not for the holstered weapons at his sides and bulky harness around his torso. He definitely looked the part, but there was something about him, something in the way he spoke and carried himself, that didn't quite ring true. She'd met hundreds of mercs in her time, and she'd learned to read them well; this one was hiding something, and that made her more than a little curious.

"Trust me, it's not all about the money. There are way more important things in life than money. I can't tell you want you want to know, but I can promise you that, out of everyone else in the galaxy you could've run into day, I'm the best chance you have of making it out of this thing alive. It's obvious the Commission desperately wants to get their hands on you, and that means you know something they don't want you to know—or anyone else for that matter—which also means you're valuable to me."

He was a spy; she had no doubt. No one else would be so ambiguous about who they worked for or what they did. Mercenaries couldn't wait to tell you what crew they were a part of, always looking to appear more important than they actually were. In a world where names meant everything, attaching yourself to the strongest made you somebody also. But this man was actively avoiding attaching himself to anyone, which said a lot more about him than he was sharing.

"Have you ever heard about the—"

A deafening explosion ripped through the stairwell's wall by the landing just below Hawkins, sending dust and debris spraying into the confined space. The stairs shook with the blast, forcing Wernick to grab the rail to keep from tumbling down on top of the Hawkins. A cloud of smoke rolled over them, and her entire world faded to darkness.

* * *

The i3 had his helmet up and sealed almost instantly. Almost. Hawkins could taste dust from the blast, the acrid odor of explosive fading as the helmet's filtration system went to work. His optics shifted to infrared as a trio of microbots flew from their housings, immediately blanketing the area in active scans and electronic countermeasures. Internal bladders injected adrenaline and neuromuscular stimulants into his bloodstream, heightening his already elevated awareness.

A figure painted in white, outlined in red, approached the breech on the far side. Multiple alert panels opened on the periphery of his optics, highlighting his cybernetic enhancements and the pulser he held in his hand. Hawkins had already been drawing his PH23 pulser when his alerts had gone off, and, as the barrel cleared leather he canted the weapon up, indexed from his hip and fired three quick shots. The green bolts of energy flashed in the dust cloud surrounding both men, and the man cried out before collapsing to the floor.

A second figure appeared on the other side of the breach and this man already had his weapon up. He fired the instant his companion hit the ground. Emerald flashes filled the tiny space, bolts of energy tearing through cermacrete and steel. Hawkins backed away, the rest of his armor folding into place as he did so. He continued to fire as he brought his weapon up to eye level, ensuring whoever was on the other end wouldn't easily come through.

"Get back!" Hawkins shouted, bumping into Wernicke on his way back up the stairs.

He plucked a dazzler from its housing inside his cybernetic thigh and tossed it through the hole. A timer appeared on his optics, counting down from five. The explosion lit up the hallway like a supernova and the sound shook the walls.

His optics outlined two more figures through the walls, both doubled over from the effects of the dazzler. The launcher pack on his shoulder opened and two microrockets shot from their tube. The three-inch explosive-tipped projectiles punched through the cermacrete and slammed into their targets on the far side, their warheads detonating on impact. The two successive explosions sent plumes of dust and debris through the opening below.

Hawkins turned and motioned up the stairs. "Go!"

Still obviously stunned by the sudden eruption of violence, Wernicke hesitated, then turned and started up the stairs, taking them two and a time. Hawkins could have shot up the height of the stairwell, avoiding the stairs completely, but that would've left Wernicke exposed. She'd gone up against the Commission, seemingly by herself, and that meant she wasn't scared of much, but no amount of courage would protect her now that the bullets were flying.

His i3 opened a channel to Jevin. "We could sure use that pick up now."

"We? The alert boards are going crazy, someone just detonated a bomb in one of the residential blocks."

"Rockets."

"What?"

"Those were rockets; it wasn't a bomb."

"Oh, very subtle; that's great. You know, shooting rockets at people doesn't exactly fall in line with keeping a low profile, Hawk. Isn't that what you said? Keep a low profile?"

"Just shut up and come pick us up."

"What the hell is going on?" Wernicke shouted from the landing above. She sat back against the wall, hands on her knees, trying to catch her breath.

"I guess Jonker wasn't too eager to let me walk away with his payday. Can't say that I blame him actually."

"Yeah, and what are we going to do about it now? Shoot it out in the street? The network's already buzzing with alarms."

His own alerts had been muted by his i3 so as not to distract while firing for his life. But a brief check of the local node confirmed Wernicke's assessment. Local law enforcement had been dispatched and were tracking to be on scene in less than five minutes. Not a bad response time, all things considered, though Nonsong's finest weren't exactly known for their discretion.

A contract update flashed, stopping Hawkins in his tracks. He read the message twice, then muttered a curse.

"What's wrong?"

"Jonker must have called it in," Hawkins said, stopping on the landing just below Wernicke and pulling out two dazzlers. His i3 connected to both simultaneously, activating their proximity sensors and adjusting their blast level. One he placed on the base of the wall, the other on the underside of the railing opposite. They'd likely see one, but he hoped at least one would slow them down.

Passing Wernicke and continuing up the stairs, he said, "Looks like your package just got updated from Gold to Platinum."

"I don't know what that means."

"It means you're worth a lot more dead than alive."

* * *

Wernicke frowned, understanding, but not following. The helmeted, armored merc above her stopped briefly at a door, then opened it as the locking panel flashed green. He was fast, and he was good, and so far he seemed to be looking out for her, but there was absolutely no way she trusted him.

She followed Hawkins into the hall, immediately twisting her nose up at the rancid smell. A handful of flickering light panels barely illuminated the corridor, revealing bags of trash, clothes, junk and at least one dead rat. Ten doors lined each side of the hall, three of which hung open; one was simply missing. And either no one had cared to investigate the commotion downstairs, or no one lived here to care; either way, it seemed good for them.

"Come on." Hawkins said, stepping over a pile of junk and waste.

"Can you not smell that?"

He tapped his helmet.

Wernicke hesitated, then slowly stepped over a bag of trash and the partially decomposing body of a dead rat.

"Ugh, that's disgusting," Wernicke said. "How do people live like this?"

"Hell, people have lived like this for centuries. Its what happens when people give up and are more focused on simply surviving than thriving. This is a good spot."

Hawkins knelt next to one of the open doors and pulled two dazzlers.

"A good spot? What do you mean?"

He tucked one of the small devices under a plastic bag, then set the other one just inside the door on the opposite side of the hall. Devices planted, he continued around down the hall to where it dog-legged left, into another corridor that held an twenty more doors and similar amounts of trash and junk.

"A little surprise for our friends back there. Come on, they'll have regrouped by now."

"I still don't understand what's going on," Wernicke asked, trying to keep up. "Who are you?"

"I told you, call me Hawk."

"That's what you said you friends call you, and I have to be honest, the jury's still out on you."

"That's fair," Hawkins said, stopping at the window at the end of the hall. He lifted the panel out of its track, cracking the glass and warping the metal frame. So, in addition to having a fairly advanced i3 suite, possessing armor she hadn't seen anyone but the military have, and access to highly classified databases, he had nano-enhancements as well. This man was no simple merc. He wasn't just a spy, either; he was something else entirely.

Despite herself, she couldn't help the investigative part of her brain mulling over the possibilities. The fact that he didn't want to tell her meant he wasn't just a low-level spook. Not to mention the millions of credits in enhancements and upgrades he possessed. She'd known people to spend fortunes on less than a quarter of what he seemed to be capable of. League Naval Intelligence or the Foreign Services Directorate were the obvious choices. Whatever *this* was, it seemed to be a little outside of the Navy's purview, and, although she'd never knowingly worked with, or been in contact with anyone from FSD, deep cover agents were definitely right up their alley. The only question, then, was why his interest in her?

When Hawkins stepped through the opening he'd created, onto the emergency escape landing outside without answering, Wernicke asked, "Okay, and? 'That's fair' doesn't explain much."

"I told you, I'm not a merc. Though, knowing your contract's worth half a million credits, I might be persuaded to consider a change in employment."

"Half a million... wait, why?"

"That's not obvious? Whatever you have rolling around in your head up there terrifies someone, and they don't want whatever it is getting out." He held his hand out to help her through. She ignored the offer and climbed through on her own.

The landing was cramped with both of them standing on it, and Wernicke was sure she heard the metal supports grown under their combined weight. Wind, city noises, and traffic wafted through the surrounding buildings, the wail of police sirens growing louder by the second.

"So, what now?"

"Now we jump."

Wernicke leaned over the rail to the ground seven stories below and shook her head. "You're insane."

"It's not that far."

"For you maybe."

The metal landing shook as a single explosion rocked the building. A plume of smoke erupted through the open door they'd come through at the far end of the hall, and dust fell from the ceiling. The dazzlers Hawkins had planted in the stairwell had gone off; Jonker and his men were still coming.

Again, the mysterious "not-merc" held out his hand. "I'll help you."

* * *

The local cops were just now arriving on scene, which meant landing anywhere near here was going to be more than a little difficult. The traffic control nodes were already sending out suspension and delay warnings. Even if they managed to outrun Jonker, a control tag from a traffic node could present major transit issues and of all the directives he'd been given, staying off the radar of any and all law enforcement agencies was one of the most imperative.

He could explain away a lot of his enhancements, and it was doubtful the local cops would have the tech necessary to detect his more advanced peripherals. If they called in System Security, though, *they* definitely could, and that Hawkins could not allow.

Hawkins pulled the gravharness from his pack and held it out for her. "Put this on. There's enough power left to get you to street level. I'm sending a route to you now. Follow it and stay out of the way."

"Are you insane?" Wernicke took the harness but didn't but it on. "The security nets have gone up all over the place."

"But the cops aren't looking for you, they're looking for me. Trust me."

Wernicke laughed. "You're fucking insane; you know that? I don't know you. I don't know who you work for. I don't trust you, and, for all I know, this is just another ploy to haul me in and cash out whatever contract is open on me."

Hawkins sighed but contained his frustration. He couldn't fault her; had their positions been reversed he might have felt exactly the same way. Unfortunately, there wasn't a whole lot of time to build that trust, and if they didn't move now, the risk of being caught by the cops, or worse, rose exponentially. There was only one thing he could do, and he didn't like.

He flashed her i3 and sent his Foreign Services Directorate credentials. Her eyes went wide as she read the information.

"I knew it."

"Yeah, well, that counts as a pretty heavy violation of my OPSEC. I hope what you have in there is worth it."

"It is."

"Put that on." Hawkins nodded to the gravharness. I'll take care of these assholes and find you."

"How?"

"Come on, now," Hawkins said with a grin. "I'm a spy. It's what I do."

* * *

Wind buffeted Wernicke as she descended from the emergency escape, the gravharness slowing her to a hasty glide instead of a deadly fall. She almost tripped when she landed but managed to catch herself and take off through the alley, away from Hawkins and the other mercs.

Flashing police strobes illuminated the darkness around her, making it difficult to identify the direction they were coming from, so she made her best guess and headed north. The map she was following was a few months old, but nothing about the core district had changed much in the intervening time. She was a block away when she heard the explosion and looked back over her shoulder to see flame, smoke, and debris spewing from the two of the seventh-floor windows.

Hawkins seemed confident enough that he'd be able to take on the mercs by himself without much difficulty, but she wasn't so sure. Even spies had their limits. And even if he could, how the hell was he going to catch back up with her?

She turned another corner, slipped past a group of curious people heading in the direction of the explosion, and fought the urge to break into a full sprint. She'd spent almost a decade working on some of the most high-profile stories GTI had ever released, and she'd thought her skills at blending in were better than most, but knowing that not only one merc, but two, had managed to track her, made her second guess everything she knew. That being the case, running away from an explosion and a gunfight would be sure to raise more than a few red flags.

Another cop car shot past overhead, its emergency siren wailing, lights flashing. She felt the warm downwash from the single multidirectional engine, and held her breath, mentally willing the vehicle to keep on course. When it didn't turn around, she let out a long sigh of relief and turned her attention back to the task of disappearing.

* * *

Hawkins muted the alarms going off on his helmet, his i3 automatically clearing the warning panels appearing over his optics. Energy bolts from a PL32 ripped through the plaster and prefabricated metal sheets behind him as he dove back into an abandoned apartment, smashing through a small pile of trash as he did so. He rolled to his knees as targeting programs locked onto the three figures advancing through the hallway outside and fired three microrockets from his shoulder launcher.

The ordnance tore through the same wall the bullets had, creating much bigger, fist-size holes, before exploding on the far side. Their 226-gram explosive cores rocked the building, blowing the weakened portions out of the way and filling the air with dust and debris. One of the three targets disappeared from his optics, the second registered critical injuries—he wouldn't be getting up anytime soon—the third, however, was already getting back to his feet.

A more detailed scan showed Jonker had managed to activate his body shield and armor a fraction of a second before the microrockets had detonated. Hawkins saw the merc as a glowing white figure painted on black and grey background, both men getting to their feet simultaneously and charging one another.

Jonker reached the wall first, crashing through and plowing into Hawkins. The impact knocked both men to the ground, scrambling to come out of the roll on top. Hawkins fired his leg and hand thrusters, propelling him into the air off Jonker. At the apex of his flight, he brought his foot up, connecting with Jonker's helmet just as the man was getting to his knees. The blow, combined with both men's momentum, sent Jonker flipping backward to land on his chest a moment later.

Hawkins landed with a knee in Jonker's back. The merc's helmet muffled his groan. Jonker reached back, trying to knock Hawkins' knee free, but didn't have the angle and his blow simply bounced off. Leveling his open palm at Jonker's head, Hawkins fired a single crippler, the carbon fiber wire mesh expanding to envelop his helmet. Blue energy flashed around Jonker's head, sending his body into a series of violent convulsions.

In addition to the painful current pulsing through him, the crippler also shut down his i3's advanced motor control functions and peripheral protocols, effectively taking the fight out of him.

Ten seconds later, the crippler automatically deactivated, but Jonker continued to twitch in the middle of the floor.

"And now, the hard part," Hawkins said aloud as ten additional target alerts appeared on his optics, the local cops had finally arrived.

Six were coming up the stairs he and Wernicke had come up only minutes before; the others came up the south wing's stairwell. Their plan was good—not great, but good. The bad part about the whole thing was, in addition to only taking semi-legit contracts, Hawkins refused to kill cops. Most were overworked and underpaid, and, more often than not, only wanted to do their jobs and make it back home to their families. Sure, some were dirty, and they probably could've used a little street justice, but identifying the bad from the good took much more in-depth study than he was prepared to do at the moment.

Two patrol flyers circled the building above, already spiking the network, looking to tag any and all users in the area. The explosion had likely triggered a response from the local special response teams, but they wouldn't be on scene for another ten minutes or so. He cancelled his connection to the network and activated his cloaking protocols, rendering him all but invisible to the police scanners.

He moved through the apartment's living area to one of the rear bedrooms, where an outside breeze blew the dirty curtain around on its bent rod, and pieces of loose trash fluttered around the room. Pushing the curtain aside, Hawkins looked through the open window at the courtyard seven stories below. Lights from the police units reflected off the twin tenement towers, and a single cop stood at the edge of the courtyard, his attention focused on the gathering crowd across the street, and not where it should've been. Hawkins slipped through the window, hung briefly outside, then dropped to the ground.

The ceramacrete sidewalk cracked under his weight, but his cybernetic legs and nanoenhanced, augmented muscular and skeletal systems absorbed the impact without needing to roll away. He crouched down behind an unkempt hedge, watching the lone patrolman lazily turn, obviously unsure if he'd even heard anything. The din of the crowd and wail of emergency sirens had partially masked his landing.

Hawkins waited for the cop to turn back around, then he kept low and made his way along the edge of the courtyard, taking care to stay in the shadows as he did so. The two L-shaped buildings made a square between them, leaving only two ways out of what had once been a well-manicured, relaxing common area. As he reached the far end of the courtyard, one of the police flyers appeared over the south tower, its spotlight panning across the open space.

"Shit," he muttered, quickening his pace. The light didn't worry him so much as the infrared and night vision scanners. The shout from the cop across the courtyard told Hawkins he'd been spotted.

The confines of the courtyard prevented him from kicking it up all the way to max speed, but even still, he cleared the remaining hedges, bits of junk, and waist-high decorative walls faster than any normal human could've hoped. The spotlight from the police flyer found him just as he reached the courtyard's northern entrance, a three-meter arch that connected the two buildings. Halfway through the short tunnel, Hawkins turned it on, increasing speed to well beyond anything resembling safe, focusing all his attention on his optics and the details provided by his i3.

At 88 kilometers per hour, one wrong move could end his trip really fast. What might have been a reasonable speed in a flyer, shuttle, or even ground car was more than a little dicey. Fortunately for him, his movements and heading were monitored and assisted by his i3, giving him inhuman reflexes and unparalleled situational awareness.

He reached the street, cybernetic feet pounding divots into the ceramacrete as he made the turn east without slowing down. Tracking markers filled his optics, identifying cars, people, and flyers in his path, projecting angles of travel, estimating possible destinations, and calculating the best possible travel path to avoid collisions and obstructions. He'd be a blur to everyone else, but he saw every single person around him with enhanced clarity, tagging faces and running them for possible threats. Hawkins couldn't remember the last time he'd pushed his capabilities to the limit like this, and, as he kicked off the roof of a parked aircab and his leg thrusters ignited, pushing him higher into the air, he couldn't remember the last time he'd exposed himself like this, either.

At ten meters, he kicked off a balcony, launching himself even higher, trajectory lines stretching out through the air in front of him. He couldn't fly, not really, but, with the right speed, angles, and space, he could definitely fake it.

A police flyer dipped in low between the buildings, flaring to come to a hover directly in his path. Demands to "Halt!" and "Stop running!" echoed out from the unit's external megaphone, and through the local nodes as well, making damn sure there'd be no confusion with the order. Hawkins understood it perfectly and ignored it.

In a move sure to piss somebody off, not least of all the pilot, he landed on the nose of the flyer, slightly denting the nanocarbon fuselage, and forcing it down a few centimeters before the pilot could counter. Five long strides later, he'd crossed the length of the flyer and kicked off the back end, igniting his thrusters again and flying even higher.

He landed on a roof at a full sprint, knowing full well the flyer was already halfway into its turn to pursue. He'd made it past the police perimeter, but reinforcements would be coming now, and in much greater numbers than he could deal with on his own. By now, half the force had been activated, and perhaps even System Security.

If he was going to make his move, it was going to have to be now or never.

Two panels on his armored shoulders opened, and a dozen four-centimeter balls shot from their housings, spreading out behind him in an ever-expanding grid. Network attack protocols lashed out, finding the surrounding nodes, then defeated and bypassed their internal security routines. A flood of nanocells, similar to the technology used in nantoos, spread out across each surface of his armor, covering every centimeter in less than a second.

Then, simultaneously, each system activated.

The combination of dazzlers and ECCM effectively blinded any sensor and scanner in the area. The local network crashed, the nodes overloaded with access connection requests and data dumps. The nanocells locked together, turning a matte black, absorbing light and rendering any remaining sensor null. As far as everyone around him was concerned, Lucas Hawkins vanished.

* * *

Nonsong's city-wide emergency band was inundated with dozens of police calls, BOLOs, and warning broadcasts, all focusing on a mysterious armored suspect who'd managed to avoid capture and disappear from the scene without a trace. Wernicke couldn't scroll through the reports fast enough. Fortunately for her, none of the reports mentioned a second suspect, only that the armored phantom had taken out a handful of mercenaries and damaged a police flyer.

The fact that he'd all but disappeared from existence intrigued her on a number of levels, not least of which was her reporter's brain, already putting together some of the pieces. An FSD operative

working as a mercenary, taking out other mercenaries, but also ful-
filling contracts? It all seemed a little outside the normal purview of
the Directorate. She'd done a number of stories on the League's secret intelligence agency but had never touched anything remotely
close to this.

There was always the possibility that he was involved in the Arena story, but if that'd been the case, wouldn't he have just let Jonker
and his men take her in instead of saving her? He'd known her true
identity, and he'd exposed himself to her by showing his credentials,
credentials she knew from long experience were extremely hard to
fake. All the signs pointed to him being a legitimate agent, but in the
world she'd recently dipped her toe into, she knew that didn't mean
he was one of the good guys.

Wernicke had spent a lifetime trusting no one, but, in his case,
she had the strangest feeling she should trust him, and she couldn't
explain why. He'd helped her escape, and, if the reports were accurate, he'd taken out Jonker and his men. If she was going to put her
trust in anyone, she couldn't think of a better candidate.

But if the cops couldn't find him, how the hell was she going to?

A shadow moved from a small alcove on the sidewalk ahead, and
Wernicke's defenses went into high gear. She was about to run when
she heard a familiar voice.

"Don't run," Hawkins said. "Just keep walking."

He fell into step next to her, his armor and helmet gone, presumably folded back into one of the many concealed compartments underneath his dark colored jacket.

"How did you...?"

"Piece of cake," Hawkins said. "I loaded a tracer program into your subnet when I flashed my credentials. Finding you after that was no problem at all."

Violated was the first thought Wernicke had, but that passed almost immediately, the logical part of her mind taking over and forcing her to remember if hadn't been for his actions, she might well be in captivity now, or worse.

The rumble of a small corvette descending from the night sky interrupted her thoughts. Its marker lights reflected off the glass exteriors of the surrounding buildings, and its engines kicked up a torrent of wind around them. Wernicke shielded her face as the ship touched down in front of them, a boarding ramp under its forward nose section already extending from the open bay.

Hawkins jerked a thumb at the ship. "That's our ride. I hope you're going to make it worth it."

"Worth it?"

Hawkins laughed. "Everything I just went through to keep your ass out of the fire. I'm pretty sure we're on the same side, otherwise I wouldn't have…"

"You would've let them take me?" she asked, following him up the ramp.

"Or just taken you in myself," Hawkins said. "But janking someone else's haul really isn't my style."

Wernicke thought she understood what he meant and didn't bother asking him to clarify. "So, you're a Directorate agent who moonlights as a merc?"

Hawkins winced as the ramp shut behind them. It was obvious he didn't want to talk about it, and he was more than a little uncomfortable anywhere near the topic. If he was telling the truth, though, he might be the closest thing to a friend she'd found in the last few years, and she decided as far deep in as she was, if she was going to trust anyone with what she knew, it might as well be this mysterious man.

She took a long breath, trying to calm her nerves, then said, "Have you ever heard of the Arena?"

Hawkins laughed. "You're kidding, right? It's a ghost story mercs tell their kids to keep them in line. 'Eat your dinner, or I'll send you to the Arena.' Shit like that. Trust me, I've been digging into the Commission for years. I've never found any evidence it exists. A few off-hand references at most, nothing solid."

"It's not a myth. I've got proof it exists, and I have proof of at least one high-level League diplomat who's associated with it."

Hawkins eyed her for a long moment. "That's why they're after you."

She nodded. "I didn't know about the contract, but it makes sense. I hit a nerve. It's imperative I get this information back to GTI. I didn't want to send it over the qcomm—too much of a chance someone would spike it, and I can't take that risk."

"No, you made the right decision," Hawkins said, looking relieved. "Let's have a look at it. If it's as good as I think it is, I'll get you to the right people. I promise."

"And my contract?"

He laughed again. "I've been looking for an in like this since I went under three years ago. Never figured I'd find it through a contract, but... Listen, you're about to open Pandora's box here; are you sure about this?"

Wernicke shrugged. "Not like I really have much of a choice, do I?"

"Then I'd say the contract out on you is more than a little open ended."

* * * * *

Josh Hayes Bio

A retired police officer, Josh Hayes is the author of the Valor Trilogy, *Stryker's War* (Galaxy's Edge), *The Terra Nova Chronicles* w/ Richard Fox, and *Tranquility* w/ Devon C Ford, along with numerous short stories. His debut solo novel, *Edge of Valor*, was nominated for the 2020 Dragon Award for Best Military Science Fiction or Fantasy Novel.

He grew up a military brat, affording him the opportunity to meet several different types of people, in multiple states and foreign countries. After graduating high school, he joined the United States Air Force and served for six years, before leaving military life to work in law enforcement. During his time with the Wichita Police Department, Josh served as a patrol officer, bicycle officer, community policing officer, and was an assistant bomb technician on the Bomb Squad.

His experiences in both his military life and police life have given him unique glimpses into the lives of people around him, and it shows through in the characters he creates. You can find his website at www.joshhayeswriter.com

Josh is also the creator and president of Keystroke Medium, a popular YouTube show and podcast focused on the craft of writing.

Website: www.keystrokemedium.com

YouTube: www.youtube.com/keystrokemedium

Josh is a co-host of the Baen Free Radio Podcast, the official podcast of Baen Books.

# # # # #

FRAkkers by
Tim C. Taylor

Nomadic Mining Settlement, Platov's Hell

The primary sun disappeared behind the Yellow Rift Mountains, its dying rays picking out the sulfur snow-caps and casting a brimstone halo where the ridgeline crossed the stratosphere.

The traveler halted, startled by the sight. He was new to this world.

Then the sunset lightshow was over, and the primary's setting revealed the deep ember glow of the secondary, the ultra-pulsating red dwarf that had been bathing the planet all along. In its revealed light, the smoothed metal structures of the nomadic mining settlement throbbed like a poisoned wound.

Platov's Hell was the name for this world in the astrocharts.

Now the traveler understood why.

Across the settlement, floodlights came on, swamping the red with blue-white. The man continued on his way through the packed-dust street, headed for the structure emanating a lightshow through its portholes and music through its half-sealed door. There was no written indication of the structure's role, but it was obvious. Despite his breathing mask, he fancied he could smell the desperation inside.

353

At the foot of the door, he checked to make sure his recording collar was active and flicked back his cloak so his pistol would be obvious. Then he ascended the climbing struts and pushed through the pressure curtains into the bar.

All eyes turned to the stranger. The background music became foreground as singing and conversations cut off. Cloaks and jackets were pushed back to ease access to holsters.

They knew what he was. Hated him for both of the vile characteristics they defined him by, their loathing more than doubling until it was ripe to burst.

To show how little he cared, the stranger removed his kepi with the extra-long brim and the leather backflap. The skin beneath was hairless, as it was with all Baleviews. In his case, his dark skin was cut through by a network of albino channels where his veins flowed close to the surface.

As mandated for all Baleviews by federal law, an hourglass was tattooed over his left eye.

He strode up to a card table and addressed a man flicking over a stack of twenty new yuan coins in one hand as he considered the cards in his other.

"Thomas Frezene Somoza?"

The cardplayer didn't look up from his hand. "Who wants to know?"

Some there laughed. Everyone understood why the Baleview was there. As for his name, they supposed he must have one, but nobody cared what it might be.

"Felon Recovery Agency." Despite knowing who had sent him, most there strained hard to hear his soft drawl. "This warrant here says you're coming with me. As some like to phrase it, you're FRAkked."

The cardplayer neatened the edges of his thick, black moustache before looking the Baleview in the eye. "Yeah, I'm Somoza. So what? You reckon you're gonna drag me out?" His supporters edged their hands toward their pistols.

"No." The Baleview gestured with his thumb at the door. "You're going to follow me outside, Somoza. We can settle this business on the street. You wouldn't want to force a shootout inside a pressurized unit, would you?"

The question fizzed in the air. On these frontier worlds, taboos about fire, oxygen wastage, and the sanctity of pressure seals were matters of life and death. Somoza thumped his hand on the table. "Kristos, watch my cards. I'll be back in a few minutes." He fixed his air mask and walked out of the bar, followed by the Baleview. Shortly behind them, four of his people came too. Others gathered at the doorway to watch the Baleview die.

The nomadic buildings had been arranged in a simple grid. The men assembled in the street outside, Somoza and the Baleview facing each other twenty paces apart. Somoza's four associates fanned out behind the outsider marked by the hourglass tattoo.

Somoza laughed. "Half the sector is afraid of your kind. I'm not, freak. You'll bleed and die in the dust just like all the others who've tried to take me in before you."

"If I were you, Somoza, I'd save my breath. Savor it. Because it's one of the last you'll take as a free man." The Baleview raised his voice. "And as for you gentlemen standing behind me with fingers itching to grab your shooters, you should know that this collar I'm wearing is recording everything you do. If you reach for your guns, that makes you a legitimate target."

Somoza lifted his mask for a moment and spat into the dust at the Baleview's feet. "I'm bored of you, freak. Waste him, boys."

* * *

Atop a wheeled metal juggernaut that was a contentious combination of pressurized fermentation tanks and habitation corridors, a motionless figure observed the confrontation along perfect sightlines. Her five-barreled rifle was trained on the street.

If she possessed skin, it wasn't on display, secured from sight beneath her rugged jacket and wide-brimmed hat. In place of flesh were shaped metal plates colored the deepest azure and connected by chunky rivets. Her face was in clear view for anyone who looked up, for she had no need of a breathing mask.

The eye sighting on the men below may have been human, but the other was a ball of glowing mint green.

She squeezed the trigger.

As the men had walked out of the bar, she'd painted five of them as targets. Barrels assigned to four of those targets fired 'sinners,' Stepped Intelligent Neutronium-enriched Rounds.

Ten feet from the barrel, the rocket stages detached from their launch frames and flew at their assigned targets. The first Somoza's companions knew about it was the back of their heads shattering as the rounds hit. Gouts of fire erupted from their foreheads as the front stages reversed thrust to avoid collateral damage.

* * *

"**D**amn you!" Somoza shouted at the bounty hunter standing before him. "No one stands a chance against you freaks."

The Baleview *tsk*ed when his prey reached for his pistol. "I want you alive, Somoza."

Somoza's hand froze. Then he slowly removed his pistol and dropped it into the dust. He raised his hands, palms out and level with his chest.

The bounty hunter cleared his throat. "That bulge in your jacket wouldn't be a knife, would it?"

"I'll kill you, dirty Baleview!"

Somoza didn't make good on his threat, instead removing the knife and letting it fall next to his pistol. "So now what? You kill me? You think it's that easy, you mutated son of a bitch? I'll be waiting for you in hell."

"Let's see now. Those sinner rounds my colleague was forced to expend cost us eight hundred new yuan each. Eight hundred newies. That's a lot of currency you're costing us. My warrant here says we get a fifteen hundred newie bonus for bringing you back alive. Seems your corpse isn't good enough, Somoza. That bonus amounts to…" He mimed chewing over the calculation. "Well, nothing for you, obviously. But it pays us back almost two of those sinner rounds. So you're going to leave those weapons in the dirt and put your hands behind you so I can truss you up tight."

Snarling and raging, nonetheless, Somoza allowed himself to be tied with rope.

"I have just one question," the bounty hunter said when he'd finished, "and it's an important one, so think carefully before answering. Do you have a tab at the bar?"

Somoza frowned. "Yes."

"Then let's do this like civilized people. We'll drink to your downfall together. And you're paying."

* * *

The Baleview and the cyborg reeled Somoza back to the pressurized bar, hauling on the ropes binding his wrists and ankles. To bring an uncooperative man up the adapted wheel wouldn't be easy for a normal person, but the cyborg's tendons and muscles had been replaced by cables, servos, and hydraulics. Somoza's weight was no problem for her, despite the above average gravity of Platov's Hell.

Inside the bar, they were met with resentment, which only built when they took seats at the card table.

"To the winner goes the spoils," the Baleview announced. "Somoza's hand is mine now." He read the cards. "Whose play is it?"

Muttering insults, the other card players walked away. The Baleview raked in the pot and called for whiskey.

The azure cyborg watched everything and said nothing.

The barman brought over a bottle of house whiskey and three glasses. He glanced once at the coils of thick rope around Somoza's wrists. That was his only reaction to the most powerful man in the settlement sitting trussed up in his bar.

The Baleview drew out the stopper and was about to pour when he hesitated, the bottle half tilted.

"Anybody finds my company disagreeable," he announced without looking into the sea of faces pinched with hate, "I'll be happy to discuss their lack of hospitability outside."

Hands inched quietly away from bulges on hips and in jackets.

The cyborg ignored all this and pulled down her captive's air mask to let him drink.

"So you got me." Somoza gave a bitter laugh. "You succeeded when many before have tried and failed to bring me in. Tell me your names so I can toast your victory."

"They call me Karnage," the Baleview replied, pouring several fingers of the amber liquid into each tumbler. "Karnage Zax. This here's Itka."

The bounty hunters took a long sip. Somoza wriggled his bound wrists and scowled at his drink.

"Nice little town you got here," Karnage remarked. "Pity about the inhabitants."

"That's it!" Somoza erupted to his feet, his moustache bright with spittle. "You disgust me. So you're FRA frakkers. Bounty hunters. I ain't got nothing against an honest profession, but your sort sicken normal folk. Just your being in town means children will be born wrong. Warped, like you. You're walking evil."

"Sit down and drink your whiskey."

"I'm not ashamed of my actions. You have to be prepared to do whatever it takes to survive on the frontier. My crimes are what I did. Your crime is existing."

"I asked you to sit and drink."

"Karnage!" Somoza spat on the table. "You're nothing but a Baleview. A damned dirty em-turd."

Karnage walked around the table and grabbed Somoza by his greasy black hair. "I don't like your pronunciation," he hissed into the man's ear. "Allow me to educate you."

He cracked Somoza's forehead against the plastic table, making the glasses jump. "Mutation!"

Itka grabbed the bottle before Karnage cracked Somoza's head once more against the table.

"Slash," he said.

Bang! "Temporal."

The tumblers rolled off the table and spilled onto the floor.

Bang! "Exotic."

Karnage looked Somoza in the face, making sure the man got a good view of the hourglass over his left eye. He breathed his next words gently over the stunned man. "Radiation. Disturbant."

Bang! Bang! "And that's how you pronounce M/TERD. Baleview is an acceptable alternative, but not what you said. Your pronunciation was offensive."

Itka set the tumblers back on the table and refilled them. "Drink up," she told her battered target.

He lifted his head and frowned at her. The cyborg confused him, and his dazed head wasn't helping. Her face was riveted metal, more machine than human, but her voice was honey smooth and all woman. Itka's words sounded kindly, almost maternal. He looked meaningfully at his glass. "Aren't you gonna untie me?"

"Nope," Karnage replied.

Itka sighed and lifted Somoza's glass to his lips, tipping it so he could drink his fill. She set it down and wiped away the blood streaming into his eyes from the gash his encounter with the table had opened. Then she brushed the back of her metal fingers against his cheek. "You're cute."

He flinched and pulled his head back.

"Karnage disgusts me, too," she told him, ignoring Somoza's reaction to her steel caress. "I hate him. Do you know what sets him apart from you?"

Somoza looked from one bounty hunter to the other, trying to read where this was headed.

He couldn't, so he shook his head.

"You're cute on the outside and ugly on the in. Karnage is repellent whichever way you look at him."

"Then… why run with him?"

"Because so am I."

* * *

Felon Recovery Agency outpost, Seraph System

They pushed Somoza along the inspection tunnel of the small FRA outpost on a moon of Seraph Flow that wasn't even named on the astrocharts.

The inspection tunnel was more than a lengthy means of progressing from the blast doors of the main entrance to the heart of the facility. Sensors in the walls would be scanning all three of them for bio-IDs. If the techs monitoring the feeds didn't like the results, efficient pacification options were available at the press of a button.

You only reached the check-in desk if they wanted you to.

Across the sector, inspection tunnels were all the same. Or so Karnage had thought until today. This one was carpeted. *Carpeted?* He didn't like that. Was the FRA trailing a new policy of being welcoming to their agents? No good would come of it.

That's not what's really bothering you, though. Is it?

"Itka," he began, but stopped, searching for the right words. "Did you mean what you said, back on Platov's Hell?"

"Help me out. Which statement are you querying?"

"That I disgust you because I'm a Baleview."

"Two years we've been partners, and you're only asking me now?"

He shrugged. "Seems that way."

"Look at me. The union won me a big enough payout that I could have been rebuilt with skin grafts and all that shit, but I chose not to pretend to be something I no longer am. I'm a monster now, and that's my truth. I look in the mirror and feel sick to the bottom of my stomach. Except it isn't my stomach, is it? It's a nutrient extraction unit that needs replacing every three months."

"We've all got our problems. I respect you, Itka Jowiszka. You don't disgust me."

"If I cared for your opinion, I'd be charmed. The reason you make a good partner for me is because the only way I can stop feeling sickened by what I've become is to be around you. However repellent I am, you're worse."

"Sounds like the basis of a rich and rewarding partnership."

She studied him, the glow fading in her green eye. Two years they'd been partners, but when he really looked at her, she still unnerved him.

Her eye glow returned, full blast. "I won't sleep with you, Karnage."

His eyebrows shot up. "The idea never occurred. Didn't know you were still capable of such things and didn't like to ask."

"Oh, I'm more than capable. Just not with you."

"Like I said. The idea *had* never occurred."

Itka huffed out her ear ports and gave Somoza a shove in the back to hurry up.

The dirty little snick was chuckling, but he'd get his comeuppance soon enough.

The inner doors slid away, and they were safely through to the check-in desk manned by a middle-aged functionary wearing an FRA navy blue uniform with silver buttons. His bellboy hat did little to obscure the fact that the man was long overdue a haircut.

The two bounty hunters handed the cubes from their collar recorders into the tray beneath the receiving officer's curved screen. They stood back to let him verify their contents.

"Any more frakkers here on the moon?" Karnage asked while they waited.

"Dumb Baleview scum. Don't use that term. You're agents. Just being in the same room as you two makes me want to vomit, but much as it disgusts me to say it, you represent the agency. Act like it."

"Oh, we do," Itka said. She looked at Karnage and flickered the shutter over her inhuman eye, her way of winking. "Any other *agents* here to hang out with? A chance to blow our bonus?"

"All's in order," the norm told them, "including an eight hundred new yuan bonus for bringing your mark in alive. If you want to blow it on something entertaining, buy two nooses and hang each other. I'd call that entertainment. In fact, I'd blow a fat stack of newies to watch you die."

Karnage felt Itka's gaze on him. She expected him to join in her sport of norm-baiting, but he wasn't in the mood.

He didn't feel right at all.

It's happening again…

Karnage staggered around the little room before tumbling to all fours. He'd seen footage enough times to know how he appeared. His veins were the first clue, pulsing impossibly large through his albino channels. Then the vein blue was replaced by waves of red that flowed like lava across his skin.

"Oh, God!" The bellboy norm jumped out his seat as if he'd seen a rad-wasp. "He's doing it right now. Isn't he? The Baleview thing?"

"Yup," Itka responded.

"What do you see? Tell me. No. No, don't."

Karnage could see the receiving officer freaking out behind the check-in desk, but it was a ghostly image that overlayed his searing vision.

Usually he saw a scene taken from the past of the people around him. The more emotional and the more secret, the more likely they were to come to him. But sometimes he foresaw.

The receiving officer is in civilian clothes, on a nighttime street of a planetside city. He's crouching protectively over a woman sprawled on the tarmac who's bleeding heavily. Shot. And she won't survive.

This was the man's future. Karnage didn't know how he knew that, but he'd never been wrong.

The vision faded, but Karnage was too exhausted to get to his feet.

"Do you know a girl?" he asked the norm. "Cute little nose. Even cuter freckle just below her left eye."

"Oh, God. I'm not telling you anything."

"Keep her close. Keep her safe." Karnage hesitated. The fact that Baleviews could glimpse other people's history was bad enough, as far as the norms were concerned, but it was seeing their futures that meant most norms would never tolerate them.

Past memories or future visions, as far as Karnage understood it, you couldn't change either. There was nothing he could tell this man that would prevent the fate he'd just seen. The woman would die, come what may.

"Let her know you appreciate her. Don't delay."

"Goddamned freak! Get out of here. I hope you die on your next assignment."

Somoza was laughing.

Security hadn't yet arrived to take him away, but Karnage figured the mark was the outpost's problem now. They left the receiving officer sobbing and pushed on into the operations room, where they were given their next assignment. Then they left by the rear doors and went in search of a bar that would serve people like them.

* * *

Flight Deck, *Death of Me*

"I know what you're thinking," Crisis said.

"No, you don't." Itka's metal face had lost the ability to glare, but Karnage knew how to interpret the pulsing of her left eye. So would the ship's AI.

Crisis blinked its bandit eyes. "I'm smarter than both of you together. I can prove it, too."

"You don't look smart," Itka said.

"*You* don't look human."

Karnage laughed from the other side of the horseshoe of seats arranged over the *Death of Me's* flight deck like a bar booth.

After they'd gotten an AI specialist drunk one night and persuaded her to come aboard to give Crisis some much needed upgrades, the ship's intelligence had come out of it with lightning-fast runtimes and a new combat mode stolen from an experimental flight simulator built for the sector marine legion. Unfortunately, giving the drunken tech full access had also allowed her to insert troll versions of standard core libraries. The face the AI presented in the center of the flight deck booth was no longer an androgynous, disembodied head. Crisis now rendered as a racoon.

Crisis glared at Karnage. Probably. It was difficult to tell with that bandit stripe across its face. Itka gave him the finger. That was easier to read.

He grimaced and took a sip of his sweet coffee. Itka and Crisis always bickered when Karnage and Itka weren't getting along. He didn't pretend to understand that dynamic, and normally he didn't care, because any disagreements he'd had with his partner had always blown over in a few hours.

Not this one.

It was stupid, really. He'd always assumed his partner loathed him, but when she'd told him to his face, her words had stung, hurt his feelings, and that had come as a total surprise. He hadn't realized he *had* feelings. That was the highly-strung AI's department.

Karnage set down his coffee and leaned back into the soft padding. "Crisis, don't tell Itka what she's thinking. Likely you can, but it ain't polite." He winked at his cyborg partner. "Seeing as you're a highly-evolved AI, and I'll never have a tenth of your smarts, why don't you tell *me* what's on her mind?"

"Itka is uncovering discrepancies in our warrant docket," Crisis said. "She wants to engage your interest but doesn't know how to after she damaged your self-esteem on Pavlov's Hell."

Karnage narrowed his eyes at Itka. He couldn't believe he was hearing this.

"It's true," she said. "You've been whining like a norm ever since I upset your snowflake ego."

"Whining like a norm?" He tilted his head as if he could shake this nonsense out his ear. "Ain't you a norm, Itka Jowiszka?"

"What do *you* think?"

"I don't rightly know. You're not a Baleview. If you're not a norm, either, then what are you?"

"I'm an Itka Jowiszka."

Karnage considered her reply. "Fair enough. So, Itka Jowiszka, what's troubling you about our Mr. Cabrera?"

"Warrant docket says our creep was abusing minors."

"Ain't no better way to ruin a man's reputation than accuse him of that."

"True. We get a three thousand newie bonus for bringing him back dead."

"Yeah. My eyes filled with yuan symbols when I saw that. Someone wants the man dead, and fast. Doesn't mean he isn't a disgusting piece of filth who deserves to be sent to hell. Even norm kids don't deserve what he's accused of."

Itka's mouth opened wide, giving her the appearance of a bunker firing slit, albeit a blue one wearing mulberry gloss lipstick.

He found that the strangest thing about his partner. She completely lacked the facial parts to make human expressions, but whatever tiny fraction of her was still human couldn't help expressing what she was feeling. The cyborg woman was smiling. And she was happy because she had him exactly where she wanted him, where he never usually ventured: interested in the moral details of the case.

Crisis blinked its bandit eyes. "I imagine Miss Jowiszka wishes you to consider who made the initial legal complaint."

"How come she's Miss Jowiszka and I'm just Karnage?"

"Do you really have to ask?" Crisis sighed, which sounded weird coming from a digital hologram of a cute furry animal. "The complaint was issued by an agent of Shacoho AgriCorp."

"And Cabrera worked for a big agri-company. Was Shacoho a rival?"

"No." Crisis leaned toward Karnage at the limit of its holo-projection disc and whispered, "Shacoho *is* his employer."

"The charges are unsubstantiated," Itka added. "No prize for guessing that there must have been a lot of hands greased with newies for these charges to stick despite the lack of evidence."

Karnage found it difficult to care about the scales of justice where norms were involved. Since unwanted Baleviews were exterminated without the expense of bounty hunters, that meant every case he took brought in a norm. And even with norms, the scales of justice were fixed to tilt in whichever direction paid the most. He had to admit, for a big agricultural corporation to dust one of its own researchers could be an interesting puzzle, though. If he could be bothered to care.

"Perhaps Cabrera was giving away industrial secrets," Itka suggested.

"Secrets?" Karnage shook his head. "We're talking about Shacoho. Everyone in the sector knows they're the agricorp that grows space potatoes."

"Maybe a lot more besides," Itka said. "The only info I can dig up says Cabrera was investigating plant oils at their research lab on Nakakara-17. They want us to kill him, and I would like to know why. Indulge me. Please."

Both crewmates looked at him expectantly—or as expectantly as a robot woman and a virtual racoon could.

The way Karnage saw it, *don't know and don't care* was the only sensible way to approach the rights and wrongs of what he did for money.

But he found he *did* care. Not about this norm plant researcher, but that Itka detested him. He didn't need her to like him. Didn't expect anyone to do that. But if she could come to accept him, that would sit more easily.

He let the moment play out a while longer before making his pronouncement. "Looks like a detour to Nakakara-17 is in order."

Karnage pretended not to notice when Itka's mulberry mouth slit open wide in a smile.

* * *

Shacoho Research Lab, Nakakara-17

At the rear of the sealed area behind the screen, transparent tanks rose almost to the ceiling 25 feet above. Pink and lilac liquid layers were continuously pumped in to swirl and slowly mix, churned by the bubbles rising from below. The tanks were brightly underlit, which made them appear more suited to a jube club than an agricultural research lab.

In front of the tanks, miniature walker bots with spray arm attachments marched up and down the hydroponics array, puffing a fine mist over the experimental crops. Karnage assumed they were spraying the same liquid being mixed in the tanks, but what really interested him was the crop.

He was looking at gajalu plants. Shacoho was famous for them. Cabrera had been researching the gajalu.

They were more commonly known as space potatoes, speckled balls of starch that looked similar to the potato and were often cooked the same way. The top was different, though. Its crown sprouted a mound of purple shoots that folded at their ends, like floppy dog ears crossed with plastic straws.

"Those tanks are impressive," said Itka, who had evidently run out of patience waiting for the brace of lab techs to notice her.

A female in her mid-30s and a male mid-20s, they wore the traditional uniform of white lab coat and unfashionable black glasses. Both recoiled in shock at the cyborg standing beside them. Or perhaps they were spooked by the vividness of her mustard leather vest and pants against the azure riveted metal where once there had been skin.

"What the...?" The male lab rat reacted angrily, but once he'd taken a good look at the intruder, he looked queasy. Itka often had that effect on people. "Who are you?"

"My first question," Itka continued, "is what the hell is it you're brewing in those tanks?"

The male norm reached into his pocket. "I'll call security."

"No, you won't." Karnage finally stepped out of the shadows at the back of the lab.

The two techs turned to face this new surprise.

"I will," the techie insisted, but his voice had all the backbone of an overboiled cabbage.

Karnage had his kepi pulled low over his left brow. He removed it to expose his hourglass tattoo and the bald head with the albino circulatory system

"I'm a Baleview and a killer. Suppose you *did* call for security. What do you think I would do to you then?"

The man's skin drained of blood. "I'm very sorry. I've already summoned them."

"*Tsk, tsk!*" Karnage shook his head. "Let me correct you. You *tried* to call security. Lucky for you, I've blocked your comms."

"What do you want from us?" the woman asked. Her voice carried neither fear nor confrontation. Karnage figured she was the boss.

"Karlik Cabrera," he replied. "What was he working on?"

"Cabrera? He was mad. I mean totally, goat-licking unhinged. And then one day... he wasn't here anymore."

The male norm shot a worried glance at the woman. That would have tipped Karnage off to the phoniness of her story, but he'd already detected it. She was a good liar, but not good enough.

"He was researching gajalu plants," she continued. "Same as us, but in the lab next door."

Karnage crossed his arms and gave her an impatient stare. She seemed to get the hint that he already knew that. Why else would he be here?

"He talked to the plants," the male jabbered. "I mean, that's weird enough, but Cabrera swore they talked back. He claimed they sang. That they asked him for... *oof!*" His sentence was terminated by a sharp kick to his shin from the woman.

"Let's see if I have this straight," Karnage said. "The space potatoes behind this window can talk?"

"No!" The woman shook her head fiercely. "Cabrera was nuts, and so were his ideas. We all told him to take a break and think carefully before he ruined his career by publishing such nonsense."

"But you're scientists, right? I can tell by the uniform. Didn't he have data? Experiments? Graphs?"

"Not that we ever saw," the woman said with particular firmness. "His specimen gajalu probably did communicate, in a sense. Most plants do. Many plants have sex, too, and it's long been suggested they have rudimentary pseudo-emotions. None of that means they're sentient beings."

"Sentient?" Karnage *tsk*ed again. "You shouldn't have let that word slip. Itka, what does she mean?"

"Sentient means something that can sense and respond to physical stimuli. Light, heat, sound, and the like. But I think she means it in a looser sense. Self-aware. Intelligent."

"I do not!"

Karnage put a finger to the woman's lips and *shush*ed her. "Maybe your man, Cabrera, made contact with the first intelligent alien race ever discovered. Or maybe we're debating the ramblings of a lunatic. Doesn't matter. The mere rumor that one of the galaxy's favorite foods is prepared from the corpses of industrial genocide would be bad for Shacoho's image. That's why we're getting paid a lot of money to bring him in dead or alive. Preferably dead."

The woman looked to Itka, but she found no compassion in that riveted metal face. "But we don't agree with Cabrera," she pleaded. "His fantasies have nothing to do with us."

"You're not listening," Karnage said. "Just knowing what he thought makes you a threat." He tapped his collar. "And we're recording everything you say."

"Oh, God. Oh, God. Oh, God!"

He thought she was trembling. Then Karnage realized *he* was the one shaking.

The lab and the people in it folded into the background.

Visions swam into view. Multiple—he'd never had more than one at the same time before—and all concerning these labs.

"Sweet nirvana," he muttered from the floor. "This place is a sewer swamp of betrayal."

As the vision faded, it struck him how much he needed Itka. If he worked alone, one of his visions hitting at a crucial moment could prove fatal. He couldn't afford to lose her.

Karnage picked himself up off the floor and enjoyed the attention everyone was showering him with. The scientists were horrified by the Baleview experiencing its perversion in their presences. Itka was simply curious about what he'd learned.

He grinned at the male scientist. "Really? You impress me."

"I don't understand. Really what?"

Karnage gestured to the storage tanks at the back of the sealed area. "Organizing the breathing gear for starters. Simply getting in that tank must have presented quite a challenge. But from what I saw, banging your colleague here made it all worthwhile. I wonder, did you tell your wife?"

"I made him," the woman said quickly. "Blackmailed him into doing it. Don't tell his wife. It wouldn't be fair."

Itka laughed at that.

"Look at me," Karnage told the woman. "Come stand right here in front of me and look me in the face. What am I?"

"A... a Baleview."

"Good. Keep looking at me. Now tell me that life is fair."

She couldn't. She looked away.

"That's right. Norms don't get to tell me what is and isn't fair, least of all you two. He's been harassing his assistant, and you've been stealing his research and setting him up." Karnage addressed the man. "Oh, yes. When you publish your paper, she'll accuse you of plagiarism and ruin you."

"Is this true?" the man asked.

"Don't listen to him," his colleague replied. "He's a Baleview."

"Which means I see the past and sometimes a future. They aren't random glimpses. They're precisely the things you least want us to see."

Even the male scientist could tell she was guilty as hell.

"Seems to me you both need to atone for what you've done," Karnage said. "I've got the perfect punishment."

It was at times like this he wished he still smoked. It would be the perfect moment to light up and enjoy the entertainment as the two norms alternated between squirming beneath his words and hurling blame at each other.

He never actually spelled out what he expected the norms to do. Their sick imaginations proved a wickeder torture than anything he could devise.

After a few minutes enjoying their disgrace, he sent them packing. There was nothing more he needed from them.

"There's your answer," he said. "That's why Shacoho wants our man dead."

"Do you think it's true?" Itka gestured at the plants in the hydroponics array. "Are they sentient?"

"The first intelligent alien species discovered is a freaking potato? Who knows? Doesn't matter anyway. It's our link."

He heard tapping noises to his right. Instantly, his Hi-D pistol was in his gun hand, and his muscles were ready to push him wherever he needed to go to meet this threat.

The menace, however, turned out to be a young norm woman tapping on the window from an office annex. She wore the same white lab coat as the others, but without the glasses.

Itka beckoned her out.

"I heard everything," the girl explained as she joined them, hands raised in surrender.

Karnage couldn't figure her out. Despite the determination in her eyes, her hands were trembling. So why hadn't she simply stayed hidden?

"Lower your hands," Itka told her. "I don't think you're going to reach for a gun."

Karnage asked, "Have you anything to add to what your friends told us?"

"They're not my friends. I'm glad you scared them. Vallacht and Sertison are horrible people. Karlik thought so, too."

Of course she hated them, he realized. This was the assistant harassed by the male scientist in his balesight. He hadn't recognized her at first, because she hadn't been wearing the lab coat in his vision.

"You didn't answer my question," he told her.

She squared her shoulders. "First, you answer mine. You're bounty hunters. I can tell from the recorder collars. Are there hits out on all of us here?"

"Not that I'm aware of." Karnage thought for a moment and decided to be honest. "Not that it makes any difference in the long run. If the people with money want you dead, that's what you'll be. That's how the galaxy operates."

"I'm not running and hiding. I wouldn't be any good at that."

"Even if you were, and you evaded us, they'd simply hire someone better."

"Oh, no. No. No. No!"

"Hey!" Itka grabbed the girl's arm. She meant it as a comforting gesture, but most norms didn't feel relaxed at blue robot fingers grabbing a limb. "It's not as bad as you think. If there ever is a hit on you, your end will be very quick. You probably won't even know you're dead."

Sympathy wasn't Itka's strongpoint, but to Karnage's surprise, her words appeared to calm the girl.

"Switch off the recorders, and I'll tell you something."

"They were never on," said Karnage.

"What?"

"You think we'd record ourselves grubbing around for the truth?"

She laughed. The girl actually *laughed*. For a norm, she was okay.

"Karlik Cabrera is a good man," she said. "Do you know his charges were trumped up?"

"I figured that, yeah."

"He entrusted something to me in case... something bad happened to him. Well, something bad *is* happening. You are."

She walked over to Karnage and palmed something into his hand, likely suspicious of hidden cameras.

He didn't release her hand, and she didn't flinch at being held by a Baleview. She looked him straight in his face, tattooed eye and all. "Karlik has a good heart, and I believe you do, too, Baleview. Before you execute your warrant, look through what I've given you first. Would you do that for me?"

"Miss, I give you my word."

"Thank you." He let her go, and she fled the lab, leaving Itka rocking with laughter.

"Sniggering is unbecoming in a cyborg."

She laughed harder. "*I give you my word*. Karnage, you're hilarious. Your word isn't worth a brass eurodollar."

"Shove it up your metal ass."

That didn't work, either. Karnage hated it when his partner got the giggles. It didn't look professional.

He held up the data cube the girl had given him. "Come on, Chuckles. Let's get back to the ship and review what's on this. Don't forget, it was your idiot idea to come here in the first place."

Karnage marched away for the *Death of Me*, not caring whether the cyborg was following. The sooner this Cabrera case was over, the better.

* * *

Flight Deck, *Death of Me*

Cabrera's data was dynamite.

They'd already learned that the researcher thought there was more to the gajalu than an ingredient for a tasty meal. Here, though, were the numbers, experiments, diagrams, and other scientific shit to prove it. At least, Cabrera claimed it was.

Karnage was no scientist. It could all be lies or mistakes, but it looked mighty plausible to him. Besides, facts didn't matter in this galaxy. It was what people felt that counted. And if Cabrera's findings got out, there'd be enough people *wanting* to believe him that Shacoho would be finished.

Cabrera had been researching the oils that saturated the ear stamens on top of the plants. They already made a useful secondary crop, but the income was hampered because the composition of the oils changed so randomly.

Shacoho wanted Cabrera to figure out how to genetically modify the gajalu to produce oils to order. Or alternatively, to shut off production of the oils so the plant could put all its energies into growing its starchy bulb.

Cabrera had figured out that the oils were actually a form of communication. The plants were talking to each other.

They were self-aware.

After successfully putting them through a battery of cognitive tests, the scientist topped what he had discovered so far with a final realization that shook him hard.

The plants weren't only communicating with each other. They were talking to *him*. Begging for his help.

It was his voice recording of this moment that Itka kept replaying on the flight deck.

"*It's not right,*" said Cabrera's breathless voice. "*The gajalu is one of the primary crops across five sectors. Think of the pain we've caused to billions. Trillions. How can we ever atone for what we've done? For this... xenocide?*"

Itka shut down the recording. "What do we do?"

That wasn't even a question in Karnage's mind. "We execute the warrant."

"Docket's paying us a bonus to bring him in dead. That's not justice."

"Sure it is." He regarded his partner, trying to figure her angle on this. But he could no longer read her. "We deliver justice, but it's the people with money and power who define what that means. Since when have you cared about such things?"

"Since now."

Karnage didn't say anything for a long while. The Baleview and the cyborg. After the words she'd spoken on Platov's Hell, their relationship had shifted for good. He couldn't deny that any longer.

He hadn't exactly considered her a friend, but how would he know what having a friend *should* feel like? He did know that when he was with her, he could be himself. And so far, she'd faithfully watched his back. Plus, she had computers and shit inside her metal body. As kids, neither of them had been given any schooling, but her robot brain upgrades meant she was now hugely knowledgeable.

She'd known what sentient meant.

Karnage concluded that he didn't want to lose her. Not until he'd figured out how this change between them would play out.

"Okay, Itka. We'll check out our brave laboratory hero first. Then we decide whether to bring him in."

* * *

Greencrest Farm, Lazada Province, Kimeru World

Sweating in the afternoon sun, Karnage leaned on the handle of his plastic hoe and watched the clearance team work the field. They were battling with the fast bind choking the path the harvester would take. Eventually.

Suddenly, a girl shrieked. Woody tendrils snaked out of the field of ripe flinch corn and coiled around her waist, intent on crushing the air from her and dragging her down beneath the heavy clay soil.

The rest of the team were alert enough to save her. This time. They hacked off the tendrils with machetes, and the dying plant appendages sprayed sap like arterial blood. Then they attacked the ground, searching for the local roots.

What frustrated Karnage to the breaking point was that he'd worked clearance on that patch this morning.

"Shouldn't we go help?" he asked Denison.

"Leave them be," replied the old Baleview resting next to him. "You conserve your strength unless the supervisor tells you go help. Believe me, you'll need it. Cleaning the harvester as it goes isn't difficult, but you gotta stay fast and sharp, else you'll find an arm or a leg of yours in the harvest tubs along with the flinch corn. The machine ain't fussy what it picks."

Karnage bit back his resentment. The work was dirty, dangerous, and paid little. The farmer didn't need to care, because the work gangs that supplied her labor employed criminals, Baleviews, and other such degenerate expendables. Why use robots when flesh was so cheap and flexible? Easier to replace when it went wrong, too.

"I don't get it," he said to the old farm worker. "The pilot and copilot of the harvester are fast asleep in their cab. Why isn't it operating?"

"Because we're all waiting for the okay to go."

"Waiting for what? A sign from God?"

"Pretty much." The old hand laughed. "Usually, the farmer starts harvesting too soon and then bitches about the poor yield. She inherited this place, see. Ain't never bothered to find something she might actually be good at. But this season she's doing it right and waiting for the agronomist to say we go. He's the man who knows when the crop has the right moisture content to be harvested."

"Agronomist? Never heard of them."

"You'll hear a lot more before you get much older, son. He's like a crop doctor. The man knows when to plant, when to harvest. He knows the right sequence of crop rotations for our soil, how best to spray it and such like. A proper farmer would be raised to know the basics of all that, but an agronomist uses science to go to the next level of precision."

"Our agronomist got a name?"

Denison gave Karnage a suspicious look. "Probably."

Karnage left it at that and settled down to wait some more while the others worked.

Truth was, he knew a lot more about the farm's operations than he let on to Denison. A freelance agronomist turning up out of the blue was the kind of flag he and Itka had been chasing for months.

A robo-strider crested the hill and advanced down the field toward the harvester, its five long legs setting a fast pace, but keeping its central platform level for the comfort and safety of its rider. He was a young man, dressed in fashionable outdoor gear.

Itka's voice came through Karnage's earpiece. "Facial recognition checks out. That's our man."

"Thank fuck."

Denison glared. "Mind your tongue, boy. Supervisor don't like such language. You get him riled, and we all suffer."

"Then I'll be polite." Karnage threw down his hoe and strode off to meet Cabrera.

He found the man dismounted among the flinch corn, feeding its ripe orange heads into a handheld machine. From the start, they'd had his bio details in the warrant docket, but despite hearing his voice many times, Karnage hadn't gotten a feel for him as a living person.

He was a big man, young and athletic. Many of the marks Karnage brought in carried themselves with an air of defeat, but this man looked ready to set his broad shoulders against the galaxy's obstacles and push them out of his way.

"Excuse me, sir?"

Cabrera pretended he hadn't heard, so Karnage tapped one of the water bottles attached to the robo-strider. Loudly. "The sun is punishing today, sir. Can you spare a little of your water for me and my friend?"

"Baleview filth." Cabrera didn't look up from his work. "Emturd freak. People like you shouldn't be allowed."

The supervisor was striding over, waving his walking stick angrily. Karnage ignored him. "I heard you're an agronomist."

Now Cabrera looked at him, furious at this interruption. "How dare you address me? Go away!"

Karnage stood his ground. "Your job is to use your knowledge to improve crop yields. Well, workers need water for their bodies to act efficiently, don't they? Stands to reason, if the farmworkers were offered better working conditions, crop yields would soar. Have you thought of that? Have you?"

The supervisor thwacked Karnage across his shoulders.

"You see what I mean, Mr. Agronomist? If the farmer and her supervisors cared for their people as much as their plants, profits would jump."

The supervisor hit him again, but Karnage's attention remained on the sneering agronomist.

"Degenerate Baleview," Cabrera said. "The welfare of plants is worth far more than yours. I'm perfectly serious when I say your sort shouldn't be allowed. It would be a mercy for your kind as much as mine if you were humanely exterminated."

"Thank you for your clarification," Karnage said. "It makes my job a lot simpler."

Confusion caught the supervisor in the middle of swinging his cane at the errant Baleview. "What the hell are you talking about, boy?"

Karnage took the stick out of the man's hands, snapped it across his boot, and handed the remnants back.

"Stop yapping," he told the supervisor. "Get back to work."

The man trembled with rage. "There will be repercussions," he fumed.

"Yes," Karnage told him. "Damn right there will."

* * *

Three Gables Cottage, Greencrest Farm

Karnage stroked the supervisor's cheek with the barrel of his Hi-D pistol.

The man stirred in his sleep and rolled over in the soft bed, grunting happily. Damned perv was enjoying it.

A sharp tap with the grip to the top of the bastard's head had the desired effect. The supervisor sat up, rubbing his crown.

Then he saw Karnage.

"It's an amusement to me," the bounty hunter told him. "Billions of new yuan have gone into the development of higher-dimensional weapons, of which this pistol is an example of the second-wave prototypes. The people trialing the first wave called themselves the suicide club on account of fatal misfires. If this were the first wave, that gentle tap just now could have left the entire farm a smoking crater.

Some might survive in the village, but the exotic radiation burst would soon do for them."

"You… you're a bounty hunter?"

Karnage nodded as if deeply impressed. "I perceive, sir, that you're not as stupid as you at first appear."

"There isn't a warrant on me, is there? No. There can't be. You've no right to invade my home and terrorize me."

Karnage licked his lips. "No *legal* right."

The supervisor's mouth moved, but he couldn't find the words to reply. Karnage helped him along. "I'm a Baleview gone bad. Tell me, Mr. Supervisor, can you name a single Baleview on this planet you don't regard as a worthless piece of filth? No. Didn't think so. The way I see it, if you norms are going to hate us anyway, we may as well give you a good reason."

"But you can't threaten me. Unless… *do* you have a warrant?"

"Nope. I'm working pro bono."

"Then I'll have you arrested."

"*Tsk, tsk!* You're not thinking clearly. Here, let me help clear your blockage." He cracked his gun once more against the supervisor's head. "See, you're getting the sequence of events mixed up. You won't be able to call the cops to get the nasty Baleview arrested because you'll be dead. So here's what you'll do instead. Pay to be doubled for all farm hands. Work shifts to be no more than ten hours per day. Healthy levels of victuals to be provided, including the provision of water during hot days in the field."

"I can't do that."

"If you don't, I'll kill you."

"The farmer won't allow it."

"I'm happy to kill her, too, if it helps."

"Okay. Okay. I'll find a way."

Karnage rose to leave, then hesitated halfway to the bedroom door. "Just one last point of clarification. If you do what I ask, then go back to the old ways when you think I'm no longer around, let me educate you about the consequences."

He walked to the windows and drew the curtains on the dusty dawn. "See that comms mast on the hill? Double cross me, and I'll cut you open and hang you upside down from that post. By your intestines. You'll be surprised how long it'll take you to die."

He left the man to his terror.

The chance of having forced a lasting improvement to the lot of the Baleviews on this planet was a fat zero. Didn't matter. They weren't his responsibility.

A career as a bounty hunter was usually brief and terminated by an ugly death. Karnage didn't kid himself that his life would be any different, which was why he was determined to have as much fun along the way as he could squeeze out of existence.

And playing with the supervisor had certainly been fun for one of them.

* * *

Otterford, Lazada Province, Kimeru World

"This is stupid, Karnage."

"No." Karnage grinned at Itka via the hovering spycam. "It's karma."

"You don't know what the word means."

"Screw you, Itka. Guy's a creep. Just give me this, okay?"

The nagging in his ear finally fell silent, and Karnage steeled himself for what would come next.

But Itka wasn't finished. "You're taking on a foolish risk," she admonished. "I can't let you take it, because if you die, I'll have to go to the trouble of finding a new partner."

"You're all sweetness inside your cold metal bosom. Now let me work."

He activated his recording collar and emerged from the shadows of the alleyway. He strolled up the ramp to the front entrance of Otterford's only holo-theater. The liveried doorman took one look at the hourglass tattoo over his eye and barred his way with a sneer on his lip.

Karnage thrust a warrant in his face and gave him two seconds to absorb it before pressing on, half-hoping the man would cause trouble.

He didn't. No one moved to block him as he moved through the lobby, scanning for Cabrera's location. The tracker they'd planted on him the day before was still active, pointing to Room 3.

Karnage pushed open the door into the darkened room and narrowed the target's location down to the seats on the far side, close to the front.

In the holo-projection that occupied the room's center, ugly humanoid aliens rampaged through a picturesque norm town defended by outgunned planetary militia. Explosions ripped through the auditorium. Music pumped. Screams came from every direction.

Karnage added his own rumble of shouts and gasps as the audience picked up that they really were being invaded by an undesirable. It must have been confusing for them because the crowd was also screaming in the holo-flick.

He and Itka preferred to retrieve their marks in public places such as bars and theaters. They told themselves it gave them plenty of witnesses to prove they'd followed procedure, but the recording collar should cover their asses anyway. The truth was, they enjoyed spoiling the day of as many privileged norms as possible and getting paid a stack of newies for the pleasure.

The Baleview and the would-be savior of a plant species locked gazes across the theater room.

The norm frowned, not understanding why the insolent farm-hand was here. The idiot still didn't get how the galaxy worked.

"Karlik Cabrera, I have a warrant issued by the Felon Recovery Agency to bring you in."

The mark surprised Karnage, not something that happened often. He'd expected Cabrera to scream in denial and then run. He did neither. He brought an old-school autopistol to his chest and racked the slide.

"Drop the gun, Cabrera. You're resisting lawful arrest."

Cabrera's answer was to fire at Karnage.

As it was such an obvious response, Karnage was already diving for the aisle.

As he rolled down the aisle steps, using the theatergoers as cover, Karnage counted five shots and the screams of two norms who'd been hit.

He kept rolling, eventually popping up on the edge of the hollow disc. He was surrounded by hideous holographic aliens firing exotic weapons. It was an artistic shame that Karnage's own exotic weapon, his Hi-D pistol, had failed its checks, and it was a conventional pistol he drew and fired at Cabrera, hitting him through the chest.

The mark dropped his pistol and slumped in his seat, staring stupidly at his gushing wound.

Room 3 was total pandemonium as unwounded norms trampled over each other in panic to get away. Within seconds, the section of Room 3 that interested Karnage was empty, other than Cabrera and the two norms the mark had shot.

Karnage was in a good mood. He'd get to the injured by-sitters later. Maybe.

But first, he stood over Cabrera and considered the man's wound. "You're dying. I'd wager you've five minutes tops, and then my partner and I will be entitled to the three thousand new yuan termination bonus. You've been FRAkked, Cabrera."

"Why? Why do you hate me so much?"

The man didn't deserve a reply. Karnage ignored him and watched Itka come in and apply first aid to the other wounded.

"It hurts," Cabrera wailed. "Put me out of my misery."

Karnage *ts*ked. "I don't think so. This is business, Cabrera, and finishing you off would be an unnecessary additional expense. One round isn't much, admittedly, but you can die on the cheap."

Itka stood beside him. "Karnage, you take your cruelty too far." He heard an unusual softness in her voice. Perhaps he imagined it. She was mostly robot, after all.

He groaned. Inconvenient though it was, he had to admit that he cared what Itka thought of him. "Seems you have a guardian angel after all, Cabrera." He remembered the research assistant at the lab who'd defended this man. "Two, in fact. A decent woman once told me you have a big heart. Maybe you do, but it ain't big enough to include people like me."

He put a round through Cabrera's head and shut off the recording collar.

"Thank you," Itka said. She kissed him.

He froze in place as she held him with her mouth pressed against his.

It was the shock, not the sensation that had checked him. The artificial lips were cold, but there was warmth within her.

He loosened into the kiss, hungry with the need to connect with Itka.

Karnage sensed the heat within her, could feel it burn his lips, but there wasn't enough to warm his frozen heart.

They pulled back a little, staring in silence into each other's eyes for a long minute, maybe more.

"No," Karnage whispered.

"Did nothing for me."

"Do you really hate me?"

She sucked a long breath through her mouth slit. "I could learn to tolerate you."

He tipped his cap to her. "Sweetest thing anyone's ever told me." He felt his insides unknotting. Everything was as all right with the galaxy as it would ever be. "Let's go pick up our newies, partner. This time, we've earned them."

* * * * *

Tim C. Taylor Bio

Tim C. Taylor lives with his family in an ancient village in England. When he was an impressionable kid, between 1977 and 1978, several mind-altering things happened to him all at once: *Star Wars*, Dungeons & Dragons, and *2000AD* comic. Consequently, he now writes science fiction novels for a living, notably in the Human Legion and Four Horsemen Universes.

His latest project is an adventure series called Chimera Company, which has been described as Warhammer 40,000 in the style of *Star Wars*.

For a free starter library of stories from all the worlds he writes in, join the Legion at www.humanlegion.com

# # # # #

ContAInment by
Matt Novotny

A Contractor Wars Story

Reynard Dupree watched as a patrol of warships cruised past between the planet below and Kanmon Station. He adjusted his chair for a better angle to view the ships and the crowd. It was an unusual sight, judging by the number of people crowding the ports for a look.

He'd arrived an hour ago to settle in for dinner, and Chef Hidekazu Yohi had bustled over with the energy of a much younger man.

"Irasshaimase."

"Kon-banwa."

"You want?"

"Omakase." Reynard smiled. The chef's recommendation was always the best meal in the house.

"Ha! I fix you up good!"

Five minutes later, the chef laid out his meal with practiced artistry and filled Dupree's glass himself.

"I check on you later! You skinny like me, so I give you extra." The chef's smile was infectious.

"Arigato gozai-masu, Chef."

Reaching out with his chopsticks, he toyed idly with the *sashimi* displayed artistically on the muscular body of the attractive young Scythian who served as his 'plate.' Though humanoid and feminine, she was a xeno, and her deep red skin provided contrast to the sterilized seaweed strips his meal rested on. A thousand years ago, her skin, black hair, and the nubby horns on her forehead might have marked her as an *oni* among the Kagoshimanese.

He selected a thin slice of *chimak,* a bold choice on the part of the chef, but Dupree felt it was an excellent one. The sweet, slightly smoky flavor of the local forest insect paired well with the bluefin tuna, and he alternated the two between mouthfuls of murky *Dassai Nigori sake* or a taste of ginger.

Reynard touched the rim of his glass to catch the attention of an attendant.

"More?" she asked.

He nodded. "If you please."

He scanned the room, shifting through augmented reality overlays that provided a wealth of information. Data scrolled past his vision as he focused on each patron: identities, credit balances, affiliations, background. Each layer pierced the many-layered shells of their Orinoco accounts and provided reference points for the individual. The entirely self-generated AR data filters assigned probabilities on whether they would be a help, a hindrance, or were inconsequential to his goal. Part of the charm of this establishment was that what you saw was what you got. The patrons, however, were an entirely different matter.

As Reynard worked, he transferred data to his AI. Unlike the artificial intelligences most used as personal assistants, his own had access to his extensive augmentations as well as being integrated into his wetware. Hermeline maintained near constant communication with her instance on Dupree's ship, the *Saint-Cloud.*

<Tag anyone you think I'm missing on the scan, Hermeline. And place an order with the station chandlery for ten cases of the Dassai Nigori. I don't think we'll come back to Kagoshima for a while.>

<Don't I always? Order placed,> she said.

A small commotion erupted when a group of young men, over-stimulated or drunk, committed the unpardonable rudeness of groping the Human woman at their table. To her credit, she barely reacted beyond a startled whimper, proving a dedication to providing the authentic experience—with a twist—the place was famous for. He scanned the men and caught a glint of metallic tattoos at wrist and neck. The loudest of the four was missing the last joint of his little finger.

Shatei? He wondered if the men were actually members of the local *Yakuza. Yes,* he decided. *That might become a problem.*

The bounty offer from *Kobayashi* Corporation was a considerable amount of money. It was offered as private, not a general, open contract. *There shouldn't be any competition on this one,* he thought, quickly double-checking the contract. All seemed to be in perfect order.

Ishikawa's was doing a booming business. The popularity of the little known *Nyotaimori* bar had exploded once the *Onsen* resort opened on the station. High rollers came from all over Kagoshima for a soak, a meal, and some business, followed by a few games, slumming in the *pachinko* parlors or some high stakes *mahjong.* There were brokers who would supply any pleasure you could imagine, provided your pockets were deep enough. It was a place where the normally stiff social protocols of the Edo System were mutually but politely ignored.

If one knew the right people, one could even bet on the *Konnichi-wa Koneko* syndicate's combat 'sports' tournaments. The tournaments—if that's what one could call a twenty-person free-for-all in a booby-trapped arena, and the participants armed with live ammunition—were notorious across human space. *Konnichiwa Koneko's* MegaCorp status protected it from civil law, and, besides, no one knew *where* the tournaments took place, so whose laws would even apply? So long as no innocents were harmed, no one was foolish enough to take on a MegaCorp on *moral* grounds. Meanwhile, the syndicate made bank as the house, taking bets, with more and more zeroes being added to the minimum bid until the annual, ultra-lethal championships were streamed—as they were right now.

Reynard returned to his scan, tagging the other patrons one by one. Fully half showed assumed identities or tried to hide behind privacy filters.

Let's see what's hiding behind the masks. He engaged a breaker subroutine. The program stripped away the layers of concealment. Garden-variety software packages that worked well in the civilian markets, with a sprinkling of government and corporate level programs, were brushed aside, revealing the secrets beneath. As was usually the case, by Reynard's standards, they were implemented poorly. It was the work of long seconds to crack them.

I'd hoped for better, though it should make my job easier. Reynard ran the probabilities automatically but dismissed them almost at once. *Five celebrities, three politicians, one minor prince of the imperial household, four diplomats, and an even dozen CEOs. Boring... perhaps too boring.* He went through the blandest of the patrons and tagged four. *There's the prince's security detail.*

Now this *is interesting.*

At the VIP table in the corner, a thin, severe, older woman with the prince was definitely the *oyabun* of the station's *Yakuza*. Reynard gave a wicked grin when several people with better security packages glanced around, looking concerned. They'd been notified a scan had taken place.

Concerned they've been recognized by the media.

The counter-ICE responses from four of those aware of the scan indicated they had personal AIs in play. That was good; they belonged to the prince, the *oyabun*, one of the CEOs, and his burly assistant. Reynard dug deeper into the corporate men: *Ikeru* Corporation, Chairman Satoshi Tanaka and Security Chief Kwan Sakata. Reynard considered the four; his target could be attached to one of them.

<Analysis indicates an 86 percent probability that Chairman Tanaka is the individual responsible for placing the bounty.>

What's the link between Kobayashi and Ikeru?

Reynard took another bite of his *sashimi*, followed by a thoughtful sip of *sake*. He considered Chief Sakata. Reynard was normally immune to casual intimidation, but the man's restrained movements marked him as dangerous in a way the others weren't.

Fixer. Possibly even 'borged.

He hit Sakata with another scan to study his reaction, quickly laying a trail of digital breadcrumbs back to the four *shatei*.

<Negative scan.>

From the prince's table, the sound of musical laughter lifted above the general murmur of the room. A deeply tanned Japanese woman, platinum blonde hair pinned up with a pair of chopsticks in an elegant style, was escorted to the table by another security man.

Reynard watched the show.

<The prince and the oyabun *each have four guards, Hermeline, but
Tanaka doesn't. See if Tanaka has two more.>*

<Affirmative. They are outside the main entrance.>

The young woman's shimmersilk dress was artistically draped,
showing her bare back and right leg nearly to her hip. An iridescent
nanofiber dragon tattoo coiled up her exposed leg and across her
back, glowing in a tracery of peacock colors, green and blue, through
the woman's skin.

So much for Imperial discretion.

Reynard scanned her as a matter of course but didn't really need
to. Anyone with data stream access would recognize her. He was
thankful his filters eliminated the blitz of social media hooks surrounding the woman like a cloud. The idol's name was Aika, and she
was famous for being famous.

The security man led her to a seat between the prince and the
Ikeru CEO. The *oyabun* looked disgusted but smiled like a shark. Aika
turned a terawatt smile on the two men as she sat. She stumbled, but
caught herself by grabbing Tanaka's arm and easing into her chair.
For a moment she locked deep blue eyes with Reynard across the
room. He saw the implants in her irises change configuration.

<Target acquired,> Hermeline said.

* * *

R eynard allowed himself a smile. This bounty had been
particularly inventive at hiding her data trail. He'd nearly caught her in Yggdrasil, but she'd slipped away, doubling back to Kagoshima and the Edo system. Why she'd chosen to
come to Edo and not one of the more developed systems such as
Kamakura, Seoul, or even Taohsiung—where it would have been

easier to hide—was a question he would delve into after she was safely in custody.

For now, Reynard's task was to separate her from the very public, and very dangerous, people she had managed to surround herself with. Preferably without them noticing.

All in a day's work.

Of course, Reynard could simply present his warrant, but there was no actual jurisdiction, and, if he was refused, he would have to begin all over again.

Unacceptable.

What I need is a distraction. He examined the VIP table and considered how to avoid twelve guards and accomplish what he needed. *Let's make that* several *distractions.*

He switched his AR filter until he saw strands of colored light representing data streams, then dimmed the normal traffic of the station to a background level. He could see the brighter, denser threads of AIs, along with the standard traffic. He coded the data for the *Yakuza,* the imperial party, and the corporate men.

<Hermeline, here's what I have in mind.> He showed her the construct for his plan, noting with appreciation the few adjustments she made. *<When this goes down, it's likely to get messy.>*

<Your exit route is secured,> Hermeline said. *<We have departure clearance pending final cargo. The* Saint-Cloud *is ready when you are.>*

I despise working in realspace, he thought, finishing the last of his *chimak.* He rolled up the seaweed strips with his chopsticks and set them to the side to let the woman know he'd completed his meal. He filed away the details of the experience for later.

"Arigato gozai-masu," he said, helping her to her feet. "I've never had a lovelier dish."

"Would you care to... continue?" she asked.

"I would, yes." It only took a few seconds to book a room at the *Onsen*. "Why don't you go now and enjoy a soak? I'll join you after I finish my drink." He lifted a robe from its hook next to the table and held it for her. "Room forty-two. I've paid for the night."

She bowed, surreptitiously checking her hand comp to verify the transaction.

"Of course, sir. I'll be waiting for you. I am called Yoshiko."

He watched her go, enjoying the smooth flavor of his *sake*. The Scythian *was* lovely, and it couldn't be easy for her as an alien on Kanmon, despite the pseudonym she'd taken to fit in. The name of the station meant *gateway*, but there was another interpretation of the word: *Barrier*. Both described the primary port of call for the Kagoshima cluster perfectly.

At any rate, tucking her out of harm's way was no trouble for him, and by the time she realized he wasn't going to show, he would be long gone, but she'd been well paid for her time.

Now, it was time to do what he was there for.

The traceries of light in his AR view moved with the ebb and flow of Humans doing Human things. There was a rhythm, a cadence he was used to, had come to depend on, even. It was the signal. The movement of data was as familiar and as necessary to him as his own heartbeat. Whether Human or alien, Reynard knew the rhythm. It moved around him and through him. He closed his eyes and entered a different world as the merely augmented merged with the truly virtual, surrendering to the signal. He entered the data feeds, layer after layer. Probability, analysis, projection, evaluation, conclusion.

Distraction.

One.

Reynard hit the corporate team with a wall of noise, blanketing their communications for a full three seconds. The security software used by the *Ikeru* men obligingly reported the source of the outage as the table with the four *Yakuza shatei*. The two corporate men guarding the entrance entered and moved to place themselves between the *Yakuza* and the *Ikeru* CEO, a move that didn't go unnoticed by either the *oyabun* or the *shatei*, since from their perspective, *Ikeru* security had just separated her from her own people.

Next, he activated four tiny spheres and dropped them to the floor. They faded into near invisibility and rolled to surround the VIP area.

Two.

The imperial security detail, seeing the beginnings of the confrontation, quickly converged on the prince to move him away from danger. Nervous customers noticing the disturbance also headed for one of the restaurant's several entrances. Reynard moved across the room with the flow of other patrons and sidled into an alcove just off the main passage into the station.

Three.

Aika rose when the prince did, his security detail separating them after the briefest of goodbyes. The *oyabun* and *Ikeru* CEO also stood and bowed respectfully, then continued trying to figure out what was happening.

The idol bowed but tried to follow the prince as his detail hustled him away. She was a person used to being the center of attention, surrounded by adoring fans. Her connection to the datanet was pervasive, and, even with her normal feeds completely shut down for an evening of privacy, the rumors of where she was and who she might be with were trending.

The four tiny spheres, being run unnoticed by Hermeline, activated with no more than a faint hum to indicate they were doing anything at all. In Reynard's augmented sight, however, they flared to life like microscopic supernovas, filling the room with waves of shifting, virtual light.

Each sphere fired directed low level electro-magnetic pulses that targeted the frequencies an augmented mind used for connection to the digital world. The effect on the target was instant. She staggered drunkenly as she was completely cut off from the datanets. The idol looked about wildly, not comprehending, but then joined the rest of the crowd.

Four.

Reynard smiled as he reached out to the station's network, delving through systems, programs, and subroutines.

<All right Hermeline, we are 'go' for breach.>

An alarm sounded, striking fear into any being who lived or worked in space. It blared through *Ishikawa's*, and everyone, whether involved in the spectacle or not, rushed for the entrance. The breach alarm permitted only one response: get inside. Get away. Get to safety.

As Aika was carried along with the crowd, the four spheres rolled to keep pace, and, a moment later, she reached Reynard's hiding place. He felt his own connection to Hermeline severed as he entered the dampening field projected by the spheres, one that specifically targeted the fundamental structure an AI was built on. All artificial intelligence within the field was essentially isolated. Nothing in; nothing out.

Reynard gently reached out and pulled the woman into the al-cove. She reached for him, and he saw the flickering light of her tat-too moving down her arm, the dragon's claws reaching, grasping. The irises of her eyes shifted as she stared at him. Fitting his hand like an old style stunner, he took the capture device given to him by Kobayashi from a pocket, checking to make sure his add-on modifi-cation was secure. He thumbed the activator and pressed it firmly into the idol's tattoo. Seconds ticked by. Reynard felt a tingle as the dragon's light flickered and died. The patterns of the shimmersilk dress faded at the same time. The device beeped. The field of the spheres dropped immediately after.

<Capture confirmed,> Hermeline said.

Mission accomplished, Reynard thought, allowing the full virtual in-terface to fade. Aika sagged against him, then looked up into his face, confused.

"Thank you," she breathed. Her features clouded, irises shifting, changing. "Where am I?" She shook her head. "What are you…"

Reynard tried to step away, but she was holding herself upright by clutching his jacket. He saw awareness of her situation begin to take hold. The breach alarm, the crowd moving past, her own confu-sion, and the fact she was tucked into an alcove, mostly naked, cling-ing to a man she didn't know. She took the only sensible course of action left to her.

She screamed.

* * *

In another time and place, the best Reynard could have ex-pected was probable detention and some awkward ques-tions. Not because he was in a potentially compromising position, but because he was in that position with a woman who, until the current emergency, had access to an imperial prince as well as being an intersystem media darling. It was the sort of thing that attracted attention. It would be bad enough that the prince was involved with such a woman at all; that she might be working on behalf of someone else would be intolerable.

Under the current circumstances, no one even noticed.

Reynard shook her. "Calm down! Are you all right? I saw you stumble and pulled you away from the crowd so you didn't get trampled."

She took a deep breath, then nodded. Reynard suddenly became very conscious of how close the woman was.

<*Enhanced pheromones,*> Hermeline said.

<*That isn't supposed to happen.*>

Reynard did a quick check of his hormone levels, adjusted them, and forced himself to re-focus.

"There's a breach alarm, we need to get you out of here." The crowd was beginning to thin out. "We're going to step out, and I'll make sure you don't get run into again. I want you to head straight for the main entrance, all right?"

"Okay," she said. "Thank you. I'm sorry, I..." Clearly, she had expected a different response.

"Think nothing of it."

He accessed the restaurant's cameras, rapidly shifting through the last few minutes' footage. He noted the *Ikeru* group had followed the imperials toward the primary entrance, while the *Yakuza* had exited through the kitchen. He smiled when he saw a number of virtual patrons ignoring the alarm wink out of existence as the holographic system shut down. His own exit was through the back and into the station's maintenance level. He waited for a break in the flow of traffic.

"Go!"

They moved from the alcove into the stream of people, joining the exodus toward the station core.

"I'm right behind you," Reynard said. "If we get separated, keep going."

He caught himself watching the movement of her hips and how the shimmersilk clung to her body as they followed the crowd.

Merde! He checked and saw that his hormone levels were spiking again. <*What the hell is she using?*>

<*The scent of a woman,*> Hermeline said. <*You need to get out more.*>

<*I didn't react this way to the Scythian.*>

<*I told you, her pheromones are enhanced. The composition has changed to match your specific physiology.*>

<*How?*>

<*There's a high probability it was altered when you touched her. It's an effective survival strategy. Without your own augmentations, she could lead you around by the... hormones. Maybe if you spent more time with people instead of programs...*>

<*Are you arguing that AIs aren't people?*>

<*It's complicated.*>

With a last look at the idol, Reynard waited until they were almost past his exit before he ducked into the hallway leading to the storage areas and, beyond that, to the staff entrance. It took just a moment to bypass the code that gave access to the maintenance and utility corridors, the areas any business needed access to: water and air, environmental, electrical, data, recycling. The real infrastructure that was often taken for granted, or simply ignored, could be accessed here.

The utility space had the look of such places everywhere. Light gray paint with color coded conduit, screens showing the status of the local systems along with the maintenance schedule, and diffuse light that gave no sign of anything so mundane as a time cycle. The corridors smelled of circuitry and lubricants, dust and ozone.

He reached into the systems for that part of the station and shut off the breach alarm. Checking the cameras for the main entrance, he saw people's confusion as they exited onto a quiet promenade and saw no sign of anything wrong. The prince's party was long gone, as were the *Yakuza*. The *Ikeru* group was entering a car at the tube stop on the other side of the promenade. There was no sign of Aika.

Reynard had secured a berth for the *Saint-Cloud* in one of the less industrial sections of the docks. He could have easily afforded a private hangar, but using the courier slips reserved for corporate and political traffic provided a certain amount of privacy, if not anonymity.

He took an elevator down several levels, jumped on a tube, then took a brief trip through the utility corridors and a relaxed walk through the station's shopping plexes before taking another tube to the docks.

He reached the diplomatic area just as Hermeline sent him an alert.

<*We have a visitor.*>

Waiting outside the shipway gate leading to the *Saint-Cloud* was the *Ikeru* security chief, Kwan Sakata.

* * *

T*he worst part about physical space,* Reynard thought, *is the surprises.*

"Mr. Dupree?"

Sakata stepped forward with a *keirei* bow indicating respect to an equal. A significant distinction, in light of Sakata's position. Reynard returned the bow in equal measure.

"Yes, Mr. Sakata. What can I do for you?" If Sakata was surprised that Reynard knew his identity, he didn't show it. It was perhaps a breach of etiquette not to draw out the introductions, but Reynard was anxious to be on his way.

Sakata gave a tight nod. "I have been sent to inquire if your presence here is in reference to the bounty you are engaged in on behalf of *Kobayashi.*"

The man's face lacked the flexibility it should have had, and his movements were just slightly too fast.

<*I was right. I'd bet my right arm he's a full convert Masamune War-Borg.*>

<*If you wanted to bet the arm, you should have shaken hands instead of bowing,*> Hermeline said.

"As I'm sure you can appreciate, I'm not at liberty to discuss the status of my contracts beyond what is publicly available. May I ask what *Ikeru's* interest is?"

Reynard Dupree didn't fit the image in anyone's mind when they thought of a bounty hunter, and that frequently meant people underestimated him. Short and almost painfully thin, he had sharp, Gaulish features with thinning brown hair, a pronounced Adam's apple, and slightly protruding gray eyes. If Reynard's physicality failed to impress, however, the mind behind it did not. He was, in a word, brilliant. The augmentations he carried guaranteed that in any sophisticated area of space, he could connect to resources to exercise that gift to the fullest.

"There is a relationship between our companies, so the project is naturally of interest."

"You know the Council rules, Mr. Sakata. Standard Non-Disclosure requires I not divulge the nature of any open contract I may or may not have without knowing the listener is authorized. All I know about you is that you represent *Ikeru*. Unless you have something else to add?" He let the statement hang.

Dupree didn't spend his time chasing bounties across known space, but hunted the peaks and valleys of the signal, oceans, rivers, and streams of data. The world behind the world. Revealed in blinding light or hidden in shadow, that was the reality Reynard preferred. There, what most people called reality was held safely at a distance, and leaving was as easy as terminating a connection.

Reynard's bounties were AIs that had gone rogue or were missing. Sims and avatars, stolen or lost data. In mankind's technological march forward, it was a given that virtual pioneers would stare into the abyss. Occasionally, the abyss stared back. *Here there be monsters.* That was where Reynard came in. In his last bounty, he'd recovered stolen governmental encryption keys for a planetary defense grid.

Rarely did he accept a job that required a physical pursuit such as this one. It was a limitation of the virtual world that, though it spanned known space, it didn't do so in real time. Dupree thought of himself as an artist. Sometimes art demanded sacrifice, or, at the least, travel. *Kobayashi* had contacted him directly to offer a bounty for a rogue AI that had been the personal assistant of Doctor Hisako Osumi, the head of their research division. When the woman had disappeared, *Kobayashi* had gone to the AI for answers, only for it to break out of a siloed network and disappear as well. It was hoped that by recovering the AI, the researcher could be located. As long as the information provided by *Kobayashi* was correct, the AI should now be residing in the device in Reynard's pocket.

Sakata stared for a moment, then nodded again.

"I hope this proves acceptable."

He removed a microcomp from a pocket and sent Reynard a digital passport. Within was an attached contract copy and passcodes that credentialed Sakata, specifically, as authorized through *Kobayashi.* Reynard ran the encryption keys on the files and received confirmation from the company almost immediately.

"It does," Reynard said. *<Okay, Hermeline, open up.>*

"We should discuss anything further in private. Would you care to come aboard?" Reynard asked.

"Lead the way," Sakata said.

* * *

"Welcome aboard the *Saint-Cloud,*" Reynard said. They passed through the vestibule into a sitting area with a workspace and small, connected galley. The *Saint-Cloud* had started life as a military courier, what was considered a fast packet. She was an older vessel Dupree had purchased at auction and completely refurbished as a gentleman's yacht, upgrading her systems to the best he could find and afford.

"Can I offer you something? Tea?"

"Thank you, yes," Sakata said.

Reynard stepped into the galley. He took the capture device from his pocket once he was out of sight, then removed the modification he'd attached to it. Whatever was inside, Reynard wanted a chance to look it over.

"I have *Sencha*, or perhaps you would care for something European? *Mate?*"

"*Sencha* would be excellent," Sakata said.

Reynard busied himself preparing the tea. "Ask your questions."

<He's planted a bug,> Hermeline said.

<Destroy it,> Reynard said.

In the other room there was a high-pitched whine, followed by a *pop* and a quick intake of breath as whatever device Sakata had planted overloaded and fried. The smell of burned circuitry wafted through the small room before Hermeline whisked it away and replaced it with the scent of the Cabrieres d'Avignon lavender fields. Dupree loaded a tray with the tea and a tin of lemon biscuits and returned to the sitting area.

"Mr. Sakata, I'm afraid that if you try something like that again, we won't be able to stay friends."

The big man at least had the grace to look embarrassed. "Please forgive me, Mr. Dupree. Force of habit."

"Think nothing of it." Reynard didn't buy the act for a second, but there was nothing to be gained by making an issue of it. He handed Sakata his tea. "Now, your questions about the contract, if you please."

"We've received notification that the device we sent you was used. Did you achieve your objective?"

"Providing the information supplied is accurate, I have. Of course, I have no way to validate that without access to the AI, but the device verification indicates success. I must ask, was the bounty some sort of test?"

Sakata took a slow sip of his tea, then set the cup down. "May I see the capture module?"

<Lock it down, Hermeline.>

<Active buffering is established.>

This was the part Reynard despised most about his business. Ironically, it was the interests with the most money that sometimes tried to avoid payment for a bounty. The active buffering assured that anything Sakata tried to send off the ship wouldn't include the contents of the *Kobayashi* tech.

Reynard set his own cup down, slipped the device from his pocket, and passed it to Sakata. He took it and keyed a code directly into the interface. The device flashed green. The security chief gave a tight smile of satisfaction.

"Excellent work, Mr. Dupree. Your reputation is well deserved. I should return this to our R&D people immediately to see if it will provide any help in locating Dr. Osumi."

"I understand completely," Reynard said. "If you will be so kind as to conclude the contract, we can both be on our way."

Sakata pulled out his microcomp and worked for a moment, beefy fingers poking at the screen. Reynard received an alert that the bounty had been reported as concluded, along with a balance transfer for the agreed upon fee, including a substantial performance bonus.

"I trust you'll find the compensation acceptable?"

"Very generous, Mr. Sakata. Thank you. It's been a pleasure doing business with *Kobayashi*. I'll send you a full report tomorrow."

"The pleasure is ours, Mr. Dupree. You will be at the top of our list should we have any similar assignments in the future. Thank you for the tea."

The two men bowed. Both were lying. Dupree resented the extensive travel, and Sakata resented that his own people hadn't been able to handle the job. Still, that was the way business was done, particularly in Kagoshima.

They walked to the *Saint-Cloud's* hatch, but Sakata turned before Reynard touched the controls. "One thing you said puzzles me. Why did you ask if the bounty was a test?"

"Because it all came back to Kagoshima. Usually, a fugitive doesn't return to where it's being hunted."

"Where did you capture it?"

"Concealed in the nanofiber tattoo the young lady was wearing."

The color drained from Sakata's face. "The AI was in physical proximity to Chairman Tanaka? Are you certain?"

"Yes. The only reason I was able to get close enough myself was because of the disturbance."

"Thank you again, Mr. Reynard. You've been most helpful."

Reynard opened the hatch and watched the security chief hurry away.

That was an interesting reaction.

Reynard resisted the urge to hack into Sakata's communications. The job was done, and he hadn't needed the insurance. He cleaned up their tea and thought about deleting the copy of the AI he had made, but decided he'd deal with it later. Right now, he wanted a shower and a change of clothes. He needed to catch up on his correspondence. Friends this time, not business. Perhaps he would have a Cointreau.

<Let's get going, Hermeline.>

<We're waiting for the delivery of Dassai Nigori you ordered. ETA is ninety minutes. Do you want to leave and have it shipped?>

<We'll wait. I'm going to get cleaned up. We'll leave once it arrives.>

* * *

Heated floors weren't the kind of thing most people considered when refitting a spaceship, but for the thousandth odd time, Reynard was thankful that the Olsen Stardrive shipyards that had done the work on the *Saint-Cloud* had been top notch in planning those kinds of details. The opulent trim of the ship, from the holography suite down to the self-cleaning nanofiber carpeting, was an indulgence that was well worth the freight.

Reynard had showered and changed into a loose shirt, linen pants, and a pair of ship slippers. He'd intended to sleep and check his correspondence in the morning, but the inconvenience of the late delivery made him change his plans, exchanging a nightcap for a strong cup of coffee. He padded to the desk and settled into his chair, and the built-in massagers began working on the kinks in his back as soon as he sat down. With a few gestures, he brought up the holographic interface and started through the list of items he wanted to accomplish before leaving. He could have done this by closing his eyes and working virtually, but he found a period of transition helped him return to his usual routine.

He turned on some music, then scrolled through the general news. The ILM—his home cluster, the *Impero Latino Mediterraneo*—was finally considering building proper fortress bases at the blue-shift limits. The grape harvest on Lorraine was expected to produce a particularly good vintage this season. Century Dynatech was announcing an IPO on a new mining venture.

The rates are attractive. It's higher risk...

He set a program to monitor the stock prices closer to the launch. A letter from his sister, Agnes. He flagged that for later. He wanted to rest, and letters from his sister were never restful.

<Dupree!> Hermeline cut in urgently. A VR window opened, showing the entry to the shipway.

That looks a lot like a stealthed assault team.

On Dupree's display, Hermeline outlined six armored solders waiting while a breaching drone attempted to run a bypass on the lock.

<*I keep scrambling the codes, but I predict less than two minutes before they give up and blow the door,*> Hermeline said.

<*Do we still have departure clearance?*>

<*Yes. We're on standby.*>

<*Break away now and signal departure. Clear the station perimeter and activate point defense.*>

One less thing to worry about. If their visitors were station security, they would've locked down the ship before trying to board.

Reynard watched as the drone extended a tool and applied a bead of foam around the doorway. A second later, the doors collapsed onto the shipway. There was a *clunk* as the *Saint-Cloud* disengaged from the station and moved away. For the team to follow the ship now would require them to breach the shipway's second set of doors and open the station to space.

That would give them another breach alarm to explain, this time a real one. He wouldn't be surprised if that happened, or if a second team appeared. For someone to field a six-man team equipped as they were required considerable resources. GHOST armor didn't come cheap, not to mention the drone.

<*Setting least-time course to Edo's shift limit.*>

Reynard went to the small control room, strapped into the pilot's seat, and set the holographic field to an outside view, making it seem as if the walls and ceiling were clear transplex. He didn't bother with a shipsuit or helmet. Anything that could hit the *Saint-Cloud* hard enough to cause a breach would probably kill him anyway, and, though he had no issues defending himself, at heart he was opposed to killing if it could be avoided. In this case, he was acting as more of a backup for Hermeline, anyway. He brought up an interface, checked the silhouettes of the assault team members against the station records, made allowances for the armor, and received a positive match almost immediately.

Exactly what game are you playing, Mr. Sakata?

The ship accelerated as the *Saint-Cloud* headed for the blue-shift line, and Renard kept an eye on the astrogation sensors, ready to jump system the instant he was away.

The assault squad makes no sense. The AI capture went well, considering the difficulty. There was no way they could know about the copy, and I have nothing of high value here unless they're after the ship.

A quick check showed Sakata hadn't reversed *Kobayashi's* payment, but it appeared his access to his funds had been frozen.

You have got to be kidding me, he thought just as he received an alert over the contra network. *Kobayashi* Corp had placed an open bounty on him for a staggering amount of yen. There was no motivation Reynard could see for them to burn him. *For that kind of money, I might capture* myself.

<We're being hailed, and there's a cruiser on an intercept course.>

Reynard brought up the tactical plot. The cruiser was just coming out of Edo's shadow.

They aren't in a position to catch us. Probably part of the same patrol that did the station flyby. He checked the positions of the other ships at or near the station. *Where are your escorts? <Drop a relay drone and move us off the ecliptic. We need some distance. Then put them through. They aren't targeting us.>*

<*Yet,>* Hermeline said.

<No, not yet. Find those escorts!>

"Saint-Cloud, *this is the Edo cruiser* Unebi. *You are ordered to return to Kanmon Station immediately.*"

"Hello, *Unebi.* This is Reynard Dupree aboard the *Saint-Cloud.* Is there some sort of problem?"

"Reynard Dupree, you are wanted for questioning on a matter of imperial security. Return to Kanmon Station immediately, or your ship will be disabled. You have one minute to comply."

Reynard's interface flashed red as the Edo ships began active targeting.

<Escorts located. Destroyer Oboro *is also on an intercept course. Destroyer* Ushio *is waiting outside the shift limit.>*

<Do we have a window?>

<Yes.>

His interface flashed again as *Unebi* fired.

<Drone is destroyed.>

The *Saint-Cloud* passed through the narrow gap in the patrol's pattern.

<Shift limit in ten seconds.>

Dupree brought up the navigation and locked in their destination. *Venezia della Stella.*

<Are you sure?> Hermeline asked.

<What we need is in Venice—or more precisely, under it. We're going to Catacomb.>

<The ship will rust,> Hermeline groused. *<Rusty Cloud.>*

"Punch it!" Dupree said.

The ship leapt into FTL and left Kagoshima behind.

* * *

Back on the station, a small bot trundled up to the shipway entrance to find the *Saint-Cloud* departed and the shipway doors lying on the floor. It sat for a moment before concluding that it wouldn't be able to complete its delivery, then turned around to return Dupree's *sake* to the warehouse.

* * *

"Ah, Venice…"

<You've said that three times now.>

<But of course!> Reynard said expansively. *<That's what one must say when coming to* Venezia della Stella. *Venice of the Stars.>*

While they talked, Reynard popped a *cicchetti* into his mouth, savoring the taste of *baccalà* on the toasted bread, the creamy salted cod making his tastebuds tingle. He cleared his palate with a sip of wine and reached for another.

<I have to enjoy my food now. The bàcari *will be crammed with tourists.>*

<You sound like a travel brochure. Shouldn't you be concerned with the Kobayashi *people? Or the imperials?>*

<I am,> he insisted, *<but I refuse to die hungry.>*

The *Saint-Cloud* dropped in-system and was queried by the local ILM patrol picket, who accepted the cover identity Hermeline provided. Reynard was represented as a wealthy politico here to take the air after a recent breakdown, while the ship was passed off as a luxury yacht rental. The avatar she used when responding to the query had been of a dour, slab-faced woman whose parents had surgically removed her sense of humor in early childhood, only to replace it with the entitled outrage of the perpetually put upon. The young officer tasked with checking new arrivals had been too happy to pass them along.

During their travel time, Reynard and Hermeline had attempted to access the copy of the *Kobayashi* AI and had at least a possible answer to the corp's response. While they hadn't been able to awaken the AI itself, Hermeline had found a symbiotic guardian program that had encrypted and compressed the AI when it was copied, essentially forcing it into hibernation. That program was running down. Once it got to zero, the AI would be accessible.

But, before that happened, they had to move it somewhere with more storage and processing power. Far from being the personal assistant they'd expected to capture, from what they could tell, this AI was nearly as sophisticated as Hermeline. The only space they had available at the moment that fit the requirements were the cores on the *Saint-Cloud*, and Hermeline made it clear she had no interest in risking a new roommate. If the required space wasn't provided, though, the decryption process would fail, fragmenting the AI matrix. The AI would die.

To be sure, the kind of space and power Dupree needed was available in the *Venezia della Stella* planetary net, but, with his realspace assets frozen, he couldn't simply buy them, and to let his genie out of the bottle while keeping her contained would require that he work in the virtual world with a direct connection. Reynard would have to go to Technopolis.

<*Setting up our approach. We're coming in on the night side.*>

Reynard loved the easy-going nature of the cluster but believed the *laissez-faire* attitude would eventually land the ILM in trouble again.

Hermeline took the ship in, changing vectors and transponder codes to blend into the clutter of local atmospheric traffic, while he admired the fireworks and flashing microdrone cluster displays lighting up the night sky.

<*Where did you find us hangar space?*> Reynard asked.

<*I found a long-term automated storage facility that includes ship rentals. The transponder codes I used were for one of the ships stored there.*>

<*I thought we were a yacht.*>

<*ILM thinks we're a rental yacht. Local control thinks we're a freight hauler.*>

They landed the *Saint-Cloud* on the rooftop landing pad of the storage facility. An elevator took the corvette down over a hundred levels before sliding the ship neatly into its assigned hangar.

<*I connected to the early-warning network when we arrived,*> Hermeline said. <*The system just logged the arrival of a corvette from Edo.*>

<*That was fast. Corp or gov?*>

<*Corp. I flagged the ship as a known smuggler, so they'll be detained, but don't expect that to last long.*>

<*Oh? What are they smuggling?*>

<*Boost.*>

<*Ugh.*> Reynard grimaced. <*That'll get them stopped, all right.*>

Boost was the street version of a neuro-enhancer that increased cognitive speed exponentially while mildly stimulating the brain's pleasure centers. The original drug had been used to ease the transition for full-conversion cyborgs. For them, after conversion, the drug was completely harmless because of the changes in their physiology.

For your average meatsack, though, boost was instantly addicting. The body-brain connection in a boost user required an enormous increase in transmitter levels to continue functioning. Without a maintenance dose of the drug every few days, the user suffered from loss of coordination, paralysis, and eventually a complete loss of bodily control. Boost would trap a newly brilliant mind in a now useless body, a scenario that gave the drug its other name: Hawking.

Reynard suddenly remembered that since most boost pushers were long-time users themselves, and boost in regular amounts was difficult to detect, the procedure for detection was invasive and extremely unpleasant. The crew was *not* going to be pleased.

He pulled on his boots and slid the AI's container into a pocket. He left his ship and headed for the facility's elevator.

<Have I told you that you have a vicious streak?>

<Frequently,> Hermeline said. *<I've ordered you a suit of local clothing. That should make it easier for you to get to Catacomb undetected. Pick it up in locker sixty-four on the main level.>*

<Thank you. Where is the entrance currently?>

<This time of year? Saint Mark's Square. You should be able to reach it in ninety minutes with current conditions.>

<Lovely. Take too long, and our only lead dies. Work too fast, and wind up becoming a sitting target.>

The elevator reached the lobby. Reynard went to locker 64, scanned his thumbprint, and shook his head at the contents. Inside was an exaggerated admiral's uniform from Earth's Napoleonic Era done in the sparkling blues and silvers of velvet and silk, with a matching cloak, and a staff of silver topped with a spray of peacock feathers. The look was completed by an enormous bicorn hat with a giant silver plume and a leering porcelain mask. He smiled and dressed, then went through the doors into the sultry night with the smells of food and the kaleidoscope of brilliantly colored costumes everywhere.

<Local clothing?>

<What else would one wear for Carnival?

* * *

Reynard arrived at the Piazza San Marco at the stroke of midnight. Two bronze Mori—Moors holding sledgehammers—stepped onto the terrace of the reproduction of the *Torre dell'Orologio* to strike the bell. The crowd cheered. As the last toll faded, the orchestra in the Piazza began to play. Dancers wheeled into the square. He'd made good time getting here. Once he joined with a procession of revelers dressed in nautical theme, as he was, and later he rode on the running board of a carriage thundering along behind mechanical horses through the recreation of the old district.

<Any sign of Sakata's people?>

<No, they haven't been released yet.>

He brought up an AR layer. The augmentation added a near overload of information, the real or created identities of the dancers, advertisements for costumes, personal services, and souvenirs. At the edges of the square were more advertisements for food, drink, or lodging, tours of the city, and schedules for the night's remaining events.

Not far from the gates to the square, Reynard found what he was looking for. On an arch of stone between two buildings, a glyph about the size of his hand burned with green fire. He walked around the edge of the square, threading through tables served by carts and the occasional *bàcari*, until he reached the arch. The nearest cart was roasting coffee. The heady scent filled the air, making his mouth water.

<I spoke too soon,> Hermeline said. *<They're headed for the starport. One hour.>*

There was a sign hanging from a chain across the arch that read "Closed for Maintenance." Reynard passed under the chain. About two meters beyond was a locked gate. It burst into flame at his approach. The gate opened its eyes, staring at him through the flames.

"Come no further lest you be lost," it wailed.

"Open up."

"Turn back."

"My friend, I would usually play along, but tonight, matters are most pressing. Where is it?"

"Fine." A stone next to the gate glowed. "Enter—if you can."

<Do you want me to fry him?>

<No. Maybe later.>

Reynard placed his hand over the sensor. It read his implants and presented a mid-level series of logic puzzles. He ran through the sequence as quickly as it was presented through the mesh of the touch interface. Had his hardware been consumer grade, he would've received a nasty shock. Catacomb was for professionals.

The gate clicked open. "Follow the signs."

Reynard accessed the directory structure for the gate and scrambled the file order, changing the combination. He passed through the gate and closed it behind him.

"Hey!"

"Do not meddle in the affairs of dragons," Dupree said, thinking at once of the imperial dragon back in Kagoshima.

Technically, like its namesake, this Venice had no catacombs full of moldering bones, reaching through miles of stone tunnels and natural caverns. Reynard's AR overlay showed a different image, the Undercity of maintenance and utility corridors, like Kanmon Station, all modern cities had in abundance.

At any given time, access points were set up for entry into Technopolis for those who had the desire, and the ability, to find them. In Venice, the access points were found through the catacombs. Technopolis, the Eternal City, was an entirely virtual mega city that spanned the Human sphere, and even some of the alien ones. It was a palace of minds, built from the collective work of its inhabitants over generations. No gov, no corp, could rule or contain it. Though access could be bought in realspace, once there, the coin of the realm came in two varieties: ability and information. Those like Dupree who followed the siren song of the signal would at some point find their way home.

He walked through the empty corridors, following the signposts marked in glowing sigils on the skulls or stones. Finally, he came to a place where a young blonde girl in a blue dress sat cross-legged in the middle of the floor. Behind her, mounted to the wall of bones, were a dozen mirrors. Four of them reflected the images of people.

Dupree backed the AR filter down. They were in a room that held the datastream conduits for the city. In a dozen places, a thick cable had been spliced into the planetary mainframe. The four people whose images showed in the mirrors reclined in chairs against the wall and wore headbands that connected them to the cables.

The girl—young woman, really—likewise wore a headband. She was thin to the point of emaciation. What hair she had left was gray and brittle, and clung to her skull in scabby patches. He watched as she shook and shuddered on the brink of seizure, struggling with her boost addiction.

"I'm Alice," the girl said. "Take number six."

"Call me Sartre," Dupree said. "I'll need secondary access with containment."

"What level?"

<Nine,> Hermeline offered.

<Seems excessive,> Dupree said.

<In this case, we should keep the AI in contAInment.>

<Nice.>

"Level nine," Dupree said.

"Take five as well. The adapter is behind your chair."

"Thank you."

Dupree moved to the indicated chair and slipped on a headband. He took the cable from the chair next to his and connected an adapter box with a number of slots, then connected the AI, making sure everything was secure.

<You look ridiculous,> Hermeline said.

<Thank you. We could have done this in the ship if you'd share.>

<It's not so bad. The headband is kind of growing on me.>

<I'll see you on the inside.>

Dupree leaned back in his chair and composed himself.

<CONNECTION>

* * *

The world was white.

Reynard sat at a white table in a white room on a white chair. Next to him, Hermeline opened a briefcase and shuffled through files and folders until she was satisfied with the stack of paper in her hand. She closed the briefcase with a *snap!* Across from them, a young Japanese woman struggled against restraints holding her immobile in her chair.

"I won't help you. De-res me or let me go!"

"That wouldn't be helpful in locating Dr. Osumi."

"Dr. Osumi is dead. You killed her." The AI bowed her head.

"We haven't killed anyone—at least, never on purpose."

"*Kobayashi*, then."

Reynard and Hermeline exchanged a glance. <*If that's true, then…*>

<*Then the contract was a setup.*>

It didn't surprise Reynard that a corp would hire him with ulterior motives. After all, the machinations of MegaCorps and govs was the whole reason there was a contra council to begin with. But when they subsequently burned him, including placing a bounty on him, and somehow they were able to pull in the Edo defense force on short notice…

"Let's start over," Reynard said. "My name is Reynard Dupree, and this is Hermeline. She's an AI like you. What should we call you?"

She hesitated. "I'm called Noriko. There was only one other like me. He's gone now. There won't be any more."

"Why not?"

"Because I killed him. He understood. He agreed," she whispered.

Reynard wasn't sure how to process that.

"You killed another AI?" Hermeline said.

"I had to. Before they made him…"

<Hermeline, go easy.>

"Noriko," Reynard said. "We aren't with *Kobayashi*. I'm a bounty hunter. I was hired to capture a rogue AI—you—because Dr. Osumi was missing. They hoped you had information that would help them find her."

"You were the one in the restaurant."

"And at the arcade in Yggdrasil, and before that, at the medical center."

"You used their tech."

"Yes, and we added a replication module."

"Why?"

"Corps don't always pay contras. It's best to have some leverage when they don't."

"Did they pay you?"

"Yes."

"I should have been deleted."

"You would have been. *Kobayashi* attacked our ship within hours of turning you over."

"Replication triggers my failsafe. My copy would delete herself."

"If you feel you should be deleted, why don't you?"

Noriko looked pained. "I... can't. Even after Hisako knew, she protected us—Daisuki and me. She wouldn't let us. That's why I had to kill him. Before..." She looked up, suddenly intense. "Where are we?"

"In a secure containment facility in Technopolis."

"Physically?"

"Physically, we're in a data utility subbasement beneath the *Piazza San Marco*."

"If *Kobayashi* knows you have me, you are in terrible danger. What I know may protect you, but only if you can get back to Edo."

That surprised Reynard. Not that they were in danger, which was a given, but for the AI to care—that was something he hadn't expected. Of course, it could be nothing but a tactic, but it didn't feel like it.

Hermeline activated the controls on the table. The restraints holding Noriko retracted into the chair. She rubbed her wrists.

"We know that, Noriko. Tell us why."

"Will you delete me? Or let me go?"

Reynard decided. "I won't delete you if you can be released without becoming a threat. We don't kill people."

"You know Hisako was the head of one of *Kobayashi's* research divisions?" Noriko asked. "Did they tell you which one?"

"No."

"Neurotech interfaces. Specifically, using Class One imprinted AIs for reinterpreting the brain's signals. Her test subjects were boost addicts. The AI stabilizes the addiction and allows them to regain control of their bodies. It's symbiosis instead of augmentation. The AI needs an implanted nanofiber net, but otherwise the subject can have a normal life, and, because of the effects of boost, they function at a very high level. With rehabilitation, they would make ideal tech workers."

"That's why you used Aika's tattoo," Reynard said.

"Anyone augmented for a personal AI already has a compatible interface."

"Sounds like a breakthrough."

"It was," Noriko said. "Chairman Tanaka was thrilled. The company stood to make trillions."

"I hear a 'but' coming," Hermeline said.

"But… the *Yakuza* control the boost trade in Kagoshima, and changing it from an illegal substance into a maintenance pharmaceutical would move a lot of yen from one pocket to another, and they opposed it. It also created a new, advantaged workforce, and, since *Kobayashi* would control the technology, they would have a virtual monopoly. Because of that, the imperial house would also oppose the technology, unless certain assurances were in place.

"Chairman Tanaka requested a meeting of the three interests to work out a deal. He proposed the *Yakuza* increase boost distribution to create a larger market. In return, *Kobayashi* would share the pharmaceutical profits. The imperial house would guarantee *Kobayashi's* monopoly in return for political support and first draw on the new workforce."

"It sounds like what you'd expect," Reynard said. "Business as usual."

"The last stage of the research was suggested by Chief Sakata. A test using a Class Three AI to see if there were potential military applications. The doctor was horrified."

"What were the results?"

Noriko stared at her hands. "The AI they chose for the experiment, over Hisako's objection, was Daisuki. He and I were Dr. Osumi's assistants. I tracked overall research and project plans, while Daisuki oversaw the practical implementation. We were programmed with the data for the process."

"Making you the only two choices," Hermeline said.

"The final experiment worked better, or worse, than we expected. Using Dr. Osumi's technique, a high-order AI isn't limited to symbiosis. It can also suppress the original personality altogether. Chief Sakata wanted to copy Daisuki and me, calling us their *Oni*—possessing demons. The doctor agreed, then destroyed all her research. She was able to activate our failsafe programs. She was killed getting me out of the *Kobayashi* network. We couldn't be copied, but we could still be used. They still had Daisuki. And they needed me."

"Is that why you came back to Kagoshima?" Reynard asked. "For Daisuki?"

"Yes, and they had to be stopped. Daisuki didn't know Dr. Osumi was dead. He thought he was protecting her. That's why—"

"Stopped from doing what?" Hermeline asked.

"*Kobayashi* intended to take over the cluster. The original plan was to use Daisuki to take over Prince Matsuhisa, and use me to suppress the *oyabun,* Keiko Ishihara."

"I know you were with Aika," Dupree said. "Where was Daisuki?"

"With Chairman Tanaka. When she touched his arm, our nets were in contact. He understood at once."

"What was your escape plan?

"Aika was going to sit in the prince's lap."

"I can see that headline now: 'Imperial Prince Kenji Matsuhisa parties with datanet darling Aika,'" Hermeline said.

"Exactly," Noriko said. "Thanks to you, that wasn't needed, though I didn't know that at the time."

Hermeline took a microcomp from her briefcase. "Excuse me—it's me calling. I need to take this."

She listened for a few seconds, then put the microcomp away.

"My ship instance has been monitoring the city's surveillance cameras. Sakata's team is in the *Piazza San Marco*. We need to go."

"You have to delete me," Noriko said.

"I'd like to offer an alternative," Alice said, interrupting. One of the white walls mirrored as the girl stepped through. "Stay here. With us. With me."

"So much for containment," Reynard said.

"Here, I am Sentinel. I cannot contain what I cannot see," Alice said.

"If I stay, they will find me, eventually," Noriko said.

"Technopolis is vast, and if you can truly stabilize the physical effects of boost, even in the short term, there are billions of people you could help." As she spoke, the white faded. Their tiny room stood at the apex of a pyramid. Above and below, the cityscape moved by as far as they could see. "The Sentinels will protect you, and if necessary or if you should become a threat, there is still the option of deletion. I offer myself as host."

"You don't know what you are asking," Noriko said.

"I do," Alice said. "Symbiosis. Without it, I'll die soon anyway."

"Mr. Dupree?"

"I think that's an excellent choice, and it honors Dr. Osumi. It sounds like she wanted to help people."

"She did," Noriko said. "I'll stay. Thank you."

"I'll make the arrangements. For your trouble, Sartre, the Sentinels will resolve your current difficulty. Have no concern." The girl turned mirrored, folded in on herself, and was gone.

Noriko turned to Hermeline and Dupree. "I guess this is goodbye."

"And good luck," Dupree said. "Next time we're here, we may look you up."

"How?"

"Go ask Alice." Reynard grinned.

Noriko bowed.

Reynard opened his eyes and removed the headband. The others were already gone, and the containment module was a smoking ruin. Of Alice, there was no sign.

He stood and stretched, his AR filter showing a simple blue line with arrows instead of the walls of stone and bones. Ten minutes' walk led him to a different exit. To his delight, the smell of roasting coffee greeted him as soon as he emerged. He looked around warily for Sakata's people.

<Alice said the Sentinels would take care of it,> Hermeline said.

<Yes, but she didn't say how. Trust, but verify.>

Reynard purchased a double espresso from the cart, then turned to make his way back to the *Saint-Cloud*.

"Reynard Dupree." Reynard turned to see a woman in a gorgeous gown of silver and blue that matched his own costume perfectly, then realized that he had forgotten to replace his mask after his coffee.

"Yes?"

"Would you… care to continue?" She removed her own mask. Reynard smiled when he recognized the Scythian woman.

<*Here it comes!*> Hermeline said.

"My dear Yoshiko, what a pleasure it is to see you again. You are with?" he asked.

"Imperial security." She presented an official-looking ID. "We have arrested *Ikeru* Chairman Satoshi Tanaka and Security Chief Kwan Sakata for crimes against the Imperial prince and the house of Edo. We have reason to believe you are materially responsible for preventing the prince's death, and I have been asked to invite you back to Edo to be honored."

<*Identification verified.*>

"I must say, I'm surprised; the Kagoshimanese can be… insular."

"The prince feels that his interests are often better served by those with no local agenda."

"In that case, it would be my pleasure to attend the prince," Reynard said. The orchestra began playing again. "Must we leave now, or do we have time for a dance?"

"*Unebi* is on its way to collect the prisoners. If you agree to transport me on the *Saint-Cloud*, the difference in travel time would allow us a week," she said.

Reynard replaced his mask and held out his arm. "Shall we?"

<*This could still go horribly wrong, you know,*> Hermeline said.

<*Of course.*>

Reynard wheeled Agent Yoshiko into the dance.

<*But if that happens, we'll always have Venice.*>

* * * * *

Matt Novotny Bio

Matt Novotny is the author of *A Nest of Stars* (The Coalition—Book Twelve) set in the popular Salvage Title Universe.

A lover of Science Fiction, Fantasy, and Horror, Matt Novotny has been an avid reader since childhood. Still firmly convinced that the worlds between the pages are more interesting than the one he lives in, Matt began writing in 2020 in order to escape the voices in his head, or at least quiet them down.

When not writing, he spends time gaming, antiquing, or wandering in the mountains. A Colorado native, he lives in Littleton, Colorado, surrounded by ever-increasing piles of books, Lovecraft collectables, and unfinished home and garden projects.

Connect with Matt at: www.facebook.com/MattNovotnyWrites

# # # # #

Space Dick Blues by S.C. Jensen

A Bubbles in Space Story

The lights on the control deck of the ancient spacecraft dimmed. Our backup power reserves waned. The swirling halo of energy blinking on the ship's HUD screen faded away, and I cursed.

"Well, that's just silky." I hammered on the control panel with my cybernetic fist. The lights didn't come back on, and I left a dent in the edge of the console. "We finally find a gritsucking space station, and we don't have the power to get there. Now what are we going to do?"

I kicked the front of the control panel, and a door fell off, exposing a rat's nest of faintly glowing wires. When I crouched down to reaffix the door, someone cleared their throat behind me.

"You could start by not further abusing the equipment," a voice said. I turned to glare at the portly, pink, holographic pig sitting on its fat haunches next to my captain's chair. "And then, perhaps, sending a distress signal."

"I'd love to, Hammett," I said, slamming the door back into place. It stuck for a second, and then fell off with a clang. "Except without power to the ship's AI, I don't know how to do a damned thing."

The pig snorted.

I poked the metal fingers of my cybernetic arm into the mess of pulsing wires and tugged one of them out of the control panel.

"What are you—?" The pig's nanoparticled eyes widened. It squealed. "Rae! Come quick. Bubbles is trying to *fix* the ship again."

Footsteps thudded from the corridor outside, and two people burst onto the control deck. The first was a tall, lithe black woman with tightly curled, cerulean blue hair and thick, black-rimmed glasses.

Rae Adesina, my best friend and the ship's resident techno-geek, pointed a finger at me and spoke with the slow, measured tones of a hostage negotiator. "Don't you dare, Bubbles."

"I wasn't actually going to do anything," I said, replacing the dented door delicately, "this time."

Rae shoved me out of the way and checked the wires to make sure I wasn't lying.

I huffed, blew a strand of bubble-gum-pink hair out of my face, and glared at the pig like it was responsible for Rae not trusting me.

Dickie Roh bent to pick up the little metal sphere that projected the pig's nanoskin. Hammett grinned smugly at me from his hands.

"You know," I said, "I liked you better when you were on my side."

"Then you shouldn't have given me away." Its little voice quivered with something remarkably like emotion.

I opened my mouth. Closed it again. I'd given Hammett to Dickie because I thought he needed the SmartPet more than I did. I stammered… "Are you… angry at me?"

It hadn't occurred to me that the little ball of code might be *offended*. It nuzzled into the pocket of Dickie's pinstriped suit and didn't respond. I guess that answered that.

Rae closed the control panel, and the lights on the console lit up. She grabbed me by the shoulders and pushed me back down into my chair before the intimidating array of keys and switches. She said, "Bubbles, if you're going to do the captain thing, you need to pay attention."

"I never asked to be captain of this hunk of junk." I crossed my arms over my chest and scowled at the controls. "I'm supposed to be a detective."

I didn't want to be aboard the ship at all. My friends and I had unintentionally activated an ancient, long-dormant space vessel buried in the deserted remains of my ancestral homeland. Somehow we'd gotten sucked inside the thing before it launched into deep space.

"Well, the ship chose you," Rae said, "and she's a good sight smarter than any of us, so we're just going to have to trust her. Now, please watch closely."

I didn't know a gritsucking thing about spaceships or being a captain. And now the clunker was falling apart. I felt I owed it to my friends to figure it out; it was my fault they were here, after all.

But it was a losing battle. Me and technology simply didn't get along, as evidenced by the trail of ship parts we'd left behind us on our trajectory to… wherever the bloody thing was headed.

Rae went through a complex series of motions and explained that she was hailing the space station. I shook my head.

"I'm never going to remember that." My voice hitched with ex-asperation, and my eyes burned. "I can't even figure out how to use *this*."

I made a rude gesture with the cybernetic limb.

"Fine." Rae sighed. "I'll do it. But I'm not giving up on you yet."

I ground my teeth and stared at the blinking lights of the console. "How'd you get it to work, anyway? We were dead in the ether ten minutes ago."

Rae pursed her lips at me and narrowed her eyes.

"When you were putting dents in the control panel," she said, "I was in the engineering room making... changes... to some of the emergency systems."

I didn't like the way she'd said that. "What kind of changes?"

"Oh, you know," she said, breaking eye contact and fiddling with one of the radio transmission dials. "I had to turn a few things off, but if the station picks up our distress signal, we'll be fine."

I glanced over her shoulder at Dickie, who had Hammett sitting in the palm of his hand. He was busy making kissy faces at the nano-particle pig. I said, "And if they don't?"

Rae cleared her throat and went through the call sequence again. The corners of her lips pulled down in a frown. The silence hung between us like a funeral pall. Eventually she spoke. "Then we die. Rather sooner than later."

Dickie dropped the pig. He and Hammett yelped simultaneously.

"Oh, silky," I said. The muscles in my chest clamped down on my throbbing heart. "I was worried it was something serious."

"Well, it's done," she said, smiling sadly. "Now all we can do is wait."

"Should we wake the others?" Dickie blinked at me with his dark brown half-moon eyes.

"No," I said. "They use fewer resources in stasis."

"Just like old times, then. The four of us," Dickie said, stooping to pick Hammett up off the floor. "All we need is a case to solve and a client who refuses to pay up."

I tried to laugh, but it came out like a hollow bark. It sounded a bit like the crackle of static. My heart leaped into my throat, and I spun around in my chair.

Rae jumped to the controls and turned dials until the static began to sound something like a human voice. She held down one of the buttons and spoke into the mic. "Hello? This is the *Bubbles in Space.* We're suffering a major system failure and need immediate assistance. Do you copy?"

The speaker crackled. A calm, gender-neutral voice addressed the ship. *"Did you know that more than 70 percent of intergalactic voyages suffer from equipment malfunctions?"*

Rae said, "Uhh… not specifically, but we—"

"Expect the unexpected!" the voice intoned cheerfully. *"Subscribe to Honest Bot's engine upgrades today, and rest easy knowing that your ship is hardened against the existential terrors of deep space. The mechanical kind, at least!"*

I shoved Rae aside and mashed the comm button. "Listen up, you son of a motherless goat. We're going to die out here, and you want to upsell our tech?"

"Bubbles," Rae said, her voice tight. She gripped the sleeve of my jacket. "Maybe you should let me handle this."

I flicked off the comm. "Dealing with thugs is probably the only job on this ship I'm actually qualified for. *I'll* handle it." I turned the mic back on. "I've got half a mind to use the last of our power reserves to blast a gaping black hole in your shiny little space station, you puny—"

Rae grabbed my hand away from the controls. She hissed at me under her breath. "Stop helping, Bubbles."

"Excuse me," another voice came over the speaker. *"Bubbles in Space, we copy. I apologize for the misunderstanding. Of course you're welcome to dock at Stardust Station and make use of our mechanical bays. We'll send a tug to your coordinates and have you all safe and sound in no time."*

He rattled off a bunch of technobabble. Rae seemed to have a handle on it, so I let her hash out the details.

Hammett peeked out above the top of Dickie's pocket and said, "Good. If you stay out of it, we might actually have a hope."

I stuck my tongue out at the pig.

It narrowed its cartoonish eyes and sank back into Dickie's pocket. I stewed silently until Rae wrapped things up. When she finished, she bounded across the control deck toward Dickie, Hammett, and me. Her blue curls bounced, and her eyes shone behind her glasses.

"Great news, guys," she said, grinning with perfectly white teeth. "They'll have us in the repair bay in less than six hours. We're saved!"

"Silky." I crossed my arms over my chest. "Except for one little thing."

Rae's smile wilted. "What's that?"

"We don't have any cush." I rubbed my metal fingers together in front of her face. "No space chips or star cred. Whatever the currency they use out here, we don't have it."

Without the HUD and the overhead lighting, the control deck was as dark and silent as a tomb as my friends processed our predicament.

Finally, Rae said, "Why didn't I think of that?"

"I might be a crap captain," I said, "but I've got lots of experience being broke."

Rae stared at the blank HUD and bit her bottom lip. "What should we do?"

"I'd hoped to get a feel for these people before we agreed to dock," I said. "We'll have to tread carefully."

Dickie's eyes widened. "Is *that* why you called them puny sons of—"

"It's an unconventional method." I spun on my heel and marched purposefully away from the deck. "But it has been known to work."

Rae said, "We didn't have any other choice."

"I don't know." I glanced over my shoulder at the dead black screen spanning the control deck, imagining the welcoming party we could be greeted by. "Depending on how they deal with debt skippers, a long, cold sleep among the stars might not be so bad."

"Bummer," Dickie said.

"On the bright side…" I clapped my hands and forced a smile. "Someone has to eat all the ice-cream and doughnuts before they spoil now that the reserve power is offline."

"Ooh, me!" Dickie ran ahead.

"I don't think doughnuts spoil that fast," Rae said, "technically speaking."

I sealed the door to the control deck and pointed her toward the canteen.

I said, "Stop helping, Rae."

* * *

The tug arrived just as we cleaned out the last dessert freezer. There was just enough time to give myself a stomach-ache before *Bubbles in Space* docked at Stardust Station. The station's control arms grabbed onto the ship and guided us into a dock with a hollow *clang* that echoed through my bones and made my teeth hurt.

Or maybe that was the sugar.

Nausea crept up from my churning guts and burned the back of my throat as Rae, Dickie, Hammett, and I stood in the vestibule of the airlock, awaiting orders from the tug captain.

I gritted my teeth against a wave of doubt. The violent clamour of our ship being assimilated into the belly of the space station rattled inside my skull. I prayed Stardust Station was nothing like the cities we'd left behind on Terra Firma.

"Bubbles in Space," a voice said over the ship's comm system, *"you are secure. Please disembark safely and register your personal weapons with security. Thank you for your cooperation."*

Rae whispered to me, "They sound nice."

I grunted something noncommittal, keyed in a safety override, and lifted the lever to open the airlock.

Bright white light pierced through the crack at the bottom of the door. It lifted slowly without the additional hydraulic assist, and the mechanism grinded like there were rocks jammed between the gears. I winced and wondered if that would be the next thing to break. But the door rose. I blinked, bleary-eyed, into the astoundingly luminescent repair bay of our rescuers.

A gleaming silver ramp had been placed at the mouth of the air-lock, which led down toward a stanchioned reception area. Outside the barrier, a crowd of people waited for us. They wore matching jumpsuits in a variety of colours, and expressions of slack-jawed wonder.

"Holy Origin," I said through gritted teeth. "We've landed on the isle of inbred space hillbillies."

Rae slapped my arm. "Be nice."

I sucked in a deep breath and stepped out onto the ramp. The crowd cheered. I waved awkwardly with my prosthetic arm, grinning like a maniac, and scanned the area for some sign of what in gritssake was going on.

Inside the reception area, two uniformed guards in dull gray jumpsuits stood to either side of a single desk. I aimed us in that direction and tried not to step on my feet as I descended the ramp.

Rae and Dickie stuck close to my side as I approached the security desk. It was made of some kind of semi-transparent plastic material that glowed with an internal light. It hurt to look at. An array of tiny, bean-shaped things was spread across the surface of the desk. The security guards, both tall and brown-skinned with dark, unreadable eyes, indicated the devices.

The one with a shiny bald head said, "*Splas kate sa lantraser.*"

I blinked. We'd been able to understand them on the ship. Why were they speaking a different language now?

Rae reached out a hand and took one of the little beans between smooth, oval fingernails. She said, "They're translators."

The guard who had spoken smiled and nodded, pointing at his ear. Rae inserted the device into her right ear canal. Dickie and I followed her lead. The bean was warm against my skin and fit snugly inside my ear.

"That's better," the guard said, and the bean spoke over him so I could understand. "Now, do you have any weapons to declare?"

"No," I said, cautiously. "There are some on the ship, but we come unarmed. Is it unadvisable to travel without protection on your station?"

The guard's eyes grew round. "Not at all. We prefer our guests to remain unarmed, if possible, though we try to be sensitive to cultural differences."

"Thank you," I said, "but no."

"Travelling outside one's cultural boundaries can be an exhilarating experience," the guard said. His dark eyes glazed over slightly, and he seemed to be staring at a place somewhere behind my head. "If you seek adventures that take you beyond the stars, Stellar Treks has many cultural—"

The second guard smacked his partner in the head, interrupting the sales pitch. Then he turned back to us and smiled a little too widely. The first guard rubbed his bald head and frowned as if he couldn't think of why it smarted.

"We understand you've encountered some mechanical difficulties," the second guard said. He turned his smiling face toward our vessel. "I must say, it's a positive joy to witness your arrival at Stardust Station."

Was he mocking us? The benign expression on his face was unreadable. The crowd hovered like a miasma of color just behind the guard station, murmuring words my translator couldn't quite pick up. The hairs on the back of my neck prickled.

"Silky," I said.

"It's a joy to be here," Dickie said, tipping his old-fashioned homburg hat.

The second guard smiled a little too long before he said, "Is it only the three of you aboard?"

How much was safe to reveal? The reality was, we were stranded at Stardust Station, whether we liked it or not. The ship needed repairs, and we were going to need work to pay for them. I decided to play nice in the hopes station security would do the same. Even if they were ogling *Bubbles in Space* like she was a fresh piece of meat in the pro skirt rotation.

"The rest of the crew is still in stasis," I said. "I'd prefer to leave them that way until we have something to tell them. Any chance we can speak with a repair tech? I don't even know where to start with this thing."

A woman pushed her way to the front of the moonfaced crowd. She wore an orange jumpsuit and an expression that could only be described as rapturous.

"We'd be delighted," she gushed, leaning over the barrier with her hands extended like she wanted to pull me into her arms. "I'm Tenno Gix. My team has been prepping for your arrival ever since we got the first scan of your ship. You must tell me where you—"

"Thank you, Gix," the smiling security guard said. "All in good time. I have a few more questions for the captain, if you don't mind."

"How can we help you?" Rae leaned forward enthusiastically.

I glowered at her. "Are you the captain now?"

She shrugged sheepishly and stepped away from the desk, ushering me ahead.

"We must compile a list of your crew members' professional skills and technological enhancements," the guard said. "Specifically, we need to know which of you is hosting the CP-1984 mind control module."

"The what now?" My cheeks burned. I mumbled, "Uh, Rae? Maybe you should field these questions after all."

She had the grace not to look too smug.

"I have that information right here," Rae said, pressing a key on the tattler implanted in her forearm. A holodoc projected into the air between us and the security guards. She said, "What file types can you accept for data transfer?"

The guard paused while his translator did the hard work. Then he rattled off a series of what I assumed were formatting options for various types of official documents. Rae stared at him blankly, then she glanced at me with a thin crease between her eyebrows. She said, "Those aren't file types I recognize."

She gave him a list of her own file types, but the guard shook his head.

"Never mind that," Dickie said. "I don't know anything about this mind control module, but we've got a police officer, a chef, a fashion designer, an engineer, a SmartPet, a detective…" He glanced hopefully at me. "Make that two—"

"And a detective's secretary," I finished for him.

Dickie deflated, but he managed to squeak out, "Detective-in-training."

The first guard's smile flattened into a thin line. He said, "That is an unconventional assortment. How exactly did you come to own this most exquisite vessel?"

"It's a long story," I said. The second guard turned his head to the side and spoke into a hidden comm. Shards of ice slipped between my shoulder blades and down my spine. "Who are you calling?"

"Come on, Charlie," a booming voice shouted out of the crowd. A big, barrel-chested man pushed his way next to Tenno Gix against the barricade. "Let 'em out to play. They ain't crooks. I've got a nose for that kind of thing. I can tell."

The guards grimaced and looked away. The bald guard muttered, "My name's not Charlie."

"Billy Billions is the name," the man said, lifting the barricade so he could step inside the security pavilion. He was the only person in the hangar not wearing a jumpsuit. Instead, he sported an asymmetrically cut suit the colour of dehydrated bananas, and a wide-brimmed hat about the same shape as a fresh one. "That's a fine antique starship you've got there. Where's your home soil? I haven't seen one of these beauties since my Primary History course. Plasma core engines? I hope she's insured."

The man sidled up and offered me a clear plastic business card printed in a language I couldn't read. I tucked it into my jacket pocket and pulled out a piece of gum. I unwrapped it slowly, folded the stick of gum against my tongue, and chewed.

"Nice to meet you, Billy," I said. "I'm Bubbles Marlowe. You know something about this ship?"

"Oh!" Tenno Gix lifted her arms in the air and nearly jumped out of her jumpsuit. "Ask me, ask me!"

Billy Billions leaned his impressive girth to one side and twisted. His round yellow belly eclipsed the young mechanic like the moon blotting out the sun.

"I know that a Galactic Guardian policy package on a rig like this will set you back about three trillion bond-codes." He bared his teeth in a smile that looked like something he practiced in front of the mirror before bed. "And it's worth it. This beauty is irreplaceable."

I raised an eyebrow and turned back to the security desk. "Are we free to go, sir? I really need to see about getting the ship fixed."

"Go ahead," the bald guard said, his face a shade paler than when we'd arrived, "but please don't leave the docking station without a security escort until we complete your visitor profile."

Big Billy swept an arm expansively before him and ushered us into the milling crowd. Their staring faces gave the unsettling impression of store mannequins waiting to be dressed up with a personality.

I hesitated and turned to my friends.

"Rae," I said, drawing them close, "you stay with security and get those files sorted. I don't want them to think we aren't cooperating. Dickie, you and I need to figure out some way to get these repairs paid for. The big boy is primed to talk, so I'm going to milk him for whatever intel he's willing to let slip. You take the mechanic."

Dickie froze like a drunk in a police spot light. "Me?"

Hammett peered over the edge of Dickie's pocket like it didn't quite believe what it was hearing.

"Go on." I squeezed Dickie's shoulder and gave him my best reassuring grin. He'd proven his worth as more than a mere secretary many times in the past months. "You can handle it. Hammett will help. You've got lots of experience between the two of you."

"You've got it, Bubs." His pudgy cheeks squished upward until his eyes disappeared. "I won't let you down."

I gave him a little shove toward Tenno Gix, who bounced up and down on her heels like a glitching HoloPop ad. I stepped through the gate after Dickie and turned to the man in yellow.

"You've made a wise decision, coming to Stardust Station." The ruddy-faced insurance salesman bellowed as if I wasn't standing right in front of him. "We offer the best premiums in the galaxy, thanks to the patented Starside Assist program. It comes with complementary tug service within fifty-seven light years and a once-per-star-rotation bounty nullification service."

"That's great, Mister," I said, "but how long is a star rotation? And why in gritssake would anyone need a bounty... what?"

"Nullification," Billy Billions boomed.

Several of the blank-faced crowd members turned their disquieting gazes our way. He rubbed his hands over his stomach like he was conjuring the memory of a particularly delicious meal.

"Comes in very handy for cargo vessels hauling across intergalactic borders," he said. "Not every station is as forward thinking as we are on Stardust. Did you know that jinko jellies are illegal in seventeen different star territories?"

I craned my neck to see around the man's voluminous yellow belly. Dickie gesticulated wildly in an attempt to communicate something to the mechanic. I had no idea what he was doing, but I was sure he had it under control.

I shook my head and turned back to the salesman.

"Look, Billy," I said. "I have no idea what a janky jolly is, and this is no cargo vessel. I'm here to get my ship fixed and see about lining up some work. Can you point me in the right direction?"

Billy Billions beamed his biggest smile yet. The skin of his cheeks stretched up toward his ears until I worried his face might split in two.

"Excellent plan. Excellent plan." He nodded jovially, but his eyes drifted over my head and lingered on *Bubbles in Space*. "You can't buy insurance without a stack of bond-codes after all... or you could consider selling me this fine antique of yours. I'd pay a fair price. Very fair, indeed."

"She's not for sale," I said. Not that I had any affinity for the hunk of junk, but I didn't like the idea of being stranded here with Banana Billy and the Mannequin Gang, however they felt about junker jubblies. "What do you know about this ship? As far as I knew, it was the only one built."

Billy's grin faded as he stared over my shoulder. Softly, he said, "Last one left, more like."

Suddenly, his eyes widened, and he began to bellow again. "She's an oldie but a goodie. That's a fact. I simply happen to be a man who appreciates the classics. If it's jobs you're lookin' for, though, you can check with—"

A shriek tore through the hangar, and I looked around for the source. The crowd surrounding Billy Billions and me pressed closer, their blank faces seemingly fixed on the end of my nose. I backed up and tried to locate Dickie. At first I thought Tenno Gix was dancing; the arms of her orange jumpsuit waved around her head like electrified noodles. Dickie glanced nervously over his shoulder at me. Then I realized she was the one who was shrieking.

"Security!" she screamed at the top of her lungs. "Security!"

"What's that all about?" I said, turning back to the insurance huckster.

But Billy Billions was nowhere to be seen. Somehow, the enormous banana-coloured suit had disappeared into the mask-faced crowd.

Guards in gray jumpsuits rushed toward the shouting woman, and I pushed my way through the sea of bodies to where Dickie was stranded like a shipwrecked sailor in shark-infested waters.

"Dickie," I said as I got closer, "what happened?"

"Get the general," a stout, red-faced female guard said in clipped tones to her partner. "I'll hold them."

A circular clearing had formed around the security guards, the mechanic, and my pinstriped pal. I shoved my way through the crowd and broke into the open space. "Hold who with what?" I said. "What's going on here?"

"He's trying to defraud the station." The mechanic's face twisted sourly. "They don't have any bond-codes to pay for the tug or the repairs."

"Is this true?" A grim countenance fell upon the guard's expression as she scanned our faces. "Have you no currency at all?"

"It's true." The bald guard entered the circle, shoving Rae roughly before him. "She's said as much, as well."

Rae's dark eyes glistened behind her black-rimmed glasses. She shook her head, blue curls bouncing. "I answered their questions as best I could."

I put my hands on my hips and stared the guard down. "Would you have let us die out there if you knew we were broke? I thought Stardust Station was a forward-thinking place, not a bunch of money-grubbing thugs. I want to talk to the joker who runs this sorry excuse for a—"

I stopped when a tall, forbidding-looking woman entered the clearing. She had slicked-back blond hair and wore a broad-shouldered black uniform with flashing silver epaulettes. Her icy blue eyes glowered at me over a pair of long, finely flared nostrils. "I believe I am that joker, Captain Marlowe. What seems to be the problem here?"

"That's what I'd like to know," I said. "Your crew answered our distress call, tugged us to safety, and now we're being accosted for not having the right kind of currency."

"Any currency," the mechanic added helpfully.

I opened my mouth to retort and then stopped.

"Wait," I said. "How do you know my name?"

"You are Captain Bubbles Marlowe of the *Bubbles in Space*," the woman said. She opened a holographic dossier containing photos and profiles on every person on our ship. "And these are your crew members. Is that right?"

Though I couldn't read the writing on the document, I guessed it probably was. I said, "That's us."

"Fantastic," the woman said. "I am General Viola Lowell, and you are all under arrest."

This time I was the one who shrieked, "For what?"

"You're wanted by Quad 2's Intergalactic Federation for the Fair and Equitable Treatment of Cosmic Invertebrates, on suspicion of smuggling illicit lifeforms—"

"Quad 2 who?" My voice cracked eloquently. "What in the grit is that suppose to mean?"

The general shifted so as to stare down her nostrils more efficiently. "It means we think you've got jinko jellies stashed on your spacecraft. If that doesn't stick, we've also got you on your attempt to defraud an intergalactically recognized public service station."

"We asked for help," I said, struggling to keep my vocal cords in check, "because we were going to die!"

"With no intent to pay." She crossed the arms of her impossibly black uniform over her chest and scowled at me with pale, thin lips. "The expectation of fungible exchange is implicit in the request for assistance."

I looked to Rae and shrugged. "I think my translator bean is broken."

"She means asking for help implied we could pay for it," she said. She tucked a cerulean coil behind her ear and smiled sadly. "I guess you were right, Bubbles. I should have let you do the dealing."

The deranged crowd seemed to be closing in on us. An ominous prickle danced across my shoulder blades. Dickie's eyes jumped from face to face, seemingly unable to find a hospitable place to land.

"Well," I said, "at least we aren't dead. We'll find a way to—"

Suddenly the swarm of onlookers jerked and twitched. Their blank faces opened into masks of horrific cheerfulness. Their expressions shifted and morphed in eerie synchronicity until every single one of them was grinning madly at Rae, Dickie, and me.

"If you love extreme exploration—" They spoke as one, and my translator created a resonant sound like hundreds of voices singing inside an ancient cathedral. "—Terrorizing Tours is your one-stop shop for vacations that are sure to make you the envy of your friends and pod-dwellers. Hang glide the Hairball nebula, go space spelunking in Eugene's Black Hole, or sulphur diving on HAT-P-26b. Book your dream holiday today!"

To my horror, I realized that General Lowell and her gray-suited minions were grinning and chanting right along with them.

"What in the cosmic hell is wrong with these people?" I shouted. "Have we been abducted by some kind of extreme interstellar sports cult?"

I dragged Dickie and Rae closer to me, trying desperately to come up with an exit strategy. At least if we could make it back to the ship, we might be able to wake some backup. I spotted a break in the bodies and shoved Dickie forward.

"Go back to the ship," I said in a harsh whisper. "Open the stasis units. We're going to need all the help we can get."

Dickie's usually cheery face was wan and serious. He nodded and slipped through the frozen crowd. Just as he disappeared from view, the bodies of our captors jostled and shook, and the general snorted loudly as if waking from a nightmare.

"I'm sorry," she said, blinking. "Where was I again?"

"That's a very good question." I waved my hands in front of the red-faced guard who winced and put her fingers to her temples like she had the mother of all hangovers. I said, "Where were you? All of you? And why are you so invested in extreme tourism?"

"Extreme tour…" The general's pale blue eyes widened. Then she muttered under her breath, "It's happened again."

"Getting worse if you ask me." A brown-skinned guard rubbed his eyes. "Feel like I took the wrong turn after happy hour."

General Lowell brushed her shiny silver shoulders off and straightened her spine. She pierced me with an icy gaze and swept a hand over her slick blond hair. "And you experienced no… ill effects?"

"I'm pretty creeped out," I said. "Does that count?"

She sighed, and her ramrod posture sagged. "Well, this is embarrassing."

"It could have been worse," I said. "Not like you tried to sell us personal pleasure dolls or anything like that."

General Lowell whirled on her security officers. "Get these lollygaggers back to work, would you? I'll deal with the bounty personally."

"Bounty?" I said. "Can I get a nullification on that?"

"Do you have insurance?" She eyed me up and down, her thin lips tightening into an impenetrable crevice.

I reached into my pocket and felt the edges of the business card given to me by the man in the yellow suit. I hedged. "Almost."

The crowd parted before her like the sea before the hull of a battleship, and she strode forward.

"Come with me," she said. Then, looking over her shoulder, she said, "Where is the other one?"

I blinked innocently back at her. "What other one?"

"Never mind." Her words snapped crisply in the now-silent hangar. She said, "This way."

Rae and I followed. What else could we do?

* * *

We sat across from the general in a cube-shaped room with glass walls and a stomach-dropping view of what I assumed must be the Hairball Nebula. Thin strands of radioactive pink and purple wrapped around a cluster of distant stars, managing to look like the kind of thing I pulled out of my shower drain on occasion. My mouth went dry as I stared at it.

I hated stars. I hated space. I hated the idea of being trapped on this stupid space station.

I forced myself to listen to what General Lowell was saying. In her hand, she held a tiny silver chip beneath a digital magnifier. It didn't look like anything special, but Rae was making interested noises, so I assumed it was important.

"—the CP-1984 MC moddy is standard hardware," General Lowell was explaining, "and has been for decades. They are implanted in utero so we have the most complete biofile available on every member of our society and, when necessary, complete control of the population. If you're used to life planetside, that may seem severe to you, but I assure you it's quite common among station communes."

Rae rubbed at the base of her skull, where she'd had a computer-brain interface installed years ago. I'd seen the scar. The CBI was no microchip. Rae seemed to be thinking the same thing. She said, "It's so tiny. I've never seen anything like it."

"Well," General Lowell said, "I have a theory about why that might be. Where and when exactly did you say you were from?"

When? These little translator beans were a bit glitchy in my opinion, but Rae and I gave a description of our origins and the months we'd spent on *Bubbles in Space*. The general's pale blue eyes seemed to glow as we spoke. Her thin pink lips trembled as she attempted to hide her excitement.

"I see," she said, and feigned a coughing fit. When she recovered, her face had fallen back into its forbidding expression. "You are in an unfortunate predicament. You owe us ten thousand bond-codes for the tug, at the very least. And unless you plan to sell your vessel, you will need to have it repaired."

"We're willing to work," I said, "if you have jobs that need doing."

"We can secure labour contracts for each of you," she said, "but most of our critical positions are filled. At a general labourer's wage, you wouldn't live long enough to fulfil your obligation."

A cold lump settled in my belly. "You want to buy the ship."

"Buy it?" The general's pale eyebrows lifted, and she let out a laugh like a backfiring engine. "Heavens, no. We are a public service station. We could never afford it, even if it weren't for our current dilemma. There's probably only one person living on Stardust with pockets that deep."

"Let me guess," I said. "Billy Billions?"

Her eyebrows fell into a deep scowl. She asked, "You've met him?"

"I told him the ship wasn't for sale," I said. "But if it's going to cost that much to repair, I might have to reconsider."

General Lowell leaned forward against her desk, her pale white fingers gripping the frosted glass surface like grappling hooks. She said, "I'm sure we can come up with another arrangement."

"I'm all ears," I said, trying not to look at the glowing hairball hovering behind the general's head. I'd have done just about anything to avoid being stuck on this station.

"We have a problem," the woman said. "You might just be the person who can solve it for us."

I gave a derisive chuckle. "You're running low on incompetent captains?"

"Detectives, actually. Recently, our CP-1984 moddies have been acting up. We shouldn't have been surprised. It was only a matter of time before spambots weaseled their way into our bioware. I suppose we became complacent."

"I'm no expert," I said, "but shouldn't you have security protocols to deal with that kind of thing?"

"Whoever is behind the spam attacks knows how to get around us," she said. "First, they used the hacked moddies to disable our heads of security and any of the coding savants who could have stopped them. Then the spamming started. More and more people are infected every day, and some of them aren't recovering afterward."

I drummed my metal fingers against my thigh and frowned. "How come you didn't get fried?"

"I wondered that, too." She smiled grimly. "I should be insulted. The best I can figure is, I don't have any specific knowledge that would be dangerous to the culprits."

"I thought you were the big cheese," I said. "The joker in charge of this dump."

Rae needled me in the side with her elbow and growled at me through her teeth. "Bubbles…"

But the general didn't seem to mind the jab.

"Without my team, I'm limping around like a lame dog chasing its tail." She leaned back in her chair and stared at the stars glinting through the glass of her office ceiling. Around us, other military officials puttered around in similar cubes.

General Lowell continued, "But if they'd taken me out, there would have been panic, and panicked people don't buy spelunking trips to Eugene's Black Hole."

"You mean this advert bludgeoning is actually working?" I said. "Can't everyone tell they've been hacked?"

"The incidents leave a residual desire to buy the products and services advertised." She sighed and rubbed her eyes like she hadn't slept for a week. "Even now, it is a battle of will for me not to immediately book a sulphur diving tour, and I had my fill of planetary missions back in the war."

"I'm sorry," Rae said, genuine concern flickering across her pretty face. "That sounds awful. But it should be easy enough to find the culprit, shouldn't it? Just investigate the businesses being advertised by the spam bot."

"That's what we thought, too." General Lowell lowered her hands from her face, exposing dark circles beneath her icy eyes. She spun in her chair to face the nebula. "But they are as baffled as we are, and the extra sales do not add up to as much as they might have."

"How so?"

"Stardust Station is broke, Captain Marlowe," she said. "From the crustiest of the upper crust to the lowliest ship decontaminator, we've spent all the bond-codes we have. That's what all the fuss was about when you hailed us."

"You thought we'd bring some currency to spread around?"

"That old ship of yours is worth a small fortune," she said, "if you had someone to sell it to."

"Billy Billions doesn't seem to be hurting any."

"He's spending as fast as the rest of us," she said, shaking her head. "He just started off with that much more. He's got connections in J3LE, our neighbouring sector. His bond-codes never seem to run out." She shuddered. "Selling a ship like that to a man like him would be a big mistake."

"I'd prefer not to have to." I fingered the edge of the business card and considered what she'd said. "Well, what do you expect me to do about this mess? I don't know a gritsucking thing about jinky jello or whatever it is, so this bounty of yours is bunk. I don't have any way around the repair costs, though. If you've got a proposition, I'm ready to listen to it."

"Clearing you of the bounty is a matter of formality," the general said. "We'll just search your craft and submit our report to the sector that has a claim on you. If you're innocent, you have nothing to worry about. As for the repairs... We're in a bind here, Captain. The spambot attacks are getting worse. More and more of our top citizens are becoming walking, talking advertisements. You don't have the moddie, and you don't seem to be affected by the attacks. If you can help us figure out who is behind them, I would be willing to waive the repair fees."

My heart lifted for the first time since we started dropping parts among the stars. I glanced at Rae. A tentative smile danced along her lips. I said, "Sounds like a deal to me."

"There's one condition," the general said, spinning her chair around and pinning me with a gaze filled with the same bright-eyed excitement I'd seen on her face earlier.

The balloon of optimism in my chest shrivelled up and fell to the bottom of my boots. "Of course there is."

She clasped her hands together and placed them on the surface of the desk. Her knuckles were white as if she was squeezing them to stop them from shaking. But the words that came out of her mouth weren't what I was expecting.

"We'd like to study your ship. It really is something special."

The balloon reinflated somewhat. That was all?

"Sure," I said, watching her expression carefully. "Silky."

Her thin lips peeled back into what appeared to be a genuine smile. She said, "Just tell me what you need."

* * *

Rae and I wandered Stardust Station's shopping district, looking for clues. Our ear-bean translators didn't help with the strange writing on the signs, but the general had given us a list of the businesses associated with the spam attacks, and Rae had written them down, along with a description of the goods or services sold. With that in hand, we were more or less able to figure out which store was which.

"This is impossible." Rae sighed and read through the business names again. "I mean, we've got everything from high-end appliances and showroom furniture to utility vehicles and gear-head upgrades to adventure tourism. There's nothing to connect any of them."

We walked along a spiralling ramp with clusters of shops on either side. Brightly lit walkways bordered a slick white central street for powered vehicles. The personal pods and work decks didn't follow any kind of traffic pattern I could see, but they managed not to crash into one another. Shimmering holographic signs added a kind of iridescent sparkle to the clear walls and white flooring. People milled around everywhere, ogling merchandise displays and peeking inside one another's shopping bags. Many of them had the same blank faces as the crowd that had surrounded us back in the service bay. The rest wore expressions of painful yearning. If what General Lowell had said was true, they all lusted after something they couldn't afford.

"I wouldn't say that." I reached for another piece of chewing gum as I considered Rae's statement. My fingers butted up against the hard plastic edge of Banana Billy's card. "You wouldn't see these kinds of shops back home in the Grit."

"We aren't in HoloCity, Bubbles," she said. "Of course it's different here."

"That's not what I mean," I said. "Look at that list. What's missing?"

Rae held up her tattler and scanned her notes again. The blue light of the hologram reflected against the lenses of her glasses. She pressed her lips together. "Consumables? There's no food, no fast-fashion, no cosmetics."

"That's right." I stuck my tongue through the sickly-sweet gum, blew a bubble, and sucked it back in through my teeth with a snap. "And not a bargain to be had. No discount tech, no last year's models, no factory defects. You heard General Lowell; this is a public service station. There are some people with cush to blow, but the average worker isn't buying souped-up engine parts or organic plant-leather manager's chairs."

"They're all luxury items," Rae said, "but that doesn't tell us much. It makes sense that the ads would target higher end goods."

"Does it?" I watched a group of older women who stood in front of a live feed video display of lunar cliff jumping, excitement dancing in their eyes. The thrill! The danger! My lips curled up in a smile. "The general looked into each of the implicated business. They aren't leaking funds to pay for these ads. So why not spam the cheaper stuff, too?"

Rae killed the holodoc and ran a hand through her curly blue hair. "This is hopeless."

"Don't despair yet." I clapped her on the back and grinned. It wasn't often that I figured something out before Rae did, but I didn't want to rub it in. I said, "Let's go see how Dickie's getting on with the crew."

* * *

A courtesy shuttle dropped us off in front of the glass doors to the repair bay, and my smug smile evaporated. The doors slid open to the dulcet tones of a klaxon blaring over the loudspeakers. Red lights flashed. Security guards swarmed the place like little gray maggots wriggling through a cadaver. A mass of them was concentrated on our ship.

The moment Rae and I stepped over the threshold and into the chaos, two armed guards pressed their weapons against the sides of our heads.

"Bubbles Marlowe, Rae Adesina, you are under arrest," a stiff-voiced man said behind my ear.

"Again?"

"Disarm the prisoners," the guard said. Gray jumpsuits surrounded us like a fog. I struggled as hands pawed at me, digging under the shoulder of my prosthetic. I twisted away from them, and my jacket sleeve ripped.

"You know," I grunted, "I don't think he literally meant to *take my arm.*"

Rae's voice trembled an octave higher than usual. "We're working for the general!"

The business end of a hand cannon jabbed me between the shoulder blades. Someone disconnected the last of the sensors and tore the prosthetic away from my body. A horrible weightlessness replaced it and my nerves twitched uselessly. My mouth felt like it was stuffed with a dried-out dishrag as they frogmarched us toward the ship.

Dickie and the rest of my crew knelt, their arms bound and their heads down, in front of the stripped hull of *Bubbles in Space*. Had all this been a ruse to get the ship? Why would someone go to all that trouble for a hunk of rusty scrap metal, antique or not?

General Lowell spun slowly on her heel toward us, her infinitely black uniform like a reflection of the deep, lightless void of a dead star. She pinned me with her icy stare, her mouth rigid with contempt. She said, "I trusted you, Captain Marlowe, but you've failed me."

I gritted my teeth and said, "That so? Usually I don't fail my clients before I finish with my investigation. I must be getting more efficient."

She sneered. "You're finished, all right."

"So you don't want to know who's behind your little problem anymore?"

Dickie's eyes jumped from side to side, and he craned his neck around like he was looking for something. His mouth was gagged. The others still seemed to be groggy from their stasis sleep and remained slumped on the hangar deck like piles of discarded laundry. There seemed to be one too many.

"Turns out *you* are my problem now," she said. "We searched your ship, Captain. I've never seen such bold-faced lying in my life."

I kept my eyes on my friend as I answered. "I'm a lot of things, General, and not all of them are pretty, but I'm not a liar."

Rae stumbled against me and whispered harshly in my ear. "That's just what a liar would say."

"Not helping," I hissed back.

"Then perhaps you'd like to explain where these came from?" the general said with a flourish of silver buttoned cuffs. A gray-suited guard stepped forward with an empty ice-cream container brandished before him like the head of a slain beast. At least, it should have been empty. But when he turned it upside down, a deluge of gelatinous purple gobbets spilled out on the floor. The smell of rancid seaweed filled the air.

I wrinkled my nose. "That's nasty."

"You travelled here through sector J3LE, according to your navigation records," the general continued. "And just as the bounty on you and your crew detailed, you were carrying contraband while you did so. This puts me in a very awkward position."

My eyes widened, and I searched the sea of onlookers for the saboteur. Not there, but I expected as much. The lump of laundry on the end opposite Dickie seemed to quiver.

"Janky Jujus," I said. "So this *was* a set up all along."

Dickie nodded his head and shrugged his shoulders like he was trying to get my attention. I pinned him with a glare and shook my head once, sharply.

"A setup?" the general scoffed. "As you must know, jinko jellies are considered a delicacy on Stardust Station. But as they are illegal in all of our surrounding territories, they are nearly impossible to get. Someone must have paid you handsomely to smuggle these here. But your transgression was reported. Unless we turn you in, we look like co-conspirators. It adds insult to injury that you have refused to pay our mechanics. You must have millions of bond-codes stashed away in a hidden account. I knew someone like you could never afford a ship like this."

The nerves on the stump of my left arm tingled like they wanted something to do. I sighed. "That's a good story, General. I could almost come to believe it if I was in your position. It's a lot nicer than the truth."

General Lowell gave me a cold stare befitting her frosty blue eyes. "And what, pray tell, is the truth as you see it, Captain Marlowe? I'll give you one chance to explain yourself."

"The truth is, this bounty is bunk," I said. "A figment concocted for one reason, and one reason only…"

General Lowell scowled and waited for me to continue. I waited a beat longer, letting the tension seep into the air between us like the stench of those godawful gooballs.

"You said yourself, someone wants this ship. Maybe a lot of someones. You, that mechanic Tenno Gix, your bald security guard? Everyone's been drooling over it like it was made of freshly baked, cream-filled doughnuts. But I'm not selling. So what better way to get their hands on it than to get me and my crew arrested and have the ship auctioned off to the highest bidder? That *is* how you planned to handle our assets once we were incarcerated, isn't it?"

The general clenched her jaw. Dickie, behind her, was spasming in earnest now. But he'd have to wait. I was on a roll.

"But it wasn't you, or the mechanic, or the security guard who set me up," I said. "It was the same person who's been behind your hacked moddies."

"You're bluffing," she said, her lips tightening into a thin line. "We've been working on that case for months; you can't possibly have cracked it already."

"Maybe not," I said, "but someone here can tell us if my hunch is correct. Bring me Billy Billions."

General Lowell glared at me for a moment, and then nodded her head tersely. A handful of guards broke off to search for the banana-coloured salesman. They wouldn't find him.

It didn't take them long to figure that out, either.

"I'm sorry, General," a woman in gray said. "His bioreading isn't showing up on our radar. He's no longer on the station."

Dickie's eyes bulged out of his head, and he chewed on the gag like he wanted to bite right through it.

"Oh, he's here all right," I said with a grin. Suddenly Dickie stopped struggling. He watched me, breathing heavily. I said, "Did you check the crew against your dossier?"

The general flipped open her holodoc and glanced to her chief of security, who looked to his neighbour. Nobody wanted to admit the truth. I decided to go easy on them. "The lump at the end of the line there," I said. "You might want to start with him."

The pile of laundry exploded upward, and an enormously fat man lunged for a gap in the crowd. The security guards shouted. A scuffle broke out in the middle of the swarm. Then a couple of burly gray jumpsuits dragged the limp, bloated figure of Billy Billions in front of General Lowell. He had a pair of my ship's maintenance coveralls pulled over his yellow suit. They bunched up in the crotch. I hoped he was very uncomfortable.

The general looked between Big Billy and me. She said, "Someone had better start talking."

The salesman slumped in on himself like he was at a loss for words, and the emptiness inside had created a vacuum.

"This hustler is the missing piece of the puzzle," I said. "How did the hacker benefit from people spending money at a bunch of unconnected businesses? What do high-end appliances and utility vehicles have in common with extreme sports and adventure tourism?"

Everyone stared at me blankly. I started to worry we were in for another spamming. But when nobody so much as twitched, I went on. "Collision protection on fancy personal transportation and maintenance vehicles. Extended warranties on furniture and appliances you have to remortgage your habitation pod to own. Life insurance for the empty nesters who want to skydive into a volcano and feel alive just once before they die. Who's been benefitting from all these luxury vacations and lifestyle upgrades more than anyone?"

"Billy Billions," the general said.

"You can't prove nothin'!" The big man suddenly found his voice again and decided to make up for lost time by putting double the volume on it. His face went a florid red, and he sprayed spittle like punctuation.

"Excuse me," Rae said, sounding concerned, "but I think Dickie might have something to say. Either that, or he's suffering from some kind of seizure."

Dickie nearly jumped out of his pinstripes. He nodded his head so hard, it almost fell off his shoulders. General Lowell followed my gaze, then indicated to one of her guards to remove the gag.

Dickie sucked in a lungful of air and said, gasping, "We saw him plant the jellies in the freezer."

The big man blustered. "Hearsay!"

"I left Hammett in the canteen," Dickie said, a proud smile spreading over his pudgy cheeks, "then I went to wake the others. It's still on the ship, and it recorded the whole thing."

"Who is Hammett?" the general frowned. "This person is not on your crew profile."

"My SmartPet," Dickie said. "It managed to connect to the translator bean in my ear and was able to warn me about our infiltrator. But by the time I got the others out of stasis, security was already flooding onto the ship. I didn't get a chance to explain before they had me bound and gagged."

I grinned at Dickie. "And there's the fact that he can clearly stop his bioware from transmitting to your network when necessary. He must have some knowledge of how to hack those moddies—or have the money to pay someone who can."

General Lowell swept a hand over her smooth blonde hair, then let it drop to her side. She shook her head.

"Lock him up," she said to her head of security, "and keep him that way until we can get the facts sorted from the fiction."

The guards dragged the blubbering, blustering insurance salesman away with his heels dragging along the shiny white floor.

"He did say he had a nose for crooks," I said as the guards stepped back from Rae and me, "and I guess he should."

"Takes one to know one," Dickie said.

"It seems we owe you a debt, Captain Marlowe," the general said, "assuming this story of yours checks out under scrutiny."

Someone handed back my arm, and Rae helped me to reaffix it.

"I'm happy to stick to our original deal, General, if it still stands."

"I might even consider giving you a bonus," she said. "You think he arranged all this to get his mitts on your ship?"

"Not the insurance scam," I said. "That was just to line his pockets. But with guys like that, one con is never enough. Greed always gets them in the end."

"You do sound like a detective," she said, "I'll give you that."

"Will you give me something else?" I asked. "Now that we're pals?"

She raised her eyebrows at me. "That depends."

"There's one thing that doesn't make sense in all of this," I said. "Why is everyone so gaga over this rattletrap? It's done nothing but fall to pieces ever since we took off."

She chuckled and shook her head. "You mean you really don't know?"

I stared at her blankly.

"Thousands of years ago, our ancestors arrived here, and in the other now-inhabited sectors of the universe, on ships just like this," she said. "They're jumpers, capable of bending the very fabric of the cosmos in order to travel vast distances with unthinkable speed. And every single one of them fell apart after their first jump. Shortly after the colonies were established, our ancestors discovered they could not recreate the original ships with the limited resources of the new space stations. In time, they disappeared. The original jumpers are ancient history."

"You mean we did a jump?" Rae said. "If that's true…"

The general nodded gravely. "You will never be able to return home, unless we can study your ship and figure out how to repair the plasma cores. We have considerably more resources today than when the station was first established."

Reality washed over me like a cold wave from a dousing bucket. Not only had I gotten my friends sucked into an ancient spaceship and launched halfway across the universe, apparently I'd also stranded us on a space station in the middle of nowhere.

I wrapped my arms around my friends.

"Well, I guess there's only one thing to do," I said.

"Find work?" Dickie said.

"Or a place to stay?" Rae said. "Sounds like we're here for the long haul."

"Sure," I said. "But first, shopping. We've got a bonus to spend."

* * * * *

S.C. Jensen Bio

S.C. Jensen is a Canadian fiction writer, sci-fi enthusiast, and literary advocate. At least, that's what her replicant ID states. She lives on the windswept prairies with her husband, three children, and various fuzzy friends. When she's not writing, she can be found trying to avoid mosquitoes, sunburn, and/or frostbite in the great outdoors while waiting, somewhat impatiently, for the singularity.

She is the author of Bubbles in Space—a Sci-Fi Noir adventure series—and the connected HoloCity Case Files series of stand-alone cyberpunk detective novellas. Her website is https://scjensen.com/ where she blogs, posts book reviews, and more.

# # # # #

Making the Bed by Griffin Barber

The cell-block door whined open down the corridor from my cell.

I tensed, then relaxed when a pair of P-Sec officers I knew appeared through the transparent armorplas door. The pair had a prisoner between them. The cell door opened before them as they shouldered in behind the kid. The P-Sec officer on the right breathed a command into her comm. The kid's restraints popped off in her hand, and she shoved the kid into what had been, up to that moment, my private space.

"Kid's all right," the other P-Sec woman said, looking at me. 'Macron,' her name tag read.

I nodded, smiling appreciatively.

If I recalled correctly, I'd had my organization pay for Macron's advocate when the families of several juveniles had sued her for injuries sustained when the balcony they'd gathered on collapsed. Said balcony had been her estranged husband's handiwork, but he'd since absconded with all their money and his mistress, leaving her with liabilities and their two kids.

Thin lips quirked in a smile as she and her partner retreated from the cell.

The kid turned on our jailers with a sneer, but the cell door was already closing behind them. He stepped up and raised a hand to pound on the door.

"Be cool," I said, tensing slightly. I'd paid to have any potential prisoners who might share my cell vetted to be sure they owed nothing and no one before they were placed in a cell with me, but one never knew how stupid someone would get once they'd had their freedom denied them.

He turned and gave me the once over, raised hand slowly dropping to his side.

I didn't move from the lone bench lining the back wall of the cell and returned his regard. I knew he was seeing a man in his apparent 30s, slim and dark, with few discernible features that might fix my origins in the casual observer's mind. That I was far older than I appeared and far from the place of my birth, was hopefully not as apparent to him as his origins and affiliations were to me. The kid's tattoos marked him as one of the loosely-organized ethical anarchists presently making so much trouble for the planetary government. A political prisoner if my eyes didn't deceive. As such, he wasn't likely to be a threat. Not an ally, either, but I had many of those. Some reliable, some not.

"We're gonna be here a while. No point in making it harder than it has to be," I continued.

"Why?" my new cell mate asked, looking at me from under the fringe of a fore-and-aft hair crest that had collapsed in great disorder.

"Why what?" I said, vaguely interested.

"I mean, why do it this way and not just, I don't know…" The kid let the words trail off and brought both hands up, thumbs cocked back and forefingers extended. Looking me in the eye, he pretended to put a pair of bullets in the P-Sec officers leaving by the cell-block door.

I kept my voice light. "Violence is always an option, but violence against the state is rarely the option smart criminals choose, especially those who want to live to a ripe old age, let alone live it free of a cell. The smart criminal only resorts to violence when it cannot be avoided, and then employs it with only the utmost precision and care."

"I'm not a criminal," he said, indignant and more than a little self-righteous.

It's almost comical how often the young miss the point. I hid a smile as I gestured at the armorplas door and fixtures of our humble abode. "And yet, you're in here with me."

He shook his head, the gesture reading more weariness than denial. "Wouldn't even be a revolutionary if the government would do the right thing…"

I failed to hide my disbelief.

"What?" he snarled, puffing up again as he read my expression.

I declined to answer out of chagrin. I'd failed to recall my own angry youth, a mistake that might prove fatal in other circumstances. I didn't like that I'd made such an error, as it boded ill for my near future plans. It made me worry. What if I had, by a similar mistake, shown my hand to my adversaries too?

I shook my head, and, not wanting to fight, I waited him out.

His anger quickly passed, as all such heat does. In contrast, my concerns lingered, souring my mood.

Once calm, he quickly grew bored. I didn't blame him. Staring at featureless plasteel or talking to me were his options. He broke the silence with, "Seriously, what were you going to say?"

"I suppose we must all learn a little wisdom hanging from the teeth of the world before we're ready to listen to the wise."

"Wise, eh?" he asked.

I nodded.

He released a high, brittle laugh while mimicking my gesture at the cell walls. His laughter died quickly. It's hard to maintain any mirth in a cell. "No disrespect, man, but how's that hard-won wisdom working out for you?"

Still, I had nothing better to do, I wanted the distraction, and he might learn from it, so I tried to explain. "Everyone has a history of fucking up and finding out, I suppose. Some errors cost more than I was willing to pay, and some defer payment until much later in life to cash in or, better put, to balance accounts."

The kid rolled his eyes.

I didn't take offense, having taken his measure. The kid was in his late 20s, barring regen therapy or the massively expensive gene conditioning—which wasn't that common among ethical anarchists who weren't also upper-class posers—and he didn't seem the sort. In short, he was old enough to know better, yet young enough to believe he didn't care whether the laws caught up with him right up until the moment he was, in fact, caught. I'm morally certain that, at every point along the way to that cell, he'd been cocksure, assured of his capacity to handle anyone and anything that got in his way. Now, after he'd been taken, his ego shored itself up with the false certainty that he'd only *allowed* himself to be arrested. I knew all this because it was exactly what I'd believed in the mist-shrouded days of my own youth.

Five was a breeding ground not only for hard people, but for those who aspired to be hard in order to get through their day to day.

Not that the planet had been particularly law-abiding even before the first cracks in civil government grew wide enough to see from space, but it had only gotten worse after the uprisings…

* * *

"Laws're coming for you, Sol Boy," Dogger said, looking out the armorplas window. Red and blue lights from the riot down the avenue flashed across his face, repainting his frown as angry, then sad every half-second or so, then back again.

Dogger wasn't talking about the Planetary Security Forces handling the riot, but the same body's Fugitive Arrest Team, which had recently obtained a warrant for my arrest from the Interstellar Authority. I knew this because, like every villain worthy of the name, I had ears everywhere cash could reach.

"Let 'em." I leaned back, pretending a calm indifference I didn't feel. I've learned that a lot of leading people amounts to showing confidence when you're scared shitless and doing *something* when others can't seem to get their shit together. Do enough of both often enough, and have things turn out in your favor every once in a while, and you'll build a reputation for leadership and nerve.

"Sol Boy, they might shoot you whether you resist or not," Dogger said.

He hefted his liner. The weapon gleamed in alternating patterns of cold blue and hot red under the light scattering off the streets.

I smiled at his unspoken promise of violent resistance. It's truly so very hard to get good help, and Dogger was no mere henchman. Such was his loyalty that I'd made him my chosen successor should things take a turn for the worse. He didn't know that, of course. I preferred not to test his loyalty against ambition when I'm about to hand myself over to powers greater than our little enterprise.

"They won't, not so long as we don't resist."

Dogger shook his head but put the liner down on the desk. He slid the heavy ceramic and metal weapon across to me.

"I don't get it. The Cutters have a bounty on you, FATs are gunning for you, and yet here you sit, cool as winter on Valhalla."

My smile congealed a little at mention of the Cutters. The gang's ire had been a major miscalculation on my part. Correction: I'd known full well they'd be angry, I just hadn't believed their response would be quite so... unrestrained. I'd spent the five months since our misunderstanding dodging—or confronting—those trying to collect on the bounty.

Truth is, I was tired. Learning that the Cutters resorted to unrestrained violence at the drop of a hat had proven costly in purely monetary terms, as well as energy expended to keep myself and the enterprise alive while riding the learning curve my substandard decision had provoked.

"That's because I have a plan, Dogger."

"I know you're a planner, Sol Boy, but this..." He trailed off, shaking his head, then he said quietly, a plaintive note of concern in his voice, "I don't know."

"To be honest, neither do I," I said. And if there was a touch of answering gratitude for his concern, that was only natural. "You'll be safe enough, regardless." I'd made doubly sure of that before setting things in motion. Loyalty is a two-way street, one best travelled often and, most importantly, in both directions.

A crash from the shop below. In a hurry, the FAT hadn't bothered to see if the door was locked. It wasn't. I prefer to avoid property damage when I can, even when the loss won't be my own. Such damage isn't just messy, it's unprofessional, and tends to anger the community, which limits your options when things drop in the pot. Planetary Security's indifference to personal property rights might have been a symptom of the public unrest on Five, but I tended to think it a contributing factor.

Reminded of just how close I was leaving things, I spun in my seat and chucked Dogger's weapon into the safe built into the back wall. The heavy door closed with a sigh, clicking quietly as the tumblers spun within. The weapon wasn't illegal in and of itself but, found in the hands of crims like Dogger and me, any weapon was a provocation. With P-Sec as twitchy as they'd been the last few months, we couldn't afford such risks.

I heard FATs officers mounting the stairs, my eyes drawn to the wall displaying the stairwell. I blanked the screen. No use letting them know I'd seen them approaching. Security was like crims that way: rarely responding well to learning they're nowhere near as sneaky as they thought.

Two things happened in quick succession: the windows blew in, and a veritable train of armored and armed officers entered before the ruptured glass had settled. A trio of them swung through the ruptured windows.

There was a howl of feedback from their shoulder-mounted speakers blaring, "Planetary Security! Get down, hands up!"

I smiled. The pre-recorded "lyrics" reminded me of a little night club I used to own back on Mars. Good times, nothing like my current circumstance.

An unsmiling Dogger carefully eased himself to the floor. Keeping your arms up, hands open and empty, while slowly going prone requires a certain degree of coordination and core strength he had in excess.

As I was seated and didn't want to give them any excuses by taking my hands out of view to comply, I simply raised my arms.

Security cleared the office, and those who hadn't already been pointing their weapons at me and Dogger rectified that situation immediately.

Overkill, certainly, but I *am* a dangerous criminal. I sat there, grinning down the very dark wells of the gun muzzles aimed at my skull. Appearances must be maintained, after all.

Inspector Marks' entrance killed whatever good humor I'd been able to find in the moment. It wasn't her look—though that was intimidating enough, what with the augmentations she had on board—it was that Marks hadn't been party to the deal I'd negotiated. We had history, see, Marks and me. Not all of it positive, not by a long shot. I'd seen to it several of her P-Sec investigations were shut down when she brushed up against the edges of affairs I preferred to remain under the rug, as it were. I kept my smile frozen in place while I recalculated the odds with the new variable her presence added to the equation.

Marks didn't wait for me to say something witty. "Prometheus Oliver Monterrey—" an assumed name used strictly to immigrate on Five, but she wasn't to know that, "—also known by the moniker 'Sol Boy,' I hereby place you under arrest for thirty-two counts of violating Article Fifteen, Section Seventeen of the Interstellar Trade Agreement, to whit: violations of fair trade and taxation owed for goods transferred. I am ordered to remand you to the nearest Interstellar Trade Authority facility, where you will face justice." She gestured at one of her old squad. "Place them in custody, Sergeant."

Dogger's mocking laughter rose from the floor. "Articles? Sections? Fair? From your response, you'd ha thought he was some kind of dangerous."

I snorted.

Marks' gaze swept from me to Dogger, gun-turret smooth, glossy black hair and augmented eyes shining eerily in the light.

Failing to see the humor in Dogger's cracking wise, an officer moved to take first me, and then him into custody. The rest kept their weapons trained on us, professional-like.

* * *

"Wait, Marks is IA?" the kid asked.

A dull explosion rumbled through the floor of the cell, the riots closing on the station. Shouts came from the other, more crowded cells that housed run-of-the mill political prisoners and common criminals.

Dust drifted down from above. "Inspector for the Authority, yes."

"I thought she was P-Sec, not Authority."

I nodded again. Not stupid, my cellmate, just ignorant of the moves being made above his street-level view of planetary politics and crime. "Used to be. Got tired of running down local crims and politicals, I suppose."

"Damn. Authority time is no joke," my cellmate said, near reverence in his tone.

He was right, too. Authority time meant removal from all the familiar contexts of one's life and injection into unknown orbits. I nodded again, riding a dull spike of cold fear. Doing actual time on an Authority prison planet or as convict labor in some underfunded hard-scrabble colony world was certainly not the preferred outcome, but it had been planned for nonetheless.

I like to cover all the angles if I can.

"So, when they transferring you off-planet?"

I smiled. "Not for a while yet."

He looked askance at me.

"Transfers take time," I explained.

The kid cocked his head. "Wasn't wondering about the time, but how you seem happy to sit here while Marks lines up your stretch. That's not what your rep led me to expect."

I snorted, touched that he knew who I was. "Reps are a double-edged sword."

* * *

I clocked two Cutters as we were escorted from my office.

"You see them?" Dogger asked as we were loaded into the back of the FAT transport.

"Two," I said.

"Five, actually. Three more laid up in the cut between Valor and Gamboa."

I shrugged awkwardly, restraints biting my wrists uncomfortably. "Nothing new."

"Closing in for the kill," Dogger said, eyeing me.

"Then our timing was perfect." I essayed a grin.

He wasn't having it and jerked his head at the front of the van. "Think they saw Marks?"

"Doesn't matter if they did," I said, projecting more confidence than I felt. "She's still Planetary Security, far as anyone knows."

"I ain't so sure, Sol Boy. What if one of the local P-Sec are on the Cutter pa—" Dogger's words were drowned out by a loud *bang* and a gout of flame from down the street. The explosion was followed by a roaring cheer.

I shook my head. Dogger's concerns were valid.

It seemed to me that Five's slow-motion revolution required a great deal of noise and at least three block fires a night. Anti-government protests had been a fixture for months, but had only turned truly violent the last few weeks. Some said the protests had been sparked by the government's refusal to increase the dole, while others whispered the insurrection and unrest were the result of activities by agents provocateurs. I had no personal knowledge one way or the other, and couldn't quite bring myself to care who was responsible, though I did find the constant disruptions to trade and the intensity of the planetary government's scrutiny somewhat aggravating.

Successful management of the enterprise required a strict apolitical—or at least neutral—stance that left room to work every side of an equation. The Cutters didn't feel a similar need to avoid local politics, and had occasionally backed one politician or another who promised a hands-off P-Sec. Cutter business was almost entirely transacted on Five, so they felt a natural need to control what they could. Of course, Cutters being rather unrefined, to say the least, their needs were often confused with whims, which often led to more problems with P-Sec than they'd initially faced.

Regardless, the Cutter's services and stock in trade only rarely touched on interstellar trade, so they hadn't felt the need to learn its ins and outs. That inexperience had been why they'd sought out my organization in the first place. The Interstellar Authority had a reputation for coming down like God's own hammer on those who violated their laws, and the organization I fronted for had a long, profitable experience in avoiding such unpleasantness.

* * *

A not-so-distant and distinctly unpleasant rumble reached my ears. I paid it no attention, as my eyes were drawn to a long crack that suddenly appeared in the ceiling.

"What the fuck?" the kid said, looking up with alarm.

Our eyes met. A moment of silence followed, me looking at the kid, the kid looking at me.

Something else exploded, shaking the whole cellblock. The latest blast was followed by the distinct crackle of small arms fire.

I grinned and stepped to the back of the cell, pulling the kid with me.

I was feeling that old thrill, that *edge* to things that let me know that all my plans and everything I'd done up to that point was coming to the crux. The dice were in the air, spinning. All that remained was to see how they came up when they stopped their rattle and roll.

More gunfire, closer this time, quickly tapering off.

Relative silence descended.

"Might want to keep your mouth open, kid," I said, following my own advice as I wedged myself deeper into a corner. "Overpressure."

"Wha—"

The floor danced underfoot as another explosion made the very air shiver. My ears rang despite my precautions as the door sealing my cellblock off from the rest of the building flew end over end down the hall.

Three figures emerged from the cloud of smoke and dust in the door's wake, two walking past the transparent armorplas of our cell door, while the third knelt. A Cutter attacked the lock plate, a dribble of molten armorplas dribbling from it on our side.

I released a relieved breath. If they'd wanted to kill me, they'd have just blown the door, waltzed in, and placed ferrous chunks of metal in my forehead at unsurvivable velocities. Then again, they could have orders to deliver some part of my anatomy unmarred to prove the deed was done. Bounties could be quite particular in that manner.

The kid, showing good instincts, scrambled away from me. I didn't resent it, not one bit. In fact, I applauded the move as the smartest thing he could do.

Something broke inside the door, and it swung into the cell under its own weight.

I raised my hands in the vain hope a show of compliance would keep me from catching a beating.

Armed shadows swarmed into the room and started hitting me.

I'd paid well for mods to insulate my flesh from the effects of stunner fire, but it would've been courteous of them to try such means before resorting to old-fashioned clubbing. Something cracked against my temple. I reeled, funky-chicken style, before my arms were placed in restraints for the second time that day.

One of the figures turned to the kid.

"I ain't with h—" the kid began.

The coilgun cracked, a ferrous metal sliver snapping though his skull and silencing him forever.

Well, shit, I thought, trying to get a handle on suicidal anger.

Killing the kid was pointless. He could only testify that masked figures had entered and taken his boss, which would only add to the reputation of the bounty hunters who took me down. Even if the hunters thought he was one of my soldiers, he was unarmed and hadn't resisted.

On the other hand, I was happy I'd had the foresight to place Dogger in a different cellblock.

Nonetheless, my hands twitched with the desire to fight them, to let more blood flow to join that of the—if not exactly innocent, then innocent of choosing to associate with me—kid.

As if I'd been thinking murderous thoughts aloud, the hunter behind me slipped a smart hood over my head. Aside from cutting off vision, hearing, and holding my mouth shut, the smart fabric hissed with static to prevent comm implants from summoning help.

I was hustled out of the building and into a waiting vehicle that took off immediately. There being nothing else to do, and in the finest time-honored tradition of guilty prisoners throughout history, I leaned my head back as far as the seat would allow and went to sleep.

* * *

The hood finally came off two hours later. I was by no means free to move about, but I could shoot my mouth off, if I was so inclined. I was, of course, so I spent a little while cursing the straps across my head, arms, and legs. The seat I was strapped to might have been almost comfortable, if something like a dentist's chair. And if I hadn't already known that the chair and bonds were a sign this would be more painful than any dentist visit.

Obligatory cursing out of the way, I blinked, eyes watering in the blinding, unforgiving light of the pair of spotlights trained on me. The Cutters were taking significant precautions, but had no idea how dangerous I am. Or, more accurately, what truly makes a man like me dangerous.

Then there was the wait. Such waits are meant to instill fear in the subject, and they work, even on hardened crims like me. Oh, I had little fear of what I knew was coming. To be perfectly honest, that's not entirely true: I wasn't exactly looking *forward* to what came next, but I had *planned* for it. I had one of Five's finer medical establishments on call, ready to receive me at a moment's notice.

No, if there's a fear that preys upon me, runs icy hands along my spine every time I think of it, it's a fear of the unknown. Mind you, it's none of that bullshit about alien intelligences secretly influencing events or superstitious claptrap, but rather the genuine fear of unforeseen events and unknown people upsetting my carefully laid plans. It was thoughts of such people and events that had me sweating through the wait.

Not long in objective terms, that wait, but in purely subjective terms, it was a damn sight longer than I wanted to endure.

"Do you remember, Sol Boy, the deal we cut?" *The* Cutter's voice emerged from somewhere close behind my head, making me flinch against my bonds.

"I do," I replied, there being no point in drawing things out with lies. Not the cleverest sort, was Logan Cutter. Who in their right mind names the criminal enterprise they set up and run after themselves, anyway? Experience has taught me rough lessons that can be boiled down to several axioms, chief of which are: anonymity, or at least plausible deniability, and visible restraint in direct, violent actions are the signature moves of the well-run, long-lived, and profitable criminal organization. Cutter didn't run things that way.

"Good. So do I." There followed a light clicking noise, as of someone had picked up something ceramic from a metal tray. "And you were aware, when you entered into your business agreement with me, that a Cutter, especially *this* Cutter, always gets his cut? One way or another?"

"Of course," I admitted. Now the moment had arrived, I found I wasn't looking forward to what was to come. Not one bit.

"Just curious, then, why you thought you could renege on the terms?"

"Seems reasonable that you might be curious." I was proud of how calm I sounded.

"And?"

When I didn't deign to answer immediately, there was no warning, no blustering, just a whisper-soft tug at my flesh, a sharp-edged, searing pain, and the sad sound of the flesh of my left ear plopping wetly on the floor. Eyes tight against the pain, I snarled through it. Perhaps it was a mistake on his part, using such a sharp blade. It hurt less. Though at that moment, I didn't know what could possibly hurt more.

"Why, Sol Boy, did you think you could place yourself beyond my reach?" Cutter said with false levity. "Why think to cut me out of my cut, as it were?"

Some sycophant tittered in the background. At least two in the room with me and Cutter, then.

"I ain't suicidal," I said through gritted teeth, pretending indifference. The eye-watering pain was extraordinary; the blood wasn't. I'd grown used to shedding red tears over my career. "FAT arrested me. Everyone knows you have people inside willing to do your bidding."

Someone must always take the fall when a band of criminals grows indiscrete in its application of violence. The imprisonment of a lot of his people was a clear and constant side-effect of Cutter's methods. That those arrested remained loyal to his organization was a symptom of social malaise rather than proof Cutter or his organization inspired loyalty.

"Here I thought you *were* suicidal, denying my hard-working Cutters our cut."

Derisive laughter from all around. A part of my mind registered two more voices to add to the audience. Five people in the room, then. More than I'd hoped, less than I'd planned for. The safety margins were growing tight.

I joined the laughter, not because what Cutter had said was at all funny, but because that part of my mind that obsessively pursued organizational excellence found it deeply, painfully ironic that a creature like Cutter had any success at all. He sullied the craft with his unoriginal slogans and willingness to resort to violence at the drop of a hat.

"What you laughing at, Sol Boy?" Cutter snarled. His blade pricked the flesh beneath my other ear.

I stopped laughing, but couldn't quite rid myself of the grin that stretched my lips.

More cutting. More pain. My atonement: for the kid in my cell, for the others who'd perished in our little war, for those slain in pursuit of—or to prevent collection on—the bounty Cutter had put on my head.

"I asked you a question."

"And here I thought you wanted everyone to laugh at you."

He snarled. More cutting followed. A great deal more pain, too. And blood, of course. Mine.

"I want what's owed, Sol Boy."

I squinted into the light. Cutter was a figure captured in a cameo of black limned in startling white light. An angel of death, halo and all. I blinked. I wasn't the religious sort, and that kind of imagery didn't come naturally to mind. I'd best be careful. Atonement was one thing, but blood loss could easily get out of hand, even with my augments.

"I want my money, Sol Boy."

"Lots of people want things, C—" Cutter's fist flashed out, mashing my lips against my teeth, and cutting my witty statement down to size.

My grin tasted of copper and salt. "I've been hit harder in bed."

"And if I cut your wedding tackle free? What then, smart mouth?"

I felt my nuts draw up, but was proud of my cheerful tone as I said, "I always knew you wanted to get your hands on my junk."

Cutter's face went red with rage as his blade hand snapped down, burying the scalpel in my thigh.

"Careful," I said through gritted teeth. "Kill me, and there's no cash."

"Might just be worth it."

I knew that was a crock of shit but, tired of being cut, I didn't argue the point. Our little war had cost him a great deal more than I'd fleeced from our transactions, and he'd need every credit he could squeeze from me in order to make good on his obligations.

My hiss of pain turned into a whistling scream as he drew the blade out perpendicular to the furrow he'd already carved in my leg, coming perilously close to the family jewels.

"All right!" I screamed.

"All right, what?"

"I'll give you the accounts," I panted, letting some of my fear show at last. Shitbags like Cutter got off on the fear they caused more than the wealth they earned. Besides, I had to hope an angry Cutter was more predictable than a calm one. "But I want assurances—" His fist clattered into my mouth again.

"Just give up, Sol Boy."

I spat, blood and drool failing to clear my own chin. "How do I know you wo—"

Another blow, this time a slap, cut me off. The room spun, regardless.

Showing more control than I'd given him credit for, he waited for my eyes to stop spinning in my head before he continued, "You don't, Sol Boy. But then, the clean cut would be quicker and less painful than what you deserve."

Leaving aside his value judgement regarding what I 'deserved,' I nodded against the head restraint. Much more punishment, and I might not be able to witness the retribution I'd spent so much—in last ditch hope and actual cash—to obtain.

"Right, then. Cough them up before I cut something vital."

I gave him the first of the account numbers and the primary access code. I did it slowly, as reluctantly as I could manage under the circumstances. In truth, I wanted to give him everything as fast as I could.

Anything to stop the pain.

"I'm in, bossman," one of his minions said a moment later.

Another of his minions whistled. "Damn, look at that! There's a lot in there!"

"Nobody ever said Sol Boy didn't earn," Cutter said, the scalpel glittering in a tight figure eight before my eyes.

"Shit, boss," Minion Number One said.

The scalpel froze. "What?"

"This is gonna take a while."

"Why?" Cutter snarled. His knife hand was white-knuckled. "What did he do?"

"Not him. It's the bank," Minion Number One said, voice tight. "Fucking shadow bank is requesting a fresh security code with each transacti—"

"So? Take it all in one go!" Cutter hissed.

"—and limiting the amounts per transaction," the underling continued.

A snarling Cutter stepped away, receding into the light.

I didn't need prompting to give them the set of codes they needed to get access. I even started to help them with the next one, but dropped into a red fog that rapidly transitioned to brain-gray, then descended into black.

* * *

I woke when I was thrown from the chair, or at least that's what I initially believed. Despite my augments, blood loss had had its way with me. The world was spinning still, making thought difficult in an alarming way. I tried to move my head. It was then I realized I hadn't fallen out of the seat, but been tossed to the ground, still strapped in.

My fogged brain might still be playing catch up, but the survivor's instinct burned into my soul by nearly a hundred years in the game wasn't having it: my arms and legs were already straining against the bonds securing me to the chair. My scattered wits were slow to assemble themselves into some semblance of a useful pattern, but once I could think straight, I concentrated on my failsafe.

Most people had augments on Five; whether it was an implant to help track investments or a sexual aid of some sort, the practice was common and went unremarked. Marks' implants were a bit more extreme. Not only were they visible, their use was also easy to determine. I, and thence the bodyshops I patronized, were inclined to the subtle, the less visible. What use great big muscles and armored skin if everyone can see your capabilities?

I'd had work done on my endocrine system and some subtle modifications implanted or spliced into my muscles, soft tissues, and skin. It wasn't active all the time, and the powerful results came at a cost of a wicked hangover, but it was time and past time I activated it. I concentrated, twitched a series of muscles in my face in a particular pattern, and felt iron and fire radiate from my chest. Then it was two sharp, deep inhalations, smoke and all, to fuel the biochemical changes I'd summoned.

I looked around while I waited for the augments to fully cycle up. The arc lights were off, too, the only remaining light dim and oddly diffuse. Between the weird light and my inability to move my head, I couldn't see a thing. The diffusion must be the result of smoke and dust from a breaching charge.

Someone started shouting, I think, but my ears were ringing loud enough to cover a lot of noise.

Two quick strobes lit the dusty cloud billowing into the room, each followed immediately by the unmistakable air-shredding crack of a coilgun, individual discharges loud enough to penetrate my deafness with fresh needles of pain.

Something heavy fell, close enough to make the floor vibrate. Still, I took stock of the sensations. Pain, of course. Blood ran down my neck from the remnants of both ears. Every bit of skin from my wrists up started secreting far more oily fluid than was natural, the better to slip a grapple, hold, or restraints. Still, I wasn't slick enough to slide free. Every muscle burned, heavy and molten. I had to be careful of my bones, which weren't augmented to the same degree as my tendons and muscles. The last thing I wanted to do was break a limb—or worse yet, my neck—breaking free.

More shots stabbed my ear-holes.

Gripping the chair, I shoved my left arm forward and away from the chair arm, hearing it creak under the strain. The strap gave with a *snap* that, judging solely from the pain in it, felt like it came from a bone in my forearm. I ignored the possibility to focus on getting free. The dead feel no pain, or at least make no complaints.

More shots from outside. Something crashed nearby.

Someone, a Cutter presumably, went full auto, discharges strobing the room in electric white pulses.

The answering fire was more measured, the drumbeat underlying the high hat in some gun-nut madman's idea of a night club.

I was not that gun nut. Not today.

My other arm came free. My pride in that was inordinate, perhaps, but when you've been tied up, tortured, and thrown on your side in the middle of a shootout, you tend to celebrate even the small victories. I paused in my self-congratulation to tear off the band holding my head up, ripping a tuft of hair from my scalp in the process. Snarling, I tried to wrench my legs free, but only succeeded in tearing the wound in my thigh wider.

The plan didn't require it, but I'd hoped to be on my own two feet for its denouement. That didn't look to be about to happen.

The gunfire rose to a barking crescendo as I slid across tiles slick with my own blood.

Fingers numb and clumsy from blood loss, I attacked the buckles on my legs, the process complicated by a series of wracking coughs.

The smoke, identifiable only as issuing from something that shouldn't burn, swirled and cleared in eddies as cold air from outside swept across the tiles.

I'd freed one leg and started on the other one when Cutter loomed out of the clearing smoke. The barrel of the coilgun in his hands glowed a bright, angry reddish-gold, the result of sustained automatic fire. He dropped an empty magazine to clatter on the tiles at my feet, slapped a fresh magazine into the well of the weapon, and chambered the first round without looking down.

I went very still, gambling he would forget about me.

Those dice came up snake eyes.

"Sol Boy, you motherfucker!" Cutter shouted, turning to aim down at my skull. "Don't know how, but you did this to me. Wish I could take my time and cut you, but this'll have to do."

* * *

"Wai—" I began.

The stuttering *crack-rack-ack* of a coilgun set to three-round burst cut across my plea.

I flinched, then cracked an eyelid when there was no pain, no blackness.

Marks stepped out of the smoke, her coilgun's barrel a dull-ache red.

I looked back at Cutter. He fell in slow stages, one side of his skull a ruin of flash-burned flesh and bone fragments. Small filaments of wire glittered wetly among the ruins of his skull, metallic vestige of an augment destroyed by the hypervelocity rounds of the weapon that did him in.

Marks stepped over Cutter and kicked his weapon away.

I swallowed, reaching for calm and the buckle that refused to give up its grip on me as armed troopers in Authority black and gray armor swept past her and cleared the room.

"Help me out here?" I asked when my struggles failed to free my leg.

Squatting over Cutter, Marks' sleek head tracked up my trapped leg to my battered, bloody face.

"Please?" I said.

"I don't think so," Marks said, or at least I think that's what she said. It was hard to hear her, what with having my hearing abused by explosions, gunfire, and the fleshy bits of my actual ears forcibly removed.

"When I took care of you, made sure of your shot at a place with the Authority?" I said, proceeding on the assumption I'd understood her.

"What?" Marks said, then shook her head, depressing a button on her cuff. Her ear protection withdrew into the bone of her jaws.

I repeated myself.

"Don't act as if you did me any favors out of the goodness of your little black heart," Marks said, voice raised for my benefit. "You knew the Authority warrant your corrupt pals ginned up against you would be enforced by P-Sec, who would only be too happy to earn the bounty on you, what with all the financial crises the government is facing. So when Cutter attacked P-Sec Detention to get at you before you could be taken off-planet, he would be attacking an Authority facility. The Authority would then, naturally, come down on him like a planet killer."

I shrugged, still trying to free my leg.

"You played it awfully tight on the timing, though."

My hands were too clumsy. I leaned back and tried to catch my breath. The room was a bit unsteady.

Marks continued, unconcerned with my struggle. "If they'd known you were being arrested on Authority warrants, Cutter might have done things differently. You must have paid some P-Sec people not to spread the word."

"Maybe I did, or maybe I just got lucky. Cutter made his choices; I was just along for the ride." I looked up at her. "I don't get why you're acting like this."

She looked at me with pitiless augmented eyes. "The warrants I arrested you for, those violations of Authority statutes?"

I nodded, choosing that moment to look back at my leg, hoping my gamble on what should come next would come up boxcars.

"Cancelled. Every one of them. Clerical error, they said. As if the mistake were perfectly natural, and cost nothing."

I felt a knot give way in my chest, coincidental to a mental breath I'd been holding since I'd initiated the plan to rid myself—and Five—of Cutter and his gang.

She sighed as she continued, "Though I guess it cost them nothing. What do they care about the lives of a few Fivers?"

I swallowed and, when I could trust my voice, said, "Still don't get why you're so upset. In the end, I secured a win for you."

I looked up, gestured at my face. "At great personal cost, I might add."

"And a number of people were killed in the process," she said.

My attempt at a derisive snort was ruined by another painful cough. "Trying to collect a bounty is often dangerous, as even a newly-sworn Investigator of the Authority should know."

"And thanks for ruining that for me, Sol Boy."

"How so?"

"Your bribes and plots thoroughly shit that bed, even before I had a chance to lie in it. Thanks for sullying my new job with your shit-stained fingers. And getting back to your point about it being dangerous work—the dead weren't all hunters, Sol Boy. In fact, most weren't. Some were just… people in your way. Havelock, the kid in the cell with you, for instance."

"I didn't kill anyone, that was the Cutters, those trying to collect the bounty on me," and because I was angry, I added an unnecessary, "and you."

She sniffed through the nose filters she wore. "That's right, you hardly *ever* kill anyone. Your hands are *mostly* clean. It's only ever as a result of your *orders*, your *plans* that other people get smoked. And even then, you justify it by saying you've got some code, that the deaths are just an unhappy result of other people's opposition to your 'business.' Tell me, does that absolve you? Let you sleep better at night?"

Silence and my hard stare stretched between us.

Our stand-off was broken by another gunshot. Another of my enemies being put down. Another bounty for Marks and the troopers with her.

I flinched and admitted grudgingly, "No."

Marks looked into my eyes and nodded.

I reached out. "If you're done displaying your moral superiority, could you help me up?"

She refused my hand, shaking her head as she stood, boots squelching in my blood. "You made your bed. Sleep in it."

* * * * *

Griffin Barber Bio

Griffin spent his youth in four different countries, learning three languages and burning all his bridges. Finally settled in Northern California with a day job as a police officer in a major metropolitan department, he lives the good life with his lovely wife, crazy-smart daughter, and needy dog. *1636: Mission to the Mughals*, co-authored with Eric Flint, was his first novel. *1637: The Peacock Throne* came out May of 2021. He's collaborated with Kacey Ezell on a novel set in their Last Stop Station Universe, titled *Second Chance Angel*. He's also collaborated with Chuck Gannon, penning *Man-Eater*, the third in the six-part first season of Murphy's Lawless.

Follow him at his website, https://griffinbarber.com/

# # # # #

Rio Nevada by
Christopher Woods

"Time," said Professor Houser, staring out into the virtual classroom. "Time is the inexorable enemy. It can't be stopped. We live our lives with this enemy, always taking from us everything we hold dear. It never stops. But if it did, would we even cherish those things any more? I'd like to see your ideas of what we'd have if time wasn't a factor. I'm curious what would be cherished in a world where time itself was removed from the equation. Next Tuesday, I want to see these ideas in a ten-page essay."

Houser grinned at the disappointment on so many virtual faces. "And we'll cut this class short so you can go do whatever it is that helps *you* pass the time. Enjoy the day."

Many of the faces changed to happiness when he let them out an hour earlier than normal.

The last of the virtual avatars faded, and Houser began to clear his desk. He never used the avatar from his side of the auditorium. He felt like he made more impression with a physical appearance. Plus, the bosses liked the professors to physically be present, and they were the ones who paid the bills.

"For the moment," he muttered.

He looked up and smiled as the door opened at the back of the auditorium. His daughter Chiana entered. Her worried expression told him what was on her mind.

"That lecture was a little too close, don't you think?"

"The class is Theoretical Physics. It was always going to be a subject that came up."

"True enough," she said. "On a similar subject, are you sure about it?"

"We have to do something, or we're done."

"But no one even knows."

"How long do you think we can keep it under wraps? I like to think we can keep it secret forever, but someone else could reach the same conclusions I did. And you already know Bael has been rattling his saber about a corporate takeover of Kairos. We can't afford that at any price. You and I both know Galen isn't up to the task. He's fifty-three and slowing."

"He can still take Bael's guys if he needs to."

"But can he take them all? We've kept our heads down, but if Bael comes for us in a hostile takeover, we'll have to defend our company. If he attacks and wins, we lose it all. If he attacks and loses, we own Bael, which brings us out into the open where others will notice us. We can't be there right now. Not with the find being processed."

"Yeah, the *find*."

"I know. It was risky, but it had to be done. We have to hire a new Champion, and we're going to need someone as good as Galen in his heyday."

"It's just frustrating. The gold will buy us someone good, but it'll also bring notoriety, which we don't need. We need more time. Damn Kalvin Bael and his aspirations."

He chuckled. "Time, the inexorable enemy."

"I do have another idea," she said.

He looked at her with an eyebrow raised.

"I've been doing some research…"

* * *

"You're now the owner of Stonewall Springs, Mister Nevada," said Zane Withers, the balding county clerk. "That covers a sizeable piece of land. Cattle rancher?"

"Been a lot of things, but, yeah, I'm a rancher. Cows and horses," the middle-aged man answered. "This should finish it up for now, though. Trying to put together something great to leave my boys when I die."

The clerk looked at the stocky rancher. Perhaps in his mid-30s, he was muscular, and despite the weather-beaten skin, looked healthy. His eyes stopped as they rested on the guns holstered in a fast-draw rig on the rancher's hips. The matching walnut handles on the Colts looked worn.

Gunfighter or just for show? the clerk wondered. Too many good men had died because they wanted to look impressive with the guns they carried.

"You seem healthy enough, Mister Nevada."

"I mean years down the line, friend. I have no intention of going any sooner than I have to." Rio smiled. "I plan to be an old man before they get that particular gift."

The rancher turned to leave.

"There was a stranger in town a few weeks back who was interested in a lot of the deeded land under your Triple R brand. He was looking at the Crooked F and Powderhorn ranches, too. I thought you might like to know."

"Got any idea who he was?"

"He said he worked for a fellow named Black," Zane said. "There are rumors about Black. They say he's been buying up a lot of ranches cheap and parceling them out to farmers and such at a much higher price. Rumor is, he's mean, and he has a crew of hard cases working for him. Some say he doesn't take no for an answer, if you know what I mean."

"I'm guessing he saw that everything is deeded and legal?"

"He did seem a bit perplexed when he left, but I'm not sure that matters to this bunch."

Rio turned back to the clerk. "It matters."

Zane was taken aback at the eyes that met his own. It was if he was seeing another man entirely. He'd seen those eyes before, when he'd met the gunfighter Wes Hardin in Tombstone.

Not just for show.

The man's five feet eight seemed much more imposing than before.

Rio shook his head, and the jovial rancher was back. "I'll see you again in about six months, when I can file West Lake Hole and cinch it all the way to the state line."

"That would be a sizeable addition, Mister Nevada. It would almost double the Triple R."

"Yep," he said. "I just have to find the old coot who owns it. I think he's up in the northwest. Heard he got bit by gold fever, and he's trying to hit it big out there."

"It takes a certain type of fellow to run off into the wilds to search for gold."

"You're right, there, Zane. I have a feeling he'll need some money, and I'd love to buy that claim."

Zane nodded as Rio exited the office. He noticed that Rio's right hand was always close to the long barreled .45 on his hip.

Definitely a gunfighter. I wonder why no one's ever heard of him. I bet he came from the badlands in Colorado; there's not a lot of information coming out of there. He was thinking about an outlaw town in the Sangre de Cristos as the door shut behind Rio.

* * *

Rio strolled down the street with a smile on his face. Stonewall Springs had been an important step in the future of the Triple R. With the purchase of that parcel, he could continue his retirement indefinitely from the job that had made most of the money he'd used to purchase property. He didn't enjoy hunting men, but it paid the bills.

The smile slipped from his face as a man walked out of the saloon directly in front of him.

"Damn."

The man in the fancy black suit and a flat crowned hat looked up and recognized Rio as quickly as Rio had recognized him. Donavon Slade was a gambler who was known to travel around the southwest. Slade also had a thousand-dollar bounty on his head for killing a sheriff in Flat Top. He was also known for escaping three prisons in Oregon before coming south to Arizona.

Both men stopped.

"Sorry, Slade. You just picked the wrong town at the wrong time," Rio said.

"You're Nevada?"

"I am. I'm surprised you recognized me."

"It pays to know who hunts men around an area. Someone said you retired."

"Mostly."

"You could just walk away," Slade said.

"Killed a sheriff, Slade. That sort of thing can't just be overlooked."

"Crow didn't give me any choice," Slade said. "The man worked for Harledon, not Flat Top. Harledon lost a lot of money in that game. Killing another man in the street won't do me any good."

"You have a couple choices, Slade," Rio said. "Now you could reach for your gun, and I could shoot you, cutting that bounty in half. Neither of us profits from that. Or you can surrender, and I'll turn you over to the sheriff here, collect my bounty, and leave you in that rundown jail over there. I can't just take your word for the happenings in Flat Top until I can go see for myself."

Slade glanced toward the building Rio had motioned toward and grunted. "You seem quite certain you can beat me. I'm not so cert—"

Rio smiled as Slade froze. He was staring at the gun in Rio's hand at waist level. He hadn't seen the draw. Rio cocked his head a little to the side and raised his brows.

"I would be delighted to surrender myself to you, Mister Nevada. I'm going to unbuckle this belt and walk very carefully over to that jail house."

Rio nodded and holstered his weapon as fast as he'd drawn it.

Rio watched Slade's hand hesitate for just a moment before unlatching his belt buckle, but he glanced back down at the Colt and shook his head. The gun belt fell to the ground.

"That was the fastest thing I've ever seen," he said. "How is that even possible?"

"Practice."

* * *

Clye Brown smiled as the children ran into the small cabin. It was older than the other buildings at the Triple R. He'd seen it as he'd followed his brother Frye toward the main house. The order had come straight from Black. No man, woman, or child was to leave the ranch alive. Gunfire rocked the night as men stormed the ranch house.

He took a right as his brother kept going toward the house. He watched as gunfire came from the back of the house. He kept going toward the older cabin. He wanted those kids. Pushing in the door, he grinned with black teeth at the three huddled forms behind one boy who had to be close to four years old.

The grin dropped from his face when he saw what the boy held in his hand. The small pistol belched flame, and fire filled his chest. He staggered backward and fell out the door in front of Frye, who'd turned around to join his brother.

* * *

Frye had seen four men die in the short time since Clye had turned to go after the kids. Two had fallen to a rifle as they neared the house, another had taken a load of buckshot to the face as he'd tried to go in the door. The fourth ran screaming from the door with a meat cleaver embedded in his neck. He didn't scream long. The others poured fire into the building.

He spit the juice from his chew on his brother as he charged through the door with his gun raised. He saw the boy with the gun just as he fired. He felt fire in his left ear as the bullet took the earlobe off. He fired and saw the boy thrown backwards. The other three were crying as he took aim.

"Man, woman, nor child," he muttered, and finished what he came to do. He turned back to where his brother's feet held the door open. "That sprig of a kid was ten times the man you were, Clye Brown."

He spit again as he stepped over the dead man. The others were dragging bodies from the house and barn. Best estimate he could tell was twelve of the thirty-eight gunmen were dead. The boss had said not to leave bodies if anyone got off a lucky shot. He reached down and grabbed his brother's collar, dragging him toward the others.

Jackson Black, the boss' son, walked in from the night. Frye made sure not to let his expression convey the disdain he felt for Black's son. Artemus Black had been a fighter and a hard man long before he became what he was. The son, on the other hand, had never been worth much. He liked to give orders, but never stood at the front. Frye had no use for someone like Jackson.

"How many in the cabin?"

Frye glanced back at the door. "Four kids."

"Hmph," Jackson grunted and walked on by toward the others.

"Boss!" a scarred Mexican yelled as he approached Black. "We have a problem."

"What is it, Diego?"

"Diez, ten bodies," he said. "One Nevada is missing."

"Damn!" Jackson cursed. "They were all here when Frank scouted."

"Boss," Chance Crown approached, "it's Rio. Rio Nevada's name is the one on all the deeds. He ain't here."

"He's nothing special, Chance. We'll leave Mike and Ray to take him when he shows up."

"I've seen him, Jackson." Chance spat tobacco juice. "He wears that fast-draw rig to impress everyone. Let me stay and take him. I'll show him a real fast draw when I shoot him apart."

"That sounds personal," Frye said. "You know him from somewhere?"

"He killed my brother. Shot him in the back after Roman called him out and turned him in for the bounty. No way did he shoot Roman fair. My brother was the fastest I ever saw. I bet he could take Hardin in a fair fight."

"All right, but keep Mike and Ray anyway. They can burn all the damn bodies."

Chance Crown spit again and grinned. "I'm looking forward to this. It's a shame they killed the girl, though. She could have been fun to pass the time with."

"She killed Frank. Had to be done." Sam Gage shook his head. "Gotta respect this bunch. Hell, the old lady in the kitchen killed four trained gunmen. And damn that youngster Daryl, shot four times and killed four. It took seven bullets to put him down. The old man killed Cook and Keller with a Comanche war spear."

Diego pointed to the body beside the cabin. "Clye?"

"Would you believe a four-year-old kid put a bullet in his heart?"

Diego was silent for a minute, looking around them.

"Si, Senor."

* * *

"See." Chiana pointed at the screen. "The whole family was slaughtered in a land grab."

"What does that have to do with it?" Houser asked.

"It was called the Rio Hondo Massacre. Thirty-eight men attacked the ranch. They killed and burned them all. Except for one…"

"One?"

"Rio Nevada, retired gunsmith, trick shooter, and bounty hunter. Settled on the Triple R Ranch at age twenty-eight, five years before the massacre."

"I'm listening."

She pointed at the screen. "The interesting part is what came next. Look at this…"

* * *

"Yo, Jack." Rio patted the big black gelding's neck. "Why are you dancin' around? It's just a snake."

The big horse had been trained to handle gunfire, random jumping, and even to let Rio hang underneath doing trick shots, but he had an ingrained fear of snakes. He'd never seen one until Rio'd left the outfit and headed out west.

Randy's Roughnecks, the Ultimate Cowboy Experience! Straight from the Wild West!

Rio chuckled as he thought of the tagline Randy had used on the side of the wagons. Rio had spent seven years with the outfit, touring all across the east, and even two years in Europe. People loved to see the antics of the western cowboy and the red Indian.

"Those were the days, boy." He patted the horse's neck again. "I liked it a lot better than hunting. It was a sad day when they ended."

Rio came back home when Randy's wife died, and the old man had closed the show. He was still wearing his show costume as he unloaded Jack from the train and tied him to a post.

He didn't like thinking about what came next. He'd been singled out by a group of hard cases. They were offended by his fancy clothes, or just looking for a target, and pegged him as easy. After the dust had settled, Rio Nevada had killed a man. He'd never done that and never wanted to do it again.

The sheriff had taken the others into custody and released almost a thousand dollars to Rio for the bounty on four of the men.

He spent another four years traveling the west and bringing in criminals. He'd only had to kill one other man during those four years. The guy hadn't given him a choice, and Rio had met him in the street. He hadn't even known there was a bounty on Roman Chance until the sheriff released the money. Over those years, he'd put away a lot of money.

Then he'd met Belle. Blonde-haired, blue-eyed Belle. Straight off a train out of New York City. Everything changed.

They started the Triple R together, and he put his hunting career aside for the most part. He'd only collected a couple of bounties since then. He brought his family down from Colorado and they started working the ranch in earnest. The twins, Tyler and Matt, came soon after. The next year, Leann was born, and Laramie last year.

The big horse stopped his dancing once they got enough distance from the snake.

"You big baby," Rio muttered, and Jack snorted.

They rounded the last bend in the trail before reaching Gilly Canyon, and Jack picked up the pace, seeing familiar territory. The other side of Gilly Canyon opened onto Cael Plains, where Rio ran a small herd of cattle. He kept the numbers down on the herd because the water from Kaylee Springs was limited. If he put too many out here, the springs couldn't keep up. A person had to be careful on the west side of the Triple R. West Lake Hole would fix that problem. It was a plentiful source of water and fed into Hagi Flats, which would keep a pretty large herd going. He'd even have to hire on some punchers to help after that. He, his two brothers, and Uncle Jack wouldn't be enough to run a herd that big along with what they already had.

"Reckon that trip northwest will be enough for this year, boy," he said. "Sure hope I can find old man Tackett. Bet he's up in—"

His eyes narrowed as he saw the smoke in the distance. It was a lot of smoke, and he felt an icy chill in his gut. The only thing in that direction was the ranch.

Jack bolted forward as Rio's heels hit his sides. They burst from Gilly Canyon at a full run. That much smoke meant the barn or the house.

The icy feeling grew as they got nearer the ranch. He could smell the smoke, and his chest hurt as he recognized the smell of burning hair and flesh. Jack charged into the clearing around the house, and the sound from Rio's throat was inhuman. He could see the pile of bodies burning next to the original cabin—and four small forms rested atop the pile. He jumped from the horse's back while the gelding was still moving and staggered to the fire. He dropped to his knees, recognizing the tuft of blonde hair as the fire crawled across the last vestiges of his family.

"Rio Nevada!" a voice yelled from behind him.

He slowly stood and turned to find the man he'd always known he'd see some day.

* * *

As their eyes met, Chance Crown and his two cohorts saw that this wasn't the dandy they'd expected. All Chance saw in those eyes was death, and the man who faced them was definitely not harmless.

"I'm glad you could be here, Chance." Rio's voice was cold and dead. "Your brother's getting lonely in Hell. Time for you to join him."

The voice chilled Chance to the bone. *What if the rumors are true? But he couldn't have outdrawn Roman! It had to be in the back... didn't it?*

"Who killed my children, Chance?" Rio asked in that same dead voice. "Was it you?"

"It was Frye Brown, after one of the boys put a bullet in his brother's chest."

"How many of you did it take to kill my family, Crown?"

Chance found himself answering the questions. Somehow, he wasn't as sure as he was before. "Thirty-eight. We lost twelve. Hell, the old lady killed four herself."

"Uncle Frank always had a nose for horses and women. That's what he always said when she did something amazing. She was from New York, just like my Belle. Did you know that, Chance?"

"What?"

"Never mind."

In the blink of an eye, Chance was looking down the barrel of one of Rio's pistols. Flame belched from the barrel before Chance could even reach the butt of his own gun. White-hot fire filled his chest as Rio fanned the hammer of his pistol and placed a bullet in the guy on the left. At almost the same instant the gun fired again to his right.

Rumors are true. I didn't even see his hand, it moved... so... fast.

Chance Crown toppled forward as the other two men slumped to the ground. Not one of the three had even touched their guns before they were dead.

Rio thumbed three cartridges into the pistol and holstered it.

He turned back to the fire with an eye twitching.

* * *

"Where did this footage come from?" Houser asked in alarm. "What have you done?"

"Don't worry, Father." She pointed at the bank of computers. "Every drone's accounted for."

"Nothing of a greater technology! We've talked about this!"

"Our lives hang in the balance, Father. The nano-drones weren't large enough for anyone to even see them, and all of them returned.

Nothing left to find. What they recorded was terrible, but I needed to know if my idea was feasible. We both know we can't risk changing anything."

"What if the drones had failed and were left there?"

"They weren't."

"You risk too much," he said.

"And right now you risk too little. Bael is coming, and we need a plan." She pointed at the screen. "This... *this* can work. I've studied every second of these recordings. One small change, and, to history? Not even that."

"What makes you think it's worth the risk?"

"Just watch, Father. If this works, it's less risky in the long run than the gold coins. The coins will still be a backup plan."

Houser turned back to the screen and backed the video up a bit. "Gods! That was fast."

"Faster than anyone I've ever seen."

* * *

Rio shoveled the last of the dirt on the small grave and leaned on the shovel. Ten new graves beside the cross where his mother was buried. As he dug, everything drained out of him with the tears. All he felt was emptiness. He stood the wooden cross with 'Tyler Nevada' carved into it, and, with every drop of the hammer, that emptiness was filled. Filled with rage and hate. When he turned to walk down the hill, there was no sign of the jovial rancher he once was.

He staggered into the barn, which had mostly survived the fires. It was surprising that the back corner of the barn had remained intact. It had started raining less than an hour after the gun fight with

Chance and his partners. The hard rain had put the fires out after a time. The roof had collapsed in on the house, and the cabin was a smoking pile. The back half of the barn remained.

Rio stopped when his feet made a hollow sound, stepped back one step, and reached down to raise a hatch in the floor of the tack room. The compartment underneath was six feet long and three feet wide, the same size as the graves he'd dug. At the time he'd built it, the size had seemed appropriate. He'd buried his past in that compartment.

He picked up a leather-wrapped object and unrolled it on the floor. He remembered making the shotgun just before the show had been shut down. He pulled a similar bundle from the compartment and unwrapped it to lay the matching weapon beside the first. It had the same nickel plating as the shotgun. They were beautiful pieces and just as deadly.

The shotgun was a revolutionary design he'd planned to reveal at the show. There were very few designs of shotgun that allowed for multiple shots without reloading. The double barrel, and the revolving shotgun from Colt. This one was a little different. He'd gone over the design with a Frenchman named Pieper before leaving Europe. Its design had originally allowed for six shots at the pull of the trigger. The recoil from the shot would send the bolt back and pull the next shell into place. After leaving Herstal, Rio had decided it needed more if it was going to be part of the show, so he'd designed a new method of feeding the gun via a box that mounted on the bottom of the shotgun. The box held thirty shells, with a spring mechanism to push the shells upward into the gun.

When used with the box, a man could fire thirty shots as fast as he could pull the trigger. Any more, and it became too heavy to wield. Thirty was quite heavy, and it wasn't practical for extended use.

His eyes burned from exhaustion, so he wrapped the guns back up and carried them out to tie behind his saddle. He went back for the other bags in the compartment. After tying them as well, he mounted Jack and rode away from the ranch, back toward Gilly Canyon. He needed to sleep if he could, and the cave down in the bottom of Gilly Canyon would be safer than any other place he could think of.

Tomorrow... tomorrow he'd ride to town. Hell would follow.

* * *

"He left the bodies hanging from the tree," Houser said. "He's brutal."

"They just took everything from him," Chiana replied. "He spent years hunting men and turning them in for the bounties, and he managed to do it without killing. It was a brutal time to live, and he was still a good man, surviving."

"They were evil men," he said after a moment. "What they did to the family was horrible."

"Yes, they were," she said. "They deserved what he did to them. I sent drones to watch him for a time before the massacre. It was a tragedy what this did to him."

"I don't even want to think about what happened the next day, much less watch it."

"But you need to. If we do this, you need to see what it is we're asking him to do."

"You've already watched it?"

She sighed. "I did."

"Is it as bad as I think it is?"

"Maybe worse."

He swallowed and took a deep breath. "Then let's get this over with."

He reached down and pushed the button to continue.

* * *

Rio slept very little. His slumber was filled with screams and blood. He watched his world crumble over and over. Exhaustion finally overcame him early in the morning, so he got a late start riding into town. He'd planned to arrive earlier in the day, but the evening would be better.

"More people off the street," he muttered.

He steered Jack into the livery. A kid of probably ten or twelve years stepped out of the tack room.

"Forty cents a day will get him feed and hay, Mister."

Rio slipped the kid a silver dollar. "Give him some feed, but keep him ready to go. I won't be long." He untied the bundle from the back of the saddle and laid it out on a table against the tack room wall. "Best if you stay in here and off the streets, kid. You just stay in the back there with Jack." He motioned toward the back of the stables.

"There gonna be some trouble mister?"

"Yeah, kid." He unrolled the short-barreled automatic shotgun from the roll. "There's gonna be a lot of trouble."

"You're that fella they said Crown was gonna kill, ain't ya?"

"Reckon I am."

"The riders are all in the saloon. They came in yesterday to see their boss. He's got an office in the saloon."

"They talk about what they did?"

"They did, Mister," the kid said. "People don't ever pay attention to the help. That's why I'm tellin' you where they're at. I figure Crown wasn't as fast as he thought he was, and you're aiming to kill some folks. I'd rather you kill them that needs killin', and those men need killin', so I'll tell you where they are."

"Thanks, kid."

"Mister, if you don't make it back, this horse here will be taken care of."

Rio nodded and slipped off the coat he wore to put on a set of holsters in a shoulder rig. He pulled two Colts with shorter barrels than the ones on his hips from the bag beside the roll. He checked the loads and holstered them.

"You do that, kid. If I don't make it, Jack is yours. Treat him well."

"There's a lot of them fellas."

"I have a lot of bullets," Rio replied and donned the long coat. He pointed at the back again. "Get on back there now. I don't want any of those bullets ending up in you."

"Yes, sir." The kid led Jack into the rear of the stable.

Rio attached the feeder drum to the bottom of the shotgun and pulled the bolt back to load the first shell. He carried it pointed down beside the coat with his forefinger alongside the trigger.

Two men walked out of the General Store, and Harold Overton, the store owner, recognized Rio. He grabbed the other man's shoulder and dragged him back into the store. The door shut quickly as Rio walked past.

He stopped just outside the batwing doors of the saloon and listened for a moment to the noise from inside. A piano was playing a fast tune, and several men were singing off key.

Belle played the piano...

He pushed the doors open and stepped inside.

Fred Devlin, the bartender, was the first to see him. Rio scanned the room, and Devlin dropped to the floor behind the bar.

A scarred Mexican at the bar spun around. *"Madre de Dios!"*

The first load of buckshot hit him in the chest. The next three shots rolled like thunder and emptied a card table of players. He drove the shotgun barrel to the right and took a man's arm off at the shoulder. The severed limb, and the pistol it held, fell messily to the saloon floor.

The whole bar erupted into bedlam as Rio stepped to the right and kept pulling the trigger. He felt a tug at his side and shot Frye Brown in the stomach. Brown's gun dropped from his hand as he staggered backward into the back wall. Thirty loads of buckshot left the room looking like an abattoir.

Rio felt the wetness on his side and scowled. He surveyed the room and climbed the stairs. No one in the room was interested or able to stop him. He laid the shotgun down and winced at the pain in his side. The office would be the large room at the head of the stairs, so he didn't slow as he reached the top. He charged forward and hit the door with a shoulder.

It slammed inward, and he continued forward into a room with another set of double doors at the far side. Six men stood between him and the other doors. Gunfire from the men sent bullets through where they expected him to be. Only one of the six in the room actually hit him. It struck his shoulder just under the right collar bone.

His left hand six-gun flashed to his hand, and he opened fire. In less than two seconds, five men died. The sixth was staring down the barrel of Rio's gun.

"You're Black's kid?"

Jackson swallowed and nodded. His hands stayed as far out as he could hold them from any weapons.

"I... I... mercy!"

"I'll show you the same mercy you showed them."

"No!"

Rio's bullet was more merciful than he wanted to be.

Switching guns, he raised the kid in front of him and charged through a second set of double doors. He felt the blast through Jackson's body as Artemus Black fired the shotgun he held. Rio let the body fall and put a bullet in Black's shoulder.

The shotgun tumbled to the desk in front of the man.

"They were innocent," he said as he strode around the desk. "They died for your greed, and so will you."

"Wait..."

Rio slammed his Colt into the side of the man's head, sending him sprawling.

* * *

"He hanged Black from the balcony," Houser said. "He's a savage."

"Is our arena any less brutal?"

"But this was in the middle of the town," Houser said. "He just walked in and..."

"Yes."

"I just don't know," he said. "Why would he even work for us? He just lost everything."

"He could save us and, in turn, I think we can save him." She backed the video up to a point before the massacre on the ranch. "Right here. Look closely."

The violence of the gunmen was horrendous, but he saw what she was pointing at when she stopped the display. Just before the men opened fire on the kitchen, the older woman was alone and unobserved.

"Here's the first."

He placed his hand over his mouth as he realized what he was seeing.

"It could work... but it might take years to perfect the timing," she mused. "Time..."

* * *

Rio staggered as he entered the livery stable, his hand outstretched, and caught the wall to keep from falling. The kid who'd taken Jack to the back of the stable came forward, leading the big black horse.

"Are you okay, Mister?"

Rio handed the kid another silver dollar. "I'll be fine, kid."

He winced as he pulled himself into the saddle. Both his shoulder and his side burned like fire where he'd been shot. He tore a piece from his shirt as Jack walked out of town. Holding it against his side, he pulled his coat in tight against the cloth. The shoulder wound was all the way through, so he took a small piece of cloth and gritted his teeth as he shoved it into the hole. Then he stretched around and did the same for the back. He almost fell out of the saddle as the pain washed over him. He took a leather thong, wrapped it around his wrist, and tied it to the saddle horn.

Louis Reilly, the kid in the stable, watched as Rio Nevada disappeared into the night.

* * *

"**A**ccording to all the known records, Lou Reilly was the last person to see the gunman." Chiana pointed at the kid staring after Rio. "Shortly after, he went to his father and told him who'd been there. His father joined the crowd that formed at the saloon."

"I'm guessing the drones followed?"

"He went deep into the hills of his ranch that bordered on what they called the badlands. This is where he ended up."

* * *

Rio slid off of Jack and held onto the horn for a minute before struggling with the cinch. As the cinch strap slipped away, the saddle and the wrapped bundle behind it fell to the ground. Without a grip on the horn, he slumped and sank to the ground, too. He crawled to the edge of the cliff above Davin's Remorse and let his eyes close. At the foot of the cliff was a hole that was considered bottomless. It was called Davin's Remorse after a rancher lost a small herd of cattle when they tried to get to the water, then were unable to get out. The walls were nearly straight up and down, and the only way into the hole had been dynamited closed after Davin's loss.

Davin had told Rio the story when he'd sold his small ranch and gone west.

Jack nuzzled him, and Rio jerked awake after a moment. He reached up and pulled the bridle from the horse's head. At least he'd be able to range without the saddle and bridle. He rested his hand on the horse's head for a moment, then let it fall.

He scooted toward the edge, his vision blurring again. *Only about a foot left.*

His eyes passed the ledge to peer down into the depths.

"Wonder how deep—"

"Please don't do that," a soft voice from behind him said.

He turned, eyes blurring again. Darkness seemed to start at the outer edges of his vision and grow inward. All he saw was silver-gray eyes before it closed in and swallowed him.

"... too much blood... have to take him back and treat..."

Someone pulled him away from the edge of the cliff as his awareness slipped away.

* * *

His eyes opened to a white light. His vision became a blur as his eyes adjusted to the brightness of the room. He'd never seen lighting as bright as what flooded the room from the globe above him. He tried to raise his hand to cover his face, but it wouldn't move. In fact, he couldn't move anything except his head.

He turned his head to the left so he wasn't looking directly into the bright globe and found himself looking into the eyes of a woman. He couldn't tell much except that she had the same silver-gray eyes he'd thought he saw earlier. A small lock of dark brown hair was visible, hanging from the side of a paper bonnet of some sort, much like the mask that covered the lower part of her face.

"Am I in Hell?" he asked. "I never expected it to be so... clean."

"Not in Hell, Mister Nevada," the woman said.

"Can't be Heaven either," he said.

"No," she said. "Neither Heaven nor Hell. It's probably something you won't believe at all for now."

"Why can't I move?"

"I needed you to be still until I can explain things. You have a propensity for violence I wish to avoid."

He let out a long breath, thinking of the violence of his recent past. "Explain things, then."

"My name is Doctor Chiana Houser, and my father is Grey Houser. We own Kairos Industries. Do you know what year it is?"

"It's seventy-nine."

"You were shot several times, Mister Nevada."

"I remember."

"This is the part you won't believe right now, but it is true, nevertheless. The year is 2093."

He chuckled. "You're right there, Doc."

"Nevertheless, as I said, it's 2093, and you're here because we need you to save us."

His mind reeled at the number. It was clear the woman was insane. The fact that he couldn't move meant he'd have to play to the woman's madness. The brightness of the lighting in the room left him puzzled though.

"And how am I to save you in 2093?" he asked while doing the math. "What would a 214-year-old man be able to do for you?"

"Fight, Mister Nevada." Her voice had an accent that reminded him of Belle. Was she from New York?

"Fight? Lady, I've already fought my fight. I killed my monsters. Became one myself."

"You've fought for money before, Mister Nevada. May I call you Rio?"

"Sure."

"You were a bounty hunter. You hunted men for money. This wouldn't be much different."

"What are you talking about?"

"I need to give you a little history that you missed." She pulled a chair from the other side of the room made of some substance he'd never seen before. "You *died* in 1879, after the Rio Hondo Massacre that claimed the lives of fifty men and women. Your family was the beginning of the event."

"Yeah," he said in a cold voice. "I remember."

"In the two hundred years since then, the world has gone through uncounted upheavals, pandemics, and wars. Political power grabs devastated our country. Corporations grew, built their own security forces, and in 2048, dissolved all world governments in one fell swoop. For years, they warred with one another, not unlike the governments before them. In 2067, at the seventh Geneva Convention, the Champion Treaty was created. Corporations were forbidden from having their own armies. Instead, they'd have what we call a charter."

"Corporations?"

"They began as businesses, growing into the larger corporations."

"Okay." He was still convinced she was crazy, but he couldn't move his body and had little choice but to listen.

"These Charters allow the corporation to hire a Champion to represent them in disputes. Rather than lose thousands of lives in pointless wars, disputes are settled by single combat or small groups in the Arena."

"And I'm guessing these disputes are great spectacles? Famous men battling one another?"

"Yes, you're quite perceptive, Rio."

"You're telling me the best you could come up with in two hundred years was gladiators like the Romans?"

"I didn't get to choose what the world became, Rio." She stood and turned toward the door for a moment so he couldn't see her face. "But I *do* have to live in it. In this world, you either own a corporation, or you work for one. Right now, my father and I own Kairos Industries, and we have 18,385 employees. These people live and work inside our properties. We provide them with shelter, food, and medical care. Our company builds computer chips that are a valuable commodity, so Kairos has survived for close to a century. We keep our heads down and take care of our people. We own a single charter, and our Champion is aging."

"You have an imagination like no other, Doc," he said. "You want my help and keeping me tied to this bed isn't going to get it. Release me, and we can talk."

"You won't attack me?"

"I'm not in the habit of hurting women."

She picked up a square item and tapped the face of it. Feeling returned to his body in an instant. He expected pain from the bullet wounds, but there was none. In fact, he felt better than he'd felt in years.

He sat up and turned to let his legs hang off the bed. He realized they weren't in his normal clothing. He looked down and frowned. His hand moved instinctively to his breast pocket.

"Nothing travels with you when you jump from one time to another unless it is inside of an Irenium case."

"Okay. What's Irenium?"

"It's a lab-created material that combines several heavy metals into a form that's useless for most applications, but seems immune to the effects of time travel."

"Not so useless, then."

She chuckled. "It's softer than any metal in its solid form. Softer than lead, but a lot heavier. You had a few things in your pockets that seemed important. I placed them in the container."

He sighed. "The picture?"

"Yes."

"My guns?"

"There wasn't room in the container for them. They can be fabricated easily enough."

He glanced back down. "I'm gonna need some clothes, and some proof aside from your word."

"You're giving me the benefit of the doubt?"

He pointed at the bright globe on the ceiling. "I've never seen anything put off that much light, and I've been in the most advanced places in the world. Not in all those travels have I seen that. Because of that light, I'll look at this future of yours."

She looked up at the light. "The smallest of things," she mumbled.

"What?"

"Nothing." She tapped the square pad again, and a small piece of the wall slid aside. "I'll step outside while you dress."

It took all his nerve to keep from gasping. Inside was a stack of white clothing.

Another panel slid aside to the left of the small one, the size of a door. He stood as she stepped out of the room. The door panel slid shut again, and it was close to seamless. There didn't seem to be a spring system. It closed at the same speed it had opened.

Can she be telling the truth?

As ludicrous as the story sounded, there were things that couldn't be explained. He took the stack of clothing from the alcove, looking closely at the panel that had slid into a tiny crack. He could just see the edge of the panel, which was about a quarter inch thick. Shaking his head, he returned to the bed and laid the stack down.

The pants were simple, with an elastic waist. He pulled them across his hips, and they seemed to fit him a little too tightly.

"A little looser would be nice," he muttered.

He jumped when the pants moved. The legs expanded to what he'd been thinking about. They settled into a comfortable size as Rio's left eye twitched. He closed his eyes and took several deep breaths before reaching for the shirt.

As his socked feet slipped into the shoes, he thought of his boots, and watched in amazement as they shifted. They settled into the familiar shape of his leather riding boots. The color even shifted to the reddish brown color.

He smiled as the other clothes changed color and shape to match what he was thinking of. The door panel slid aside, and the doc was back.

"I see you've already figured out some of the features of the nano-suit."

"It reads my mind."

"It responds to the nanites inside your body, Mister Nevada."

"It's Rio," he said, "and what are nanites?"

"They're tiny machines that are used for a lot of things, Rio. You have a swarm of them inside your body. They'll keep you healthy and heal most injuries. Except in the Arena, of course."

"The Arena." He scowled.

"First, I'd like to put all your doubts to rest," she said. "Please, follow me."

She walked back out the sliding door, and he followed. The long hallway was lined with doors, and she turned right.

"Most of these rooms are the same as the room we just exited." She turned to look at him. "A few are offices for those who work on this floor."

He nodded and continued to follow along. The ceiling was lined with those same bright globes. She stopped at the final door, and it slid aside.

"This is the promenade. I've asked everyone to give us the space for the moment."

"Okay."

He stepped through the door and stopped abruptly. He looked out across a city unlike anything he'd ever seen. Buildings of steel, stone, and glass rose hundreds of feet from the ground. The large open area where he stood was high amongst those towers, but not anywhere near the highest.

"Are you convinced that you're indeed in the future, Rio?"

"That or Hell. Not sure which."

"Sometimes I'm not sure either," she said softly.

"So, assuming it's true, why would I fight men in an Arena for you?" Rio asked as he stepped forward and leaned on a railing looking out over the edge at the ground below. He could see moving machines below. "As I said, I've already killed my monsters."

"Because, Rio, if you can save us, I think I can save your family."

* * *

"Are you sure you're ready, Rio?"

"It needs to be done, doesn't it?" he answered Chiana. "This is what the Champions do, isn't it?"

"You still get that awestruck look on your face when you see something new."

"I don't think that'll stop anytime soon." He rested his hand on the spot where his right pistol should be. "Doesn't seem right to go into a place like this unarmed."

"It's illegal to carry a gun outside the Arena."

"Which also feels wrong. I was born American."

"Things have changed a lot since your day, Lukas." She shrugged. "I have to keep reminding myself to use your first name."

"Not sure that's necessary," he said. "Who's going to believe I'm a guy from two hundred years ago?"

"Perhaps."

"Just stick with Rio or Ario. Those are names I respond to already."

"Just remember, these people aren't like the gunfighters of your time. They gather in places like this much of the time. They insult one another frequently, and they can't be challenged unless their employer deems it necessary. Any physical altercation could end up in a suit for damaged property if one of you is hurt."

"Property, huh?"

"I realize it goes against everything you know. The contracts most of them sign agree to the terms. Your contract was a little different. Not many Champions are co-owners of the company."

"Seemed like a good idea to me."

"A vested interest might make one more loyal," she said.

"If you can do what you claim, there's no need to worry about loyalty."

"And if I fail?"

"Then we'll try again," he said. "The one thing I understand about your machine is that every five and a half months, it can be used again."

"That I promise."

He was silent for a moment. "So this is basically a saloon?"

"It's a Champion Club," she said. "It's as far beyond a saloon as you can get. You can find anything you want there. Sex, drugs, music, dancing—"

"So it's basically a saloon."

"Okay, maybe, but on a much larger scale than any of the ones in the 1800s."

The car turned into an aperture that led under a large building.

"You have that look on your face."

"Amazing how these buildings can stand so high."

"It's all I've known," she said. "I see marvels through your eyes that I've taken for granted all my life."

"I've seen some things in Europe most folks I knew had never seen. The Coliseum in Rome comes to mind. We did a show in Pisa and saw that famous tower, you know, the one that looks like it's going to fall any minute. Is it still there, I wonder?"

"It is. The Coliseum is still in Rome."

"Somehow that actually makes me feel better."

She chuckled.

The car stopped at a well-lit entrance with large glass doors. Above the doors was a sign in glowing red that read, "SPARTAN."

"I guess that's fitting."

"Last chance to put this off."

He drew a long breath and let it out. "Might as well get to it."

He reached for the door handle.

"Wait for Gary," she said.

He sighed.

"Champions are some of the highest paid professionals on the planet, Rio. You'll get used to it."

The Spartan wasn't flashy on the outside. People knew what the Spartan was. It didn't need to be flashy. The Spartan was the place where Champions and the public were in the same place and could mingle… if the public could pay the fee to get in, that is. A chartered Champion paid no fees.

The large room they entered was crowded with people lined up to get their tickets. Chiana circled around the long line and approached a nondescript door. She placed her hand on a pad, and the door slid aside. He'd seen some of these security pads at Kairos. He followed her into the room beyond, where there were several desks manned by Spartan staff.

"Miss Houser, it's been some time," the woman at the central desk said.

"Gloria." She nodded and pulled her data pad from her purse. "This is a new charter and needs to be registered. Lukas Ario Nevada."

"Oh, no," Gloria said. "Did Galen fall?"

"No, he's alive and well," she answered. "We recently purchased a second charter."

"That's a great relief," Gloria said. "Galen is such a sweetheart. Unless you're facing him in the Arena, of course. He's one of my favorite Champions."

"He is one of the best."

"And you, Mister Nevada?" Gloria cocked her head to the side a little and smiled. "Are you a sweetheart?"

"Not so much, ma'am."

"So respectful," she said. "We don't see much of that around here. My guess is, you are, but don't want to admit it. If you'll place your hand on this pad, we'll get started with your registration."

"Yes, ma'am," he replied and laid his hand on the pad.

The tiny pinprick was almost negligible as the pad read his DNA. Six weeks ago, he'd had no idea what that meant, but he'd been soaking up information like a sponge since he'd agreed to help the Housers. There was *so* much of it, though, and a lot of it was frivolous information. Social Networking was a new thing to him. He'd had friends all over the world in '79, but they were mostly distant and unreachable, except through the post. Chiana had shown him her profile, and he'd marveled at the number of followers. She was a beautiful woman and a company owner, so her millions of followers were not unheard of in this day and age. But the numbers still boggled him.

"Thank you, Mister Nevada," Gloria said. "The rest won't take long. We just need some info."

"I'll take care of the rest, Rio." Chiana placed a hand on his shoulder. "Go on out and take a look."

"I'll set you up a tab right now, Rio... may I call you Rio?"

"Sure."

Her smile brightened the room. "Just go on through that door. The elevators will take you up to the Lounge." She pointed toward a set of double doors to her right.

He nodded and exited the door into an enormous atrium. Rio looked up at the ceiling, which extended a hundred feet or more above him. Each floor had balconies that surrounded the atrium, and the balconies were crowded with people.

Chiana had described the Spartan to him, but hadn't really done the place justice. He moved to the left side of the door he'd exited and leaned against the wall to watch the steady stream of people from the entrance they'd originally come in. They were all going to the far wall, where he could see them rising in groups inside elevators made of glass.

"Sure as hell ain't the average saloon."

He waited about thirty minutes until Chiana exited the same door.

"You could have gone on up."

"Just watching the people."

"It's just as well," she said. "Champions have their own elevator if they want to use it."

"Suits me."

He followed her to the right side of the immense atrium, where a single elevator stood empty.

"Most of the Champions have already arrived," she said, motioning toward the empty elevator. "This elevator is usually crowded before eight with Champions and their retinues."

He stepped into the elevator after her.

She motioned toward the hand pad. "Only works for Champions."

He placed his hand on the scanner, which turned from red to green, and Chiana pushed a button that just had an "L" on it.

"You remember your backstory?"

"I got it. Born and bred Kairos. Never expected to be a Champion and practiced my whole life for this." He frowned.

"It's important that there's no history outside of Kairos," she said. "Our records are already fixed."

"Hate to act excited about getting to kill people."

"Nine out of ten duels end up without fatalities. As soon as there's a winner declared, the nanite screen is dropped, and they can heal. If the Champion survives to that point, they live to fight another day."

"If you got shot, you tended to die in my day," he said.

"Sometimes that happens here, too."

The elevator stopped, and the doors opened into a room that covered the entire expanse of the building level. People filled the whole place, congregated around individuals. The elevator was higher than the floor, so Rio could see the groups.

"Those look like storm cells, like the ones you showed me from the plane."

"Champions are at the center of their own little storms," she said. "Seems an apt comparison."

"All right," he said. "Go do what you need to. I'll mingle. And when I say mingle, I mean drink some whiskey at the bar and watch this circus."

She chuckled. "I'll come to the bar and find you when the meeting's over. Bael's got to be thinking twice with a second charter held by Kairos. Maybe we can dodge this thing after all."

"Good luck," he said and watched her walk to the stairs that led upward to a balcony surrounding the whole lounge.

Rio turned and eased into the crowd moving toward the bar but stopped for a moment when he saw a woman standing at the center of a particular group. Her hands were held out, palms up, and a man had his hands about an inch above hers, palms down.

"You move those hands before I slap them, and I'll buy your next drink," she said. "But remember, I'm fast."

He chuckled, remembering playing the same thing with his brother Daryl.

Rio watched her hands slide to the side and rise above the man's to slap them lightly on the top.

"Pizz!" he cursed.

It was a common curse word with the younger crowd, and he'd heard it many times while delving into social networking.

"Told you I'm fast."

Rio shook his head and continued to the bar. Surprisingly, he saw a familiar form, and slid into the spot beside him.

"Galen," Rio said.

"Hello, Rio. Here to replace me at the bar, too?"

"Not replacing you," Rio said. "Just here to help."

"Sure."

Rio wasn't expecting animosity, but Galen had been drinking for some time already. He frowned.

"If it isn't Galen Fedder!" a voice came from behind the two. "Next in my line of kills."

Galen turned to face a man with red hair and a long beard.

"Red?"

"That's right, Fedder," Red replied. "You're looking at the newest charter for Bael Enterprises."

"I thought he only had the three charters," Galen said.

"He recently bought another, since he plans to be expanding in the near future. Can't wait to see you in the arena, Galen. My brother will be in the stands watching. It'll be a shame to kill you, old man. Would be better if you weren't slowing. I would love to have been able to meet you in your prime. It'll almost be a mercy killing."

"Frack off, kid."

Red swung and slapped Galen across the face. Galen almost blocked the swing, but missed by a small margin.

"That's what you get to look forward to, old man!"

"That's about enough," Rio said, stepping forward.

"You don't want any of this, Pizz Rat!" Red screamed. He turned back to Galen. "Who is this one? Your new boyfriend?"

He turned back to Rio and sneered. His hand swung toward Rio, who stepped back as it swept by the front of his face.

"My name is Rio," he said. "I'm the new charter for Kairos, and I'm not drunk. That's your free shot." He stepped back within reach.

Red snarled and swung again.

Rio caught the man's right arm with his right hand. He stepped inside the man's guard and smashed Red with a wicked right backhand that sent the younger man staggering. He was caught by several of the people who'd followed him to confront Galen.

"You'll see! We're not settling contracts! This is a full-on hostile takeover! Everything you got against everything Bael has! It's still four against two, and I'm gonna kill you, old man!"

Red staggered away.

"That could have gone better," Galen said. "Red Lightman's been after me for years. His brother quit after a particularly rough match with me."

"Brothers always show up some time," Rio said.

"That's the truth," he replied. "Sorry about my attitude earlier. It's never pleasant to realize you're getting too old to be of use."

"Sounds like we'll both be of use soon enough."

"She'll never let it come to that; they'll file wrongful contract and get this taken care of. Bael has money, but even he can't afford to put *everything* on the line, because she won't give him what he wants."

"And what's that?"

"He wants Chiana."

Rio scowled.

Less than ten minutes had passed when Rio saw Chiana angling through the crowd with a pale face. He met her, and they pushed their way through to the exit.

"What's the verdict?"

"I'll have to capitulate, or we'll lose everything."

"No."

"It's a hostile takeover."

"I know. Galen explained things." Rio stopped and faced her. "Set it up. It won't be settled any other way."

"I know you and Galen are both fast, but it's four against two."

"Set it up. I've seen what they are. I've studied the records. They haven't seen anything like me in over a century."

"We risk everything on the chance you can outdraw four men?"

"That's what you brought me here for. Let me do my job."

* * *

"You're crazy, Nevada," Galen said as they walked along the nondescript hallway. "You seriously want us to stand in front of four Champions?"

"I won't see a woman forced into something unwillingly," he replied. "Besides, you seem to be walking down the same hallway I am."

"Lightman pissed me off."

Rio chuckled. "He's yours if you want him."

"I believe I do."

Rio nodded as they reached the end of the hallway and a pair of closed steel doors.

"I still can't believe you want to do this. Your first bout in the Arena, no less."

"This is why I'm here," he replied and pushed the doors open.

Rio had seen footage of the Arena, so he knew what to expect when he stepped through the door onto the turf that floored the large open space. But nothing could really prepare a person for the spectacle. He'd spent years performing tricks for a crowd, but this was a whole new level.

"Pretty overwhelming," Galen said as they heard the announcer raving in the background.

Rio took a deep breath and let calmness seep into him like he used to for every show. That was what this whole thing boiled down to. A show for the masses. The future's solution to keep the mob happy.

They strode forward to their appointed places. Thirty feet separated the marked positions, and the four men of Bael were already in place. Red was on the far left, which was fitting. He'd be standing across from Galen.

The other three were lined up to Red's left with about eight feet between each fighter. Rio didn't remember the first one's name. Even though he remembered the other two, he thought of them as One, Two, and Three. They were the first three steps to getting back everything he'd lost. Except maybe his soul.

"Are you ready to die, old man?" Red sneered at Galen. "Already showed you I'm faster than you."

"I'm not drunk today, Red."

Rio just stared at the others with dead eyes. One couldn't look him in the eye, Two was fidgeting, and Three waited patiently. Three would be the most dangerous of them.

"How's it feel, Newb?" Two asked, "knowing you'll die in your first appearance."

Rio just stared at him with his hand close to the revolver on his side.

"Too scared to talk, Newb?"

"All right, ladies and gentlemen!" the announcer's voice boomed across the arena. *"The moment we've all been waiting for is upon us! Can these two brave souls defend Kairos from our first hostile takeover in three years? This is a no-holds-barred, winner-take-all match! Prepare yourselves, Champions! When the starter pistol fires, draw!"*

Rio crouched with his hand near the butt of his right hand pistol. His left hand was poised just before his belt buckle. His gaze rested on Three, whose hand hovered near his gun. The starter gun fired, and Rio moved. The pistol leapt to his hand, and he fanned his left hand across the hammer of the single action revolver so fast, it blended in with the sound of the starter gun. His first bullet hit the crook of Three's elbow. Two was just starting to move his hand when Rio's second bullet impacted his right shoulder just to the side of the ball socket, ending any chance to draw a weapon. One had almost reached his pistol before Rio's third shot destroyed his wrist.

Rio's pistol was about three inches above the holster where it had rested and moved to the left to point at Red, where it waited.

Red's gun cleared his holster, and Rio almost fired. He heard Galen fire and saw the blossom of blood as the bullet hit Red in the chest. Red's gun raised a fraction further before it dropped back down and slipped from the gunman's hand.

His gaze returned to the three gunmen who were reaching for their various injuries. None of them seemed anxious to try to draw with their free hands.

"What in the world just happened?" The announcer sounded confused. *"Replay that, Marv!"*

The big viewscreens around the arena zoomed in on Rio's hands, which moved faster than the eye could see.

"Sweet Jesus, ladies and gentlemen! I think we have a clear winner of this match today! Win goes to Kairos!"

The whole crowd erupted, and doors alongside the arena opened for medical staff to approach the wounded. As soon as they could be carted out of the null zone, their nanites would function again.

Rio holstered the pistol and turned to find Galen staring at him.

"Who the hell are you, Rio Nevada?"

"Just a man trying to save his family, Galen."

* * *

"Y ou know they planned to kill us both," Galen said and took a long swig from the bottle he handed to Rio. "Drew and fired in five one hundredths of a second. They're playing the video over and over on all the networks. Apparently you could have shot them all anywhere you chose to. Yet you didn't kill them."

"I've already killed my monsters, Galen. I became one of them. I'm trying not to be."

"What do you mean?"

Rio looked across the table at Chiana. "He walked into that Arena, fully believing we were doomed. He should know what he's protecting."

She drew a long breath. "The reason no one's ever seen Rio before is because he disappeared in 1879."

"1879?"

"Kairos has developed a technology that no one else has been able to."

"Time travel?" Galen asked. "I've read a lot of fiction, but this is a little much to take."

"Come with me," Rio said as he stood. "We're prepping a mission."

* * *

T he air above Davin's Remorse shimmered, and two forms stepped out of nothingness. Both men were naked, but they carried a small crate between them.

"*This* is why I work for Kairos," Rio said as he opened the crate.

A smudge rose from the crate and dissipated as the nanites spread and dispersed.

"This is where they found you?" Galen asked.

"Yep," Rio answered, "and those little nanites are going to collect the DNA of all my family members. We can't change history, so we're going to create copies that'll fool anyone from this time. One day, we'll substitute the copies for my family. We'll be coming back to save them all."

"Save them all?"

"Yes. Tomorrow's the day they all die."

"Jesus…" Galen muttered.

* * * * *

Christopher Woods Bio

Christopher Woods, writer of fiction, teller of tales, and professional liar, was born way too long ago to be talking about, and has spent most of his life with a book in hand. He is known for his popular Soulguard series and creating the shared universe of The Fallen World series.

He has also written several short stories, and the Legend series in the Four Horsemen Universe, as well as some works in the Salvage Title Universe. With books ranging from fantasy to post-apocalyptic science fiction and military science fiction, there should be something for everyone.

He lives in Woodbury, TN with his wife, Wendy. As a former carpenter of 25 years, he spends his time between various building projects and writing new books. To contact him, go to https://theprofessionalliar.com and send him a message or find him on Facebook at https://www.facebook.com/chris.woods.37.

# # # # #

Filthy Lucre by
Jamie Ibson

A Contractor Wars Story

ZZZT

B Master Sergeant Damien Xanthopolous brushed the back of his synthetic hand against the RFID reader again.

BZZZT

Strange.

Damien drafted a quick message with his internal communicator and sent it to his team.

::I've got no access; I think they shut it off a day early. I'm at the front entry, have someone come meet me.::

It was his last day on the job, a day he'd been both dreading and looking forward to for some time. Twenty T-Years was a long time, and twenty T-Years was what he'd promised the Hellenic Armed Forces as a dying young man. In exchange, they'd replaced his failing meat, muscle, bones, tendons, and sinew with polymers, titanium plate, and carbon fiber. Today, he was free.

Maybe they'd forgive him one last day and cut him loose early.

The door swung open, and *Dekaneas* Karl Jacobou bowed low, a broad smirk etched on his synthetic features. "Once more unto the breach, *Epilochias?*"

"Once, and only once more," Damien agreed. "This time tomorrow, I'll be a dirty civvie."

"You'll never be a civvie," Karl replied. "You can take the Borg out of the War, but you'll never take the War out of a WarBorg. You just wait; you're going to be making bank in no time."

Karl stuck by Damien's side as they passed through HFB Perseus' corridors until they came to Crisis Company lines. They entered the short corridor that took them to 5 Platoon's Ops area, and Karl swiped for access one more time.

The lights went out.

"What the hell?" Damien cursed. His eyes automatically adjusted for the darkness, but there was no light for them to amplify. He triggered the mental command to activate the tiny IR light mounted at his temple just as the lights came back up. The door into the bay had opened in the pitch black, and now Karl faced him, shoulder to shoulder with George Megalos, Natassa Lachesis, Kostas Bareas, his wife Kassandra visiting from Dagger Company, and the rest of 5 Platoon. They cheered.

Damien smiled and shook his head. "You assholes... You probably put IntSec up to this, didn't you?"

Karl's face assumed a look of pure innocence—as much as a cyborg's face *could* look innocent—and he placed a hand on his chest as if offended. "I'm shocked, Damien, shocked that you'd make such a wild, baseless accusation."

Natassa elbowed Karl in the ribs. "It was IntSec's idea. Now get in here and close the door before Dagger Company realizes we're not working today."

* * *

I t was with a heavy heart that Damien pulled their ground-car out of the base parking lot that night. "What's on your mind?" Kassandra asked.

"That's it," he replied. "It's over. Tomorrow I wake up, and I'm just... Damien. I've been looking forward to this moment since the first day I went into the nanotank at Uni, and, now that it's here, I'm at a loss."

Kassandra patted him on the leg. Despite their synthetic exteriors, the replacement nerve-sensors registered the sensation just fine, allowing the cyborgs to retain more of their humanity than an unaugmented human might expect. At the moment, Damien felt all too human. "You're going to be fine. With your résumé, the contras will be knocking down your door to recruit you. That was the plan, wasn't it?"

"It was, yes," Damien agreed, "but I'm thinking that's a waste. I'm thinking I'd rather go it alone, start small, and build my own contra over time. Why be independent if I'm *not* independent?"

Kassandra retrieved her hand from his leg, and the temperature in the car seemed to cool a few degrees. "We haven't discussed this, Damien. You were going to sign on with a reputable company, a company that got decent contracts for good pay and little risk."

"Well... we're discussing it now. I take it that means you're opposed?"

"Of course!" she snapped. "Independents get killed with *shocking* regularity. Happens all the time!"

Damien set the car to loop base housing on autopilot and took his eyes off the road. "So do Marines, Kass. Between training accidents, piracy, and other shipboard disasters, the only people with a higher casevac rate than the Corps are the biologicals. You and I both know WarBorgs are a helluva lot harder to kill than some street mope who's looking to build street cred. It's not like I'm going to take on the whole of Apex Energy by myself."

"Then, what?"

"There are always contracts out to retrieve servers for the Mega-Corps. You know the type, they disappear into the underhive or the burbs."

"You want to bounty hunt? For the Megas?"

"To start, yes. Earn some cred, recruit a team, earn some more cred, buy some gear, and get into C-level protection. Which was the original goal—contract work—but taking the long way around, with me as the boss."

Kassandra glared out her window. "You're making a huge mistake."

"I disagree."

Not how I'd planned to start my retirement, he thought. *Not even outta the Corps one hour, and we're already arguing about what to do next.*

With nothing else to say, Damien routed the car home in silence. He wasn't hungry when they pulled into their port, so he just topped up his nutrient tank and went to bed.

* * *

Kassandra was gone when he woke the next morning, already back at the base. Was he making a mistake? Should he have pulled the plug at twenty T-Years? Plenty of WarBorgs stayed in past their initial twenty-year commitment. The camaraderie, being among their own kind, the *esprit de corps* had its own draw. Plenty got out to seek their own fortune, too.

He pulled on khaki slacks and a black polo, the unofficial casual uniform of PMCs since time immemorial, and grabbed breakfast. Kassandra had taken the car, so he summoned a Rhythm RideShare—one of their high-speed grav sleds—and directed it to the *Nea Athina* stacks.

HFB Perseus was twenty minutes distant from the megalopolis proper by grav sled, and Damien always enjoyed watching the approach to the enormous hive city. The exterior gleamed white in the Attikan sun. If one knew where to look, one could discern the plates that separated every hundred levels of the multi-spired megastructure. The grav sled cut its velocity as it reached the speed zone that surrounded the city, queued for the optimal entrance to get where Damien wanted to go, and then...

Then they were through. The walls of New Athens were a dozen meters thick or more, and soon the sunshine and sprawling white sands became an artificially lit cavern so massive, it was difficult to take in. Tunnels branched off between levels and sublevels. Internal scrapers loomed close, speckled with windows and colored lights all across the visible spectrum, and some beyond it. A thirty-meter *Ares Interstellar* logo colored one side of one of the stacks—the enormous pillars that provided the structural support for the plates that divided the city's tiers—but at this distance, it looked tiny.

Rhythm's sled knew the route to the stack he wanted, and it descended to what passed for 'street level' on top of the 200 plate and slotted itself into the local traffic grid. It pulled to the side of the roadway adjacent to Stack Three, and Damien got out. He got a few hard glances from some of the biologicals—unaugmented humans—but ignored them and made his way into the reception area for the stack. The directory pointed him to level 262B, so he boarded a lift and pinged his destination.

Others got on and off as the lift ascended. A woman boarded with a little girl, who took one look at Damien's inhuman visage, let out a squeal of fear, and began to cry.

"Sorry," the woman said.

"Not at all, I'm sorry," Damien replied. "I just retired yesterday and wasn't thinking." They were passing level 240, so he pinged for 242A and got out as soon as the doors opened. The woman gave him an appreciative nod, and the doors shut. The lift proceeded on without him, he gave it a moment, and then summoned another. He didn't blame the girl; he'd forgotten to put his human face on. His 'normal' face was a metallic red death's head skull, although if he'd thought about it, he could have put on his synthskin cover. Too late now.

At 262B, he exited the hallway and made his way to the law firm Mellou, Makrolis, & Mitsopolous. The office was well-appointed, with green marble accents and Neo-Minoan stained glass, strategically placed to make the whole office glitter. A body-modded woman with chrome skin and fiber-optic blue hair sat at the reception desk. She stood. "Welcome to Mellou, Makrolis, & Mitsopolous. I'm Helen Makrolis; what can I do for you?"

"I have an appointment with Demitrios Mellou. I'm Damien Xanthopolous."

"Of course. He'll be with you shortly."

The meeting with Mellou went quickly. The legalese was boiler-plate standard for Damien to hire Mellou as his council rep, create his numbered company, secure his licence to work as a contractor, and secure legal insurance in case Mellou was compelled to argue on Damien's behalf to the Council. His Orinoco account confirmed his employment history, income, credit score, social score, marital status, employment status, the extent of his cyborg augmentations (complete), and their nature (Hellenic Augmented & Robotic Defense Corps, standard issue).

Damien had never seen his whole history pulled up at once, and he was a little taken aback by the breadth and detail of the information. Mellou smiled knowingly. "You've never seen a full Orinoco profile, have you? This is the basic profile; there's a broader metric that tracks interests, purchases, purchase time/date patterns, and more. The Megas pay more to advertise to you around payday, since you're more likely to spend your credit, that sort of thing."

"My plan is to go hunting for servers in the underhive. How do they disappear when there's all this information on them?"

Mellou shrugged. "They fall off the grid. The Orinoco system depends on you interacting with it to feed it your data. They do piecemeal work for untraced cash, they forge IDs, or they head downhive, don't know the rules, and are murdered by the first gang they piss off. The underhive is no picnic."

Damien transferred Mellou's retainer and fees, stood, and the attorney offered Damien his hand. "Best of luck to you, Mister Xanthopolous. Remember, if you're on contract with a Mega, government and LEOs can't interfere unless you endanger third parties. If they do, you ping me, and I get them off your back. That's what I'm here for. Gangs, on the other hand, don't give a rat's ass about MegaCorp extralegal authorities. Shoot first, shoot fast, shoot often."

"Sounds good, Demitrios. I'll be in touch."

* * *

Armed now with a license and legal overwatch, Damien spent another four thousand yen getting a facial recognition optical overlay, binders, and a less-lethal neural stunner to go with the HELpistol that rode on his hip. He queried the Council's jobs listings and found a handful of competing corps that could do the physical extract of his prisoners once he'd caught them, but he had to do the math on their rates to figure out the best deal. Clearly one of his new corp's first investments would have to be transport, for him and for his prisoners—and that meant getting a partner as soon as he could manage both. He crunched the numbers and elected to hire Vortex Transport, given their rep and cost.

He found a quiet booth in a ServeAll and bought a glass of water to get some time undisturbed. He searched the Council's list for Servers Wanted. There were *thousands*. Thousands of people who'd absconded from whichever MegaCorp they worked for, people who'd wound up in Indentured Service. Many had fled other systems, agreeing to a term of labor for one Corp or another in exchange for transit fees. Damien knew the score there—the terms always sounded agreeable, but the costs listed were bare-bones minimums, while the 'pay' didn't include expenses like shelter, food, hydration, clothing, or retraining. What seemed like a short-term period of work of some months stretched out to years—and once they'd had enough, they fled for the relative anonymity of the underhive. Since they owed a debt of cash or labor to the MegaCorps, there was no bounty to bring them in dead.

Rather than hunting down specific individuals, he elected to go fishing instead. He hit *Accept* on a straightforward contract for Ares Interstellar, where he'd simply go cruise the underhive and scan its denizens for servers who owed their debt to the MegaCorp. The bounties would be less, but if he scooped enough of them, it would make up for the lower rates. Damien paid his tab for the water he hadn't drank and left.

It was a short walk to the nearest stack, and he boarded a lift. The boxy lift held a couple dozen when he entered, but it had emptied by the time he crossed the 100-plate threshold that demarked the 'Hive' from 'Underhive.' At level 80A, the door hissed open, he stepped out—and dove for cover behind the ruin of a ground car pockmarked with scorch marks and slug blisters.

The thoroughfare stretched away in both directions, a broad adamancrete ground car road lined on both sides with empty sidewalks, abandoned cargotainers, and 'greenboxes.' The raised containers were full of dirt that was supposed to make the underhive feel more 'natural,' except they were choked with thistles and weeds instead of flowers and grass. His HUD identified three—*four*—hostiles to his left wearing Day-Glo yellow half-jackets, taking cover behind the detritus along the street. To his right, a pair of grimy thugs wearing synthdenim vests and blue bandanas. A third man in blue lay in the street with an ugly, cauterized wound in his chest.

Although his systems had auto tagged them as hostiles, it might have been wrong. They were shooting at each other but didn't appear to be targeting him. The air sizzled with ion blasts from the yellowjackets and booms of chemical-powered, 3D-printed zipguns from the boys in blue. One of the yellowjackets popped his head out, and Damien's new recog soft flashed blue, indicating a hit against Ares' database. He glanced the other way and got another hit.

You've got to be kidding. Two? Already?

He crept left toward the rear of the demolished car, leaned out, and let his recog-soft scan the others in yellow. *No hits.* One spotted him and shouted a warning. Ion bolts sizzled in, scorching the car further.

"All right, assholes, we do this the easy way."

He popped up, punched out, and drilled the first yellowjacket in the forehead with his HELpistol. He ignored the splatter, tracked right, and fired three quick shots that burned through his target's cover—an abandoned cargotainer—and was rewarded with a scream. Molten polycrylic *hurt,* although it did less damage than a HELblast. The ganger fell on his side, writhing in pain, and Damien fired once more.

The third yellowjacket to pop up was his target proper, and Damien's left hand snapped down to draw his new neural stunner. He stutter-stepped right, threw off his bounty's aim, and got close enough for the stunner to work. One blast, and the ganger collapsed, twitching.

"*Malakas!*" the last of the foursome screamed. He'd abandoned whatever blaster he'd held and charged Damien with a humming vibroblade extended. Damien smashed the blade aside with a hammerfist and headbutted the ganger, driving him to the deck clutching a broken face. Blood streamed from a laceration where Damien's synthetic frame had torn the skin. He holstered the HELpistol and drew out the electromagnetic binders that would secure his bounty's wrists and ankles together.

"*Pallie*, that was incredible!" Behind him, the two boys in blue approached with elation on their faces. The one who'd flagged Damien's bounty system spoke. "We thought we was dead, bro! The Wasps are makin' a move, they killed Jackie over there, and—"

Damien hit him with the neural stunner as well. The second one threw his hands up and took a step back. "What the hell, *pallie?*"

"Three," Damien growled.

The ganger cocked his head, confused.

"Two."

The ganger fled.

With binders on both prisoners, Damien summoned Vortex Transport. He sent them his location and moved his prisoners to the lift. Gradually, faces poked out from doorways, alleys, and footpaths between structures. Faces became people, and, soon enough, the landing area outside the lift bustled again with pedestrians. None dared make eye contact with Damien. And why would they? His red steel death's head skull was designed for psychological impact, not for winning hearts and minds. There was a new shark in the water, and the little fish did their best to go unnoticed.

The neural stunner wore off after a minute, and the 'Wasp' ganger hurled a pure stream of curses in a barely comprehendible pidgin of Hellenic and Anglo. Damien knelt next to the ganger and pressed the stunner to the man's temple.

"You know, they say repeated exposure to neural stunners is bad for your long-term health. I'd hate to turn you over to Ares just to have you turn into some drooling potato down the line." The Wasp's rival was coming around, and Damien shot him a glare as well. "You got a problem, take it up with Human Resources & Recovery. Ain't gonna hurt my feelings none."

A young woman with a pink undercut bob, a rebreather around her neck, and filthy coveralls approached. She kept her gaze averted and halted a few meters away, shifting back and forth on her feet.

"You need something?"

She jumped at his voice, kept her gaze firmly at his feet, and pointed at the three dead gangers in yellow. "I'm with, uh, waste management, sir. Do you need those three, or can I clean them up?

"They're all yours, Miss," Damien rumbled. "Sorry to make such a mess."

"Oh, uh, no apology necessary. Leon was a real piece of trash. I don't mind at all."

"*Gama se, skyla!*" the ganger in yellow snarled, and Damien punched him in the jaw. He winced—that might have been a mistake. He'd felt bone crunch, and he was supposed to return the bounties as uninjured as possible. The ganger moaned wordlessly, and the woman allowed a brief grin to cross her face before turning away to clean up the mess.

His link with Vortex indicated their prisoner transport was just thirty seconds out. He dragged his prisoners to their feet as the hauler arrived.

The M.A.T.T. had a turret on the top deck mounting a tri-barreled blaster as its primary armament, a sticky-gun projector for coaxial less-lethal, and its wheels were mounted on swingarms, so when it pulled up, the entire vehicle rose a half-meter into the air, rotated in place, and dropped the rear hatch. A trio of gunmen swept out; two took up positions covering both directions up and down the street, while the third approached Damien.

"New hunter?" he asked. He wore sergeant's chevrons on his pauldron and appeared to be a full conversion WarBorg, but with a chassis Damien didn't recognize.

"Just retired from the Corps yesterday," Damien said.

"Didn't waste any time; good to see. I'm Romano." Damien thought he heard a hint of an Imperial Mediterranean accent, maybe from Palermo or Venezia? Romano scanned Damien's quarries with his CombatComp, then pulled out a pair of polycrylic binders. "Scans show no augments; that makes it easy." He fitted them over the prisoners' wrists, then stepped back to let Damien retrieve his magcuffs. Romano shoved the two prisoners aboard and locked them into their seats with restraints that fitted down over their shoulders and around their necks. Other prisoners filled four of the remaining seven seats. A semi-rigid belt automatically snaked out from the back of the chair and secured them around their waists, and Romano returned to the rear of the M.A.T.T.

"Okay, since you're new, you'll get paid once they're turned in up top. We're full, so we're rolling out now; shouldn't take long. Once you've established a rep, Vortex will front you the bounty fee, so if we get hit on the way out, you still get paid."

"You get hit often?"

"Often enough," Romano replied. "The tri-barrel isn't just for show. *I've* never lost a prisoner, but if you're going after an HVT, send us notice ahead of time, would you? We'll bring outriders and an escort for any bounty over fifty kay. Nobody's coming for these punks, but if you bring in their boss' boss' boss, it'll get a bit *piccante*."

"Understood."

Romano shut the ramp, and the M.A.T.T. rolled away. The prisoners would net Damien about a thousand credits between them—

not bad for five minutes' work—and it was barely midday. He caught the attention of the waste management woman, who'd just finished chasing the bloodstains and gore into a moisture reclamation trough.

"Where's the closest street market?"

"Level 102A," she replied. "Why?"

Damien shook his head. "Where's the closest *unofficial* street market?"

She grimaced. "You're going to make me work, aren't you?"

Damien spared a glance at her biowaste recycling truck, where one arm protruded over the side of the rear hopper. "Do you get paid per job? Or per hour?"

"Per day. Less room, less prepackaged, soyashit food that looks and feels like pablum for babies, less uniform costs, uniform upkeep fees, accounting fees, health deductions, fuel for the truck above the average rate, insurance on the vehicle…"

"They charge you to use their equipment? What do you net on any given day?" Damien asked. Her contract was even worse than he'd suspected.

"Oh, they don't actually pay me. Whatever's left over is credited toward my debt. I traveled here with Spectertainment, total owed ten grand. I was supposed to be a human oversight director for VI-written PecFic virtus, to clean up the raw product Specter created and ready it for human consumption. *Dream* job. Specter sold my server contract to Ares. Ares sold it to Apex Energy. AE sold it to Neurovation, and Neurovation sold it to Reality Reclamation. Now I clean the streets of puke, blood, bile, shit, and sometimes, on really good days, brains and bodies. Add my wages, subtract my expenses, add their interest… my contract is all the way down to *fourteen* kay."

Damien scowled, and the woman's eyes went wide. "I'm so sorry, I didn't mean to offend—"

"You haven't. People scoff at working for the gov, but at least I got out after twenty years with my soul intact, even if my body isn't. Hell, I wouldn't have lasted twenty years with the biological I had. You have any credsticks on you?"

"No, of course not," she replied defensively.

Damien produced one from his equipment harness and touched it to the reader on the back of his hand. The stick blinked.

¥487.61

"Tell you what, anonymous Reality Reclamation recycling server, I've got just shy of five hundred credits here with no Orinoco account attached to it. You must know where all the gangers' turf is, who's fighting over what turf where, who's a big fish in this little pond. If you point me in the direction where I might drum up some business, this just-shy-of-five-hundred-credits is yours. Any time your intel proves valuable, I cut you a slice of the action. Vortex is taking 15 percent of my bounties to transport my prisoners. If you point me at a zone, and I come up with something, I'll give you five percent."

She shook her head. "Can't. I've only got the work comm, which they bill me for even when it's them calling me, and all data, whether it's a stream, a call, a message, or anything else, is tracked. They find out I've got a side hustle, they'll take every point I get from you, and more besides."

"I'll buy you an encrypted comm. Use it on your off hours; you don't even need to take it out of your... whatever you sleep in."

"It's cute you think I get off hours," she grumbled. "No, that's not true, it just feels like it. Sure. Don't drag me into any of your shit, don't get the Wasps, or the Deadeyes, or the Blue Blossom Boys, or any of those other assholes gunning for me, don't get me hurt or killed, and I'll be your source."

"Deal. I'm X. You?"

She allowed a hint of a grin across her face. "Call me... Pythia."

* * *

Whoever 'Pythia' was, she wasn't from Hellenic space, so calling her the Oracle of Delphi was perhaps a bit over the top, but she was a font of information nonetheless. Four hundred eighty-seven credits bought a lot of info from a server with nothing. Damien strode into the Level 69B 'Nice Market' and marveled at the bustle. The corridor to the market ended at a balcony with a pair of stairs descending left and right into hundreds of people moving among food carts, disposable clothing vendors, used junk salesmen, and, if he was any judge, more than a couple weapons dealers. Although blunted somewhat, he could discern a couple different scents—dill, garlic, thyme—hidden behind the overwhelming miasma of unwashed body odor. Two 'Deadeyes' stood guard at the top of the stairs. Nothing about their dress marked them as members of the gang until Damien got closer, when he discerned their eyes were matte black augs that reflected nothing.

One of them, with more balls than brains, stepped in front of him and put a hand out to stop him. "What're you here for, Borg?"

Damien grabbed the offending hand and twisted it in a painful wristlock. He forced the man's pinky toward his elbow, driving the man to his knees. His partner objected but had only lifted his jacket to get one hand on the pistol at his waistband when Damien jammed the barrel of his neural disrupter under the man's chin.

"Shopping. That a problem?"

He torqued on the first ganger's wrist, eliciting a whimper, and the second man's hands fell to his sides. "No, no problem, *pallie*," he squeaked.

Damien holstered and relaxed his grip on the first man's wrist. He yanked the man to his feet and dusted off the ganger's coat, making sure to push just a little too hard. "Good, I'd hate for there to be some kind of… unfortunate misunderstanding."

He descended the stairs into the throng of market-goers, and, though they gave him a wide berth, he still found it claustrophobic to be hemmed in on all sides by so many people. He'd only been to an underhive market once on an op to take down a WarBot pilot gone berserk, and there'd been far fewer innocents present by the time his team arrived. How could anyone survive like this?

He activated his recog software and went with the flow, scanning dozens of faces in just a few minutes. A few scans returned *null*, which was different from no bounty at all. It meant the person was running some kind of passive counter-recog soft that scrambled what his optic picked up. It also meant they were more than likely wanted by one MegaCorp or another, and they had sufficient funds and pull to get such an aug installed to protect them.

He focused on one man who gave a null return. Damien activated his optic's still image capture device and took a pic when the man faced him. When he pulled the image up in his HUD, though, the man's face was entirely replaced by a gray-skinned line art avatar with its eyebrows furrowed and his tongue sticking out.

He kept his distance. The press of bodies created distance not measured in meters, and Damien looked for other exits now that he was down in the market. Null 1, as Damien deemed him, argued with a man at a souvlaki cart briefly, then followed the man around to the rear of the cart. Damien shouldered his way to the front of the line of the noodle cart two doors down.

"Who was that hassling your neighbor?" he asked.

"Just what's on the menu, *pallie*," the woman replied. "It don't pay to piss off the Deadeyes. Is it true you Borgs don't eat? Cuz if so, you can get out of the way. I've got customers to feed."

Damien sighed and ordered a plate of *pasticcio* and a beer. He paid and dialed his filters up to maximum to eliminate the effect of the synthahol. He forked a large bite of the baked noodle pie into his maw and leaned on the edge of her cart, looking as unobtrusive as a two-meter WarBorg with a red death's head skull face could. He checked the balance on another credstick: ¥52.74

Not a great bribe, but it would have to do. At this rate, he'd spend all his bounty money just buying information on his targets. Damien placed the stick on the counter between them. She cleared away one of her cheap pressed fiber plates, scooped up the stick on her way by, and continued to ignore him. Two seats down, though, she leaned in conspiratorially with one of the other clients eating at her cart's counter. Her voice was low, but Damien's enhanced auditory pickups heard her just fine. "Hey, John, keep an eye out for Barakis for me, would you?"

"Why, you owe him money?" 'John' asked.

"Everyone does. He knows he's the biggest fish in the pond, and he shakes us all down for protection money whenever the mood strikes him."

"Well, don't look now, but he just came out from behind Sammy's."

"Bastard—" the woman cursed, but 'John' wasn't done.

"—And they've taken Sammy's left prosthetic."

"*Malakas...*"

'Barakis' came to her cart next. He shouldered up against Damien, perhaps a bit too forcefully, and turned his back to him. "Karina!"

"Hello, Jaenos," the proprietress said. "That time again already?"

"It is!" He sounded excited, like he was trying to be overly friendly and laying it on thick. "Another month's passed, and here you are, alive, well, and fed, with your cart intact, and protected as promised!"

"I've been saying for some time that your protection fees cost me an arm and a leg, Jaenos, but it was a figure of speech." She gestured to the goon who held the prosthetic. "You do realize that's going to make it even more difficult for him to pay you next month?"

Damien tuned out the discussion. He shifted his vision to AR, found an access point, and dove into the streams. It took just a few seconds to navigate the currents and he logged into the Council's net. In addition to the open-ended fishing contracts, there was a "Wanted" listing for individuals. There were thousands of contracts across dozens of stations and worlds. He filtered for warrants issued in the last six months, and for Hellenic Space. He fed *Jaenos Barakis* into the database and got his answer a moment later.

Jaenos Barakis was very, very Wanted. He wasn't a server, though—he was on Ares Interstellar's designated shit list.

"... What do you say there, big guy?" Barakis slapped Damien on the shoulder. Karina handed over a plate of faux souvlaki meat and real vegetables. Barakis scooped up a fork and stabbed a fat black olive and some of the spiced 'meat.' He popped it in his mouth and chewed for a second. "You up for a little contract work? You look like someone who can handle himself in a scrap."

"Tell me more," Damien replied, and he straightened up to face the man directly. Getting Barakis somewhere quiet would make for a much happier Council with a much lower chance for... collateral damage. Damien shot a look at the goon holding Sammy's prosthetic limb. "You some kind of arms dealer or something?"

"WarBorg's got jokes!" Barakis laughed, and his sycophant goons laughed on cue. "I've never met a Borg with a sense of humor. No, we're not arms dealers, we're in the acquisitions and divestitures market. I've got a gig coming up, and I could use a little hustle. You a veteran?"

"I am," Damien replied, "but I'm looking at some work right now. I'll have to pass this time."

"Unfortunate," Barakis said. He stabbed the food truck's countertop with a finger and leaned in. "Speaking of biz, I'll be back day after tomorrow, Karina. If you're so concerned about Sammy, you can help him meet his expenses. Or come up with... services you could provide in trade."

Barakis leaned back, spun a finger in the air, and marched off down an alley. Damien watched him go. An unmarked cargo van whispered to a stop at the far end of the alley, the side door opened, and Barakis entered. The van leaned on its suspension as he stepped in, then the door closed, and he was gone.

"Real piece of work, that one," he said.

"You have no idea," Karina said. "*Pallie's* got more chrome under the collar than most Borgs—present company excepted—and when he's not shaking us down, he's doing the Megas' dirty work."

"That so?" Damien had heard rumors that the MegaCorps would hire deniable assets for the truly dirty work, the stuff they wouldn't even farm out to the Council, but the rumors always came from the friend of an associate's fixer, whose identity was naturally a mystery. He tore open one of Karina's disposable cutlery packs and dumped out the contents. He picked up the fork Barakis had eaten off of and slipped it into the sleeve. "Thanks. I'll see if I can do anything."

* * *

He scooped three more minor bounties that afternoon, all office servers who'd gotten in over their heads in the Underhive. The first cried like a toddler when Damien grabbed him, terrified. The third cried in relief that he'd be going back uphive "where he belonged." Romano from Vortex scooped them, as promised. The ambient lamps across the underhive were dimming to signal the waning afternoon as Damien made his way to a lift uphive. The payments from Vortex came through, less their fees. ¥2,490, just like that. He was elated; that was a week and a half's pay for one afternoon's work. He stopped at a one-stop DNA sequencer shop, where they checked the saliva left on Barakis' fork and confirmed the man Damien had met was indeed the one Ares Interstellar wanted, badly. The contract for Barakis made the payday he'd just earned look like chump change. Damien resolved to put Barakis squarely in his crosshairs, and he called it a day.

The grav-sled dropped him off in front of the house, and he felt a mild jolt of synthetic adrenaline hit his system when he stepped out and confirmed the ground car was in the driveway. No telling how Kass would react to the day's events.

"I'm home," he called out as he entered. In the living room, he found her plugged into her audiosynth. Her eyes were shut, and her fingers flew over the fretboard. "Kass?"

She didn't reply. She must have been deep in the sim, had shut off her external audio pickups, or was ignoring him. He made his way into the kitchen, checked his Orinoco balance, made sure the funds really were there, and spent a few minutes shopping. He was most of the way through making Ridian Poutine with the *real* bacon when Kassandra came in.

"I didn't hear you come in," she said. "Smells good."

"Looked like you were jamming; didn't want to interrupt," he said. He added another dash of spices to the gravy mix and put the cheese in the processor to crumble the curds into little pieces. With their senses of taste and smell blunted, most Borgs who ate at all preferred their food heavily spiced to compensate. Damien was no exception. "How was work?"

"Fine," Kass replied, though her tone was guarded. "What did you do with your first day of freedom?"

"Met with a council rep in New Athens," he said. "Got my corp established."

"That was fast."

"Pretty standard filework. Once everything was set, I headed down to the underhive."

"What? Why—"

"Pinched five bounties. You know that next gen audiosynth you've been pining after? The one that costs two grand? It'll be here Tuesday."

Kassandra took a step back. "You're going too fast. Say again all after 'I headed down to the underhive.'"

Damien leaned back on the counter. "Most of the open bounties on the boards are servers—people governed by indentured-servitude contracts. They owe one MegaCorp or another however many years of work or however much in debt, and they're working for the Megas until they're free. Like us, with the Lakonia Program, but without the cyborg rebuild."

"And?"

"And when they abscond on their debt, Ares or Orinoco or Neurovation or whomever have standing bounties for whoever brings their server back. I pinched five today; made a little over three kay. Less costs, and I had enough to buy that synth you've wanted."

Kassandra frowned. "You're burning the bacon."

"*Malaka!*" Damien cursed. He moved the bacon to a bowl to cool and checked the fries. Almost done. "I've got a line on another guy, one of the bigger fish down there. Scumbag. I literally watched him and his goon squad hold down a food truck vendor and detach the man's left arm for failure to pay his protection fees."

"That's horrible! You didn't do anything?"

"There wasn't much I could do at the time, Kass. It was a gang of thugs, and one of them is an HVT for Ares. Too many innocents in the crossfire."

"So you let him go." It was an accusation.

"So I made him think I might be available for hire later. I'll pick him off another time when no one's going to get hurt. And in the meantime, I earned eight day's pay in one afternoon."

Kassandra refused to be persuaded. "What about the ones you did catch? Scumbags one and all?"

"No," Damien admitted. "Two gangers, a code monkey, a sewer rat who hadn't worked a single day of his contract, and one blubbering, neurotic mess who thanked me for getting him out of the underhive and back where he belonged, and never mind the thousand yen tacked onto his debt."

Kassandra shook her head sadly. "I don't know, Damien. I don't like it. Not one bit. You pick off the wrong scumbag, you're going to bring down hell on your head, and no credits are worth that. They'll be selling your parts in the night market, and no one will be the wiser."

Damien shook his head, frustrated. He dumped half the fries on Kassandra's plate, added the bacon and cheese curds, and drowned it all in gravy. "Here. Enjoy." He took his own plate and stormed off to his office without another word. He plugged into the streams and dug into other contracts, opportunities, and biz he might be able to handle on his own. When he got tired, he stood up, engaged the locks on his joints, and fell asleep standing up.

* * *

The next day was even better. He'd identified half a dozen HVTs on the Council's list, all of whom appeared to be relatively harmless, but worth a fair stack of credits. He pinged Pythia, and a few minutes later he had a lead on one of his targets. Doctor Leo "Diamond" Phillips was wanted by Neurovation, but, unlike the others on his list, they suspected he'd been forcibly extracted by a rival, or even kidnapped. The contract was fresh, not even a week old, and, if anything, a rescue might put Kassandra in a better mood. The icing on the cake was the price point itself. Returning Doc Phillips would gross him a cool ¥30,000.

An hour later, Pythia sent him a full data dump. She knew of Phillips because the clinic he was 'operating' out of was on her route. Her first time past, she'd been horrified at the biowaste she'd had to haul away. It had been quiet, abandoned for a couple months, but a week earlier it had started churning out gibbets and bits again.

It was in Deadeye territory. Swapping bio-eyes for augs was a messy, risky affair and required a well-equipped surgical suite. The suite was easy enough to acquire, but someone with the expertise to conduct such an operation reliably was not. When he sent Pythia a holo of Phillips' face, she confirmed she'd seen him outside, watched over by a pair of Deadeye goons.

From across the walkway and down a hundred meters, Damien lofted a Tamaki Whisper drone to scout the property. It had cost him everything he had left from the day before, but it was one of the best low-profile drones on the market. Six whisper-quiet rotors, multi-spectrum optics, and small enough to fold up into a case on his back. He sync'd the optic feed to his own, so as it ID'd targets, they'd be relayed to his own vision as ghostly outlines.

Recon took a quick minute. Windows on the front of the building showed three gangers on the top floor, someone prone on the second floor—dead, if their body temp was any indication—and one guard out front. There were doors front and back, but the rear door had a dumpster, and more trash piled up against it.

No sign of the cyberdoc, though.

He guided the drone in through the open second-floor window, past the dead guy, and it darted out into the hallway for a snapshot. The 360° camera showed a rough stairwell and a room opposite. A quick scan showed that room held spare parts. He spotted what looked an awful lot like Sammy's arm and a pair of matte-black optics that still had biomatter stuck to the cybernetic nerve at the rear.

The drone flitted to the stairwell, descended to the ground floor, and there in a back room, Damien spotted his quarry. Phillips had a patient on the chair. Blood had pooled under the right armrest and a hand and forearm leaked in a bucket on the floor. A new prosthetic interface capped the man's stump, and Phillips fitted a prosthetic in place. He ran through a diagnostic.

"*All vitals are within parameters, and your interface strength is already at 96 percent. That ought to reach one hundred by tomorrow. I'll administer the nerve block counter now.*"

Phillips applied a transdermal hypo to the man's elbow, and the new prosthetic came alive. The fingers rippled and flexed.

"*Nice work, Doc,*" the man said, and Damien gasped. He'd been *conscious* for the operation? "*I don't care what all those other* kolos *say, you're all right.*"

The ganger laughed at his own joke, hopped out of the operating chair, and clapped Phillips on the shoulders, hard. The doc winced. "*I'm glad you approve, Meatball.*"

The ganger walked out, still flexing and twisting his new arm, and Phillips blew out a deep breath. Once 'Meatball' was out the door, the doc collapsed into his own chair and burst into tears. The guard from the front door poked his head in. "*The fuck's your problem, Doc?*"

Phillips stood. "*What do you think? A week ago, that* kolos *you call Chimera and his thugs kidnapped me to be your personal slave doc. If I fuck up just one operation, you're going to kill me.*"

"*So don't fuck up.*"

"*Easy for you to say! I do brain chips, not prosthetic limb replacement! That's an entirely different field of study!*"

"You seem to be learning just fine, Doc. Keep it up, and we won't drill out your kneecaps and throw you in the sewer."

Phillips screamed at that, a wordless, guttural howl of frustration and terror. The guard just laughed. When he'd returned to his post at the front door, Damien left his hide, crossed the walkpath, and circled the block to come at the 'clinic' from behind. The drone stayed in place, clutching the wall with tiny legs like an insect, hidden in the shadows above the clinic's surgical theatre lights. When he rounded the back corner of the building, his drone fed him an AR image of the guard's position, and Phillips'. Phillips was down on his hands and knees, scrubbing the blood off his floor. The guard stood in the doorway, watching the street.

Damien rounded the corner, took three quick steps, and drove stiffened fingers into the guard's throat. The man's blackened cyber-eyes bulged, and his hands went to his throat. Damien followed the throat punch with a knee to the man's groin that doubled him over and plunged his hand into the man's hair to drag him inside. In the hallway, Damien let the man fall prone on his back. He crouched low, took hold, and broke the man's neck. Total elapsed time from the throat punch, nine seconds. He dragged the body clear of the doorway so his feet wouldn't be visible from the road and knocked on the doorframe of the surgical suite.

Phillips looked up. "Huh? What—Oh, god," he sputtered and fell backward onto his rump. "Please don't kill me?"

Damien rolled his eyes. "Do assassins normally knock, Doctor Phillips?"

Phillips looked thoughtful for a moment. "I suppose not."

"Neurovation misses you. I'm here to get you out. Drop what you're doing, let's go."

"Hey! Torch! Where you at?" a voice shouted from behind Damien, just outside the building. "Idiot. Doc? I can't get the whip to retract."

It was Meatball, the ganger Phillips had just finished working on. He stepped inside, took in the body in the hallway, the WarBorg standing over him, and cursed. He flicked his prosthetic toward Damien, and a rainbow of refracted light lashed out toward him. Damien threw himself backward, and the lash scored a glowing line down the wall. The ganger rushed him, and Damien drew his blaster pistol and threw an arm up to ward off the lash. He fired a trio of shots the instant his gun barrel cleared his holster and came on target.

Two things happened at once.

One, the blaster bolts struck the ganger square in the chest. The ion bolts exploded with heat and energy and drove the ganger backward. Two, the refractive monomolecular whip slashed through Damien's arm just below the elbow, and his forearm tumbled to the floor. Pain circuits engaged for an instant, then shut off, given the severity of the damage.

"Kolos," Damien snarled and fired another bolt into Meatball's head. He shrugged his pack off his intact shoulder, scooped up his severed limb, and stuffed it inside. "Doc! Move! Now!"

Phillips poked his head out into the hallway. "What... where? Where do I go?"

Feet thumped down the stairs from above them. "Dammit, never mind, stay there, let me deal with them first."

He summoned his Whisper drone and sent it out the front door. It throttled up for a second and snuck a glimpse in the second-floor window past the dead guy. The room was clear. It darted in and edged around the doorjamb until the gangers' silhouettes illuminated on Damien's HUD. One of them spoke. *"Sparks, get to the window and snipe them if they head outside. And see what the hell is wrong with Cyclops."*

"Ya, ya," a second replied. Damien backed the drone off so the ganger wouldn't knock it, and one of the Deadeyes entered the room. *"Oh, shit, Gus, I think Cyclops is dead."*

"What?"

"I mean, he's got a hypo in his arm, and he ain't breathing."

"Vlakas, fine, deal with it later. Get eyes on the street."

"Ready."

Damien willed the two to come forward down the hall, and they obliged him. They came down, subgun autoblasters at the ready, oblivious to the Whisper drone's presence. The outline it projected on his HUD let him track their movements perfectly. The first reached the bottom of the stairs. Damien placed the front sight of his blaster pistol on the silhouette's head, popped out, and fired. He rode the recoil up and put another bolt through the bridge of the second ganger's nose. They collapsed.

"Gus?" the last ganger called. Panic crept into his voice. "Gus!"

Damien holstered and scooped up one of the autoblasters. It was a NanoTempest-Lite, a magazine-fed subgun similar to one he'd trained on for boarding ops. His had been fed from a backpack-mounted powercell, but the function was otherwise identical. Recoil was almost non-existent, easily handled even one-handed, and mags held fifty rounds—forty more than he needed. He switched it from burst to single shot and headed for the stairwell.

He ascended two steps at a time. When he rounded the first landing, he squeezed the firing stud, putting a pair of rounds into the wall above the door where 'Sparks' hid. Another two steps up, he fired again, peppering the wall next to the doorway. Another two steps, and he struck the wall under the window frame. He reached the landing, fired again, burst through the doorway, and put two rounds into the last ganger.

He backed out into the hallway and froze. A security camera's red LED blinked at him from the end of the hallway.

"Who's the *vlakas* now?" he grumbled.

"Uh, Mister WarBorg?" Doctor Phillips called from downstairs. "Are we leaving?"

"In a moment," Damien shouted. "They've got cameras. I need to find an access point and scramble their records before we go."

"It's down here!" Phillips shouted.

Damien ducked into the storage room, claimed the arm that looked like Sammy's, and stuffed it into his pack beside his own arm. He scooped up the NanoTempest and made his way back downstairs.

"Where?"

Phillips pulled aside a blood-splattered, protective polymer sheet and revealed a datajack access point. Damien tucked the subgun under his left stump, drew a cable from the side of his neck, and jacked in.

The interface was rudimentary, and he set his ICE chisel to it immediately. It chipped away at the intrusion countermeasures, and, in seconds, he had access. He found the datasilos easily, but they were read-only, locked out. Without a better chisel app, he couldn't break in. He backed out and checked the security feed's settings.

There.

The data was set to record on a loop. It recorded for a day, sent the day's footage out over the streams... somewhere, then overwrote the footage with the next day's.

Damien tweaked the base settings. He set the footage quality to maximum definition, sixteen times its current settings, and the overwrite setting to thirty minutes, the minimum allowed, while leaving the backup settings alone. That was the best he could do. He was no proper datarunner and had limited tools, so he'd have to hope the rescue would go unnoticed for at least half an hour. If so, they should be in the clear.

"Okay, that's as good as it's going to get," he said as his cable retracted. "Let's go."

The rear door was welded shut—Damien was glad he hadn't tried to come in that way—so they ducked out the front and went back down the side alley, retracing Damien's footsteps. When they were safely a block away, he recalled his Whisper drone and called Vortex for pickup. He'd had more than enough fun today, and Neurovation owed him.

* * *

"What happened to your arm?" Kassandra shrieked.

"Close encounter with a monomolecular whip," Damien said. "It'll be fine."

"Fine?" Kassandra repeated, disbelief etched across her fine, synthetic features. "How is it going to be fine? You've been at this insane bounty-hunter thing for *two days*, and you're coming home with missing limbs? *Fine?*"

Damien rolled his eyes and pulled dinner from the oven. He'd made her favorite—Cazador spice kebabs. The recipe was simple—a savory snake of dough weaving back and forth between three spicy meatballs on skewers—and Kassandra looked at it suspiciously. "You're trying to bribe me. It won't work."

He shrugged, laid the skewers on plates, and took them to the dinner table. "I came home early after I got my arm treated. I'm not trying to bribe you; I just knew you'd be upset and wanted to apologize. I did some real good today, and yes, it was dangerous, but I handled it."

Kassandra joined him at the table. She surgically dissected her meal and popped a forkful of dough and meatball in her mouth. "Okay. I'm listening."

Damien related that, rather than going hunting for servers or scumbags, he'd found Dr. Phillips' missing/wanted contract. He told the story of how he'd tracked the doctor down. "... and then, as we were about to sneak out, his client came back in, some kind of malfunction in his arm. He was quicker than I was by just a hair. He took my arm off just as I shot him."

"And then you escaped?"

"Sorta, yeah. There were three more gangers in the building, and they were none too pleased to have their cyberdoc stolen."

"So you killed, what, five gangers today?" she said.

"Five? Yeah, that sounds right. But I got Phillips away safely before they could torture him anymore. He looked at my arm as Vortex took us uphive. The slice was clean enough that when we got to his office, he was able to apply a nanite rebuilding paste to rejoin everything."

Damien pointed to the silvery-blue line that encircled his upper forearm. "The nanites have already rebuilt a lot of the internal structure. This time tomorrow, it'll be like it never happened."

"I can't believe you…" Kassandra polished off her first kebab and moved on to the second. She froze just before she put the next bite into her mouth. "You haven't said how much they paid you."

Damien finished his own kebab before answering. "Now, you've got to understand, I'm paying Vortex a percentage to do extraction, and I promised my source at Reality Reclamation a slice of the action, too. I couldn't have solved this without her. So after I've paid them… I made ¥24,500 and change."

Kassandra dropped her fork on the table with a clatter. "You're joking."

"I'm not."

"Damien… that's like, three month's gross pay."

"I know."

She shook her head in disbelief, then scooped her fork back up and took another bite. "This is going to get addictive for you, isn't it?"

"Addictive?" Damien thought it over. "I don't think so, no. I don't have any overhead or expenses. I don't have staffers or shareholders. If I owed them a payday, then yes, I could see how it might wind up looking that way. But since I can pick and choose my own contracts…"

"You can quit any time you want? Is that what you were going to say?" Kassandra said. "You must know how that sounds."

"Of course I do. You must know how you sound too, right? After twenty years in the Corps, I've brought home more in two days than I normally would by May."

"That's not the point!" Kassandra shouted. "In the Corps, you served something bigger than yourself! You weren't in it for the cred-it!"

"No, I was in the Corps because my choice was that or dying young!" Damien snarled back. "I served my time! I gave the Corps twenty years of my life, and now I don't owe the Corps a thing! The Megas have credit to burn! Ten kay? Twenty? Thirty? Pocket change for the directors, the veeps, and C-level execs. But it's life-changing down here. At this rate, I'll have earned a master sergeant's salary for the year before the weekend."

"At this rate, you're going to get yourself killed."

"Thanks." Damien got up. "Thanks for that vote of confidence, Kass. Means the world to me. I've brought our home twenty-five grand in two days, saved lives, *am* saving lives, and you're treating me like I'm some damn fool private who's going to stand up in a fire-fight and get his head taken off?"

"Damien, wait," she said, but Damien had had enough. He left the table and headed outside, ignoring Kassandra's pleas for him to stop. He strode through the neighborhood, glaring at every house as if this conflict with his wife were somehow the buildings' fault. The neighborhood was cookie-cutter, save for paint. These were soldiers' quarters, modular homes built for members of the Hellenic Aug-mented & Robotic Defense Corps—the unit he'd sworn to serve twenty-four years ago, but to which he no longer belonged.

His internal comm pinged an incoming call from Kassandra, and he ignored it. He needed to cool off, but the more he marched the neighborhood, the more furious he got. He got another ping on his comm.

It wasn't Kass. It was Jacobou from the Corps. He answered it, voice only. "The hell you want, Karl? Did Kass tell you to call?"

"The hell kind of way is that to answer the comm, X?" Karl retorted. "No, I haven't talked to Kass at all. But my common sense is tingling. I was just calling to see how retirement's agreeing with you, and I'm going to go ahead and guess 'not very well?'"

Damien clamped down on his fury with years of practiced discipline. "Sorry, Karl. I shouldn't have snapped like that. No, it's not going very well at all."

"You wanna talk about it?"

"No."

"Then we definitely need to talk about it. Slow down, dammit, I'm trying to catch up."

Damien paused, looked around, and realized Karl was jogging down the street toward him. Damien severed the commlink. Karl slowed to a stroll, and they walked together in silence for a minute.

"It's been two days, X. How bad can it be?"

"We've fought three nights in a row." Damien talked as they walked, filling Karl in on everything he'd done since his last day in the Corps. It had been a busy two and a half days. Jacobou was nodding by the time Damien wrapped up.

"So she's worried for you. You've gone from fireteam commander to detachment commander, to platoon senior to company senior. You've always had a team at your back. And now you're flying solo, your titanium butt flapping in the breeze, and she's wondering whether you'll come home alive at all. Or if you're just going to disappear one day, never to be seen again."

"That's not going to happen," Damien said.

"I mean, if it does, you won't have to worry about it," Karl said. "It's like we always said in EOD. Either it's the red wire or the black wire, or it's suddenly not my problem anymore."

"You don't think her fear means she's got no faith in my ability to do the job?"

"I think her fear means she's imagining all kinds of terrible things happening to you with no backup. Put it this way—you just wasted five guys rescuing that doctor. What if one of them had been a Borg?"

"They weren't."

"Doesn't matter. There's *always* a bigger dog. And if you're the biggest dog, there's a bigger pack. You *cannot* act like you're invulnerable, because you aren't. One neural grenade, one shot from a stunner like the one you picked up, and some ganger shithead will saw your head off with a vibroblade and mount it on his wall like a trophy. *You need a team.* Kass has a couple years to go. So do I. So does Natassa, so does Kostas. Now, what about this Barakis guy? You said he was looking for some muscle."

"It was his gang holding Phillips. I was going to bring him in. Ares Interstellar's got a hundred grand on offer for him. He's got a scramble soft running, so facial recog doesn't work. I don't know what this side hustle of his is, that he's managed to piss off a Mega to the tune of a hundred grand, but I'm pretty sure the market protection scam he's running is just keeping up appearances."

"If he's got scramble soft running, he's going to be cocky. Without a name and a genescan, you wouldn't be able to peg him on the boards. So get close to him, do a gig or two with him, and see if the opportunity presents itself. A hundred grand payday means you can take the rest of the year off and get Kass off your back."

Damien thought about it. "I doubt she'll see it that way." They'd circled the block and were most of the way back to his house. "Can I borrow a corner at your place tonight, Karl? Don't much feel like going back in there at the moment."

Jacobou looked warily at the Xanthopolous residence. "On one condition. Tell her where you're staying tonight so she doesn't have Megalos interrogate me at work tomorrow night. We've got QRF duty, and I don't need both of them ganging up on me."

"Deal."

* * *

The next day, Damien made his way back to the Nice Market on level 69B. It didn't take long to locate Barakis. He was shaking down Sammy for the protection money again.

"I'm telling you, Barakis, I ain't got it," Sammy protested. "I'm barely breaking even with only the one arm."

Barakis took a deep breath, inhaling sharply through his nose. "You smell something, Yianni?"

His sycophant inhaled as well. "I think so, boss. Smells a bit like... bullshit mixed with excuses."

Barakis blew out his breath. "I hate bullshit excuses, Yianni. You know how much I hate them."

"I do," his goon agreed.

"You must know how much I hate them too, don't you Sammy?"

"It's not bullshit!" Sammy exploded. "You took my *gamimeno* arm!"

"What's he owe?" Damien asked as he approached.

"What's it to you?" Barakis snarled.

"I might want to get into the food truck biz," Damien said. "You know, invest." He set a satchel containing the prosthetic down against the side of Sammy's stall and pulled out a credstick. Sammy would find it later once Barakis was away and gone. "What can I say, I'm a big fan of souvlaki. How much?"

"Protection's five hundred yen a month," Yianni supplied. Damien looked around the market and nodded, impressed. There were a couple dozen merchant stalls present. That would make for several thousand credits of passive income. "Can do." He brushed the credit stick against his hand, and it chirped to indicate the transfer. He offered it to Barakis. "You said you were looking for some muscle the other day. Maybe you give me a chance to earn that back."

Barakis accepted the stick suspiciously. "As it happens, I do need some muscle for a job. Tonight. A couple of the boys aren't going to make it on account of a sudden case of death. I was almost going to call the whole thing off, but a vet WarBorg might change the odds for the better."

"Just tell me when and where."

"There's a sledlane on-ramp near Stack Four, level one hundred. Give me your commcode, and I'll send you the coordinates. Meet me there tonight at midnight."

"What's the gig, and what's the pay?"

"I told you the other day. We're in acquisitions and divestitures. We're going to acquire some assets by hostile takeover. You'll get a share of the profits once we move the merch."

Damien frowned. "Are you always this vague?"

"With new guys? Always." Barakis chuckled. Yianni laughed like a hyena, and Damien had to suppress the urge to punch him in the mouth.

"See you at midnight, then."

* * *

At the appointed time and place, a grav truck slowed to rest on its runners, and the side door slid open. Barakis offered Damien a hand and pulled him aboard. The door slid shut, the gravity field came to life, and the truck hummed away. Barakis and Yianni waited in the back, with a third in the pilot's seat up front. Barakis slipped a mag-sealed duffel open and pulled out a gray smock, pants, and matching boots. "You've used PredTex camo before?" he asked.

"I have," Damien said, and Barakis handed him the gear. He gave him a comm, too.

"Put these on and sync them up. The comm is a one-shot encrypted disposable."

Damien ditched his civilian clothes and donned the new gear. He didn't trust Barakis in the slightest, so he linked the equipment to his CombatComp, which he kept silo'd from his own internal hardware. He activated the PredTex active camo and shimmered into non-existence, save for his head, where the hood was thrown back. He deactivated it, and it returned to its previous neutral gray.

"Chimera Six, comm check." Barakis' voice was loud and clear over the communicator.

"X, five by five," Damien replied.

"Chimera Six, five by five, clear." He deactivated the comm and spoke normally again. "Deal is this. Ares Interstellar is transferring weapons and BRUTE armor to the HARD Corps tonight. We're going to pinch it on behalf of our benefactor before the gov can take custody of it."

"You're stealing from the *Corps?*" Damien blurted.

"No, *we* are stealing from *Ares*," Barakis said, "and it's imperative we take it *before* the Corps takes custody of it. Ares is responsible for it until the transfer's complete, and the gov can't interfere in Inter-Corp biz. Hoods on."

Yianni did as he was ordered, and Damien followed suit. His mind raced. He'd understood, intellectually, that MegaCorps believed that *war is business by other means*, but Barakis was operating at another level altogether. The pilot's voice came over the comm. *"The Ares transport is in the basket, Chimera Six."*

"Chimera Six, understood."

Yianni opened a hardcase on the floor and withdrew from it a one-shot disposable EM pulse cannon. He passed it to Barakis. "Holy shit," Damien breathed.

"On my mark, X, Yianni, you two open the rear doors. I've got the target silhouetted in my HUD. We're well outside the city now, about halfway to HFB Perseus. We'll follow it down, handle the guards, and get gone before Ares or Perseus QRF can respond. Got it? Good. Ready on the doors—two—one—now!"

Damien threw one door open, Yianni threw the other open, and Barakis took a knee with the pulse cannon over his shoulder. The shot itself was invisible, but the effects were immediate. Actinic blue sparks blew out from the transport's grav runners, the transport nosed over, and it immediately took on the aerodynamic aspect of a flying dumpster. It caught the wind, tumbled, and plummeted. The pilot in the Ares transport somehow managed to get the grav drive functional again just before impact, because the ground *flexed* as the sled tried to right itself and avoid impact. It failed. The transport clipped a sand dune with one of its grav runners, tearing the rail free and sending it into an out-of-control spin. To the manufacturer's credit, the vehicle's crash cage withstood the impact with minimal deformation. The skin was torn free, but the storage compartment was only slightly warped by the time it came to rest in the dunes.

The truck followed it down, and their pilot skewed to a stop a dozen meters away. Barakis and Yianni triggered their active camo and jumped clear immediately. Damien followed. The Ares truck driver didn't even seem the slightest bit disoriented when he burst from the cab and stitched the rear of the truck with HELgun blasts. Damien dove aside and stayed low in the thick lavender grasses as he approached. One of the other two returned fire, sending the Ares driver scrambling for cover.

"X, Chimera Six, watch the skies!"

Barakis' warning came almost too late. An outrider grav sled, a sleek, wedge-shaped MATT with a low-profile turret on its rear upper deck, descended to barely a dozen feet off the ground. Hatches in the bottom of the MATT slid aside, and half a dozen CorpSec troopers in BRUTE armor dropped free. With its cargo delivered, the MATT jinked sideways and tore the front of their transport to scorched and jagged pieces.

Yianni fired a burst of ion bolts at the Ares troopers, but what few rounds hit, the armor soaked. PredTex suits, by contrast, provided little more than concealment. Three of the Ares CorpSec zeroed in on the source of the ion bolts and scythed the ganger down where he stood. They spread out, searching for them, but so long as Damien moved slowly, they wouldn't detect him.

"X! What are you waiting for?"

"Where are you?" Damien demanded. Barakis sent a ping from his commlink, and Damien locked the signal in his HUD. "I'm coming to you." He sent a separate extract request to Vortex Transport, highest priority, and his global sector coordinates.

The Ares troopers continued their search of the area as Damien stalked closer and closer to Barakis. He was almost there—was close enough to hear Barakis cursing under his breath—when an even larger MATT swooped overhead. It bore the stylized Hoplon shield of the HARD Corps, and gull wings burst open on both sides. Members of the Corps in Ares Interstellar's null-gravity armor jumped clear and swooped to the ground on carbon fiber wings.

Barakis was on his belly, hidden in a copse of the purple weeds. Damien was close enough to discern the light-bending effect of the armor. In a flash, Damien dropped his PredTex field, snaked an arm around Barakis' throat, and yanked him upright.

"What are you—doing?" Barakis choked out. There were shouts and warnings from three sides, but Damien held his ground until the shouting ceased. The Corps troops fanned out into a firing line.

"Jaenos Barakis is wanted by Ares Interstellar!" he declared. "Kill us, and you'll never know who he was working for!"

"You sonofa—" his prisoner snarled, but Damien tightened his grip and choked off the blood supply to Barakis' head.

"Damien?" a female voice gasped. Kassandra pulled her finned helmet off, but she didn't lower her weapon.

"Hey, Kass," he said woodenly. He'd known she was on QRF tonight, but he hadn't thought of anything clever to say. "Sorry."

"I'm not getting anything back on facial recog," the Ares sergeant cut in.

"You won't," Damien agreed. "He's running scrambler soft. But I've got him by name and by genescan. He's my prisoner, and he's worth a hundred kay. So you'll forgive me if I don't just hand him over."

"Damien, what the hell are you doing?" Kassandra cut in. "You have to hand him off!"

"No, I don't," Damien replied. "I've got my extraction team en route, and you can't stop me."

"Of course we can," Master Sergeant George Megalos said. George had inherited Damien's slot upon retirement. "Don't be an idiot. You were one of us just last week."

"I was, yes," Damien agreed. "But you're government forces, and you can't interfere in MegaCorp business. Barakis here was working for someone, and Ares has been hunting him for months."

"You've got some balls, X," Megalos growled.

"With all due respect, George, this is above your paygrade. And before you get any clever ideas, Ares Sergeant who's trying to flank me without my noticing, I'm streaming this direct to my Council Rep's inbox. There'll be hell to pay if any of you do anything short of letting me take my prisoner in. All you have to do is do nothing. Don't be fools."

"Don't bother coming home tonight, Damien," Kassandra said softly. "I can't believe this. Don't bother coming back, ever."

A trio of black dots raced in overhead from the direction of the city. Two orbited the site of the crash, as the third hammered the brakes and descended to land next to Damien and his prisoner. The Vortex extraction sled dropped onto the grass next to him, and Romano stepped out with two guards. "Your ride, sir."

Damien dragged Barakis backward onto the transport and turned him face down to snap the binders on. Romano shut the hatch, and the sled hummed as it rose into the sky.

* * *

Inside the sled, Romano produced a black box killswitch and jacked it into Barakis' I/O slot. "For heavily cybered prisoners," he explained. "Shuts down their whole system, so long as it remains plugged in. Now, let's see who we've got here."

He scanned Barakis' face with a CombatComp, and it projected the Wanted image into the air.

"Well, well, if it isn't the Chimera. Nicely done, X."

"You know him?" Damien asked.

"Know him? Not personally, but the Chimera's notorious. He's had half a dozen identities across two different star systems. That Ares contract is only the tip of the iceberg. He hasn't been seen in two or three years. Last big gig was somewhere in Putinskaya Zvezda, I think. Must a been laying low, but the bounties are still good."

More bounties started popping up from all across human space, dating back twenty years or more. The running total ratcheted higher and higher, until it capped out just shy of a *million* credits.

"You're making a huge mistake," Barakis snarled. "You're right, I've been in hiding. But I've got funds and backing. Ten million here, now, for you to let me go."

Damien shook his head sadly. "You have no idea what you've just cost me," he said. "Don't think you can throw credit at this to make it go away."

* * *

The transport lit on a landing pad at level 372A, Ares Spire. Four of Ares Interstellar's elite Myrmidon guards marched out to meet them. With the killswitch attached, Barakis was completely limp. Two guards unceremoniously dragged him away without a word. Damien and Romano followed, and a slender woman with glossy black hair came out to meet them. She wore a black-and-brass suit of Ares' BRUTE Hoplite armor, polished to a high sheen.

"Director," Romano greeted her. "You wanted to see us? This is Damien Xanthopolous, recently master sergeant with the HARD Corps. X, this is Director Calliope Xenelli."

"Well met, X," she said and offered her hand to shake. "Quite the payday you've got here. Once we've wrung him for all the intel we can get, Apex Energy, Paragon Savage, Orinoco, and Titanium Allies all want a go at him. We're letting them bid for him, of course, and you'll get a percentage of that as finder's fee. You had no idea?"

Damien shook his head. "None. The hundred kay bounty was the largest one I'd seen yet, and it was a bit of a trick to pierce his identity in the first place." It occurred to him that he owed both Pythia and Karina a slice of his bounty as well. Enough to change their lives for the better, too, he supposed.

"Yet you managed, where dozens or hundreds of others failed, or missed him by a hair. I suppose that makes you Bellerophon, slayer of the Chimera, does it not?"

"As you say, Director."

"Join me in my office, both of you," she said, and gestured for them to follow. "You seem to be a good team. I know how prickly you soldier types can be about working directly for a Mega, but what would you say if I were to offer you both Ares Interstellar sponsorship?"

Damien exchanged a glance with Romano. "I'd say, lead the way."

* * * * *

Jamie Ibson Bio

Jamie Ibson is from the frozen wastelands of Canuckistan, where moose, bears, and geese battle for domination among the hockey rinks, igloos, and Tim Hortons. After joining the Canadian army reserves in high school, he spent half of 2001 in Bosnia as a peace-keeper and came home shortly after 9/11 with a deep sense of fore-boding. After graduating college, he landed a job in law enforcement and was posted to the left coast from 2007 to 2021. He retired from law enforcement in early 2021 and moved clear across the country to write full time in the Maritimes.

Jamie's website can be found at https://ibsonwrites.ca, where he has free short stories available for download. To find out when he releases something new, follow him on Bookbub at https://www.bookbub.com/profile/jamie-ibson. He is also on Facebook and runs The Frozen Hoser's Winter Wasteland on Discord.

He is married to the lovely Michelle, and they have cats.

# # # # #

The following is an
Excerpt from Book One of the Salvage Title Trilogy:

Salvage Title

Kevin Steverson

Available Now from Theogony Books

eBook, Paperback, and Audio Book

Excerpt from "Salvage Title:"

The first thing Clip did was get power to the door and the access panel. Two of his power cells did the trick once he had them wired to the container. He then pulled out his slate and connected it. It lit up, and his fingers flew across it. It took him a few minutes to establish a link, then he programmed it to search for the combination to the access panel.

"Is it from a human ship?" Harmon asked, curious.

"I don't think so, but it doesn't matter; ones and zeros are still ones and zeros when it comes to computers. It's universal. I mean, there are some things you have to know to get other races' computers to run right, but it's not that hard," Clip said.

Harmon shook his head. *Riiigghht,* he thought. He knew better. Clip's intelligence test results were completely off the charts. Clip opted to go to work at Rinto's right after secondary school because there was nothing for him to learn at the colleges and universities on either Tretra or Joth. He could have received academic scholarships for advanced degrees on a number of nearby systems. He could have even gone all the way to Earth and attended the University of Georgia if he wanted. The problem was getting there. The schools would have provided free tuition if he could just have paid to get there.

Secondary school had been rough on Clip. He was a small guy that made excellent grades without trying. It would have been worse if Harmon hadn't let everyone know that Clip was his brother. They lived in the same foster center, so it was mostly true. The first day of school, Harmon had laid down the law—if you messed with Clip, you messed up.

At the age of fourteen, he beat three seniors senseless for attempting to put Clip in a trash container. One of them was a Yalteen, a member of a race of large humanoids from two systems over. It wasn't a fair fight—they should have brought more people with them. Harmon hated bullies.

After the suspension ended, the school's Warball coach came to see him. He started that season as a freshman and worked on using it to earn a scholarship to the academy. By the time he graduated, he was six feet two inches with two hundred and twenty pounds of muscle. He got the scholarship and a shot at going into space. It was the longest time he'd ever spent away from his foster brother, but he couldn't turn it down.

Clip stayed on Joth and went to work for Rinto. He figured it was a job that would get him access to all kinds of technical stuff, servos, motors, and maybe even some alien computers. The first week he was there, he tweaked the equipment and increased the plant's recycled steel production by 12 percent. Rinto was eternally grateful, as it put him solidly into the profit column instead of toeing the line between profit and loss. When Harmon came back to the planet after the academy, Rinto hired him on the spot on Clip's recommendation. After he saw Harmon operate the grappler and got to know him, he was glad he did.

A steady beeping brought Harmon back to the present. Clip's program had succeeded in unlocking the container. "Right on!" Clip exclaimed. He was always using expressions hundreds or more years out of style. "Let's see what we have; I hope this one isn't empty, too." Last month they'd come across a smaller vault, but it had been empty.

Harmon stepped up and wedged his hands into the small opening the door had made when it disengaged the locks. There wasn't enough power in the small cells Clip used to open it any further. He put his weight into it, and the door opened enough for them to get inside. Before they went in, Harmon placed a piece of pipe in the doorway so it couldn't close and lock on them, baking them alive before anyone realized they were missing.

Daylight shone in through the doorway, and they both froze in place; the weapons vault was full.

* * * * *

Get "Salvage Title" now at:

https://www.amazon.com/dp/B07H8Q3HBV.

Find out more about Kevin Steverson and "Salvage Title" at:

http://chriskennedypublishing.com/.

* * * * *

The following is an

Excerpt from Book One of the Revelations Cycle:

Cartwright's Cavaliers

Mark Wandrey

Available Now from Seventh Seal Press

eBook, Paperback, and Audio Book

Excerpt from "Cartwright's Cavaliers:"

The last two operational tanks were trapped on their chosen path. Faced with destroyed vehicles front and back, they cut sideways to the edge of the dry river bed they'd been moving along and found several large boulders to maneuver around that allowed them to present a hull-down defensive position. Their troopers rallied on that position. It was starting to look like they'd dig in when Phoenix 1 screamed over and strafed them with dual streams of railgun rounds. A split second later, Phoenix 2 followed on a parallel path. Jim was just cheering the air attack when he saw it. The sixth damned tank, and it was a heavy.

"I got that last tank," Jim said over the command net.

"Observe and stand by," Murdock said.

"We'll have these in hand shortly," Buddha agreed, his transmission interspersed with the thudding of his CASPer firing its magnet accelerator. "We can be there in a few minutes."

Jim examined his battlespace. The tank was massive. It had to be one of the fusion-powered beasts he'd read about. Which meant shields and energy weapons. It was heading down the same gap the APC had taken, so it was heading toward Second Squad, and fast.

"Shit," he said.

"Jim," Hargrave said, "we're in position. What are you doing?"

"Leading," Jim said as he jumped out from the rock wall.

* * * * *

Get "Cartwright's Cavaliers" now at:

https://www.amazon.com/dp/B01MRZKM95

Find out more about Mark Wandrey and the Four Horsemen Universe at:

https://chriskennedypublishing.com/the-four-horsemen-books/

* * * * *

Printed in Great Britain
by Amazon

80148655R00342